An Old-Fashioned
Christmas
ROMANCE COLLECTION

An Old-Fashioned Christmas

ROMANCE COLLECTION

*9 Stories Celebrate Christmas Traditions
and Love from Bygone Years*

Kay Cornelius, Rosey Dow, Rebecca Germany,
JoAnn A. Grote, Sally Laity, Loree Lough,
Gail G. Martin, DiAnn Mills, & Colleen L. Reece

BARBOUR BOOKS
An Imprint of Barbour Publishing, Inc.

Contents

Dreams and Secrets

DiAnn Mills

Every good gift and every perfect gift is from above,
and cometh down from the Father of lights,
with whom is no variableness, neither shadow of turning.
JAMES 1:17

Chapter 1

November 1851, near Philadelphia

Falling always came easy for Emma Leigh, especially when she had her mind on other matters. She smoothed the skirt of her worn, brown-and-pink-flowered dress, lifted her chin, and marched toward her employer's office at the Jones Inn. Abruptly, she slammed headlong into Thad Benson's armload of firewood.

The smell of freshly cut wood enveloped her senses mere seconds before the impact knocked her to the floor. Thad's bundle fell with a crash, but thankfully, none of the pieces hit her. Emma Leigh's hoop skirt, however, soared upward in a less than dignified manner.

"Oh my." Her cheeks flamed. She scrambled to push down her heap of snowy white petticoats and restore some semblance of balance and poise.

A calloused hand reached for hers overtop her hoop skirt and righted her to her feet.

"Thank you, Thad," she said, unable to look at him. He should have seen her coming. A combination of ruffled feelings and a bruised backside produced a bit of irritation.

"Are you hurt?" he said, shoving aside the pieces of wood. "I'm really sorry, Emma Leigh."

Forcing herself to stare into his face lined with concern, she swallowed a stinging remark and braved a smile. After all, sweet Thad, the young man in charge of the stables and all the outside grounds, would never intentionally harm anyone.

From the office came the sound of someone clearing his throat. Towering in the doorway, Alexander Jones, the owner of the inn, looked indeed formidable with his permanent frown. "What's all the racket?"

Thad whirled around. "Sir, I collided with Miss Carter. I do apologize for the incident."

"Is the young lady injured?" Mr. Jones crossed his arms over his narrow chest and leaned toward Emma Leigh.

She met the owner's gaze, feeling more humiliated than before. "No sir." *Only my pride.*

Mr. Jones pressed his lips tightly, but his mustache and beard jiggled, betraying his gruff reaction. The scene must have looked amusing, further intensifying her humiliation. "Gather up the firewood, Thad. You are dismissed." Nodding to Emma Leigh, he stepped aside from the doorway. "Miss Carter, I'll see you now."

Emma Leigh followed him into his office. She'd felt nervous before the fall, but now every part of her trembled. For a moment she feared toppling over his desk.

"Are you certain you are uninjured?" He peered down over his long, pointed nose.

"Yes sir." She hoped her voice sounded stronger than the weak reply rising in her ears.

Mr. Jones, impeccably dressed in a black suit, eased into his chair. She'd heard some of the staff refer to him as Old Matchstick. Although Emma Leigh didn't comment on his skeletal frame, she did wonder if he'd blow away on a blustery day. He smiled on occasion and greeted those who graced his inn with the utmost of hospitality and respect, but he insisted upon a meticulous establishment. Most of the staff feared him. He had the type of voice that carried—rather rolled— like thunder. Perhaps his mannerisms had something to do with his military background. But in any event, Emma Leigh had been summoned to his office.

"Sit down, Miss Carter." He gestured to an empty chair in front of his desk. His booming voice, devoid of passion, further alarmed her. "I've been observing you as you interact with the guests, and there's a matter we need to discuss."

The lump in her throat grew to boulder-sized proportions, and she rubbed her clammy hands together. A dozen grievances flashed across her mind. He surely must believe she shirked her duties. She lowered herself onto the chair, sitting stiffly on the edge, and gave him her attention.

"Christmas will be here before we're prepared." The grandfather clock in the main entrance struck ten times to punctuate his words. "In the past, the staff has engaged in merriment, which I believe is appropriate for the celebration of our Lord's birth. This year—" Mr. Jones cleared his throat. "This year I'd like for us to partake in something different, and I believe you can be of assistance."

Emma Leigh dug her fingers into her palms. "In what way, sir?"

He drew out a sheet of paper from his drawer and placed his spectacles on his nose. Picking up his quill, he dipped it into the inkwell. "Miss Carter, you have a way of exhibiting excellent social skills in your duties as the inn's hostess— however, you do at times overindulge." He scrutinized her over his spectacles.

"Yes sir. I mean, I'm sorry, sir."

He paused. "Very well. I'm assigning you the task of organizing a frugal yet highly enjoyable Christmas party for the staff. In the past, too much emphasis has been placed on an abundance of gift giving. This year, I'd like to see the holiday made more simple and meaningful." He painstakingly wrote something on the paper, then handed it to her. "This is your budget and your orders. Mrs. Weares will be notified of your extra duties, and that you will be assisting her in selecting the menu for the Christmas dinner."

Emma Leigh hastily read her new directives. "Thank you, Mr. Jones. When would you like for me to have this completed?"

"Ten days hence," he said. "I plan to call a holiday meeting to appoint those who will be decorating the inn and such. You can present your findings then. Of course, I need to approve them beforehand."

Humility washed over Emma Leigh. "Yes sir. I. . .I am greatly honored."

His eyes widened. "Goodness, girl. I don't bite. Calm yourself and go on about your business." A slight smile tugged at his mustache. "After all, we're talking about a Christmas celebration. Just remember I want a memorable holiday." With those words, Mr. Jones dismissed her with a perfunctory nod.

Ah, he wasn't so fearsome after all. Stepping into the entranceway of the inn, Emma Leigh saw the polished floor had been swept spotless. Not a trace of bark or splinter remained to tell of the collision. For the first time, she realized she could have been badly hurt with the firewood flying in all directions. Poor, shy Thad. He must feel terrible. At her first opportunity, she'd reassure him the happening was indeed an accident and as much her fault as anyone's. She'd been so caught up in meeting with Mr. Jones that she hadn't paid attention to anything else.

Clutching the paper outlining her new duties, Emma Leigh took her position at the front desk where she greeted guests, showed them to their rooms, and helped them in any way she could. Excitement caused a smile as though Christmas were tomorrow. During the moments when her services were not needed, her thoughts and prayers would be engrossed in providing a memorable celebration for the staff at the Jones Inn.

∽

Thad lifted the ax high above his head and sent it crashing into the log. Sawdust and splinters flew every which way. Tossing aside the split wood, he set another log in its place.

He should have seen Emma Leigh coming.

He'd been thinking about those large doe eyes and the sound of her sweet voice when he sent her sprawling to the floor.

And right in front of Mr. Jones. The owner had just spoken to him about raising his pay and extending his duties to include inside maintenance of the inn. Thad grimaced. He'd left such an improper impression.

Most likely Emma Leigh would never speak to him again, and Mr. Jones would forget about elevating Thad to a new position. Both probabilities ended his dreams of saving additional money and someday inviting Emma Leigh to spend the rest of her life with him.

Thad lifted the ax and rested it on his right shoulder. He'd known Emma Leigh since they were children in school. Back then his parents were living. Those were happier days, when laughter swept through their clapboard country home like a breeze on a hot day. His father, a country doctor, and his devoted mother never said no to a single person in need—whether the need be medical or financial. But all their goodness ended when his parents drowned in a tragic buggy accident.

Thad had spent the first three years since their deaths living alone in Boston, but then he had returned to his home village and moved in with his uncle and Swedish-born aunt. He could fend for himself in his parents' home, but he simply chose not to spend time alone. Sometimes he visited the homestead and tidied up a bit, often reflecting on more pleasant times, but he didn't allow his thoughts to be consumed with bitterness or regret. God had taken his parents for a reason, and they'd left a legacy of unselfish giving. In their memory and with the peace God had given him, Thad chose to live his life just as his parents had: serving the Lord with all his might. Like his father, Thad had committed his life to medicine.

Kicking aside the split wood, he set the last piece in place and sank the ax all the way through. The chunk divided into two separate pieces, just like Emma Leigh and him.

His favorite memory of her occurred when she was about nine and he nearly eleven. George, one of the older boys, had insisted upon bullying a younger one, and Emma Leigh must have had her fill. She marched over to the children watching the badgering and pushed her way through. She stomped her feet and shook her fist in the bully's face, her light brown pigtails bouncing with her denunciation of the ignoble deed.

"Jesus doesn't want us hurting other people," she'd said. "When you do, it hurts Him!"

Thad still recalled the way Emma Leigh's turned-up nose wrinkled when she concentrated—like poor George that day. Oddly enough, George had released the younger boy.

Even then, Emma Leigh possessed the ability to make folks see the error of their ways. Yet she always did so in a tender fashion. After confronting George, she shared her noon meal with him. Years later, George had become a preacher—a good one, too.

Back then, Thad had cared for the little girl, and now he found himself hopelessly in love with her. But she needed an outgoing man, one who could give her a good life and show off her grand beauty. Because of her father's long illness, she knew nothing but poverty, and Thad had medical school to complete. He couldn't ask her to marry him until he had something more to offer.

Thad needed to apologize. And he must speak with her today.

Evening shadows danced across the quiet yard of the inn before he finished his chores. Already the ground beneath him crunched in anticipation of another frost. Glancing back at the barn, he saw the moonlight reflecting in a silvery glow from the weathered side of the structure. Beauty in simple things. Perfection in God's creation. They served to remind him of Emma Leigh.

He entered the inn through the back near the kitchen and stomped his feet until no trace of debris could be tracked inside. His gaze noted the cook, Sarah, placing the finishing touches on a platter of beef, garnished in potatoes, carrots, and onions. Her white bonnet accented her red hair, and the warm glow of the fire spiced her cheeks like red apples. The woman smiled.

"Aye, Thad. Working late, are ye?"

"Yes ma'am. Mr. Jones is expecting a large party tomorrow from Philadelphia, and I wanted the harnesses shined before I fetched them in the morning."

"Good boy. Are ye a-needin' something?"

Thad felt his cheeks warm and his toes tingle in his boots. "I needed to speak with Miss Carter."

Sarah tilted her head and gave him a sad smile. Did the dear woman read his heart? "Her father already came by."

Determined to hide his disappointment, Thad thanked her kindly and trekked outside. Emma Leigh lived about three miles from the inn. He'd gladly walk the distance to ease his conscience. There'd be no resting for him tonight until he knew she'd forgiven him for the fall.

Chapter 2

Emma Leigh chatted with Papa all during the wagon ride home from the inn. The cooler air caused her to wrap her arms about her as she told him about the meeting with Mr. Jones and her new assignment. Of course, she bent poor Papa's ear until she knew he must be ready for her to hush.

"I'm sorry, Papa. I'm talking on and not bothering to ask about your day."

Papa reached to give her shoulders a squeeze. "I daresay the happenings at home were not as exciting as yours. With the grain harvested, my hours are starting to slow a bit. We have good apples this year—I believe plenty for the months ahead."

"They will taste good when the wind is blowing and the snow is piled high."

For the past year and a half, neither Papa's crops nor his health had done well. Emma Leigh had taken the job at the inn to help her family, despite her father's protests. Her duties at the inn interested her, and she'd stayed on. The extra money provided additional food and clothing for her family.

"Talk to your mother about the inn's Christmas. I'm sure she can help you much better than I."

Once home, Emma Leigh greeted her five brothers and sister before helping Mama ladle tender chunks of rabbit, potatoes, and a few scant carrots into mismatched pieces of cracked crockery for dinner. The enticing aroma of apples and spices slowly simmering over the fire and transforming into thick, dark apple butter tantalized her senses. The wind whistled around the meager cabin, ushering a draft through the cracks in the rough-sawn logs. She glanced at the children and saw they were warmly dressed, but patches were worn thin. A shiver raced up her spine from fear for her siblings in the winter ahead.

Oh, Lord, keep them healthy. We've already lost three to putrid fever. Charles is still not well. Help me not to complain but be a humble servant.

Emma Leigh roused the dog and ordered him to play next to the younger children where the animal's heat would keep them warm. Taking a deep breath, she turned her attention to Mama and explained her dilemma about the inn's Christmas celebration.

"What can I do?" Emma Leigh accidentally stuck her finger in the hot stew and yanked it back. Poking the finger in her mouth, then rubbing it vigorously, she glanced up at her mother expectantly.

Mama wiped her hands on a clean apron and silently examined her finger. Hearing a howl, she cast a disapproving glance at one of her sons, who had pulled his brother's hair. "It's Emma Leigh's turn for your mama's attention. Mind your manners." She lifted a crusty brown loaf of bread from the hearth. "Emma Leigh, I think you need to pray about the matter. I will say those fine people at the inn want a holiday that knits their hearts with friendship and love. Simple joys and laughter are the best gifts of all, especially when they are tied with a ribbon of love."

Emma Leigh always paid attention to her mother's wisdom. *Simple joys and laughter.* "How can one give joy and laughter? They can't be wrapped and tied with a colorful piece of yarn."

"But those things are everlasting, the kind of treasures from which memories are made." Her mother snapped her fingers in the direction of the children. "Joseph, do not tease your brother again or you will forfeit your supper."

"I'm confused." Emma sighed and picked up baby Charles, who had crawled to her feet and tugged at her skirts. His little shirt and drawers bore knee marks from the day's adventures.

"Emma Leigh, you will find a way." Mama smiled and planted a kiss on Charles's cheek before motioning for the other children and Papa to gather around the table.

As soon as Papa had asked the blessing, Emma Leigh buried herself in thought. The hum of children's voices rose and fell in the wake of contemplating Mr. Jones's request. The stew tasted delicious, and the hot bread thinly coated with freshly churned butter filled the empty spot in her stomach, but she still had no idea how the staff should celebrate Christmas.

Midway through the meal, a pounding at the door seized her attention. Papa rose from his chair and answered it. The heavy wooden door with its leather hinges squeaked open.

"Evenin', Thad. Come on in. You haven't visited us in a long time." Papa shook his hand. "You're just in time for supper."

Emma Leigh couldn't believe Thad stood before her. Whatever could he need from them? He looked a bit troubled. She hoped nothing terrible had happened to his aunt or uncle.

"Evenin' to you, too, Mr. Carter." Thad removed his cap and nodded at Mama. "Hope everything is well with you, ma'am. Sorry to disturb your supper, but I will only be a minute."

Emma Leigh noted how broad his shoulders had become. Since they were in school together, he'd grown to quite a handsome man. She felt herself blush. She shouldn't be thinking such thoughts, but Thad had always captured a soft spot in her heart.

"If you don't mind, sir, I'd like a word with Miss Emma Leigh." Thad's clear blue gaze bore into hers as though he'd read her earlier thoughts.

She felt her skin tingle and knew a bright shade of red glistened on her cheeks.

"You have a fine-looking family, Mr. Carter. I know you must be proud."

Thad's kind mannerisms and carefully chosen words told of his Christian upbringing. If he weren't so shy, Emma Leigh would set her cap for him.

Papa glanced at Emma Leigh. "Daughter, this gentleman would like a word with you."

"Certainly, Papa." She rose from her spot on the well-worn bench and snatched up her shawl from a peg near the door.

"Thank you," Thad said to Papa.

Thad stepped aside from the door, allowing her to pass. Emma Leigh caught a glimpse of his reddened face and assumed the color came from the dipping temperatures. Once again she smelled the rich scent of wood, so much a part of him and his position at the Jones Inn.

Once the door shut, she whirled around in the twilight to face him. "Is something wrong?"

"I believe so." He replaced his woolen cap. "Emma Leigh, I wanted to make sure you were all right after I knocked you down this morning."

He'd walked all this way to check on her? The thought stole her breath. "Thad, how very sweet of you. I'm fine, perfectly fine. I never gave the matter another thought."

He nodded slowly. "Good. I worried you might be hurt, and I needed to apologize again."

"And I looked for you before I left because I feared I was rude to you earlier in the day."

His eyes widened, and a slow smile spread across his thin face. Thad had been a frail-looking child, but it seemed as though he'd suddenly filled out the hollow places. Those deep-set robin's-egg blue eyes and striking features were now those of a man.

Oh my, what is wrong with me?

"You tried to find me?" He jammed his hands into his pockets. His breath puffed into an icy cloud, giving evidence of the plummeting temperatures.

"Of course. Thad, we're friends—have been since we sat next to each other in school. I always welcome a conversation with you."

He shrugged. "Thank you, Emma Leigh. You have a knack of being able to talk to people easier than I do. I wouldn't want to embarrass you."

"Never! Oh my, have I turned into some dreadful person? I certainly hope I haven't given you the impression we should be friends in secret." The horror of being rude to him curdled her stomach.

"No, not at all. It's. . .it's simply I can't always think of clever things to say."

She lifted her chin. "Nonsense," she said as gently as possible. "You have always found plenty to say to me." Her mind raced. "Thad, you have given me a wonderful idea."

"I have?" He raised a brow.

"Yes." Delight danced across her mind. "Mr. Jones gave me an assignment today. He wants me to come up with a memorable way for the staff to celebrate Christmas. I couldn't think of a thing until now." She touched his arm. "Oh, thank you. Thank you ever so much."

"For what?" He clearly looked baffled.

She laughed. "Secret friends. Don't you see? We can all be secret friends for Christmas." She placed a finger to her lips as she considered the particulars. "All the staff could place their names into a basket, then each of us would draw a name. The person whose name we receive will be a secret friend for. . .for about ten days before Christmas. On Christmas Eve when we have our dinner, we'll find out who's our secret friend!"

He chuckled, and she liked the sound of it. "Emma Leigh, your idea sounds like fun."

"Do you really think so?"

"Absolutely. Mr. Jones will be pleased, I'm sure."

She clapped her hands. "I can't wait to tell him. Oh Thad, thank you so much. And I will tell him it was your idea."

"But it isn't."

"But it is. You deserve the credit. After all, you're an answer to prayer."

A sudden gust of wind chilled her, and from Thad's stance, she gathered he must be cold, too, for his face looked rather pinched.

"You need to come inside and warm yourself before heading home." She offered a genuine smile. "I'm sure Papa would hitch up the wagon and take you."

"It's not necessary. Once I start walking, I'll get plenty warm." He glanced toward the road and shifted.

"Are you certain? At least let me make you a hot cup of tea." He'd been so good to walk all this way, and now she had the perfect plan to propose to Mr. Jones.

"I appreciate your thoughtfulness, but I must be going. Please give my best to your parents." A gust of wind caught his scarf and he paused. "I will see you tomorrow."

"Tomorrow it is." Emma Leigh felt a sudden twinge of timidity. Certainly a new emotion for her.

His familiar smile, the one she'd grown up with, now caused a flutter in her stomach. What had happened to the skinny little boy, Dr. Horatio Benson's only child?

He plodded across the barnyard on his way to the road. Emma Leigh watched him curiously, her mind recalling the many lazy hours they'd played together as children.

He'd chased rabbits scampering into the brush. She'd raced after butterflies.

He'd fished in the lazy creek in the back corner of his parents' small farm. She'd waded in the cool stream, allowing her toes to sink into the soft mud.

He'd carved their names into an old oak. She'd picked wildflowers. And when Emma Leigh had tried to make friends with the neighbor's bull, Thad had pulled her beneath a fence just in time.

Then a tragic accident took the lives of his parents. For the next three years, Thad had lived in Boston. Emma Leigh hadn't seen him until she began working at the Jones Inn and discovered he had sought employment at the same establishment.

"Thad," Emma Leigh called out.

He whirled around, and she waved. An unexplainable impulse caused her to hurry in his direction. "I'm so thoughtless. Please forgive me, but how are you doing?"

He waited until she caught up with him. "Fairly well. I'm able to help my aunt and uncle with their farm and still keep up my parents' place."

"I'm surprised you're not living at your parents' home."

"I thought about it long and hard, but this seemed the best way for me to put aside money to attend medical school and help out my aunt and uncle at the same time."

Her heart raced. "Thad, you're going to be a doctor?"

He scuffed at the hard ground before lifting a smiling face. "Yes, just like my father. Once I'm finished with my schooling at the medical school in Boston, I'd like to tend the same folks here as he did."

Her heart felt a distinct comfort. "I'm proud of you. And you'll make a fine doctor. You've always been so gentle and caring."

He massaged his hands. She wished she had gloves to offer him. Maybe next winter she'd have some of her own.

"I appreciate your encouragement, Emma Leigh. You have a real gift with words and making folks feel good about themselves. God willing, I'll do my best. My father gave his life to the people of this community, and I can do no less."

She felt chills mounting on her arms. "I won't keep you any longer. Good-bye and Godspeed."

As she trudged toward the cabin and the firelight flickering in the window, she had a sudden urge to turn around.

Thad Benson stood in the same place she'd left him. He lifted a hand and waved. Perhaps they'd collide again. . .real soon.

Chapter 3

T had walked the miles home in the dark and cold, but his heart felt as light as a spring day. No matter that snow dusted the road before him and the wind attempted to find solace inside his coat. He had reasons to rejoice. Emma Leigh was neither hurt nor upset with him.

He'd even seen such rosiness on her cheeks. How he'd like to think he might have put the color there. Thad's mind danced with pictures of Emma Leigh—her hair as dark and rich as the soil on his parents' farm and her skin as fair as thick cream. To him she looked like a queen, from her sweet ways to her lovely features. He envied the lucky man who won her heart.

The cold dissipated with more warm thoughts of Emma Leigh, and only when he lifted the latch on his aunt and uncle's wooden door did he notice the frigid temperatures.

"Thad, I've been so worried," Aunt Klara said, rushing from a chair at her spinning wheel to the door to meet him. Her Swedish accent soothed him, and he stepped into her motherly embrace. "Warm yourself by the fire, and I'll get you something to eat. I have beef stew." She released him but not before patting him on the back.

"I'm sorry to have alarmed you. I needed to pay a visit to the Carter family, and it took longer than I expected."

Uncle Albert lifted his gaze from his Bible. A concerned look etched additional wrinkles into his leathered face. "Is everything all right there?"

"Yes. I—I accidentally caused Miss Emma Leigh to take a spill today and wanted to make sure she escaped unharmed." He grasped his uncle's hand. "I apologize if I caused you any unnecessary discomfort. I'll do the evening chores now rather than after I eat."

"They're finished. You're home now, and the load is lifted from my mind." Uncle Albert offered a reassuring smile.

Thad scraped a chair across the wooden floor and sat at the table. "Thank you, but I could have done them." Weariness suddenly settled in his bones, and for the first time that day he relaxed. The aroma of Aunt Klara's *kalops*, Swedish beef stew with special spices, caused his stomach to rumble. She dished out a hearty bowl and sliced a thick piece of rye bread to go with it.

The comforts of home kept him at his aunt and uncle's. Perhaps selfishness ruled a part of his heart, but he despised being alone—and knew he'd starve with his cooking.

"The health of the Carters could be better. Mr. Carter is still pale, and the younger children have runny noses," Thad said after quietly blessing his food. "Looks like two new additions to their family since I was there, too."

"Elizabeth and Charles," Aunt Klara said. "Nearly lost the boy that first year, but he's getting stronger."

The thought troubled Thad. "Makes me wish I already practiced medicine."

Uncle Albert closed his Bible. "You'll be a fine doctor when the time comes."

Emma Leigh had made the same comment earlier.

"God is with you," Uncle Albert continued. "He's given you a sound mind and a gift for wanting to heal. I saw the same attributes in your father."

"Thank you, Uncle. I'm anxious to begin my studies. If I can be half as good a doctor as my father, I will be pleased."

His uncle chuckled. "The young—anxious to be about their business."

"I have enough money saved for the fall session," Thad said. "Although I will miss both of you. All I need to put aside now is money to live on and purchase my textbooks."

"I heartily approve of your frugal ways." His uncle returned to his Bible reading.

Thad thanked Aunt Klara for the stew. When he first came to live with his aunt and uncle, her Swedish mannerisms and traditions often confused him. He hadn't always been pleasant. Later when he apologized, Aunt Klara quickly forgave.

"It would have been easier if I'd been more like your mother." She'd tilted her head as though she understood the grief plaguing his heart.

Often he wondered why God had not blessed Uncle Albert and Aunt Klara with children. They gave so much of themselves.

She poured him a cold glass of buttermilk. "I keep thinking the sooner you leave for school, the sooner you'll be a fine doctor for our community. This time for good."

Uncle Albert stood and tucked his Bible under his arm. "Mornin' comes early. I'm heading to bed."

He dutifully kissed Aunt Klara's cheek and ruffled Thad's hair as though he were but a boy.

"Good night, Uncle. Sleep well."

Uncle Albert disappeared into a darkened room and closed the door behind him.

"You need your rest, too," Thad said to his aunt. "I'm fine, and I'll be ready for bed as soon as I finish eating."

She pulled a chair closer to him, folded her hands in her lap, and took a deep breath. "Thad, is there a matter plaguing you?"

"I don't think so." *Unless you consider my useless feelings for Emma Leigh.*

"Are you working too hard with the farm and at the inn? Every day you do chores at your parents' home and then here." She leaned closer.

"Not at all. I enjoy hard work."

Silence crept between them. The fire crackled, and the dog snored.

"Is your heart hurting for Miss Emma Leigh?"

Thad closed his eyes. Did it really show?

"Love can be a painful thing," she said, gray tendrils framing her oval face.

He nodded. "She's a fine lady."

"And you're a fine man."

"If I had my schooling done, perhaps I could think about. . .well, consider the possibilities. I could make a few repairs on my parents' home and clean things up proper-like."

Aunt Klara touched his arm. "Sounds to me like you have done a lot of thinking about the matter."

Thad never lied, but offering information about his private thoughts was another matter.

"Well, you finish your supper, and I'll leave you to your thinking." She rose from her chair and bade him good night.

If Aunt Klara read his heart so easily, did others know, too?

◦∂—

Monday, November 17, 1851

"I'd like the inn ready for Christmas by Monday, December 1," Mr. Jones announced at the morning staff meeting. He dug his hands into his trousers' pockets, and the motion revealed a festive plaid vest of red, green, and gold. He teetered back and forth on his heels, grinning broadly. "This is our favorite time of the year. Don't you agree?"

Thad glanced at the staff of eleven—seven women and four men—nodding and voicing their approval. The spirit of Christmas had arrived at the Jones Inn. The enthusiasm would mount until it seemed the walls would burst with laughter and merriment. He'd joined the staff a little more than a year ago, and he well remembered last year's joy in celebrating the Lord's birth. Guests loved the atmosphere of the inn during this special time, and the staff took pains to make their stay memorable. The mirth could not be equaled at any other season of the year.

Mr. Jones cleared his throat. "Thad, you are in charge of finding the tree—a tall, full one for the entranceway. Make sure you take someone to help you. Mrs. Jones and I will decorate it. We rather enjoy that part of Christmas. Mrs. Weares, as in years before, your responsibilities are to oversee the overall trimming of the entire inn. I'd like every room to hold a bit of Christmas cheer."

Mrs. Weares nodded, her thin face breaking forth into a smile.

"Sarah, as head cook, I want you to provide the guests with the best of food. Spare nothing when it comes to their pleasure." Mr. Jones nodded at Emma Leigh. "Miss Carter, are you ready to explain the details of how all of us will spread 'goodwill towards men' amongst each other? My wife and I are looking forward to what you've planned."

So Mr. and Mrs. Jones planned to be a part of the celebration. Thad stole a glimpse at Emma Leigh. Her rosy cheeks brightened, and as always when she was excited, her big brown eyes sparkled.

"Yes sir," she said, rising from her chair.

"Come along then. We're all ready to hear your plan."

Emma Leigh grasped a small basket and made her way to Mr. Jones's side. He stepped back, making a formal gesture for her to begin. The staff laughed. For certain the holiday season reigned in their bones.

Emma Leigh moistened her lips. "This year, our Christmas party will be slightly different. Oh, we'll have a marvelous meal on Christmas Eve, but there will be one addition." She took a deep breath. "In just a moment, all of us will write our names on a piece of paper and place them in this basket. Then we will take turns drawing out a name. The one you select is your secret friend from December 15 until Christmas Eve. As often as you like, you may select something for your secret friend and leave it on the wooden table in the kitchen for him or her to pick up. The items are to be small, a sweet treat or a note—or anything you feel appropriate. The idea is to spread love and cheer in ways that don't involve a great deal of money. We simply want everyone to be remembered. On Christmas Eve, we all find out who our secret friends are. Is this fine with everyone?"

From the sounds of the women clapping, Thad surmised the secret friend proposal suited all of them. Although the men looked a little less pleased. To Thad, it really didn't matter. He merely wanted to see the joy on Emma Leigh's face.

"Oh my," Sarah said and covered her mouth to stifle a giggle. "I hope I get one of you skinny maids so I can fatten you up."

Mr. Jones held up his hand. "Nonsense. I've been trying to add a little meat to my bones for years. I hope you draw my name."

The hum of the staff's chatter rose like pealing bells. Thad remembered the days before Christmas when his parents were alive. His father loved to tease, and his mother always pretended mock indignation. On Christmas Eve, she'd take the time to bake an apple pie to enjoy after they'd selected a tree. Father would declare it sour. "You're a fine doctor's wife," he'd say, "but at Christmas I need a woman who can bake a sugary crusted pie." Of course, he always chuckled with his words and ate every bite.

Thad missed those days.

One by one each member of the staff dropped his or her name into Emma Leigh's basket. Closing her eyes, she waded her fingers through the pieces of paper. "Mr. Jones, would you like to be the first one to select your secret friend?"

He dutifully stepped forward and made a grand production of inserting his hand into the basket. He winked at his wife, a quiet, gentle woman who never spoke ill of anyone. Mr. Jones pulled out a name. He lifted his chin and read the paper. "This is grand," he said. "I believe I have the best name of all."

His wife or Sarah, Thad speculated.

One by one the staff filed up to select a name. One of the stable boys drew his own, causing much laughter until he replaced it and reached down into the basket for another. Thad watched the expressions on their faces—and on Emma Leigh's. Surprise. Elation. He waited until the end of the line. How grand if one dark-haired beauty became his secret friend for an entire ten days.

"You have the last name, Thad," Mr. Jones called out.

Thad felt the others study him. They all knew him to be a shy sort. Forcing a faint grin, he reached inside the basket for the lone slip of paper.

Emma Leigh Carter.

Chapter 4

Emma Leigh finished her work promptly before Papa came with the wagon to drive her home. She could very well walk the three miles and did when Papa had a full day in the fields. But now a nip of winter tugged at her heels, and he took her each morning and came by every afternoon. Emma Leigh understood his need to do all he could for her. Ever since he took ill, Papa had troubled himself with her working. Emma Leigh realized he felt inadequate as provider for his family, but in truth she loved her position at the inn. Greeting guests and making sure they were comfortable suited her fine. Admittedly, she loved the Jones Inn.

Glancing about, she looked for signs of Thad. Odd, he'd been on her mind since last night, more so than she deemed proper. She hoped he'd drawn an easy name for the Christmas celebration. In fact, she'd hoped all the men found her plan easy. The secret friend project should be fun for everyone, or it wouldn't suit Mr. Jones's idea of a memorable holiday.

Taking a peek into the kitchen, she didn't see signs of Thad there either.

"Can I help ya, Emma Leigh?" Sarah said, giving her a quick smile. Her sleeves were rolled to her elbows, revealing forearms dusted with flour. She took both hands to the dough and kneaded it again, putting all of her strength into the white mound.

"Have you seen Thad?" Emma Leigh said, sensing embarrassment for inquiring about the man.

"Not in the past hour. He's probably in the carriage house or the stables at this time of day."

"Thank you. I'll try those places." She avoided the curious look on Sarah's face.

The moment Emma Leigh closed the outside door, she regretted leaving her shawl behind. But she'd only be a moment with Thad, just long enough to see if he was content with the name he'd drawn. After all, he'd given her the idea of a secret friend.

She spotted him instructing a stableboy on how to properly escort the guests to and from the carriage. Emma Leigh listened, wondering why she'd

24

never heard the deep timbre of his voice before. After all, they'd worked together for more than a year and grown up together on neighboring farms.

She smiled at the scene before her. A few days ago, a pine bough had been draped across the shiny back of the carriage, adding a festive touch.

"If you are in the position of assisting the lady into the carriage, always offer your hand and address her appropriately. Think of her as a royal queen. Greet the men as though they were kings, and you will never disappoint the guests or Mr. Jones."

The young man nodded in Emma Leigh's direction. "Good afternoon, Miss Emma Leigh."

She stifled a giggle, knowing his mannerly words came as a result of Thad's careful instruction. "Hello, Baxter. I see you're having a fine lesson with an excellent teacher."

Thad grinned broadly. He bent low and offered her his hand. "My lady."

This was the Thad she remembered, the fun-loving boy who played make-believe with her. With a deep curtsy, she reached for his outstretched hand and allowed him to lead her to the carriage door. He opened it wide and assisted her inside.

"Have a pleasant and safe journey, Miss Carter," Thad said. "We look forward to having you return as a guest of Jones Inn." He closed the door and tipped his woolen cap as though he wore a top hat.

"Bravo." Emma Leigh clapped. "I shall recommend you to the owner of this impeccable establishment," she said, no longer able to contain her laughter. "Your manners are exquisite."

"I appreciate your generous compliments." He opened the carriage door and took her hand as she stepped to the ground.

She caught his gaze, and its warmth branded her heart. *Oh dear, Thad will be able to see I'm clearly flustered.*

"I understand the formalities now," Baxter laughed. "Thank you for helping me. I'll do my best not to forget a single thing."

Thad shook the young man's hand. "You won't have any problems. You have a quick mind."

Baxter disappeared from the stable, leaving Emma Leigh and Thad alone.

"You were very kind to him," she said, willing her heart to cease its incessant pounding.

"He's a fine lad." Thad leaned against the carriage and rubbed a dull spot on the carriage door.

"You reminded me of when we were children." Emma Leigh shook her head at the memories. "You were always so good about playing the games I suggested."

"Oh, but you never refused climbing trees or marching to my soldier's drum."

Laughing with Thad came easily. She sighed happily and relaxed a bit. She recalled her errand. "Are you satisfied with the name you drew today?"

"I'll manage," he said. "It's a challenge, but your idea was excellent."

"You inspired it."

A rooster strutted past them with two hens trailing behind. "Best you watch your manners," he said to the chickens. "Sarah will have you for dinner tomorrow if you venture too close to the kitchen."

Emma Leigh joined him in laughter and realized she needed to get back inside. Papa would be coming soon, and she didn't want to detain him. "Please give your aunt and uncle my regards." She turned to leave. "And my parents said you were welcome to stop by anytime."

Immediately color tinge her cheeks. What had happened to her?

❧

Thad set the pail of milk inside the front door of his aunt and uncle's frame home. He smelled dinner, and his stomach rumbled.

"Hungry?" Aunt Klara said, wiping her hands on her apron.

"Enough to eat a horse." He washed his hands in a basin, all the while thinking about the Christmas happenings at the inn. *Thank You, Lord, for allowing me to draw Emma Leigh's name. Now if I can only come up with the right gifts.*

"I sure could use your help, Aunt Klara," Thad said, drying his hands. "Can we talk later?"

When Aunt Klara smiled, her whole face radiated, reminding him of how an angel must look. "You can have all the time you need."

He hugged her waist, and Uncle Albert wrinkled his brow in mock annoyance. "Find your own wife, Thad," he said. "Klara is mine, and I've seen you looking at her—especially at mealtime." He winked and stuck his pipe into his mouth.

I know the wife I want, but I'll never have her.

As they ate, Thad reflected on the past year with his aunt and uncle. He'd still been grieving for his parents when he arrived from Boston, and the guilt of lashing out at Aunt Klara when she tried to comfort him still stung. Praise God he had finally come to his senses and realized this precious woman was a gift. Every day he thanked God for Aunt Klara's love and wisdom.

Once they'd completed the meal, Thad read the scripture aloud while Uncle Albert listened and Aunt Klara bustled about tidying up the kitchen. He made certain she heard his voice in the next room, clear and strong. Tonight he chose Psalm 37. Verse four seized him as though God had lifted the words from the page: " 'Delight thyself also in the Lord; and he shall give thee the desires of thine heart.' "

God knew how Thad's heart longed for Emma Leigh. Dare he ask for so great a blessing as to have her always? Thad took a deep breath and continued reading. Still, Emma Leigh should have a husband who had mastered witty conversation. She'd be bored with the likes of him. What could he possibly be thinking? Medical school lay in the near future, and he had little money to support a wife.

Soon after, Aunt Klara joined them for prayers. Once Uncle Albert concluded with a hearty "Amen," he stood and yawned. "I'm in need of some sleep."

"Are you going to bed because I want to talk to Aunt Klara?" Thad laughed.

"Of course not." His uncle joined in the laughter. "Mind you, don't be making plans to run off with my wife, hear me?"

Thad bid his uncle good night. He pulled an extra chair around the cozy fire. How he loved this house and the many ways Aunt Klara graced the room with touches of beauty. She'd brought countless reminders of her homeland from Sweden. Near the fireplace rested a huge, hand-painted wooden chest. The top and sides were bordered in a deep blue vinelike pattern. Yellow outlined lighter blue flowers in the middle. The chest held many treasures from her native land. Every box, tool, and dish had been intricately painted. Shades of blue, green, dull reds, and oranges made up the background colors while greens, reds, whites, yellows, and different hues of blue formed the designs.

Thad remembered the first time Aunt Klara had opened the box to show him her handsomely carved distaff called a scotching knife, and her mangle, used to smooth the wrinkles from wet clothing. Both were painted in green and orange-red. She called the colorful technique rosemaling, and on long winter nights she busied herself in painting plates, chests, and even some of Uncle Albert's tools with the beautiful designs. The chest also contained a Swedish hymnal and a pair of hand-painted gloves.

Thad glanced at the ceiling beam near Aunt Klara and Uncle Albert's bedroom. Aunt Klara had bordered some of the walls with flowers and leaves. A beam was draped with a handwoven blanket in green and orange. Upstairs in his loftlike room hung another blanket in blue-green, light green, and red.

"How can I help you?" Aunt Klara said, interrupting his reverie.

He rubbed the legs of his breeches. His carefully chosen words had slipped his mind. He might as well leap into it all. "Today at the inn, everyone drew a name for a secret friend. We're supposed to give this person a token of friendship as often as we desire. On Christmas Eve we all find out who has our name. Mr. Jones wants this Christmas to be memorable, and the gifts are to be more from the heart than the purse."

Aunt Klara nodded. "And whose name did you receive?"

Thad took a deep breath. "Emma Leigh's."

Aunt Klara tilted her head, and her clear blue eyes peered up into his. "My dear boy, are you happy about this?"

He sighed. "I think so, but I only have a few ideas. That's where I need help."

Aunt Klara touched her finger to the dimple in her chin. "In Sweden, we celebrate Christmas for a whole month. Perhaps I can help you with some of the gifts."

He felt himself smile from the inside out.

"What are your thoughts?" she said.

Thad swallowed hard. "I can write a little, but not fancy words. I can whittle some. Candy would be nice. She doesn't have any gloves, and I don't remember her having any last winter either." He shrugged. "Maybe a pretty ribbon for her hair. And I know her family is so very poor, so maybe I could give her food to share. I know the things I have in mind will cost a little, but there are so many things she needs." He remembered the small pot of stew on their table the night he visited her. They were all thin, too slight to fight the cold of winter.

"Those all sound like fine ideas."

He forced a hesitant smile. "I also wondered if you could show me how to do the rosemaling—I mean a few simple strokes that I could add to a small box."

Her eyes moistened. "I'd be honored, but when will you have the time? Your days and evenings are so full."

"I'll simply stay up later."

She seemed to ponder his words. "We could work on the painting together. You can learn, and we both can add touches to it in our spare moments."

Thad took a deep breath. "I don't want you to have added work."

She patted his arm in her familiar affectionate manner. "It's not work when you use your hands for someone you love."

"I love you," he whispered, then grinned. "I dare not say those words too loud. Uncle Albert may come out of his bed with a gun after me!"

"Ah, I believe I know where your heart lies, and the young woman is most lucky indeed."

He hesitated. "Aunt Klara, she is a beautiful woman inside and out. Look at what she's doing for her family, and she is always happy."

Aunt Klara caressed his cheek. "I pray God grants you the same as in the psalm you read this night."

The desires of my heart. Great heavenly Father, should I dare even ask such a thing?

Chapter 5

Emma Leigh took a peek into Mama's cooking pot to see if she could ladle a few more beans and broth into her bowl. The day had been long and busy, and for some reason the joy about introducing the Christmas celebration had made her hungrier than usual.

"Would you get us some more, please?" eight-year-old Simon said, holding up his empty bowl.

She gazed into the eyes of her younger brother and then at the other children who looked expectantly. Such sad, hungry eyes. Would life ever get better? How could she be so selfish and not think of them? God forgive her.

"I'd be happy to," she said cheerfully.

"And bread, too," Simon said.

Emma Leigh held her breath. Not a crumb remained.

"The bread's gone," Papa said, a bit harshly.

"Here, take the rest of mine," Mama placed her remaining quarter piece of bread into Simon's palm.

Emma Leigh fought the overwhelming urge to weep. The wooden spoon scraped across the bottom of the pot as she placed every bean she could find in the empty bowls. She hated this constant turmoil over food. At least she could get a good meal at the inn. That fact alone made her feel guilty when the pangs of hunger tugged at her siblings' empty stomachs. Sometimes Mr. Jones asked Sarah to send the day's leftovers home with Emma Leigh. Papa disliked the charity, grumbled about being able to care for his family, but he took the food nonetheless.

Mama cleared her throat. "How was your day, Emma Leigh? Did everyone like your idea for Christmas?"

Nodding, Emma Leigh set the food before her brothers before taking her place on the bench. "Everyone seemed excited and talked about it most of the day. Even Mr. Jones and his wife participated in the drawing."

"Whose name did you receive?" Mama said, reaching across the table and taking Emma's hand into hers. Mama's thin hands felt comforting despite the sadness that constantly threatened the family.

"Sarah, the cook."

Papa raised his brow. "What do you plan to give her over the next ten days?"

"I'm thinking of scripture, and I already have paper."

"Excellent choice." He sat straighter in his chair. "I think tonight would be the perfect evening for me to bring out my fiddle. Anyone feel like singing?"

Mama smiled, and the children clapped. Christmas would be celebrated in spirit only at the Carter cabin, but they had enough love to fill a large house. If only she could provide a fine Christmas dinner for them.

Later on that night, Emma Leigh snuggled Charles and Elizabeth close to her, wrapping her arms around their little bodies in an effort to keep these two youngest members of the household warm. She allowed delicious thoughts about the day to occupy her mind.

Spending time with Thad in the stables had kindled something in her heart. Something she dared not allow herself to dwell upon except in moments like these. His lighthearted antics with Baxter carried her back to those wonderful days when they played together as children without cares or worries.

The desire to have a home of her own one day tore at her heart, especially when many of her friends were already married. But how could she desert Mama and Papa when they needed her income? Papa had borrowed money to help through the frightening period when he nearly died, but he must pay his debts. God had blessed him with renewed strength, and this year's harvest had been better than the preceding year's. Yet the scant supply of food on the table proved that her destiny, for now anyway, was at home helping her family.

Those working at the inn must surely know of her destitute situation, but she'd never spoken of it. Although she wore the same thin dress day after day, she refused to complain about her poverty. After all, God did supply her needs.

Emma Leigh clung to the hope of a better life for her family. Perhaps then she might meet a man as fine and godly as Thad. Until life proved easier, she'd keep smiling and giving, just as the Lord wanted.

~

Thad woke before dawn, excited about his gift for the first day of the Christmas celebration. He'd gotten the idea just before falling asleep last night—or rather God had given him the answer to his prayers.

"My, you're bustling about early this morning," Aunt Klara said, once she opened her bedroom door and saw Thad had already stoked the fire and added wood to the embers. It crackled like a welcoming old friend.

"I needed to talk to you this morning," he said, rising from the rug by the hearth.

She laughed. "Seems like you are needing to do a lot of that lately."

He couldn't stop the smile. "Uncle Albert worried again?"

"Never know," she said. "I guess we need to be careful. So how can I help you?"

"I'd like to buy a dozen eggs."

"Certainly not."

Thad lifted a brow in a silent question.

"I know you want those eggs for Emma Leigh and her family. God be my witness, I would never sell food meant for a hungry family."

"But I'm the one doing the purchasing." Thad felt somewhere between helpless and frustrated.

Aunt Klara pointed her finger at him. " 'Tis your uncle and I who owe you for all your hard work. Now you take those eggs and don't say another word about it. Hear me?"

Later, Thad chuckled all the way to the inn. Aunt Klara had scolded him until he'd agreed to take the eggs. He'd carefully printed Emma Leigh's name on a piece of paper and slipped it between two large brown eggs, and he'd left early so he could set the small basket on the wooden table in the kitchen before Emma Leigh arrived.

***

Laughter from the inn's kitchen nabbed Emma Leigh's attention. Part of her wanted to see if her secret friend had left a token of the season, and the other part didn't really care.

All morning Emma Leigh had tended to guests and helped the maids change bed linens. She'd feigned the anticipation of the season in hopes no one would see her fatigue. Shortly after she'd fallen asleep the night before, Emma Leigh had been awakened by little Charles coughing uncontrollably. His flesh seared hers. She roused Mama, and they prepared a hot mustard plaster for his chest and gave him chamomile tea mixed with honey. When she noticed Mama felt feverish, too, Emma Leigh offered to stay up with her brother. Mama reluctantly agreed to go back to bed when Emma Leigh pointed out that the children needed a healthy mother. Throughout the long night, Emma Leigh prayed for her family.

Poor little Charles didn't sleep until nearly dawn, and his fever didn't diminish by the time she hurried to the inn. She'd managed to carefully write out the Twenty-third Psalm on a piece of paper and place it on the wooden table in the kitchen before Sarah arrived.

The scent of pine filled the air, and although Emma Leigh did not feel like celebrating, the aura of Christmas cascaded around her like a rushing waterfall. Emma Lee forced a cordial greeting to Mrs. Weares as the older woman descended the stairs, her heels clicking on the wood flooring and her lips humming "Silent Night." The gangly woman looked a bit manly with her severe hair pulled back sharply. The style accented her long nose.

"I received the best gift today," Mrs. Weares said, fanning herself as though the excitement might cause her to faint.

"And what did your secret friend leave for you?" Emma Leigh said, pleased to see the woman happy.

"Oh…" The older woman turned her head and laughed lightly. "A peppermint stick. Can you imagine enjoying candy at my age?" She fanned her face, the wrinkles around her eyes deepening with each precious giggle. "And I see your gift is still on the table."

Emma Leigh's eyes widened. "Mine?"

"Why, yes!" Mrs. Weares leaned closer. "I couldn't help but see your name sticking out from it."

Glancing toward the door, Emma Leigh suddenly had an urge to see for herself.

"Run along now. I'll mind things while you see the pleasant surprise in store for you."

Emma Leigh scurried off to the kitchen. In all of the worries about her family, should she rejoice in a gift left for her?

As she reached the kitchen, Emma Leigh greeted the cook. "Hello, Sarah. How are you today?" The red-haired woman was busily peeling potatoes, but she had time to offer Emma Leigh a wink.

"Aye, perfectly wonderful, lass. I've had a beautiful psalm to keep me content all this morning long."

"I'm glad for you," Emma Leigh said, her heart warming at Sarah's words.

"Indeed. I have a secret friend who knew exactly what I needed today. Yes indeed, the Lord is my Shepherd."

Emma Leigh advanced across the room to hug Sarah and hide her own tears that threatened to spill over. She fretted so much about her family, although the Bible said not to worry but trust God. Constantly, she asked the Lord for healing and a way for her family to receive their basic needs.

"And your secret friend blessed you," Sarah said, when the two ended their sweet embrace.

Emma Leigh's gaze flew to the wooden table where a small basket rested. She stole a look inside. Several lovely light brown eggs nestled together like delicate rolls. Catching her breath in her throat, Emma Leigh nearly cried. "Eggs. Little Charles's favorite."

Bless you, my secret friend. Whoever you may be.

Chapter 6

Emma Leigh forgot her aching body for the remainder of the day. She couldn't wait to get home. Surely the eggs were a sign of God's healing for Charles and Mama, as well as for Papa's continued strength.

She spotted Thad in the entranceway just before Papa came by. Her heart lifted at the sight of him. She could only be his childhood friend. Nothing more. He'd be a fine doctor one day and would need a wife who was much smarter than she. But her logic didn't stop the yearning in her heart.

He smiled, but a guest requested his attention and the two disappeared outside. Tomorrow perhaps she and Thad might have an opportunity to visit.

❧

Thad regretted not talking to Emma Leigh before she went home, but he treasured her response to the eggs. He'd been standing behind the door when she discovered them, and he found it difficult to remain hiding once she shared her enthusiasm with Sarah.

Later that evening, Aunt Klara began instructing him in rosemaling by demonstrating a few simple strokes. At first he believed the art impossible to grasp, but as he persevered, he found success.

"Are you taking Miss Emma Leigh a gift tomorrow?" Aunt Klara said as he practiced two brush strokes—C and S curves.

"I think so." He concentrated on the task at hand. "I'd like to."

"Do you need any help selecting something?" Aunt Klara leaned closer, a habit when she wanted to make sure she was heard.

"Not this time. I kept one of the cinnamon sticks from my last trip to Philadelphia." He arched his back, which felt a bit stiff from bending over his work. "And late tomorrow afternoon I need to drive some guests to the city. Mr. Jones said for me to take my time in returning, so I plan to purchase a few things."

"What a lovely idea."

The following day Thad drove two fine chestnut mares along the brick streets of Philadelphia. The rhythmic clopping of the horse hooves mesmerized him as he listened to the sights and sounds of one of the nation's largest cities, the birth-place of America. He drove the carriage down Chestnut Street to view Independence Hall. Thad never tired of this sight. A mere glimpse filled him with pride. The Georgian-style edifice stood as a symbol of liberty and freedom for all Americans.

He reined the horses right onto Fifth Street and on toward Market Street where he could view Christ Church. Many wonderful stories surrounded this beautiful building that silently commemorated those who had worshiped within its sacred walls and was rich in history. The Second Continental Congress had attended its services, as had Benjamin Franklin and George Washington.

Thad took a moment to reflect on the beautiful landmark before gathering up the reins and urging the horses onto Third Street and on south.

Outside Philadelphia, he passed through a small community that held a sizable dry goods and general store. He pulled alongside, secured the horses and carriage, and made his way through the establishment. Thad knew exactly what he wanted for Uncle Albert and Aunt Klara, but his Emma Leigh proved the most difficult.

When had he begun to think of her as his? Pressing his lips together firmly in contemplation, he realized she'd always been his—nestled somewhere in a treasured part of his heart. But this time next year, he'd be in Boston attending medical school. Asking her to wait for him didn't seem fair, but he selfishly admitted he didn't want to tell her good-bye in a few months. He simply must enjoy the time with her now and leave the rest up to God.

Thad found a warm, woolen scarf for Uncle Albert and a new shawl for Aunt Klara. He felt like being extravagant, mostly because he had the money saved for his education and he didn't know what his circumstances might be next Christmas—or even if he would be able to come home. So this year he would give his dear aunt and uncle the best gifts possible. A trace of nostalgia for Christmases past when his parents were alive passed through his mind. He allowed a few pleasant thoughts, but when sadness ushered in painful memories, he shoved them all aside.

Practicality ruled a large portion of Thad's life, and he believed a gift should be something the recipient needed. Glancing about, he saw many things Emma Leigh and her entire family could use. Poverty and indebtedness hammered at their door, and until Mr. Carter repaid all he owed, the family would continue to suffer. Nothing would give Thad more pleasure than to give all of the Carters a splendid holiday. Just to see a spark of joy in those children's eyes would make him extremely happy, but the Carters were a proud sort.

An idea began to form, and while he meandered through the store, peering at and examining the many items upon the shelves, he prayed for guidance and wisdom.

"Do you need some assistance?" an older gentleman said, his face akin to a dried apple.

Thad stopped and considered the question. "I'm looking for a few small gifts for a young lady, something useful. I definitely want a ribbon for her hair."

The man offered a smile. "Right this way, sir." The storekeeper led the way to where bolts of beautiful fabric and notions rested on shelves and a long table. "Would this do?" He held up two spools of ribbon in red and green.

"The red one, please." Already Thad could envision the bright color woven in Emma Leigh's dark curls.

"Do you see anything else here that catches your fancy?" the man said.

Thad studied the notions, buttons, and other sewing items. If she were his wife... *What am I thinking?* Anyway, Emma Leigh did need a new dress, but fabric didn't fall within his responsibility, nor was it proper.

"A thimble?" Thad lifted his gaze questioningly to the storekeeper.

"Excellent idea."

Together they selected one. Thad remembered the night he'd walked to the Carter home and the chill permeating the air.

"The lady needs gloves and a thick scarf," he said aloud.

By the time Thad finished, he'd found a beeswax candle and enough penny candy to give to each of Emma Leigh's siblings on Christmas Day. By then she'd know he'd been the one to draw her name. A flutter arose in his stomach, and the fear of her shunning his gifts settled like a gray cloud.

As Thad drove the carriage back to the Jones Inn, he added up the gifts and the nine days remaining: the hair ribbon, cinnamon stick, thimble, candle, the deep green gloves, matching scarf, the small box he planned to paint with the rosemaling technique, perhaps some freshly churned butter, and perhaps a piece of bobbin lace that his aunt Klara had made. He counted nine, and the eggs he'd already given made ten. Except he wanted to do more.

Truth be known, he must surely be courting. The thought scared him, especially with the uncertainty of the future. Still, he couldn't put the idea out of his mind. Poetic words began to form in his mind, slowly at first, then more freely as thoughts of Emma Leigh wrapped around him like a thick quilt.

> *A candle's flicker in the darkness,*
> *A fire's warmth to greet the weary,*
> *Only Jesus shines more brightly*
> *Than my lovely Emma Leigh.*

Would she think him foolish? Laugh at his attempt of showing his affections through verse? Thad's stomach twisted into a painful knot. Giving a poem to her required more courage than venturing to medical school. At least he knew how to study. But with Emma Leigh, he didn't know what kind of reaction to expect.

❧

Emma Leigh balled her fists and dug her fingernails into her palms to keep her hands warm. Soon she'd be at the inn where a toasty fire would stop the ache in her hands and feet. But what of the little ones left at home? Last night's snowfall only made her feel more dismal about the long winter ahead.

"Papa, why don't you and I patch the walls after I'm finished this afternoon?" she said, willing her teeth to cease chattering.

"The drafts are making the others sick," he said, his voice echoing with despair.

From the corner of her eye, she saw his pallor. He looked so old and beaten.

"You and I could have the chore done in no time. And Simon, he's able to help, don't you think?" She tried to sound cheerful, optimistic about the work that should have been completed more than six weeks ago when a heavy rain and windstorm dislodged much of the mud and straw used to chink their cabin.

"You work too hard." Papa coughed, a deep gut-wrenching sound that seemed to originate in the soles of his feet. Once he gained control, he continued. "I'll see to it today."

"Papa, why don't you rest and let us attempt it together?"

He shook his head, and from the determined look upon his face, Emma Leigh knew not to argue. His pride dug his grave.

At the inn, she kissed him good-bye and hurried into the warm building. How dreadful of her to prefer the atmosphere of this fine place to her own home.

The staff bustled about their work, eager to find out if their secret friend had remembered them. Whoever held her name had been most generous, for two days ago she'd received a delicious cinnamon stick that she had shared with the younger children at home, and yesterday she'd received a lovely red ribbon for her hair. She had no idea who had drawn her name, but it didn't matter. Thad occupied her thoughts more than any plan devised to celebrate Christmas. She wondered if she appeared ungrateful to her benefactor and quickly asked God to forgive her. But a few words from Thad or his cheery smile meant more to her than material things.

As if knowing her feelings, he called her name from the kitchen. "Emma Leigh, your secret friend left you something."

She glanced up at his face, seemingly brilliant in his wide smile. How incredible that each time she saw him, he became more handsome. . .and more dear.

"Again? Oh my, I'm not worthy to receive yet another gift."

"Why not?" he said, opening the kitchen door for her to step inside.

"I didn't mean for others to become extravagant." Trouble loomed over her. She never wanted to cause problems.

"Nonsense. Today I received a peppermint, and I do enjoy sweets."

She made her way the short distance to the table. Her eyes widened, and she gasped. "Surely Mr. or Mrs. Jones have my name, for the giver is most generous." She picked up the gloves with tears in her eyes and slipped them on. Her fingers were still cold from the morning ride. "I can't accept this," she murmured. "It's too much."

Thad moved to her side. "Why don't you let the one who gave you the gift decide what is appropriate?"

She lifted her gaze to meet his. "I simply feel uncomfortable when I can't do for my secret friend what is being done for me."

His eyes reflected a certain tenderness, or did she simply wish they saw only her? Her bold thoughts brought a flush to her cheeks.

"God requires we give our best, whatever that may be," he said.

"Thank you, Thad. You always have a way of making me see things differently."

The smile lingered on his lips, and she memorized it for later when the burdens of home threatened to overwhelm her.

"How is your family?" Thad said.

Melancholy crept across her heart, but she masked it as best she could. "Little Charles has been ill, but he's doing much better. The others have coughs and are feeling a bit poorly with runny noses and such. I'm so glad we grew herbs to help them through the winter."

"I'm sorry."

"Oh, it will be remedied soon. Papa and I are going to patch the outside walls this evening."

"Tonight?" He frowned, looking disconcerted.

"Yes," she said, forcing a smile.

"Would you like some help?"

Emma Leigh shook her head. "Papa doesn't approve of charity."

Thad appeared to ponder the matter. "What if I came by for a visit? I could help while I talked to your father."

Oh Thad, you are so good to do this. "I suppose he'd agree, but are you sure you want to work in the cold?"

"Of course. I'll send a note to my aunt and uncle, explaining where I'll be." He pointed to the gloves. "Please, wear these so whoever got them for you will know you are pleased."

She nodded happily.

"Would you like to go ice skating on Sunday afternoon? I believe a few from church are planning a Christmas party."

"Yes. . .why, yes. I'd love to." How good of God to give her such a fine friend as Thad Benson.

Chapter 7

T had knew mixing mud with straw to patch the Carter cabin meant a tedious task. The hard ground and frigid temperatures combined with working at dusk didn't appeal to him at all, but the thought of helping Emma Leigh and her family set well in his spirit. He remembered when high winds and a thunderstorm did tremendous damage to nearby homes and barns. Obviously those hit included the Carters, and Mr. Carter had barely enough strength to harvest the fall crops, much less repair the cabin.

Within an hour after Emma Leigh departed from the inn, Thad made the trek after them, thankful that he'd ridden his horse to work that day. Taking a quick look at the sky, he realized they'd most likely be working by kerosene light long before they finished the job. Anger swept over him as he considered the arduous task ahead for Emma Leigh. He wanted to ask her father why the rest of the family hadn't patched the cabin instead of leaving it all for his precious lady.

But Mr. Carter has been ill. I've no right to judge.

He spotted Mr. Carter and Emma Leigh along with two of the boys daubing the north side of the small structure. As he grew closer, he saw the east side had already been completed. The sight pleased him; Emma Leigh need not carry all of the work on her frail shoulders.

"Good evening," Thad called heartily.

Mr. Carter looked up and waved. "Good to see you, Thad."

"I dropped by to say hello. Looks like you're busy." He secured his horse and advanced at a sharp pace. The wind blew at a brisk speed, inviting a nasty chill up his spine. If he felt the cold, how badly did the others feel? "Evening, Emma Leigh." He glanced at the other two boys but couldn't remember their names.

Emma caught his gaze and smiled knowingly. "The one beside me is Simon, and by Papa is Joseph."

Thad rubbed his hands together. "You folks got yourself a big job here."

Mr. Carter continued to work, the mud dropping from his fingers onto the cold ground. He'd mixed straw with it for durability. Normally moss and clay made the mud harder. "Yes we do. I started earlier today, and I think we'll finish tonight."

"Can I offer a hand?" Thad said.

"It's not necessary," her father said. His voice sounded raspy, and he coughed as though consumption nailed at his chest. Thad prayed not.

"I'd like to talk to you, and I can say my words just as easily working."

Mr. Carter appeared to deliberate the matter. His pale skin alarmed Thad. The older man didn't need to be in the cold.

"I guess that will be fine," Mr. Carter said.

Thad peeled off his gloves and bent to stick his hands into a pile of dirt already dampened by water. Ice cold. All of them would be sick. Adding a little straw, Thad worked the mud, then slapped it up against a bare spot. He reached down and did the same thing again. . .and again.

"So what did you want to talk about?" Mr. Carter said after another series of coughs.

Thad figured Mr. Carter thought he'd come to ask about courting Emma Leigh, and the truth of the matter was the older man probably guessed correctly.

"Well sir. The matter is rather delicate."

"I see." He rubbed his nose. "Emma Leigh, you and your brothers go get us some more straw from the barn."

She nodded, but before she turned in the direction of the barn, a slow blush ascended her cheeks.

After daubing another hole and making sure they were alone, Thad began. "Mr. Carter, I'd like permission to stop by now and then."

"For what reason?"

Another handful of ice-cold mud hit against the wall. "To visit you and your family."

"I'm not so certain you're being honest here."

"What do you mean?"

Mr. Carter dipped into the mud and grabbed a handful of straw. "I mean I believe you want to court Emma Leigh, but you don't want to ask me for permission because you're leaving for school."

The sting of Mr. Carter's words held more truth than Thad cared to admit. "I hadn't considered the situation in that way." He attempted to give the impression of studying the patched wall while he pondered Mr. Carter's observations.

"And how do you view it?" the older man said, taking a deep breath.

Thad shrugged. "Friendship."

"Do you care about my daughter?" the man blurted out before he broke into another coughing spell.

"Yes sir. We grew up together."

The coughing ceased. "Do you care for her in such a way that you'd expect her to wait while you're studying to be a doctor?"

For an ailing man, Mr. Carter didn't mince words when speaking his mind. "I don't know, sir."

"Well, as her father, I'm saying you'd better decide about the future before talking to me about Emma Leigh."

Thad's face reddened. "Are you telling me no?"

"I'm saying I care too much for my little girl to have some fellow break her heart."

"I'd never hurt Emma Leigh!"

"What do you think would happen if I give my permission for you to come visiting, then you up and left for Boston?"

Thad realized how selfish he'd become. Bringing Emma Leigh gifts as a secret friend was a ruse for her affections. How despicable of him.

"Mr. Carter, I apologize for not considering her feelings. I will not see her again unless I am prepared to make a decision about my future. I'd asked her to go skating with me on Sunday, but I see an afternoon together is not considerate of her feelings."

The older man neither smiled not frowned. "I see the way she looks at you. The damage may already be done. I'll tell her she can't attend on Sunday."

◦⌒

Emma Leigh approached Papa and Thad with the straw. Neither looked happy. Neither conversed with the other. What had happened? She'd so hoped Thad wanted to ask Papa if he could come courting. Lately she and Thad had found plenty to talk about, and her mind often wandered to dreams about him. Oh yes, she knew he needed to leave in the spring for Boston. But if they truly cared for each other and God meant for them to enjoy the special gift of love, then He'd show the way.

Or am I acting foolishly?

Why would Thad be interested in a poor girl with nothing to offer? And her family. Who would take care of them if Emma Leigh no longer had a job to help support them? She shouldn't think about such things. Her life—everything about it—lay in God's hands. Taking a cleansing breath, she lifted her head to the dark blue sky and smiled in the direction of Papa and Thad.

"We have straw," she said. "My, we're already working on the final wall."

"Yes, we'll be finished here shortly," Papa said as he continued to daub the holes.

"How good of you to help," she said to Thad.

He didn't acknowledge her.

"Thad needs to get home," Papa said firmly. "Darkness is upon us, and we're taking advantage of a good neighbor."

"Sir, I don't mind seeing this to completion," he said. "My aunt and uncle are not expecting me until late."

"And I would not want to abuse our good friendship with Albert and Klara by keeping you any later." Papa stopped long enough to give Thad a steely glance. "Thank you, and may God bless your endeavors."

Emma Leigh watched Thad head down the road until he disappeared from sight. He'd been cordial when he left and taken the time to bid a proper good-bye to Mama and the younger ones, but something terrible must have happened between Papa and Thad.

By kerosene light, she stole a glance at her father. She could tell by the determined set of his jaw she dare not interrupt his thoughts with questions. He coughed and spurted, the effort obviously draining his strength.

"Papa, let Simon, Joseph, and me finish this," she said, wanting to embrace him. He'd be angry if she touched him. She'd tried in times past and failed.

"Not when we are this close to having the job done."

Emma Leigh chose not to respond. Most likely Papa would spend tomorrow in bed, and she intended to talk to Thad about this evening.

Later on, Papa pulled her aside. "It's not a good idea for you to attend any skating events with Thad Benson."

Her heart cried out for an explanation, but she must not be disrespectful.

The next day she walked to work. Papa had a fever and his cough worsened. She trudged through the snow, praying to keep her mind from the cold and despair. At least she had gloves to keep her hands warm. Papa simply had to get better. She didn't dare think of anything else.

At the inn Thad avoided her, or so she thought. In the afternoon she stepped into the carriage house in hopes of finding him there, but he walked out with Baxter as soon as she entered. He greeted her kindly, but his gaze never met hers.

Her secret friend once again remembered her. In the kitchen she found freshly churned butter. Although her spirits sank with thoughts of home, she praised God for the food.

The next day, she spied Thad with Sarah in the kitchen.

"Do you have a moment to talk?" Her hands trembled, and she instantly thrust them behind her back.

"I can't right now, Emma Leigh. Perhaps later when my duties are completed. The Christmas guests are keeping me extremely busy." Thad shifted from one foot to the other. He excused himself and stepped out into the cold wind.

She swallowed her disappointment and glanced at the gift table. There sat a thimble. She remembered patching a shirt for Joseph without one and how her thumb had bled. The thought of anyone caring enough to give such useful gifts had brought tears to her eyes on more than one occasion. But the gifts didn't ease the aching in her heart.

Chapter 8

On Saturday, Thad gave Emma Leigh the green wool scarf to match her gloves. Sarah had discovered he'd Emma Leigh's name, so the cook reported the young woman's reaction to his gifts.

"Aye." Sarah wiped her eyes with the corner of her apron. "I don't believe she has ever been given such fine things."

"She has needed everything I've given her," Thad said, genuinely pleased at Emma Leigh's sentiment, even if he couldn't talk to her like he wanted.

"Your heart longs for her?" Rather than irritate, Sarah's question soothed Thad's turmoil over Mr. Carter's ultimatum.

He shrugged, not sure how to pose his reply.

"Have ye talked to her father?"

Thad nodded slowly and gazed up into her round face. "I can't talk about it, Sarah, but I know you mean well."

She smiled sadly, and he believed she really understood. He pulled the beeswax candle from inside his jacket. "Would you make sure she finds this tomorrow? I shan't be here until Monday."

Sarah agreed. "A prayer for your Miss Emma Leigh might help."

"I keep asking God for wisdom. Perhaps tomorrow, the Lord's Day, He will give me some answers."

The next evening by firelight, Thad toiled over the small box where he'd begun a reddish-orange chrysanthemum. Aunt Klara had instructed him to outline the flowers in white and add leaves around it. The finishing touch would be a leaflike scroll outlined in the same reddish orange. All the while he worked at the painting, his mind spun with thoughts of Emma Leigh, his plans as a doctor, and what God intended for his life.

"My dear boy, you look so troubled." Aunt Klara placed a comforting hand upon his shoulder. "Has something happened?"

He glanced into the wrinkled face he'd grown to love. "I spoke with Mr. Carter the night I helped patch their cabin."

"About Emma Leigh?"

"Yes ma'am. He doesn't want me seeing her until I make a decision about my future." Thad bent over the box, his heart heavy. "He doesn't believe it fair for me to see her now and leave in a few months for school."

"I see," Aunt Klara murmured.

"Unfortunately, I agree with him."

She pulled a chair beside him close to the fire. "Do you love her?"

"Yes, I most certainly do."

"God gives us the gift of love to glorify Him. He will help you find an answer."

Shaking his head, Thad released a pent-up sigh. "I listened very hard to the sermon this morning but heard nothing about what I must do. I'm spending extra time pondering over the scriptures and in prayer. Still, I'm confused."

"What is your dream?"

He peered into the fire, listened to the cheerful sound of its crackle. "I would like to marry her and take her with me to Boston." Simply speaking his secret longings aloud made him feel as though they threatened to vanish into ashes.

Uncle Albert joined them by the fire, pulling a rocker near his wife. "Forgive me for listening, but Thad, why is this not possible?"

For the first time, Thad realized how much his uncle resembled his father. Even his uncle's deep voice and the gentleness reflected in his eyes reminded Thad of the man he sorely missed.

"I have enough money saved for my tuition and to live meagerly—but certainly not with the lifestyle Emma Leigh deserves."

Uncle Albert cleared his throat. "What does the dear child have now? She works all day and goes home to take care of her family. Surely you could offer her more than she now receives."

Thad considered his uncle's words. True, in being his wife, she would not exhaust herself day after day. Another realization saddened him. "Her father may refuse me because she supports the family."

"Surely not!" Aunt Klara said. "He is an honorable man."

Uncle Albert studied Thad. "Isn't Mr. Carter improving?"

"Slowly, but I believe he's harboring a hard cough."

"Do any of us have anything we could offer to make their lives easier until he regains his strength?" Aunt Klara said.

Thad straightened. A warm sensation spread through him. "I have no need for the seven cows and bull on my parents' farm. Do you think if I offered them to Mr. Carter in return for him keeping a watchful eye on my land, it would help?"

"An excellent idea," Uncle Albert replied and chuckled. "You and I tire of keeping them milked, and I was going to suggest you sell them before you left for Boston."

"Perhaps the Carters could grow a season of crops there, too," Thad continued. "Enough for them to eat and to sell."

Aunt Klara smiled, and her eyes moistened. " 'Tis an answer to prayer, Thad. See, God did hear your heart."

"I believe so," he said, his heart picking up pace to match his new hope. "I'll talk to Mr. Carter tomorrow."

Emma Leigh spotted Thad heading her way Sunday morning after church. For the first time since he'd helped patch her home, he smiled at her freely. She'd never learned what transpired that night, except Mama said it was best to not speak of it to Papa.

To her dismay, as soon as church dismissed, she needed to help Mrs. Weares at the inn. Oh, for a day to help Mama with the children and not have to spend herself between responsibilities at work and at home. Mama said she felt fine and didn't need an extra hand, but Emma Leigh still longed to give her mother a rest.

The next morning she spotted Thad as she made her way into the inn.

"Good morning," Thad called with a wave.

"Yes, it's a beautiful morning." Emma Leigh allowed herself one long look at him. The thought of his leaving in a few months for school grieved her—not because she regretted his desire to be a doctor. She'd simply miss him.

"Are you excited about tomorrow's Christmas Eve celebration?" he said, rubbing his gloved hands together.

"For certain. I want to find out who my secret friend is so I can thank the person properly for all of my treasures." She felt the familiar trembling that so often came these days whenever Thad was near. "But I do believe it is Mr. or Mrs. Jones. Who do you think has your name?"

He laughed. "I've had sweet treats nearly every day. I'm convinced my secret friend is Sarah." Thad's gaze seemed to search her face. "You look very nice this morning."

She grew warm with his compliment. "Why, thank you. I feel wonderful on the inside."

"It shows," he whispered.

"Did you have a grand time skating?" At once, she wished she hadn't brought up the canceled Sunday afternoon activity. No matter that Mr. Jones had asked her to work; she simply wished she could have been there with Thad.

"I didn't go."

"Why?" *Do I dare think you wanted my company?*

He shuffled and dug his hands into his coat pockets. "Emma Leigh, I didn't want to attend without you."

She gasped, unable to believe her ears. What had brought about the change in him?

Silence prevailed, and for a rare moment, Emma Leigh couldn't think of a single thing to say.

Thad broke the silence. "Shall we see if we have anything in the kitchen?" Before she had an opportunity to respond, he offered her his arm, and they walked up the back wooden steps of the inn.

Inside the cozy kitchen where Sarah and her helper fried thick pieces of bacon and broke eggs into a huge wooden bowl, other staff members bustled about the gift table.

"Ah, sweet bread," Thad said, inhaling the tantalizing scent of apples and cinnamon. "Sarah, I know you must have my name—trying to fatten me up like a Christmas goose."

Sarah said nothing, but a smile caressed her lips.

Emma Leigh glanced down to see a piece of delicately made bobbin lace, finer than anything she'd ever seen. "This is beautiful. I don't know how I will ever be able to thank my secret friend."

"I imagine the smile on your face will be enough," Thad said.

She heard something in his voice, more tenderness than before. Could she hope for more than friendship?

"Emma Leigh," he began softly. "Do you have a moment?"

Startled and pleased all in one breath, she agreed. "Of course. Would you like to walk with me to Mr. Jones's office? I need to see him about the dinner tomorrow."

Thad opened the kitchen door, and the two stepped out into the huge front entrance of the inn. A floor-to-ceiling pine tree was decorated with crystal stars and angels, some of Mrs. Jones's heirlooms from England. Neatly tied gold and red satin bows adorned its limbs. The scent—the fragrance of Christmas—swirled through the air.

"I'd like to visit your father this evening, if you don't have any objection," Thad said.

"I'm sure he will be pleased to see you." Her heart fluttered, especially when she remembered Papa and Thad's parting the last time.

Thad glanced about. "I want to ask him if I can come courting."

Holding her breath, she feared she'd heard incorrectly.

"I want to make sure this is something you want before I seek permission," he said, his gaze fixed on the floor.

Excitement raced through her veins. "I think that is a most pleasant idea."

"You do?" He looked up, and his robin's-egg blue eyes sparkled. "I'm deeply honored, Emma Leigh."

By this time they had reached the front of Mr. Jones's office. Emma Leigh remembered the moment, just a short time ago, when she had collided with Thad in that very spot.

"I hope we have time to talk this evening," Thad said, "providing your father approves of me."

She wanted to shout her delight for all to hear, but at that instant Mrs. Weares made her way across the wooden floor. She frowned disapprovingly. "Is there a problem?"

"Not at all, Mrs. Weares." Thad nodded at Emma Leigh and turned on his heel to leave before she could offer him a reassuring smile. Emma Leigh was certain her father would approve.

Chapter 9

No matter what consolation Thad offered himself, the fact remained that he feared speaking with Emma Leigh's father. Once Thad had decided to ask permission to come courting, anxiety took a strangling hold of him. By now, Mr. Carter might have concluded Thad was not suitable for Emma Leigh or that her family needed her to help support them.

Lord God, I pray Your will be accomplished in this endeavor—whatever that may be.

Once he finished his work, Thad saddled his horse. He'd ridden to work because of his planned visit at the Carters on his way home. Now he wished he'd walked so he could clear his mind.

A startling revelation occurred to him. He was embarking upon what was, next to accepting the Lord as his Savior, the most important step of his life. God had given him a peace about the future, but Thad felt ill prepared to converse with Emma Leigh's father.

A wisp of smoke from the chimney of the Carter cabin came much too quickly. Thad's stomach tightened as he recalled his last encounter with Mr. Carter.

As Thad dismounted, Simon and Joseph rushed from the barn to greet him. "Hello, Thad," they chorused. He noted Simon didn't have a coat, and the sight made him want to give the boy his own.

"Hello, boys. Finishing up your chores?"

Simon nodded. He and Joseph were both shivering. "We're done now," Simon said.

"Your father at home?"

Simon motioned to the cabin. "He's inside."

With a deep breath and a prayer, Thad crunched through the snow to knock at the door. Emma Leigh answered. Her face radiated an ethereal glow, giving him courage to take on a dozen difficult fathers who might protest his courting her.

"Is your father at home?" he said.

She nodded shyly. "Papa, Thad Benson is here to see you. Won't you come in?"

"I'd rather wait outside for your father," he said. He smelled chicken and remembered Sarah giving Emma Leigh the remains from dinner at the inn.

As soon as Mr. Carter stood in the doorway, Thad stuck out his hand and eyed him squarely. "Good evening, sir. May I have a word with you?"

Not a trace of emotion settled upon the older man's face. He nodded and snatched a coat from a peg. "Let's talk in the barn away from the wind." He caught sight of Simon and Joseph. "You boys head inside now. Your mama has food nearly ready."

Thad tried to think of something clever to say, but the only thing bursting from his mouth sounded more like a snort about the weather than polite conversation.

"I remember the last time we talked," Mr. Carter said, sauntering into the barn.

The scent of fresh hay, sweet and clean, met Thad's nostrils. The horse whinnied, and a single chicken scurried past them. "I'd like to continue our discussion."

Mr. Carter leaned against a horse stall. "I thought as much."

Thad cleared his throat. "Sir, again I apologize for sounding selfish the last time when I talked to you about Emma Leigh."

The man nodded. Still no emotion. Mr. Carter would not make this easy.

"I don't want to request permission to come courting Emma Leigh."

The older man's features hardened.

Thad braved his way forward. "I want to ask for her hand in marriage." His heart thumped like a scared rabbit. "I have the money saved for my schooling and some besides to live on. While I'm learning to be a doctor, I can't give her fine things like she deserves, but I can take care of her."

"Hmmm," Mr. Carter said, his face stoical.

"With this in mind and providing I get your blessing, I'd like to ask you a favor, one that might help both of us."

"And what might it be, providing I approve of your marrying my daughter?"

"Uncle Albert and I have been tending to seven cows and a bull on my parents' farm. It's more than my aunt and uncle need once I'm gone, and they are getting on in years as well. Since my land borders yours, I'm wondering if you would take care of the cattle for me during my absence, and in return you could have all the milk you needed and any calves born while I'm away at school. I do need to sell one of the cows though."

"Sounds like charity to me," Mr. Carter grumbled.

"We'd be family," Thad said. "I also wondered if you'd help me out by tending to my apple trees. You might want to use some of the land to grow a few crops."

"Still sounds like charity."

"Not if we split the sale of the crops. I could use the extra money to take care of Emma Leigh."

Mr. Carter rubbed a bristled chin. "Not once have you told me your feelings for my daughter."

Where are my thoughts? "Mr. Carter, I do love Emma Leigh. I want to take care of her always. Why, we grew up together, and I can't imagine any woman in my life but your fine daughter."

Mr. Carter said nothing, and Thad believed the man just might order him to leave. He prayed as Emma Leigh's father slowly paced the length of the barn.

"Emma Leigh works much too hard," he finally said. "She never stops to rest, always wanting to do more. We'd be lost without her, but it's not a good reason to stop my daughter from having a life of her own. She deserves more than waiting on all of us like a servant." Mr. Carter shook his head and wiped a single tear from his cheek. "I am getting better. The good Lord has seen fit to restore my health. You've given me a generous offer—one by which I could pay my debts and take care of my family proper. But more importantly, you've offered a way for my precious Emma Leigh to do better for herself."

Thad swallowed hard. *Is this a yes?*

"I misjudged you, and I'm the one who owes you an apology. If Emma Leigh will have you, then I give my blessing for her to wed."

Thad reached for his hand, a smile bursting through his face from deep within his heart. "Thank you, sir. I'm deeply grateful."

Mr. Carter held on to Thad's hand. "You'll be a fine husband and doctor. I see much of your father in you, and I'm sure he'd be proud." He glanced about the barn. "Would you like me to get Emma Leigh for you?"

"I'd rather this be a surprise," Thad said, tripping over his words like a schoolboy. "So I don't want her to have any idea of what we've discussed until tomorrow night."

Mr. Carter chuckled. "I understand." He released his grip and nodded toward the house. "I imagine she's in a tizzy wanting to know what's going on out here, but I'll not say a word."

"I appreciate that. You see, I drew her name in the secret friend celebration at the inn. I have an idea for tomorrow, something special."

Mr. Carter smiled broadly. "You're going to make her very happy."

They walked toward Thad's tethered horse. "Sir, may I come by tomorrow night and escort Emma Leigh to church?"

"By all means," Mr. Carter whispered. "She will have the best Christmas ever."

Thank You, Lord. I'll not disappoint You. Thank You for showing me the way.

⌒

Emma Leigh found it nearly impossible to mask her disappointment when Papa entered without Thad. "Where's Thad?" she said, searching her father's face. "I thought he might want to stay for dinner."

Papa hung his thin coat on the peg and moved toward the fire. "He's gone home."

She hastily blinked back the tears. What had gone wrong? Why didn't Papa want Thad to come courting?

Thad sang all the way home, making use of every Christmas carol he could remember. Neither the darkness wrapping its blanket around him nor the cold air nipping at his fingers and toes could chill him tonight. Thad understood God's plan for his life and was confident that He intended him to marry Emma Leigh. They'd have a rich life together, rich with the blessings that come only from the heavenly Father.

He stopped at his parents' farm and tended the cattle. Odd, he always referred to it as his parents' when, in fact, the house and land belonged to him. *Emma Leigh's and mine.*

Once at his aunt and uncle's, Thad took care of his horse and hurried in to tell them the good news.

"I plan to ask Emma Leigh to marry me tomorrow night," he said. "I'm not worried in the least about it. God has brought me this far, and I know His hand rests in this."

"She won't refuse such a handsome, caring man," Aunt Klara said, unable to conceal her excitement.

"Or a godly man," Uncle Albert added.

"Simply pray for me," Thad said. The seriousness of asking Emma Leigh to marry him weighed heavily upon him. What had he just done?

"Delight thyself also in the Lord; and he shall give thee the desires of thine heart."

Chapter 10

Emma Leigh dutifully kissed her father good-bye at the inn. She didn't feel much affection though. Tears were ready to surface each time she thought about Papa refusing to let Thad see her.

Either Papa didn't like Thad, and she didn't know why, or he needed her to give all her attention to the Jones Inn and home.

No matter what the reason, the situation deemed unfair. Christmas was tomorrow, the inn staff's celebration this afternoon, and she should be rejoicing in the Lord's birth. But how could she when her heart threatened to break into irreparable pieces?

"But I must," she whispered. "Mr. Jones expects me to be cheerful for the guests and the activities planned for today." She stiffened her spine. The Lord would help her.

Opening the back kitchen door, Emma Leigh pasted on a smile and greeted Sarah with a hug. "Merry Christmas, Sarah. Are you excited about today?"

"Oh yes. I want to find out who's been sending me such sweet scripture messages. One day last week, I came in to work and found the eggs, bacon, and potatoes all ready for me to cook."

Emma Leigh smiled. Sarah's face glowed as though she'd just seen Jesus, and indeed she had through all those excited about celebrating His birth.

All morning Emma Leigh looked to see Thad, but Mr. Jones obviously kept him busy—or perhaps Thad was avoiding her. In any event, his absence made it even harder for her to wish merry Christmas to the guests and staff.

While Emma Leigh set the extra long-table with Mrs. Jones's fine English china and silver in the main dining room for the guests, the smell of turkey basted in herbs and butter wafted around her. What a splendid dinner the guests and the staff would enjoy with an array of vegetables, bread, and sweet treats. The thought made Emma Leigh a bit sad. How she longed for her family to partake in such a fine meal. She could only imagine the sparkle in her siblings' eyes at the sight of such wonderful food.

"Are you ill, Emma Leigh?" Mrs. Weares peered into her face.

Snapped from her thoughts, Emma Leigh produced a smile. "Of course not.

Merely thinking about our Christmas party this afternoon."

"Very well. Let's not dawdle about our duties then," Mrs. Weares said with her typical firmness. "We all want to enjoy Sarah's cooking." She fanned herself furiously. "Oh my, I forgot to tell Thad about the guests wishing a sleigh ride as soon as dinner is completed."

Will he not be here for the staff celebration?

The hours passed swiftly in a flurry of joy and Christmas carols. The time came for the staff to eat. Sarah prepared the same menu as she had provided for the guests, but she put aside a plate for Thad since he'd not returned from the sleigh ride. All were in attendance, except the man Emma Leigh longed to see. The man to whom she longed to give her heart.

She knew selfishness reigned in her heart but she longed to see Thad.

At the completion of the meal, Mr. Jones rose from the table. "I see we have gifts to be opened from our secret friends. Miss Carter, would you do us the honor of presenting the final mementos?"

The items were brought into the dining room and set on the walnut sideboard. Mr. Jones motioned for Emma Leigh to come forward. She tired of smiling, and Thad wasn't there for any of the celebration, and he'd given her the idea.

One by one she picked up the small notes and tokens and distributed them to each staff member, setting aside a brown paper wrapping with her name and another small parcel for Thad. She'd open hers at the end.

Ooh's and *ah*'s rose from the group as each one discovered their secret friend. Sarah hugged her soundly. "Such a blessing you've been to me. Thank you."

From the corner of her eye, Emma Leigh saw Thad slip into the dining room. Mr. Jones greeted him and presented him with his gift. Emma Leigh watched Thad open a small prayer book and a note that identified the item as being from Mrs. Jones. Thad caught Emma Leigh's attention and their gazes met. She saw tenderness, and her heart nearly burst.

"Now it is your turn, Emma Leigh," Mr. Jones said, handing her the gift.

"I am excited to learn who has my name." For the first time, she sensed a lilt in the celebration. Now she could properly thank the giver.

Mr. Jones handed her the brown parcel, and she sat to open it. Pulling away the wrapping, she gasped at the small wooden box embellished in red-orange flowers and an ornate border. "How beautiful," she whispered, tracing the flowers with her fingertips. Curiously, she lifted the lid and saw a piece of paper inside. Now she'd learn for sure that Mr. Jones had indeed drawn her name. How she appreciated his generosity.

Unfolding the paper, she read:

A candle's flicker in the darkness,
A fire's warmth to greet the weary,
Only Jesus shines more brightly
Than my lovely Emma Leigh.
Love,
Thad

Tears brimmed her eyes, and her gaze flew to his face. "You." She swallowed her joyful tears. "I never thought. . . I never imagined."

It seemed she and Thad were the only two people in the crowded dining room. He stood before her and bent to one knee.

"Then you are pleased?" he said.

"Oh Thad, all the things you gave me—so extravagant, so generous. I don't deserve your goodness, but I do thank you."

A smile spread over his face, and she saw an image of herself in his blue eyes. "Good. I'm pleased. Tonight we can talk, for your father has given me permission to come calling."

A tear trickled over her cheek. Emma Leigh quickly wiped it away. "This is the best Christmas I've ever had." Her cheeks flushed warm, and joy abounded through every inch of her.

Thad rose to his feet. His adoring look promised what her heart felt. Never had she known such contentment.

⌒

Thad counted the hours until he could leave the inn and ride to the Carter home. Once Mr. Jones had learned about Thad's plans for the evening, he'd given him use of a carriage to escort Emma Leigh to church. He could return it later when he came by the inn to get his horse.

Too excited to think, his stomach toying with a game of leapfrog, Thad drove to the Carter home. In his pocket, he had his mother's ivory cameo brooch as a token of his love and devotion to Emma Leigh.

Once he caught sight of the cabin, he believed the firelight from the windows shone more cheerfully than usual. Tonight, he'd ask Emma Leigh to marry him and later escort her to Christmas Eve services.

Mr. Carter answered the door as soon as Thad's gloved knuckles tapped against the wood. "Welcome, Thad, and merry Christmas to you."

"And the blessings of Christmas to you, too, sir."

Mr. Carter stepped back to usher Thad inside. The older man winked. Surely the 'goodwill toward men' sentiments had taken hold. "Emma Leigh, Thad is here to see you."

Thad's gaze flew to her face and took in the sight of her. She'd woven a red ribbon through her dark hair, and the bobbin lace decorated her throat, but their beauty did not compare to the love he saw in her eyes—eyes reminding him so much of an innocent doe. For a moment he couldn't speak until the sound of the children's laughter shook him to his senses.

"Hush, children." Mrs. Carter's face blushed nearly as radiantly as Emma Leigh's. "Good to see you, Thad."

"Good evening, Mrs. Carter." Thad swung his attention to Emma Leigh. "Would you like to take a ride with me before going to church?"

She glanced at her father, and he nodded. "You have my permission."

Once she gathered her scarf and gloves, Thad offered his arm, much to the giggling of Simon and Joseph, and stepped out into the cold, crisp night.

"Oh," she breathed. "You have one of the inn's carriages."

"Only the best for my Emma Leigh," he said, glad for the darkness settling around them so she wouldn't see his reddened face.

"I don't know what to say except thank you."

He assisted her up onto the seat, marveling at her lightness, then lit the kerosene lanterns on both sides of the carriage.

Soon they were on their way down the road leading to his parents' farm. Thad had so much to say, but the words simply wouldn't form on his lips. He'd thought of little else but this moment for the past twenty-four hours.

"Are we going past your land?" Emma Leigh said. The wind whistled, and she snuggled against his shoulder.

"Most assuredly. Remember all the winter days we skated on the pond behind the barn?"

She laughed. "And all the times we fell until we learned?"

We'll have many more times to skate together—years of memories. "I remember the time you threw a snowball and bloodied my nose." He laughed heartily in remembrance, causing him to relax a bit.

She shuddered. "Dare you remind me? I ran all the way home and hid in Papa's barn for fear I'd get thrashed." She sighed in a mellow sort of way. "You never told anyone."

He pulled the horse in front of the house, his and Emma Leigh's future home. "Would you like to come by here tomorrow?" He took her hand. "I'd like to walk through the rooms and remember Christmases past."

"Of course. Is everything there as before?"

He nodded and smiled, recalling every piece of furniture and handmade item from his mother. "But tonight, I have something else on my mind." His heart began to pound furiously.

"Is everything all right?" She stared into his face. "You seem distressed."

The overwhelming urge to kiss her nearly drove him to distraction, but not yet. Soon enough he'd claim her lips. Taking her hand, he began. "Last night I talked to your father about more things than courting you."

Her eyes widened, but she said nothing.

"We discussed matters about the future."

Emma Leigh was always chatting away. Having her say something, anything, would help his scattered nerves.

Taking a deep breath, Thad forged on. "Emma Leigh, I love you. I can't remember ever loving anyone but you. So I'm asking you to marry me. Now we might have a difficult time while I'm in school, but one day I'll be a doctor, and things will be easier."

In the faint light, she quivered. "I love you, too, Thad, but I can't marry you. I simply can't."

"Why?" he blurted out. Hadn't he felt God leading him to take Emma Leigh as his wife?

Tears fell swiftly from her eyes, and she did nothing to stop them. "Papa and Mama need me to help them take care of the family."

He removed his glove and with his thumb brushed the wetness from her cheeks. His heart swelled with love for his precious Emma Leigh. "No, my darling. Your father and I have an agreement. He is going to take care of my cattle, and in return he will have the milk to use and sell. He will also have any calves to start his own herd."

She held her breath as though unbelieving of his words.

"Come spring," Thad said, "he's going to take care of my apple orchard and till the land to plant crops. We'll split the difference come harvest time."

"But his health?"

Thad lifted her chin. "Granted, he had a deep cough less than ten days ago, but look how he's doing now. God is healing him, Emma Leigh. By spring he'll have his strength, and by midsummer, you and I can be married. If you will have me."

She continued to cry.

Desperate and confused, Thad couldn't even pray. "What is it? Do you not care for me?"

She stiffened and shook her head. Then she took a deep breath. "No, I do love you. I'm crying. . .I'm crying because I'm happy."

He gathered her into his arms and held her close. Slowly he bent to kiss away her salty tears now chilling against her soft cheeks. His lips trailed to hers and tasted their sweetness. "You will marry me in midsummer?" he whispered.

"Maybe sooner, if you would like," she said, standing back and offering a smile.

Reaching into his coat pocket, he pulled his mother's brooch into his palm. "I'd like for you to have this," he said. "I know you can't see it very well in the darkness, but it's a cameo that belonged to my mother." He slipped it into her hand.

"Thank you," she said breathlessly. "I'll take such good care of the brooch— just as I will of you."

"No," he said. "I'm taking care of you, and God will do the rest."

◦━

Before dawn on Christmas morning, Thad and Uncle Albert quietly unloaded the wagon and set its contents by the Carter door. Two smoked hams large enough to feed a family of growing children for much more than one meal, flour, potatoes, red cabbage and bacon, squash, turnips, green beans harvested from the summer, stewed apples, and Aunt Klara's delicious rice pudding—all ready for the family inside. Atop the food, Thad placed six cinnamon candy sticks, one for each of his soon-to-be brothers and sister. In a bundle, he'd placed warm coats for each member of the family—the result of selling one of his cows and taking a small portion from his savings.

As he and Uncle Albert drove away, Thad looked back to see the cabin door open and Emma Leigh wave and blow him a kiss. God had indeed given him the desires of his heart.

Miracle on Kismet Hill

Loree Lough

Prologue

Blood oozed from the colonel's left temple as a dozen of his men knelt in a protective semicircle around his battered body. Daubing the officer's forehead with the corner of a dingy neckerchief, Trevor Williams caught the eye of one soldier and demanded, "Where's that water I told you to fetch?"

"What's the point, Sarge? He's bleedin' like a stuck pig. We ought to be fetchin' a shovel, instead, and start diggin' his. . ."

"Quit talkin' a fool," Trevor growled. "The Colonel's strong as an ox. He'll pull through this."

Shrugging, the private rolled onto his belly and, using his elbows to propel himself forward, dodged flying debris as he headed for the water trough.

"Be a cryin' shame iffen that boy dies tryin' to save a dead man," came a coarse whisper from the back of the group.

Trevor stood, fists clenched at his sides, oblivious, it seemed, to the constant barrage of cannon fire exploding around him. Glaring at each man in turn, he said through clenched teeth, "Get back to your posts. Anyone who has any other ideas will be talking to the front end of my musket!"

Without another word, the small crowd dispersed.

"You were a might hard on 'em, don't you think?"

On one knee again, Trevor studied his colonel's black-bearded face. "Good to see you're awake," he said, ignoing the question. "Billy'll be back with some cool water any minute."

The colonel waved the offer away. "Don't need water. What I need is. . ." Arching his back, he winced with pain. "How long was I out?" he gasped when the agony released him.

"To tell the truth, Colonel, with all that's been goin' on, coulda been an hour. . . or a couple a minutes. All's I know is, a block of stone knocked you cold when the east tower came down." Trevor nodded at the colonel's bloodied pant leg. "Hurt much?"

Richard Carter forced a half-hearted snicker. "Hurts plenty," he managed to say. He'd been hit enough times to know this was no mere flesh wound. It would be bad—the sticky dampness in his boot and the unending throbbing told him that much—but how bad he wouldn't know until he mustered the courage to look. Summoning all his strength, Richard levered himself onto one elbow, took a deep breath, and focused on his right foot.

The sight sent waves of nausea and dizziness coursing through him.

His once slate-gray trousers leg now glistened with the deep maroon of his lifeblood, and the squared toe of his boot was missing. . .along with three of his toes.

Whether his light-headedness came from what he'd just seen or loss of blood, Richard didn't know. He slumped wearily back onto the brass-buttoned jacket his men had wadded beneath his neck. A rasping sigh slipped from his lungs as the image of the mangled foot flickered behind his closed eyes. Even if the injury healed, he'd walk with a limp for the rest of his life. And if gangrene set in. . .

But he couldn't allow himself to dwell on the grisly possibilities just now. He focused on his men—mere boys, some of them—who were counting on him to lead them to safety. "What're the damages elsewhere, Sergeant?"

With quiet efficiency, Trevor Williams gave his commander a rundown.

The assault that began in the early afternoon had continued until Union General Terry aimed his navy's guns to targets inside the fort. As the Yanks at sea struck the north facade, two thousand troops stormed the seaward wall. But armed only with cutlasses and handguns, the Bluecoats were no match for Fort Fisher's soldiers, and after hours of bitter hand-to-hand combat, the Northerners retreated. When they returned, better armed and more determined than ever to win, they forced the Confederates to fall back.

"We lost hundreds of men," Trevor continued, his voice soft with reverence, "and hundreds more will likely die of their wounds." Hanging his head, he took a shaky breath. He frowned deeply, and his eyes and lips narrowed with fury and disgust. "The Bluebellies're loadin' up every Reb who's breathin'. " He rubbed the furrow between his brows, his hand casting an even darker shadow across his sooty face, and snarled, "Well, I ain't goin' to no Yankee prisoner of war camp!"

Richard surveyed the surrounding terrain. Lifeless bodies of boys and men lay alongside the wounded, the blood of Blue- and Graycoats puddling together on the rust-red North Carolina clay. The smoky air thickened overhead, trapping the stink of gunpowder and burning wood—and death—beneath it. The boom of exploding Colombiad cannonballs echoed within the fortress as horowitzers, carbines, and musketoons discharged deadly lead balls.

Amid the melee, Richard remembered the *Albermarle*. He'd been on board the sturdy boat when it attacked Plymouth. The North hadn't been prepared for its enemy's ingenuity, and the shallow-draft gunboat, secretly constructed in a cornfield beside the Roanoke River, defeated a squadron of eight Union gunboats, giving the South reign over the western end of the Sound. None of the North's vessels could match the ironclad's power. . .until Cushing's torpedo sank her. Afterward, Richard and a handful of stalwart survivors were quickly reassigned to Fort Fisher. . . .

"Worst of it is," Trevor was saying, "they've cut us off from reinforcements."

Richard acknowledged the seriousness of the sergeant's statement. The North was better armed. Better fed. And in many ways, better led. Still, Richard refused to believe the South would be defeated. After all, no one, least of all northern forces, had expected the *Albermarle* to succeed. Yet she had. . . .

"We're not licked yet," Richard grated. Then, with a fortitude that surprised even himself, he wrapped his bloody fingers around Trevor's forearm. "There's a letter," he began, "in the pocket of my coat. If I don't. . ." Clamping his teeth together, he hesitated. "If I don't make it through this one, I want you to see it reaches my family."

Trevor grimaced. "Ain't like you to talk this a way, Colonel. What is it you're always tellin' us? 'You lose only when you give up.' Seems to me you oughta take a little of your own good advice."

Eyes wide with fear and desperation, Richard tightened his hold on Trevor's arm. "Get the letter," he hissed.

Gently, Trevor slid the coat from beneath Richard's head and rummaged through the pockets until he found an envelope, addressed to the Carter family in Spring Creek, Virginia. He held it up for the colonel to see.

"Put it somewhere safe," Richard insisted.

Trevor stuffed the envelope into his shirt and patted it. "Snug as a bug in a rug," he said, feigning a lighthearted grin.

Only then did Richard release his death grip on Trevor's arm. His relieved smile disappeared as a coughing fit devoured his remaining strength. Eyelids fluttering and arms flailing, he reached blindly for Trevor. "Is it getting dark, or. . . ?"

"Ain't got a watch," the sergeant interrupted, squinting into the powder-gray sky. Giving the older man's shoulder an affectionate squeeze, he added, "You ain't gonna die, Colonel. Least. . .not if I have anything to say about it."

But Trevor's assurance fell on deaf ears, for Colonel Richard Carter had once again blacked out. His sleeplike state rendered him dumb to the fact that his men were being seized. Somewhere, from deep within the fog of unconsciousness, he pictured his beautiful brown-eyed daughter, Brynne. His burly son, Edward, who he'd heard had been wounded in Nashville. His loving wife, Amelia. *Oh, how I miss her sweet smile. . .and that way she has of fussing over me,* Richard thought. *How are they faring, with me gone three long years?*

He seemed to recall seeing Trevor, picking his way through the ruins of Fort Fisher, ducking and dodging, weaving and bobbing. . . . He'd always admired the young man. Like himself, Trevor believed in leading by example. *He'll be a fine officer someday, if he doesn't. . .*

Richard's buzzing brain would not allow him to complete the grisly thought. *Take care,* was his silent message to the sergeant. *Take care, and get that letter to my Amelia.*

The very thought of her comforted and calmed him. The vapor in his mind cleared just enough for the hard-voweled voices of two Union soldiers to break through. "This one'll never make it," the first said as he and a mate roughly slung Richard onto a dirty wagon bed.

"Doesn't matter," said the second. "We were told to take every one that was breathing, and this one's breathing."

"Maybe so," replied the first, "but he won't be breathing long."

Richard hadn't talked to God in a very long time. Hadn't had time to do anything, really, but attempt to survive this miserable war. But the smoky haze cloaking his mind felt cool and comforting. It stanched the throbbing in his foot and the ache in his head, too. In the white mist, he smiled, feeling whole and healthy and pain free, as boyhood images of heaven echoed in his memory.

Lord Jesus, he prayed, *if You decide to take me home to Paradise, let them bury my bones on Kismet Hill, near that stubborn little pine....*

Chapter 1

Brynne had been working since dawn, trying to put the house back together after the last Yankee raid, when a persistent rapping at the front door interrupted her work. She had played hostess to enough Yankees to recognize their "calling card" when she heard it.

She had to admit that, by and large, the regular troops of Bluecoats passing through had been gentlemen, but a few ragged stragglers were another story. As a result, half of her father's cherished book collection had disappeared, along with her mother's wedding rings, and the cameo Brynne had inherited from Grandma Moore. They'd also helped themselves to chickens and sheep, cows and horses, bushels of potatoes and sacks of flour.

If the two- and three-man parties that regularly showed up without warning had known she'd gladly have shared the family's quickly dwindling food supply, would they have stolen heirlooms and keepsakes anyway? And if they'd been given advance notice that she considered it her Christian duty to tend their wounds and mend their uniforms, would they still have found it necessary to break windows, trample flowers, destroy fine upholstered pieces that had been in the Carter family for generations? Brynne's cynical answer, after years of dealing with these blue-coated marauders, was yes.

The very first time Yankees had approached Carter soil, Brynne hid her father's pistols and hunting muskets. The weapons, as yet untouched by Northern hands, still nestled beneath the parlor floorboards.

Now, Brynne climbed down from the stepladder and knelt to pull up the plank nearest the fireplace, where Richard's rifle lay wrapped in a bedsheet. Balancing it on palms that trembled with fear and rage, Brynne stared at the weapon. *Do you have what it takes to use it?* she wondered, biting her lower lip.

As she searched her heart and mind for an answer, Brynne recalled what a raiding party had done to her neighbors to the east: The Smith house had stood majestically on Spring Creek soil for nearly a hundred years before the drunken infantrymen burned it to the ground—with the family trapped inside. And no one would ever forget what the next group had done to the Warner's twin daughters. . . .

Before the war, had anyone asked Brynne if she could aim a gun at one of God's children for any reason, the answer would have been a quick and resounding "No!" But now. . .

"Please, Lord," she prayed under her breath, "don't let them give me a reason to use this. . .because we both know that if I must, I will."

Had her mother been home, she'd have reminded Brynne in not-so-gentle tones that it was not Christian to take up arms against her fellowman. "A true lady leaves the fighting to the menfolk," Amelia would have scolded.

But her mother was not at home. As Spring Creek's only midwife, she'd been at the Andersons' since dawn, helping bring their first baby into the world.

Brynne hoped the soldiers would be satisfied with a bite to eat and a cup of weak coffee, because she had little else to offer, and she would not be satisfied leaving the fighting to the menfolk any longer!

She tucked the hem of her full blue skirt into her black belt and slipped into her boiled wool jacket. Hoisting the rifle, she tiptoed through the house and sneaked silently out the back door. Crouching low in the shadows, she worked her way around to the side of the house, doing her best to time each step to coincide with the soldiers' knocks. *There's no telling how many of them have descended upon Moorewood this time,* she cautioned herself. *You mustn't reveal your position. . . .*

Once she rounded the corner and peeked over the winter-browned honeysuckle, she halted in surprise: just one soldier stood on her porch. He appeared to be a young man, tall and lanky, with broad shoulders that slumped a bit under the oppressive weight of war.

He carried no weapon that she could see, but experience had taught her the wisdom of the old proverb, "An ounce of prevention is worth a pound of cure." Creeping alongside the forsythia hedge that led to the front door, she made it to the bottom porch step. . .and rushed him. "Turn around slow, soldier," she snarled, the rifle barrel mere inches from his blue-coated back, "real slow."

He did as he was told. "No need to be afraid, ma'am," he said in a soft Southern drawl.

"You've got that right," she snapped, giving him a gentle poke with the end of her gun. "No need to be afraid if you have enough firepower."

If someone had been pointing a gun at her, she'd be shaking in her boots. That he could stand there, calm as you please, amazed her. What amazed her more was that he wore neither the arrogant smirk nor the malicious grin of those who'd come to Moorewood before him. The expression on his bearded face seemed genuinely gentle, seemed. . .

Stop it, you little ninny! she warned herself. *Could be he's just a good actor, like your precious Ross Bartlett. Could be he'll grab this gun and point it at you if you're not careful!*

"I'm on your side," he said quietly.

Brynne knew better than to judge all Yankees by the behavior of a despicable few. Still, she refused to be fooled by this one's friendly demeanor. "The last bunch of your buddies didn't leave much behind," she said, sneering, "but they generously left my eyesight, and I can plainly see that you're wearing blue. You, sir, are not on my side!"

Looking down at the brass buttons on his jacket, the soldier nodded. "I know this looks bad, ma'am, but I can explain. Y'see, I knew I'd be traipsin' through enemy territory, so I sort of, uh, I borrowed this here jacket from a Union soldier." Moving nothing but his pointer finger, he gestured toward the haversack at his feet. "My coat's in there. Ain't too perty after the last fight, but. . ."

She was scowling by now. "Oh please. Give me credit for having some sense."

Shrugging, he sighed. "Reckon I can't blame you for bein' suspicious, ma'am. But you're more'n welcome to check it out."

No doubt if she did, Brynne would find a Confederate jacket in the bag. *But that doesn't mean it's his.*

Suddenly, something he'd said earlier gonged in her mind. "You. . .you stole that coat from. . ." Brynne swallowed hard. "From a dead man?"

Wincing, he said, " 'Fraid so, ma'am." In a more serious tone, he quickly added, "But I never kilt him; he was dead when I found him."

The mental picture of him peeling the uniform from a corpse sent a shiver up her back. Blinking rapidly, she took it all in: his shaggy blond hair and beard, the badly scraped boots, trousers that likely hadn't been washed in an age, cuts and bruises on the backs of his hands. . .hands that had touched a fallen comrade. He'd wrapped those same hands around the handles of his bag. . .

Wrinkling her nose with disgust, Brynne used the weapon as a pointer. "You open the bag. And take care not to pull any stunts," she warned, narrowing her eyes, "this gun has a hair trigger. . ."

She watched carefully as he crouched, unbuckled his knapsack, and withdrew the contents, item by item. First, a gray fez. A small and well-worn Bible. A pair of holey socks. And a bonafide Confederate jacket. The soldier stood slowly and held it out for her inspection. "In the inside front pocket," he said, "you'll find a letter from your pa."

A letter from Papa? Brynne repeated mentally. She whispered the words out loud, as though their meaning had some sacred significance that demanded hushed tones of reverence. Why, the soldier had said it as casually as he might have said, "Nice weather we're havin', ain't it?" Her heart began to hammer so hard, Brynne could count the beats in her ears. She wanted that letter, and she wanted it now.

But she had only two hands. How would she search the jacket and keep the soldier at gunpoint at the same time?

Frustration got the better of her. "Here," she said, handing him the rifle. "Hold this while I have a look-see."

The soldier obligingly exchanged the gun for the jacket. She paid no mind to the grin that split his face as she excitedly dug through the pockets. "It is from Papa," she sighed, holding the envelope at arm's length. "I'd know his handwriting anywhere!"

Quick as it appeared, the joy that brightened her face dimmed. Flustered and furious at the same time, she grabbed the rifle from him and shoved the letter into her apron pocket. "How did you get this?" she demanded. "Did you pick through his pockets the way you went through that dead soldier's. . . ?" Brynne simply couldn't finish the question. "If you harmed him," she grated, "I'll, I'll. . ."

He'd relaxed some when she handed him the gun. Now, as her agitation escalated, the soldier's arms slid slowly skyward again. "Harm him! Why, I'da sooner been gutshot!" He shook his head. "Last words he said to me were 'See that my family gets the letter.' When my unit was captured by the Yankees, I slipped away. Coulda headed south, to be with my wife an' young'un." The soldier frowned. "Came here instead, on account-a I gave your daddy my word."

Brynne tucked in one corner of her mouth. His voice, his face, even his stance communicated sincerity. The man was either a very good actor or telling the truth. It was all she could do to concentrate on keeping him in her gunsight. She wanted nothing more than to tear open the envelope. She wanted to shout for joy, for no one had heard from her father in so long that the family had begun to think. . . A sob ached in her throat as the blood pounded in her ears. Brynne tightened her grip on the rifle's burled wood stock.

"The Colonel told me he hadn't heard a word from home in nigh on to a year," he continued, "but that didn't stop him from writin' y'all ever' week. Weren't no easy feat, let me tell you, what with pencils and paper in such short supply, and one confounded Yankee or another tryin' to blow us to smithereens at ever' turn."

Brynne said nothing. As he talked, she felt her resolve ebbing away. Still, she trained the gun on him.

The soldier looked toward the shrub to the right of the porch. "Forsythia ought to be buddin' soon." Meeting Brynne's eyes, he added, "Your daddy said spring is your mama's favorite time of year. Your brother's, too." He brightened some. "Speakin' of Edward, did he make it home all right? Last the Colonel heard, the boy had got himself shot down in Nashville."

Brynne's brows drew together as she attempted to make sense of all he'd said. If he was the type who could steal a coat from a dead man, he was the type who could use force to extract personal facts from a dying man. "How do you know so much about my family?"

Despite his raggedy uniform and haggard face, he stood taller to say, "Fought alongside your daddy ever' day for a year. We had time a-plenty to talk 'bout families. Got me a son back home, name of Ezra, like in the Bible." His eyes took on a faraway look as he smiled wanly and added, "Weren't even walkin' when I left, but he'll turn four in a month."

Brynne watched as tears glistened in his eyes. He shook his head, as if to summon his former control. He spoke with the dulcet tones of a southern gentleman, she couldn't deny that. But what if like Ross, he'd been born with a gift for emulating accents? And where was his gun? Edward had told her that no self-respecting soldier went anywhere without his standard-issue six pounder. "Where's your rifle, soldier?"

He nodded toward the end of the long, winding drive. "Hid it in the bushes 'longside the road," he said, grinning sheepishly. "Didn't think it'd be smart to come down here, wearin' a Union coat and brandishin' artillery!"

Something told her he was everything he professed himself to be. *Lord,* she prayed, *if he isn't a Southerner, show me a sign; help me protect Moorewood.*

When a minute ticked silently by, and no such proof materialized, Brynne lowered the gun. "Tell me, soldier, when was the last time you had a decent meal?"

⌒

Patience had never been one of Brynne's strong suits. If the letter had been addressed to Amelia Carter instead of the whole Carter family, she would have waited to read it until her mother returned from the Andersons'. But this was Mary Anderson's first baby, and Brynne knew how long it sometimes took to bring a firstborn into the world. Her mother might be away for hours yet.

She lit a flame under the big kettle on the cookstove to heat up the vegetable soup she'd cooked for supper last night. Without any meat to flavor it, it was thin and watery, but she figured it would make a fine snack for the hungry soldier after his bath. Pouring herself a cup of tea, Brynne sat at the kitchen table and began to read.

December 1, 1864

My dearest family,
I can only hope this reaches you. It seems the only messages getting through these days are from general to general!

No doubt you've tried to contact me since I left Moorewood in '62, but only the letter dated December 22, 1863 reached my homesick hands. I have read it so often, I could recite every word by heart.

December 5, 1864

Fell asleep at the General's writing table, and was awakened by artillery fire to the south. This is the first opportunity I've had to get back to the writing.

I'm sure you've heard by now that supplies are scarce for our side. I won't insult you by denying it, but I will assure you I am fine. "Every cloud has a silver lining," or so the sages say. One bright side of this dismal war has been that I've learned to appreciate cornmeal mush. Think what a good example I'll set for our little grandson when at last I'm home again!

I'm told the blame for our food shortage rests squarely on the shoulders of the governors, who demand "protocol" be followed to the letter. I have half a mind to run for office myself if this miserable war ever ends, and as my first official duty, I'll pass a law making arrogance and self-importance illegal!

Colonel William Lamb has been an able leader. Fort Fisher is the strongest fortification constructed by either side. We are nearly two thousand men strong and have fifty powerful guns at our disposal. All landward approaches are protected by palisades, with land mines buried around the perimeter. As I told you in one of my earlier letters, the only way the Yanks can get us here is if they should attack by both land and sea.

Often, I find myself comparing our situation to that of our forefathers. When the Minutemen stood up against the British nearly a hundred years ago, they, too, lived off the land. Some of our boys are calling themselves "The Savages" instead of "The Confederates," because they've taken to trapping varmints and eating them raw so the shooting and the cookfires won't give away our position. I can almost picture you, my sweet Brynne, wrinkling your nose at that one!

January 1, 1865

Now, where was I?

If we're to believe the latest scuttlebutt, Southern agents are overseas, begging for shoes, clothing, medicines, ammunition, and firearms. If you ask me, this war is serving no purpose other than to make the French and the English rich! But enough talk of politics.

I hope all is well in Spring Creek. I think of Moorewood and everyone there often. But it is you, my darling wife, that I remember most. In the dark of night, when all is silent, I picture your beautiful eyes. If I close my own eyes in the light of day, I can imagine myself touching your velvet-brown hair. When the skies darken with storm clouds, I have only to think of your smile, and I see blue skies. You are my heaven in the hell that is this war.

Oh, how I yearn for the day when I return. That is the tonic that warms me when cold winds blow. And neither the cannons' blast nor the rifles' report can blot your loving voice from my memory.

Your love has sustained me thus far, my darling, and it will keep me safe until this dreadful fight is won. I promise to move heaven and earth to come home to you. Please never stop believing that I will come back to you.

Well, the bugler is blowing, and I must muster the troops. There's a rumor afloat that the Union has sent ships to test our mettle. If that's true, the Yanks are in for a rude awakening, for they'll be "welcomed" by a fierce defense of the Stars and Bars!

Sleep deeply and well, Amelia, and know that as you do, I'll be dreaming of you. All of you are in my prayers—Amelia my dear wife, my beloved daughter Brynne, my brave son Edward and his sweet wife Julia, and last but not least, my little grandson Richie.

All my love, eternally, to all of you,
Richard

Chapter 2

Hours later, snuggled deep in the cushions of her window seat, Brynne drew up her knees. With trembling fingers, she held the pages on which her father had created a link between the scarred battlefield and his home. She brushed them against her cheek, as if the feel of them could replicate the gentleness of her father's touch.

Her dark eyes drank in every word that described the torment and suffering of war, as she hoped against hope that he would survive it, as her brother had. Yes, Edward had hobbled home on crude wooden crutches, but he would walk on his own again eventually.

Something told Brynne she ought to put the letter away the moment she began reading the loving words her father had written to her mother. Tall and powerfully built, no one—not even his only daughter—would have guessed that inside this burly man beat the heart of an incurable romantic. Captivated by his endearments, by his confessions of the deep and abiding love he felt for her mother, Brynne read on, despite the fact that doing so made her feel a bit like an interloper.

Will a man ever love me as Father loves Mother? she sighed dreamily.

Quickly, she got hold of her emotions. *Not very likely,* she told herself, tucking the letter back into its soot-rimmed envelope. Ross Bartlett had been the only one to woo her, but he had tossed her aside for a fancy Boston-schooled girl.

Like her father and brother, Brynne's fiancé had gone off to war. But unlike Richard and Edward, Ross had decided to live by the code of the jungle: "Survival of the fittest" became his battle cry, and he sold himself to the highest bidder. With nary a backward glance, he turned on Virginia—on all the South—by putting his talents for mimicking accents to use as a double agent. Ross's spying paid off quite handsomely, she'd heard. And one of his rewards had been the hand of a wealthy general's daughter.

To add insult to injury, Brynne learned of his marriage from Camille Prentice when the girl returned from Massachusetts where she had been visiting relatives when the war started. If Ross had given her the news in a letter, that would at least have been preferable to hearing it from Camille's smirking lips.

Common sense told her that her wounded pride would eventually heal, but her shattered spirit would not. Much as she yearned for it, Brynne believed she would never know love as her mother knew it. Because, to put it plainly, she didn't trust her judgement when it came to men.

Laying her father's letter aside, she thought of her conversation with Trevor earlier. Because Richard had described Brynne as a strong young woman, Trevor had felt free to tell her the truth, with no frills or soft touches.

"I did my best to bind his wounds," Trevor had said quietly, reverently, "but he was bleeding badly. Last I saw of him, the confounded Bluebellies were loading him onto a wagon."

Trevor said that he'd hidden in the trees until the Yankees headed north. His intent was to follow them, and when they bedded down for the night, he'd set his comrades free. But he hadn't eaten in days, and he carried a Union lead ball in his own leg. Bleeding and near starved, he'd hadn't been able to keep up, he admitted dismally, and he lost their trail.

The tears she'd blinked back earlier flowed freely now. Her wounded, weakened father had been roughly carted off to a prisoner of war camp. She'd heard about those places, so crowded and dirty that even younger, healthier men had died within their confines. He was dead, and suddenly she couldn't continue to pretend otherwise.

Brynne threw back her shoulders and lifted her chin. Drying her tears on the backs of her hands, she took a deep breath and rose from the window bench. *Grieve Papa's passing later,* she told herself. *For now, you must be strong and brave, for Mama.*

No doubt when Amelia returned from the Andersons', she'd be exhausted. With one last sniff, Brynne marched toward the kitchen and started supper. After the rest of the family heard her news, only little Richie was likely to be hungry. But cooking would give her something to concentrate on besides her father's letter.

"Why so glum?" her brother said from the kitchen doorway.

No point in telling the story more than once, she decided. Hopefully, by the time their mother returned, Trevor would have awakened from his nap, and he could explain to all of the Carters at the same time.

She felt him studying her face for a moment, and she worried he might want to know why she'd been crying. She prayed he wouldn't ask.

God saw fit to answer her brief prayer, for Edward lifted the lid of the pot she'd just sealed. "Mmm, smells delicious." Then, wrinkling his nose, he added, "What is it?"

"Potato soup."

"How many potatoes are in there? One?"

"No, two. But there's a piece of an old turnip, too." She gave the back of his hand a gentle pat with her wooden spoon. "Now put the lid back on so the flavors won't escape. I'm rationing the herbs and spices, you know."

Edward affectionately mussed her hair. "Anything you say, sister dear. . . provided I'll get a bowl when it's time."

The day Edward left to fight, Amelia had insisted that his wife and son move into the big house with her and Brynne. "What will we do with all this space, just the two of us?" she'd asked in her typical lighthearted way. "Besides, I wouldn't sleep a wink, worrying about Julia and my grandson, alone over there on the other side of the knoll with all these Yankees prowling about."

Brynne had come to think of Julia as the sister she'd never had, and of four-year-old Richie as a young brother. If her brother and his family ever moved back into their own home, Brynne thought she'd die of loneliness.

"Of course you'll have a bowl." She wiggled her eyebrows and winked. "And maybe, if you fetch me a bucket of water for my dishpan, I'll dip you up a second bowl. . . ."

Grinning, he dampened her cheek with a noisy kiss. "What will two buckets get me?"

"Sparkling clean dishes, that's what," she responded, grinning right back. "Now get on out of here before I take the broom to your backside!"

Edward stood at attention and saluted. "Yes'm," he said, and headed for the door.

It still broke her heart to watch him walk—but not as it had when first he'd returned from Nashville in November of '64, minus his left leg.

Edward had always been proud and stubborn. Why, even as a boy, he felt duty-bound to outlift, outrun, and outshoot every other boy in town. Everything was a game, everyone a competitor. No one was surprised then, when within a week of his return, Edward began hobbling about on the crude wooden crutches the army sent home with him. She'd been so proud of the way he refused to be pitied and insisted upon trying to do his share around Moorewood. By mid-January, his grit paid off, for the gnarled stump that had been his leg had healed enough to strap on the peg he'd whittled for himself. Seeing his drive and determination dwindle each time the prosthesis slipped and caused him to fall nearly broke Brynne's heart. But it had given her a drive and determination of her own. . . .

Late one night, after everyone had gone to bed, she tiptoed into the room he shared with Julia and took the peg from where it leaned near the door. Sitting at the kitchen table, she'd turned it over and over in her hands, trying to puzzle out a way to connect it to a brace, a holster. . .something that would secure it to Edward's body.

The idea struck like lightning, and Brynne had barely been able to contain her excitement. She'd lit a lantern and headed for the shed, where her father had kept an old leather wagon tarp.

Night after night, Brynne worked by lamplight, sewing straps to the body of the brace. Day after day, someone demanded an explanation for her swollen bloodied fingers. She couldn't very well tell them she'd done the damage trying to drive the needle through the deerskin, lest one of them let the cat out of the bag and spoil Edward's surprise. "I'm trying to get the blackberry hedges under control so we'll have a hearty crop next summer," she'd say, smiling as she hid her aching hands behind her back. She was working on the blackberry hedges during the day, but that wasn't what was turning her fingers red and sore.

And then one night, after three weeks of secret struggling, Brynne completed the brace. The sky turned the deep purple shade that signalled the dawn as she added the padded liner that would protect Edward's scarred stump from the hard wood. She'd slipped the peg and its brand-new brace into Edward and Julia's room, thanking God he'd never noticed it was missing, and then Brynne returned to the kitchen to wait. . .and pray the brace would fit.

It did, Brynne discovered just after sunup. She'd been at the stove, tending the biscuits she'd baked, when she heard an unfamiliar sound. The *step-slide-clomp, step-slide-clomp* began at the front stairs and echoed down the hall.

Edward thumped into the kitchen, beaming. "When did you do this?" he'd asked, his voice foggy with emotion. "How did you do this?" Wiggling his brows, he smirked wickedly. "I'm stumped, sister dear!"

It had been good to see him standing there on his own, grinning like his old self, with no crutches to support him. So good that Brynne couldn't answer. Instead, she'd covered her face with both hands and wept softly.

He'd limped over to where she stood and took her in his arms. "Brynne, Brynne, Brynne," Edward had sighed, stroking her hair. "I know why you're such a good teacher—because I've never known a gentler, more kindhearted woman." There had been tears in his own dark eyes when he'd held her at arm's length to add in a raspy whisper, "I haven't felt much like a man since I got home. . .till this morning." He'd kissed her forehead. "Thank you, Brynne. And God bless you."

She watched him now, moving about at almost his old speed, and smiled ruefully. When he'd walked into the room, she'd tried to sidestep his question, but she had seen the telltale eyebrow arch that was proof her quick change of subject hadn't fooled him in the least.

She wondered how long he'd wait before demanding an answer to his question. Wondered, too, how she'd phrase her response.

Ah, to be a child again, she thought, sighing, *like Richie, and never have to worry about protecting others from bad news, always able to believe in happy endings.*

Because right now, she'd give anything, just about anything, to believe that her father was still alive.

Chapter 3

March 1865

"Cullen Adams, this is the third time in a week you've come to school late," Brynne scolded gently. "What do you have to say for yourself?"

She didn't expect the boy to respond, for Cullen hadn't said a word since his parents died in a Yankee raid on Petersburg. Why Clay, his older brother, made the child come to school at all seemed as big a mystery to Brynne as Cullen's silence. If sitting in her makeshift classroom all these months had made a difference in his behavior, Brynne would have been the first to insist that he attend. But he sat alone in the last row, staring blankly ahead, never speaking, barely moving. It was time to discuss the matter with his brother.

~

First thing next morning, she set out to do just that.

Brynne had heard much about Clay Adams, but though she had seen him around town, she hadn't exchanged more than polite nods with the somber-faced man. Once, in response to something Buster the postmaster said, she'd seen Clay smile. Until that moment, she'd guessed his age to be thirty or thirty-five—but the smile had so completely transformed his face, that she decided he was closer to twenty-five after all.

She felt a strange interest in this man who was now the guardian of her silent student, an interest that had first begun to grow when she had talked with his parents about him. The Adamses had moved to Spring Creek from Louisiana in the summer of '59, and as their younger son's teacher, Brynne had had occasion to talk with the parents, first at school functions and then at numerous church gatherings. Ernest and Claudia had been so proud of their eldest son who was attending a Boston college. When he graduated, they said, he planned to put his education to use improving their tobacco plantation.

The war killed the plans of thousands like the Adamses. Clay, his mother tearfully told Brynne one Sunday morning, felt duty bound to defend his beloved South and had enlisted in the Confederate Army the moment he heard about what had taken place in South Carolina. He fought long and hard...until an injury suffered during the Franklin-Nashville Campaign in November of '64 sent him home, just weeks before his parents became victims of the slaughter in Petersburg. The war had put a heavy hand on Clay's family, just as it had on Brynne's. Maybe that was why she felt this strange sense of kinship with him....

Since childhood, Brynne had made a hobby of tracing the meaning of folks' names. Her own meant "the heights," a fine name for a girl with her head in the clouds, Brynne told herself, but not at all appropriate for a young woman like herself, with both feet planted firmly on solid ground.

Clay's name meant "of the earth." *Now there's a name*, she'd told herself, *that fits like a comfortable shoe.* He stood tall and broad as a mighty oak, with hair the color of acorns and eyes as blue as a summer sky, and he looked as though his feet, like hers, were planted solidly on the earth. She just wished that one day she could see him smile again....

As she guided her two-wheeled buggy over the bumpy road toward Adams' Hill, Brynne wondered how he would react when she told him to keep his brother home from school. The time, she'd say, would allow the boy to heal privately from his emotional wounds. Would Clay be the kind of man who'd understand that her idea had been born of concern for his brother—or the type who'd tell her to mind her own business?

She pictured the determined set of his jaw and the deep furrow that lined his brow. "I have a feeling he'll be a bit of both," she told herself.

༄

He'd been so engrossed in repairing the pasture fence that Clay never heard the buggy's approach. When he finally caught sight of it from the corner of his eye, he nearly hammered his thumb. *Cullen's teacher,* he acknowledged, grimacing as he drew a sleeve across his perspiring brow. If she had come this early on a Saturday, it couldn't be good news that brought her.

Jamming the hammer handle into the back pocket of his trousers, Clay tucked in his shirt as she smiled and waved in friendly greeting. "Good morning, Mr. Adams," she called, bringing the buggy to a halt at the end of the drive. "My, but you're up and at it early."

He cocked one dark brow and tucked in a corner of his mustachioed mouth. "What can I do for you?"

He winced with guilt at the startled expression his gruff tone had etched on her pretty face, but thankfully she recovered quickly. Wrapping the horse's reins around her left hand, the pretty young teacher adjusted the bow of her wide-brimmed hat. "I need to speak with you about your brother," she said, squaring her shoulders and lifting her chin.

He'd been casually leaning on the fencepost, but now he straightened in response to her statement. "What about him?" Clay crossed both arms over his chest. "He givin' you some sort of trouble?"

She blinked several times, as if trying to read the reason for the anger in his voice. "Quite the contrary. Cullen is the best-behaved boy in class." Pursing her lips, she added, "Trouble is, he isn't learning a thing."

"That's impossible," he grated, shaking his head. "I see to it he does his lessons, every night after supper."

She raised a brow in response to the heat of his words, then leaned forward slightly to say, "I realize this visit is impromptu, Mr. Adams, but. . ."

He watched as she bit her full lower lip and tilted her head. *I like a woman who thinks before she speaks,* he thought, hiding a smirk. *It's a right rare commodity these days.*

"I seem to have completely forgotten my manners," she said, holding out her hand. "I don't believe we've ever been properly introduced. I'm Brynne Carter, Mr. Adams."

Frowning, he focused on the tiny, lace-covered hand for a moment. He tried to shake off the gentle feeling growing inside him toward her. *She's just more of what I've had too much of lately. . .trouble,* he told himself. "I know who you are," he growled, meeting her eyes. "What do you take me for, some kind of simpleton? Spring Creek has but one teacher."

When she realized he had no intention of taking her hand, she made a fist of it, then rested it on her hip. After a moment of intense scrutiny, she climbed down from the buggy seat and tethered her horse to the post Clay had just repaired. Tapping a fingertip to her chin, she gave his dusty work boots a cursory glance. "It appears you're putting most of your weight on your right foot, Mr. Adams." She met his eyes. "Would you mind very much shifting it to your left?"

Clay's brow wrinkled with confusion. He hadn't moved a step. How could she have noticed his limp? He looked at his feet, then focused on her face. "What?"

Mischievous light danced in her dark eyes. "It's the most sensible thing to do, since we seem to have gotten off on the wrong foot."

"The wrong. . ." When understanding dawned, Clay chuckled softly and shook his head. Extending his own hand, he said, "Pleasure to make your acquaintance, Miss Carter."

The power of her grip amazed him even more than the way her hand all but disappeared in his. And the way she stood there, blinking up at him, made his heart lurch. The sunlight glinting on her hair reminded him of ripe chestnuts.

Clay's ears had grown hot. His cheeks, too. He turned her hand loose and tried to recall why she'd come here in the first place. "Now, tell me about this trouble Cullen is giving you."

She glanced toward the house. "Where is he?"

"In the barn, mucking out stalls. Why?"

Brynne untethered her horse and climbed back onto the buggy seat. "I don't think he should overhear our conversation." Pausing, she swung her gaze to his eyes. "Do you suppose we might go on up to the house?"

"You're not a woman who beats around the bush, are you?" he asked, grinning slightly.

Brynne grinned right back. "I find bush beating a terrible waste of time. . .and unnecessarily hard on the shrubbery." Smiling, she patted the seat beside her. "You're more than welcome to drive," she added, offering him the reins.

He hesitated, but only for a moment. "Well," he grumbled, "I reckon the sooner we get this over with, the sooner I'll be able to get back to work." Clay climbed up beside her and relieved her of the reins. He didn't say another word until he parked near the front porch. Neither did Brynne, and something told Clay this was not typical behavior for the lovely little teacher.

Though he'd stared straight ahead as they made the ten-minute trip from the road to the house, he could see from the corner of his eye her every reaction to the sights around her. As they rode over the narrow drive that curved like a gently flowing river of crushed stone, her eyes had widened. A little smile curved her lips as they passed beneath stately magnolias that lined the entire length of the drive.

He'd had the same eye-popping reaction the first time he'd seen the big house, with its black-shuttered, many-paned windows that offset wide double doors on the first floor. A dozen red brick steps led from the drive to the massive portico. Tall columns supported either side of the porch roof, crowned by a second, equally grand porch, enclosed by a white picket rail.

A sense of well-being had wrapped 'round him like a mother's hug the first time he caught sight of those four imposing chimneys, silhouetted against the blue, sun-bright sky. And the two gigantic oaks that flanked the porch. And that sea of velvety white crocuses. . .

"White crocuses," she sighed. "They're my mother's favorite flowers." Brynne turned a bit on the buggy seat to face him. "How did you avoid the Yankee raids here at Adams' Hill?" she asked, incredulous. "Why, they completely burned the Smiths out. And it'll likely take us years to repair the damage they did at Moorewood."

Clay shrugged. "Don't rightly know," he admitted, stepping down from the buggy.

She was watching him, he knew, and making note of his limp. *Dear God,* he prayed, *don't let her feel sorry for me. I can take just about anything from her but that.* Just in case pity was shining in her eyes, he avoided her gaze as he reached up to help her from the buggy.

But Brynne wasn't having any of that! "Mr. Adams," she said brightly, forcing him to look at her, "you are a true gentleman indeed."

He didn't see a trace of pity on her face, which only made her all the more beautiful to him. He clamped his hands around her waist—a waist tinier than any he'd ever seen—to lift her from the seat.

"Now, don't strain yourself, Mr. Adams."

He bristled for a moment, but the gentle look on her face told him her comment hadn't been motivated by pity. "Why, I've hefted sacks of wheat and corn that weigh more than you, Miss Carter," he said, putting her gently onto the ground. She seemed so small, so vulnerable. And yet, if all he'd heard about her in town was true, she'd more or less single-handedly run Moorewood while her father and brother were fighting. Suddenly, Clay didn't want to let her go. He wanted, instead, to draw her close and wrap her in a protective hug.

"Forgive my boldness, Mr. Adams, but do you have anything warm to drink inside? I know the sun is shining bright as can be, but I'm afraid I've caught a bit of a chill. . . ."

The question broke the trancelike connection that had fused his eyes to hers. He quickly unhanded her, and with a grand, sweeping gesture, invited her to precede him into the house. If he led the way, she'd have to walk behind him and watch him shuffle along like a three-legged dog. "Could be there's some coffee left from breakfast," he said.

She lifted her skirts and dashed up the stairs. "That'll be just fine." She stopped suddenly and faced the barn. "You're sure Cullen won't overhear?"

Clay held open the front door. "Not if we get this matter settled before sunset."

Brynne pursed her lips. "Well," she huffed, smiling only with her eyes, "you're not one to beat around the bush either, are you, Mr. Adams?" And with that, she breezed past him and into the house.

"Do you mind talking in the kitchen?" he asked, closing the door behind them.

"The kitchen is my favorite room at Moorewood." She leaned forward as if telling state secrets. "Kitchens are the coziest rooms in any house, where people can gather around the table and have a companionable conversation and. . ."

If he had to stand there and listen to her chatter like a magpie for another minute, he was likely to sweep her off those tiny feet and give her a big kiss, just to shut her up. Clay grinned and quirked a brow. *Not such a bad thought,* he told himself.

". . .the very best place to discuss the day's events. Don't you think so?"

"Yes, yes," he agreed, though he hadn't the foggiest idea what she'd been babbling about. "The kitchen's right down that hall."

She headed in the direction he'd pointed and helped herself to a white mug from the shelf above the cookstove. She hadn't even taken her gloves off yet when she touched a palm to the coffeepot. "Good. It's still warm." And as though she were the lady of the house rather than the guest, Brynne smiled. "May I pour you a cup?"

Clay had to admit she looked lovely standing there at the stove, his mother's coffeepot in one hand, his father's favorite cup in the other. More than that, she looked as if she belonged. He shook his head to clear his mind. "I, uh, I'd just as soon get down to business, if you don't mind." He nodded toward the yard, visible through the window beside her. "There's that fence to finish repairin', and. . ."

"Then I suggest we sit," she broke in, settling herself in a ladder-backed chair. Brynne placed her mug on the table and wrapped her hands around it. "Tell me, Mr. Adams, how long since Cullen has spoken?"

Clay turned his chair around and sat across from her, leaning both arms across the seat back. "My folks were killed in Petersburg in December," he said matter-of-factly. "When I told Cullen about it, he said, 'You're lyin'. Ain't no way they're dead!'" Clay frowned, linked his fingers. "Then his eyes filled up with tears and he ran out to the barn." He met her eyes. "Hasn't said a word since."

Brynne clasped both hands under her chin. "Oh, how dreadful," she sighed, shaking her head. "I heard how your folks volunteered to travel south, to interview the seminarian who would replace Pastor Zaph."

Tears shimmered in her eyes as she absently stroked a scratch on the tabletop, the nonchalant action, it seemed to Clay, an intent to hide her tender side from him. It touched him deeply that she would cry for his losses when she'd suffered so many of her own.

"So much death and destruction. So much suffering," Brynne was saying, more to herself than to Clay. "I wonder if, when it's over, either side will think it was worth it."

He had heard what happened to her father. To her brother Edward. To her precious Moorewood. Yet there she sat, head up and shoulders back, determined to take it on the chin. What and who she was showed in her determined smile, in her warm brown eyes. Brynne Carter was a woman who cared deeply. What more proof did he need than the concern for his brother that brought her here today?

Clay didn't know what prompted him to do it, but he blanketed her hand with his own. "Now, about Cullen. . ."

She looked at their hands, and he was pleased that she didn't draw away. He was still more pleased when she put her free hand atop the stack of fingers. Brightening a bit, she smiled. "As a matter of fact, I have several ideas I'd like to discuss with you."

Grinning, Clay gave her hand a gentle squeeze. "I had a feeling you might."

Chapter 4

June 1865

When Sergeant Trevor Williams had left Moorewood in late February, he made two promises to Amelia: "Yes, Miz Carter, I'll take good care of myself, and don't you worry, if I hear anything about the Colonel, I'll get a message to you."

Almost four months had now passed without a word from him—or any army official, for that matter. Not that Brynne was surprised. Amelia still insisted that her husband would return to them, but in Brynne's heart, she knew she'd never see her father again. Sometimes, when the pain of her grief seemed too heavy to bear, Brynne wished that, like her mother, a little childlike faith beat in her heart.

Because, oh, how she missed him! Not a day went by that she didn't think of him, for there wasn't a man like him on earth and likely would never be. *If Papa were here,* she thought, shaking her head at the irony, *he'd know how to make Mama face the truth. . . .*

Brynne had been taught both at home and in Sunday school that worrying never solved any problem. "Prayer, faith, and patience," her father had always said, "are the ways to ease a troubled mind."

Well, she'd prayed morning, noon, and night that God would give her the words to help Amelia deal realistically with what had happened to Richard. And she'd clung to her faith, hoping the Almighty would answer those prayers. But day by day, it grew more obvious that Amelia could spend the rest of her life clinging to the hope that her husband would return. If only God would show the poor woman a sign!

Having been born and bred in Christian fundamentals, Brynne couldn't make herself believe the Lord had simply turned His back on her family. Compared to the war, Amelia's delusions were a small problem; surely the Lord had plenty more important prayers to answer. . . .

Still, it had shaken her faith a bit that the Lord had not provided a solution to her mother's problem. Brynne was feeling a bit lost. A little less trusting in the God who had promised peace to all those who put their troubles at the foot of the cross. . . .

Not once in her life had Brynne spoken a disrespectful word to her mother. But one evening, four months to the day after the Andersons' baby was born, the day Trevor had brought them her father's letter, all that changed.

Amelia had visited little Jake at least a dozen times since bringing him into the world. "Just seeing the little tyke grow and thrive makes me feel better." Just back from yet another visit, she hung her hat on the peg near the door. "It's proof that life goes on, even as this horrible war rages on all around us."

Brynne wanted to point out that death was very much a part of life, because of the war. But she held her tongue. The subject of Richard's survival was by now a sore point that both mother and daughter scrupulously avoided. Brynne could not understand how, after so many months with no word from her father—or about him—Amelia could still be so certain he was alive, that he would return.

Her mother had not shed a tear, not while reading the letter Trevor delivered, not as she'd stuffed it back into its envelope. Instead, she'd held up her chin in stubborn denial of the obvious and shook her head.

She was looking at Brynne that same way now, and Brynne didn't know if she possessed the strength of character to continue pretending she shared her mother's faith. Life had taught her that such naivete could only bring pain and disappointment.

"Don't wrinkle your brow at me, young lady," her mother scolded. "You're not too big to turn over my knee, you know."

Brynne sighed. "I mean no disrespect, Mama. It's just. . ."

"Just nothing! Remember what Jesus said: 'If you have faith as a grain of mustard seed, you can say to that mountain, move, and it will move.'"

"Papa isn't Lazarus, Mama," Brynne said dully, "Christ isn't going to bring him back to life."

Amelia planted both hands on her hips. "If your father was dead, don't you think I'd know it?" She pressed a fist to her chest. "He's. . .he's. . ."

Her mother's hesitation surprised Brynne, and she sat in stony silence as Amelia stared at an unknown spot beyond Brynne's shoulder.

For a time, soon after Richard's letter had been delivered, she'd tried to share her mother's unwavering optimism, but whenever her mood darkened, reality set in, and when it did, her father died anew in her tortured mind. And so she'd turned loose the dream that could never come true, and clung instead to the tried and true: Expect the worst, and when it comes, you can say "I told you so!" And if the worst never happens, it'll be a blissful surprise.

While Brynne had been daydreaming, Amelia had gathered her former resoluteness. "'Christ isn't going to bring Papa back to life,'" she quoted Brynne. "Well, the disciples spoke just as plainly of Lazarus's death." She gave her words a moment to sink in. "And they were just as wrong."

Nodding, Brynne stared at her hands, folded in her lap. She knew the verse well, for she'd read it a hundred times since her father's letter had been delivered: "And Martha fell at Jesus's feet and said, 'If you had been here, Lord, my brother would not have died,'" Brynne quoted the book of John. She met Amelia's dark eyes, unaware of the rage that rang in her voice. "Jesus wasn't on that battlefield. If He had been, Papa wouldn't be—"

"I'm surprised, Brynne," Amelia interrupted, "that I need to remind you the Lord is with us always, everywhere."

Expelling an exasperated sigh, Brynne closed her eyes in an attempt to summon patience. "If that's true," she said slowly, her voice quiet and cool, "how do you explain all those who died fighting, and your own son, who came home wounded beyond repair? How do you explain the destruction of the South and our beautiful Moorewood?" *How do you explain the way Ross turned his back on his own people, on me, and. . . ?*

Amelia wrapped her daughter in a hug and sighed. "I can't explain it, Brynne, because I don't understand it myself. But it isn't our place to understand such things. God calls us to believe, nothing more." Smiling gently, she cupped Brynne's cheek. "I only know that God promises to give us the strength to bear up under any burden. 'He will not let you be tested beyond your strength, but with the test, he will provide the way of escape, so you may be able to endure it.' He knows our limits better than we do."

In a blinding flash, Brynne realized that Amelia needed to believe in the impossible every bit as much as Brynne needed to stare the truth straight in the eye. Could her mother's heroic demeanor be a disguise that hid her true fears? If so, her mother needed loving support.

"Your father will come back to us. I'm certain of it!"

What harm can it do to pretend you share her sunny view? she asked herself. "Of course he will," Brynne said, feigning a smile. "Now I really must get to bed. I have a busy day planned for my class tomorrow."

Amelia pressed a gentle kiss to Brynne's forehead. "I was so proud when you suggested to Pastor Gentry that the congregation use our barn as a temporary church and school after the Yankees destroyed the church and school. The shed will be plenty big enough for Bessie until the new church is built."

Once, Bessie had been one of dozens of dairy cows that stood side by side in the big wooden structure. Now she stood alone in what was little more than a ramshackle lean-to behind the house. "True, but Bessie is awfully spoiled," Brynne said, heading for the door. "I hope she doesn't decide to stop producing milk, just to get even for being reassigned to such tiny quarters."

Smiling sadly, Amelia shook her head. "Goodness, Brynne, when did you become such a pessimist?"

When our great nation was divided by a ridiculous war, Brynne wanted to say. When Edward came home mangled. When the list of the dead soldiers on the post office wall doubled, then tripled. When Ross chose money and social position over doing the right thing. When Papa's letter came and. . .

But remembering her decision to be loving and supportive for as long as her mother needed it, Brynne grinned and affectionately patted her mother's hand. "I promise to try and keep my negative comments to a minimum, starting now." She gave her mother a quick hug and a peck on the cheek. "Good night, Mama.

I love you." She hurried to her room, hoping that a good night's sleep would help her continue the pretense tomorrow, and the next day, and the next.

᠀

Brynne's pessimism, as it turned out, had not been completely unfounded. Though Bessie dutifully continued to pour out an ample supply of milk, European support of the South dried up. Everyone, it seemed, was hungry and, according to all reports, desertion in Lee's army had increased alarmingly.

The Yankees were bored. There was little else for them to do but pillage and rampage and complain about the war that would not end. Rumor had it that Lee's remaining veterans, despite their skilled—if not grim—determination, had spent the last of their fighting strength.

Rumor became reality midmonth when word came by way of a fleeing Rebel soldier that on April second, the Confederate government, guarded by a stalwart few, fled Richmond by way of the railroad. By the fourth, said an article in a special edition of the Gazette, President Lincoln arrived, unescorted and unannounced, to inspect the grand old city, now under Union control. "Let 'em up easy," he was quoted to have told General Grant. "Let 'em up easy."

But there was no letup, and by May tenth, the war that would not end officially ended.

The suffering in the South did not end however. Hunger, homelessness, illness, and poverty afflicted people who, before the war, had never experienced physical or monetary discomfort. The Carters, like their neighbors all around them, attempted to get back to living life as they had prior to April 12, 1861, when the ten-inch mortar that screamed over Charleston Harbor blasted Fort Sumter.

Brynne held tight to a hope of her own. Colonel Richard Carter had died a hero's death and deserved a hero's burial; someday, perhaps, his family could bury his remains in his favorite place. . .at the top of Kismet Hill, beside the scraggly pine that had somehow grown in a bed of rock.

Chapter 5

July 1865

It wasn't an easy hike to Kismet Hill, and Brynne had decided to spend the night there rather than making the long trek back before nightfall. She started out late in the afternoon and walked along the stream, as her father had taught her. Part of the beauty of this country, he'd always said, was that it never changed. Brynne recognized trees and trails she'd marked as a little girl, using her father's big hunting knife as he supervised with a watchful eye. Finally, as the sun slid down the backside of Moore's Peak, their special place opened up to her.

Brynne sat on a fallen tree trunk, hands resting on her knees, and drank in the territory like a woman lost in the desert might suck at the wet lip of a canteen. This was where her father always came when he sought to escape life's hectic pace or yearned for the privacy to thank God for his blessings. She'd been honored that he'd shared his secret place with her. Over time, it had become a place of respite for her, too. Since he'd left to fight for Moorewood, it had become a place to hide.

Not until a cardinal peeped in a nearby tree did she rouse from her memory and begin setting up camp. The temperature here could dip low at night, even in summer, but Brynne had come prepared. Nature couldn't do anything to her up here to equal what the war had done! She constructed a makeshift tent from an old blanket and several ropes, strung from low-hanging tree branches. If it rained, she'd climb inside. Otherwise, she'd sleep under the stars.

Staring up at the shimmering darkness, she felt Richard's presence. He'd been nothing but the poor son of a pig farmer when he met Amelia. "She fell for him like a lumberjack's tree," Grandpa Moore often said with a wink and a grin. "And so did the rest of the family. I saw brilliance peekin' out from under that bent straw hat he wore, and decided to take a chance on it."

Richard, Grandpa insisted, had been born with a head for business. Less than two years after marrying George Moore's only daughter, he'd tripled the worth of Moorewood. "It's only fittin' that it become yours when I leave this old world," Grandpa had written in the letter accompanying his last will and testament.

Brynne had often acknowledged her father's intelligence, but it was his heart that she admired most. Yes, he'd slaughter pigs and sheep and cows to put meat on the table, and yes, he'd sell whole herds to assure there'd always be money to care for his family. He was a crack-shot hunter, too, but Brynne understood better than anyone how it pained him to take a life for any reason.

They'd been here, on Kismet Hill, overlooking the valley when he'd spied a doe and two fawns in the distance. "Look there," he's whispered. "Isn't it the most beautiful sight?"

Puzzled by his awestruck expression, young Brynne had frowned. "But Papa," she'd said, "you're here to kill them."

He'd taken her face in his hands to say, "The Lord created every creature on earth for man's benefit—some for food, others for coats and hats. . ." An eagle screeched overhead just then, and he'd said, "And some, we're to admire from afar." Gently chucking her under the chin, he'd winked. "It's up to us to know when and how He means for us to use what He gave us." Only then did he raise his rifle and fire.

Brynne missed Richard more at that moment than in those first hard days after he'd left home. She and Clay Adams had been going for some long walks together. At first, they had discussed Cullen and his problems, but lately their conversations had ranged far and wide. On their last walk, Clay had held her hand, and Brynne had been filled with confusion ever since. If she'd come to her father for advice on the thoughts she'd been thinking about Clay Adams, he'd have known exactly what to say. . . .

Am I being foolish, she'd ask him, *giving my heart away so soon after Ross's betrayal? And do you think Clay will ever give his heart to me?*

She snuggled under the blankets she'd brought and smiled. Papa and Clay would have gotten along famously, she acknowledged, missing them both more than she cared to admit. Brynne remembered her first meeting with Clay, when she'd spelled out ways they might help Cullen learn to talk again.

He hadn't rejected a single one of her suggestions. Instead, Clay had nodded in agreement with everything she'd said, right down to and including her idea that he start attending church services again.

"Haven't been inside a church in a while," he'd admitted on a heavy sigh, "but if you believe it'll help the boy, I'll give it a try."

"Someday, perhaps you'll tell me why you've stayed away so long," she'd said.

An array of emotions had flickered over his handsome, mustachioed face in response to her simple request. Like storm clouds that blot out the sun, his secret reasons dimmed the light in his blue eyes. The furrow between his brows deepened, and the corners of his mouth turned down. His soft, rich voice took on a hard cold edge, like a blade scraping across a dry stone. "Don't hold your breath," he'd grated. But his hand had still been sandwiched between hers when he'd said it, as if he hoped that "someday" would indeed come.

With her heart and head full of these memories, Brynne slept deeply for the first time in months. When she woke at dawn, she felt as though she'd slept six nights instead of one. She sat up to stretch and breathe in the sharp pure scent of pine.

She got onto her knees and faced the sun. "Dear Lord," she prayed, hands folded and face tilted toward the heavens, "thank You for a night of peaceful slumber. Thank You for this glorious morning and this beautiful view and everything else You've given me. Bless this day, and see that I do Your will throughout it. Amen."

When she was finished, Brynne set about the business of having breakfast. Poking at her smoldering campfire, she carefully placed dried leaves and sticks atop the coals and blew gently until they glowed red. When the tiny flames licked at the twigs, she added larger limbs, until the fire blazed hot and bright. Now Brynne dumped a handful of coffee grounds into the bottom of a blue-speckled pot and poured fresh mountain spring water over them. While she waited for it to bubble, she tore off a chunk of bread and popped it into her mouth as she looked out over the valley beyond.

Tears stung her eyes as she surveyed the pristine scene. "How could anyone plant their boots on ground like this and not believe in God?" Richard had said. Brynne couldn't help but agree, for only a powerful and mighty Being could have created anything so vast and magnificent. The vista was an explosion of color and scent, from the sun-glinted hilltops to the twisting aqua river below, from the pale azure sky to the pillowy green of faraway treetops.

Wiping her eyes with the back of a hand, she slid her father's letter from her skirt pocket. Most of the time, her mother kept the letter with her, in her pocket, but she had let her daughter borrow it, and now Brynne stared down at the blackened paper. Her father's handwriting, like the man itself, bespoke power and determination. He had promised to move heaven and earth to come home to them, but even Richard Carter didn't possess that kind of strength.

He'd left them in May of '62 and hadn't gotten a letter through until July. In it, he told his family there had been a lot of activity near the Rappahannock River. As his unit continued to push south to block the enemy, it had grown smaller and smaller. "You know that I believe in the truth," he'd written, "and so I shall never lie about my situation." He'd closed that letter with a promise to return, too.

They didn't hear from him again until November of '63. This time, he wrote that the fighting had escalated in the area. They were thinking of building a secret weapon, he'd told them. But he hadn't said what sort of weapon, and since the family hadn't heard from him again, no one knew if it had been a success. All they were left with was his second promise to come home.

The next letter described his move to Fort Fisher. "The Yanks will never defeat us here," he had promised. "Not unless they should be foxy enough to come at us both by land and sea. But I believe the Northern generals are not as clever as the Southern." And then again he had promised, "I promise to be home as soon as I am able."

If this, his final correspondence, had not been delivered in person by the young sergeant, it would have been easy to believe that maybe Richard could keep his promise. As it was, Trevor's description of the colonel as he'd last seen him made it only too clear there was little hope her father had survived.

Head in her hands, Brynne sobbed and remembered those last precious moments with her father.

"Why must you go?" she'd demanded. "No one expects it of you, not a man with all your responsibilities. . ."

"I expect it of me," he'd said, buckling his haversack. "What kind of man would I be if I didn't do my share to protect what's mine?"

She'd read newspaper accounts of the fighting that had already taken place. And she'd done her Christian duty, standing among neighbors and friends as they buried sons and brothers and husbands. Brynne wanted no part of any obligation that would have her saying a final farewell to her father! "But Papa," she'd pressed, "we need you here. Why not leave the fighting to the younger men?"

He'd put both hands on her shoulders and given her a gentle shake. "I realize I seem ancient to you, daughter, but there's plenty of fight left in me."

She'd wriggled free of his grasp and stood at the window, hugging herself to fend off the cold chill that had wrapped itself around her. "What if. . . What will we do if. . . ?"

Resting his chin atop her head, he hugged her from behind. "Nothing is going to happen to me, sweet girl."

"You can't be sure of that," she'd said, facing him. And with the last of her hope, she'd added, "Can you?"

"'No man is sure of life,'" he quoted from the book of Job. "But you can be sure I'll do everything in my power to come home." Drawing her into a comforting embrace, he'd added, "Home is what I'm fighting for, remember?"

Now, Brynne folded the letter and returned it to the worn envelope and resigned herself once more to the inevitable. She had hoped that in coming here, to their special place, she might find reason to share her mother's optimism.

Here, he'd told her breathtaking stories that simplified the miracles of life. Her favorite was his explanation of how one lonely scrub pine had been able to grow from a fissure in a boulder at the top of the hill.

"Some time ago," he'd said, "a tiny seed parted from its mother plant and soared through the heavens in God's palm, searching for a place to rest. From on high, God pointed to a minuscule crevice. 'There?' the little seed asked. 'But Lord, nothing can grow in solid rock!' And God said, 'You can grow there, if you believe enough in Me.'

"So the seed coasted to earth on the breath of God, and nestled deep in the darkness of the crook where nothing else had had the courage to go.

"God smiled upon that brave little seed, and because it had trusted so completely in Him, He saw to it there was soil enough, and water enough, and the seed took root and grew, and it survived."

Though she had always loved the way he told tales, with wonder and awe rumbling in his deep voice, Brynne had never understood its application to her own life. It seemed to her the little pine had endured many hardships by blindly doing as God asked it to do. For one thing, it stood completely alone all these many years, without grass or flowers or another tree to keep it company. And the wicked wind had blown cold for so long that the spindly thing had needles on only one side, and leaned hard toward the rocks, as though seeking shelter from the constant blasts of tempestuous air.

It had been here for as long as Brynne could remember, yet the tree stood barely taller than she, while pines that had rooted in the forest's loamy soil for half as long had developed trunks as big around as barrel hoops and needly branches that raked the undersides of the clouds.

Well, she told herself, *it's a nice story, all the same.* She didn't have to learn a lesson from every tale he told, did she? And Richard had taught her many valuable lessons here, like how to find her way through a dense forest, where to find drinking water, how to tell which berries and mushrooms were poisonous so she could survive in any locale.

Much to Brynne's dismay, though, she realized her father had overlooked the most important lesson of all: He hadn't taught her how to survive the loss of him.

Chapter 6

The community of Spring Creek had finally built themselves a new church building where they could meet to worship God. Clay chose the same seat in the new building every week, hoping that as few people as possible would notice him and his brother.

"Sit front and center," had been Brynne's advice, "so Cullen can hear God's Word, loud and clear!" Third row from the altar, at the end of the pew nearest the stained glass windows was as close to front and center as Clay intended to get.

He found himself daydreaming during the services, a practice that would have earned him a heated scolding from his mother, even at his age, had she lived. Try as he might, he could not focus on the music or the words filtering around the tidy chapel, for just as he had chosen this seat near the wall each week, Brynne found her own favorite spot every Sunday, too: in the pew right in front of his, but in the center, right where he couldn't help but see her pretty profile.

Like an earthly angel, he thought, smiling inwardly as he watched her sitting there, looking serene and beautiful as she stared ahead, hands folded primly in her lap. Her students, he'd noticed in weeks past, scrambled and shoved for the opportunity to sit beside her. Mary Scott and Sammy Barber had won the contest this week, and though neither child had yet seen a tenth birthday, each sat almost as tall as their teacher.

She moved with the grace and agility of a doe, and something told him that despite her fragile-looking bone structure, Brynne was anything but delicate.

He remembered that day when she'd ridden out to the farm in her dainty two-wheeled buggy to discuss Cullen's emotional problems. Her diminutive size and stature had given him a powerful urge to wrap her in a protective embrace. When she bounded toward his front door, he couldn't help but grin, for everything about her, from the smile that lit her eyes like a beacon to the surefooted way she moved, forced him to see her as larger than life.

The congregation rose in unison. "Please turn to page one hundred twenty-one in your hymnals," the preacher said, nodding to the organist. Smiling, Mrs. Henderson nodded back, leaning hard on the ivory keys as the first melodious strains of song filled the new church.

"Sing praise to our Creator, O son of Adam's race," the parishioners sang.

Clay stood, open hymnal balanced on one palm, head bowed and eyes closed. After years of loss, he had something to sing praise about again, he realized. Brynne's suggestion that he bring Cullen to church, for starters. Before, the boy barely lifted his chin from his chest. Now, at least, he made eye contact from time to time. He sent a heartfelt "thank You" heavenward.

"God's children by adoption, baptized into His grace," the song continued.

He regarded Cullen from the corner of his eye. The boy was staring hard at his songbook. Though he'd turned to the right page, he stood as silent as a statue. Clay sometimes wondered what might be going through his brother's head. Was he picturing the explosion that killed their parents? That would certainly explain the shadows that so often dulled Cullen's dark eyes and twisted his face into a tortured scowl.

Granted, it had been a difficult piece of news to hear. Still, despite the slight improvement Cullen had shown, until Brynne had confronted him, Clay's patience had been wearing thin. After all, Cullen had turned thirteen on his last birthday, older than some of the boys Clay had fought with in the war. They had performed many tasks to assist their older comrades, from handing rifles down the front lines to reloading muskets. They filled canteens and sewed rips in the men's shirtsleeves. Sometimes, in the quiet of the night, their soft angelic voices could be heard in the distance, singing sad old ballads that lulled the tired soldiers to sleep.

"Praise the holy trinity," the congregation continued, "undivided unity. . ."

Lovely as it was, the hymn couldn't begin to compare with those simple tunes created by the youngsters on the battlefield. Those boys had walked side by side with the foot soldiers, straight into the bowels of battle. They'd seen all manner of death and destruction, yet managed to keep their fears at bay as the unit marched toward the next skirmish, and the next.

Clay remembered one in particular. As second lieutenant, Clay had been ordered to report to General Hood's quarters for a top-secret conclave. The officers were bending over the map table, studying their options, when the youngster barged into the tent and stood at attention. "Dale Allen Jones, reporting for duty," he'd said in a loud, official-sounding voice. "I can play a fife and drum; I know how to shoot. And I'm an orphan, so it don't much matter iffen I get back to Chattanooga alive or not." Looking straight ahead, he'd concluded his little speech with a snappy salute: "Brung my own bedroll and canteen, too."

It was hard not to be impressed by a boy like that. Tough through and through, he more than made up for his smaller than average height and weight. "All spit and vinegar, that one," the men often said of Dale. The boy never complained, not when the blisters on his feet bled, not when his flute was destroyed by enemy fire. He didn't whine when the men who'd become his substitute fathers took direct hits, didn't cry when they died. Even when a Union cannonball exploded near him, pocking his puny frame with shrapnel, Dale did not whimper. He would have been quite a man, Clay acknowledged, had he survived that last battle. . . .

Dale, like so many boys who did their part for the South, understood that a man couldn't hide from pain any more than he could hide from himself. Clay had begun to wonder when Cullen would learn that lesson. Did he enjoy the pitying stares and whispers that floated round him everywhere he went? Had he no pride at all?

The voices of his brethren united in a resounding tribute to the Almighty. "Holy God, mighty God, God immortal be adored."

"Please be seated," the pastor said. Amid the din of shuffling feet and hymnals dropping into bookrests, the flock sat on the hard wooden pews.

"Bow your heads and ask for God's blessing," came Gentry's booming voice. "He will cleanse you of your sins, if you will only ask Him to." The preacher raised both arms and closed his eyes. "Does something trouble your heart? Give it to the Lord! Have you done a deed that separates you from His love? Give it to the Lord! Do you harbor a grudge that darkens His light in your soul? Give it to the Lord!"

A hush befell the church as members of the flock searched their hearts and minds for sins to confess. As their murmurs sought God's ear, Clay's heart pounded. For while these good people of Spring Creek had been compassionate regarding his brother's condition, Clay had not. Until Brynne had shared her opinions with him, he had believed that the boy didn't need sympathy and mollycoddling, but a firm hand. *The trouble with Cullen*, he'd told himself time and again, *is life's been too easy. He's a spoiled, weak boy.*

"Give it to God!" Pastor Gentry repeated.

I was ashamed of him, Lord, Clay prayed. *I thought he should be standing at the crossroads to manhood by now. . . .*

He watched as Cullen repeatedly folded and unfolded his hands. Clay shook his head. *Lord, how can I help him?*

". . .give it to your Father in heaven!"

"Give it to the Lord!" the congregation repeated.

I give it to You, Clay prayed, *and I beg You. . .bring Cullen around. Help me to forgive him for his weakness.*

৩—

"So good to see you," Pastor Gentry said, smiling and nodding as he greeted each parishioner in turn. "Good morning, Brynne. Don't you look lovely this morning."

Blushing, she tucked a flyaway curl under her bonnet. "That was quite a sermon, Reverend. Why, I believe your voice will vibrate in my ears till well past dinnertime!"

"You have a gift for changing the subject," he said, taking her hand, "but I have one, too. My dear mama called it a stubborn streak." Patting the hand he held, Gentry leaned close to say, "You make it difficult for me to do my job."

Her eyebrows drew together in a confused frown as she took back her hand.

"Your job? I'm afraid I don't. . ."

Chuckling, Gentry grabbed her other hand. "It isn't easy preaching fire and brimstone when you're staring into the sweet face of an angel."

Clay stood at the back of the church, waiting his turn to descend the stone steps. He'd never been overly fond of the hand-shaking ritual that concluded every Sunday service. Today, he found it even harder to bear. Look at him! *Why, he's flirting shamelessly with her,* he fumed mentally. *Him, a man of God, and here, on the steps of the church!*

The conversation between the women in front of him captured Clay's attention.

"Pastor Gentry is quite a specimen, don't you think?" the Widow Jenson whispered.

"Mmm-hmm," her elderly sister agreed. "I've always been particularly fond of blond-haired, blue-eyed men." Winking, she added, "If I were a few years younger. . ."

The widow giggled. "A few years! Why, Annabelle, you're old enough to be his great-grandma!"

Her sister sighed. "Well still, I wouldn't mind a few minutes in Brynne Carter's shoes right about now."

A heavyset gray-haired woman barged to the front of the line and shoved Brynne aside. "Pastor Gentry, I am appalled!"

"Ah, Mrs. Anderson," he purred, ignoring her angry tone, "Lovely day, isn't it?"

The woman tucked in her chins. "If you think you can sweet-talk me the way you sweet-talked her," she spat, casting a glare in Brynne's direction, "you've got another think coming!"

Gentry bowed slightly. "Can't have too many 'thinks,' I always say."

"Save your charm for someone who appreciates it," she snarled. "What sort of preacher carries on so shamelessly in the House of God?"

The pastor drew himself up to his full six-foot height. There wasn't a trace of a smile on his face when he said, "The sort who's tired of the bachelor's life." He directed his next comment to Brynne. "And if Miss Carter would agree, I'd like nothing better than to escort her to the church picnic next Saturday."

Mrs. Anderson huffed off without another word as Clay watched Brynne's cheek flush crimson. It seemed to him she didn't want to attend the picnic as the preacher's companion. "I'm afraid Miss Carter is already spoken for," Clay blurted. Marching to the front of the line, he pumped the pastor's arm. "She will be going to the picnic. . ." He cast a glance in her direction, and nothing could have pleased him more than the relieved smile on her face. ". . .She'll be going with me."

It was the reverend's turn to blush. "Oh. I, uh, I see." He tipped an imaginary hat in Brynne's direction and shot her a disappointed smile, then turned to greet the next person in line.

Clay offered Brynne his elbow and together, they headed down the flagstone walk. "Thank you for coming to my rescue," she said, grinning up at him, "but I know how you feel about church events, so you needn't feel obliged to. . ."

"Obliged?" he broke in, facing her. "Why, I'd be honored."

If she continued looking up at him, blinking those long-lashed dark eyes and smiling that way, Clay thought he might just be obliged to kiss that very kissable mouth. "I've been meaning to have a word with you," he started, "about. . ."

She walked through the gate. "And I've been meaning to have a word with you."

Clay felt like a schoolboy in the throes of his first mad crush as he stepped along beside her. "Oh? About what?"

"About the wonderful things you've done for Spring Creek." She stopped walking and faced the church. "Just look at what all the scrap wood you donated has created. It's a lovely church. A wonderful schoolhouse. Better, even, than what we had before. Why, there was enough to build a new home for the pastor." Brynne met his eyes.

Clay tucked in one corner of his mouth. "The pastor's house," he grated, his eyes narrowing as he glanced at Gentry. "Maybe I should have been a little less generous." He met her eyes to say, "But how did you know I donated. . ."

Shrugging, she smiled. "The only person in a small town who knows more than the doctor is the schoolmarm. Children are filled with all sorts of delightful— and personal—facts." She leaned in close to add, "Billy Donnelly's pa is. . ."

". . .the fellow who designed the buildings," he finished, shaking his head incredulously. Clay heaved a sigh. And grinning, he said, "Well, I'm glad you let me in on your secret. It's a good thing to know if a man aims to be, uh, friends with the teacher."

She crossed both arms over her chest and tapped one foot. "Go ahead. You may as well confess the rest."

"Confess?" Clay's brow wrinkled with confusion. "The rest?"

Rolling her eyes with feigned exasperation, Brynne began counting on her fingers all she knew about him. "You not only donated the wood from the outbuildings on your property, you handed over windowpanes and hardware as well. And," she said with a tilt of her head, "you did quite a bit of the work yourself."

He was certain his cheeks were redder even than Gentry's had been moments ago. Clay took her hand and led her away from the church and didn't stop until they were shrouded by the low-hanging branches of a weeping willow tree. "I've been thinking a lot about you."

"Cullen's doing quite well, don't you think?" she injected.

He waved the comment away. "Mmm. Yes. A little better." He looked at her distractedly, then blurted, "I dreamt of you last night."

A small gasp escaped her lips as her eyes widened. Pressing a hand to her bosom, she glossed over his comment. "Did you see the A-plus Cullen got on his last arithmetic test? And did you know that I saw him following along as one of the other students read a passage out loud," she rattled, "his finger underlining every word in his history book. He was even moving his lips! And—"

Clay grabbed her by the shoulders and pulled her to him. "I'm glad Cullen has finally decided to come out of his confounded self-induced, self-pitying trance.

It's high time he started behaving like a man, if you ask me," he said through clenched teeth. "But—"

"You shouldn't be so hard on him, Clay. He's barely more than a boy."

Boy, my foot! he wanted to counter. But then he remembered what he had prayed during church, and he felt his impatience being washed away as he looked at her. The way she stood there, hands pressed against his chest and trusting eyes searching his face, made his heart beat fast.

Clay was a man who never did anything without first devising a careful plan. He hadn't planned what he might say if he got her alone. Hadn't planned to get her alone! But now that he had, he wouldn't let opportunity slip by.

"Brynne," he rasped, "have you any idea what a difference you've made in—"

"Helping Cullen was just part of my job," she interrupted.

Clay smiled as his hands slid slowly from her shoulders to cup her cheeks. "And what about the difference you've made in my life? Is that part of your job, too?"

"Your life?" Her lips parted with surprise as Brynne glanced left, then right. "I suppose. . .I guess. . .It's only natural," she stammered, "that any positive effect I've had on Cullen would also. . ."

His thumbs followed the contours of her jaw. "The effect you've had on me has very little to do with what you've done for my brother," he grated. "I've been watching you, almost from the moment I limped back from the war, and—"

"How did it happen?" she interrupted, straightening his tie with a wifely nonchalance that made his face burn.

"How did what happen?" he asked, confused.

"Your wound of course."

"Mortar shell." Clay shrugged one shoulder. "Blew a chunk of my thigh away." He searched her face for any trace of sympathy.

As though she could read his mind, she lifted one brow and grinned. "Well you'll get no pity from me, Mr. Adams." Nodding at his injured leg, she added, "Your leg got you here, alone with me under this tree, didn't it?"

"That it did," he said, smiling.

Still grinning, she put a hand on a hip and narrowed one eye. "Exactly why did you bring me. . .?"

Brynne never finished her question, for her words were swallowed up by Clay's insistent kiss.

Chapter 7

August 12, 1865

To the Carter Family
Spring Creek, Virginia

    When I left your warmth and hospitality, I promised to find out what I could about the Colonel.
    Well, I met a man who spent some time in the camp where they took the Colonel. He says he never met anyone name of Richard Carter. Could be he never heard of him because the Colonel was one of a dozen or so soldiers who escaped one night during a thunderstorm.
    I am not one to believe in false hope. I can only say that I pray the Colonel was one of the lucky ones who stole their freedom that stormy night.
    If I hear anything more, I will get word to you. My thoughts and prayers are with you.

        Very truly yours,
        Trevor McDermott Williams

*W*hy does bad news always arrive right on the heels of bad news? Brynne wondered. Guilt hammered her heart as her mother flitted about the kitchen, giggling happily.

"I told you he was alive!" Amelia gasped, flapping Trevor's letter in the air. "Your father escaped from that nasty old prisoner of war camp, and right this minute he's making his way back to us!"

Brynne's heart ached with fear and dread—fear that her mother would find out that she'd been an unwitting accomplice in her father's death, dread that her father would never rest in peace, as she'd hoped, on Kismet Hill—thanks to the information she'd stupidly passed on to Ross Bartlett.

Over and over again, her mind replayed the memory that was torturing her: the day when Ross had wrapped his arms around her and he told her he'd be leaving on the morning train. He'd looked so handsome in his wide-brimmed black hat and many-buttoned uniform, a gleaming cutlass at his hip. She'd thought at the time it had been concern for her family that prompted Ross to ask where her father and brother would be stationed. If she'd known how he intended to use the facts, she'd never have willingly shared what her father had written in an earlier letter: "The only way into Fort Fisher is by way of a narrow channel, so fear not, family, for I am safe, so long as the Yankees don't try a land and sea attack!"

It wasn't until she paid her respects to the Prentices last week that Brynne learned what Ross had done with the information....

Joshua Prentice had also served—and died—at Fort Fisher. After church, Joshua's sister Camille told Brynne a long story, all about how Camille's father, who had been an officer at Fort Fisher, explained the fall of the fortress: The Union army and navy had attacked simultaneously, and the South, though well-manned and well-armed, had not been equipped for the two-pronged attack.

"My daddy says he saw your ex-fiancé leadin' the Bluecoats in," Camille added with a baleful glare. "One minute, Ross was givin' orders to the Yankees, next minute the east tower was toppling over on my poor sweet brother." Her eyes narrowed. "And I wouldn't be surprised if your own father was there, too."

Camille had paused to dry her eyes on a dainty hanky. "They nearly caught Ross, slinking away from the melee." All ladylike decorum was set aside as Camille made her final statement. "If that low-down polecat ever shows his face 'round these parts again, he'll wish they had hanged him."

Brynne had gone over and over it in her head, and try as she might, she could not escape one ugly fact: because of her loose tongue, hundreds of men—her own father included—had died!

She made an effort to pull her thoughts together and pay attention to her mother. "Mama," she said, a hand on Amelia's arm, "seems to me the sergeant made it clear there isn't much sense in holding out for. . ."

"Brynne Amelia Carter," her mother hissed, shoulders hunched and fists bunched, "I'll not have such talk in this house." Her eyes blazed with indignation. "Your father is alive, and he will come home." She shook the balled-up letter under Brynne's nose. "You promised once that you'd keep your negative comments to yourself. I'm holding you to it, do you hear?"

In all her life, Brynne had never seen her mother so angry. At least, she'd never been as angry with her. "I'm sorry, Mama. I never intended to hurt you. I only thought. . ."

"I know what you thought," Amelia bit out. "You thought if you were patient long enough, I'd stop behaving like a dotty old woman and come around to your way of thinking." She took a deep breath, then lovingly smoothed the letter against her stomach and put it back into the envelope.

Fresh tears filled her eyes. "I believe your father is alive, and I'll go right on believing it," she said past the hitch in her voice, "because your father can read me like a book, and I won't have him seeing a trace of faithlessness on my face when he walks through that door. Not after all he's been through."

More than anything, Brynne wanted to console her mother. But words and actions would seem empty and hollow to this woman who saw her daughter as a disloyal skeptic. Tears brimmed in her own eyes as she hurried to the back door. "I'm sorry, Mama," she repeated as she ran outside, "so sorry. . ."

Brynne didn't stop running until she'd reached the summit. There, she fell on her knees and looked toward the heavens. "Lord," she cried, "help me deal with this horrible secret. . .and to discern between false hope—and faith in what is possible."

Brynne did want to share her mother's steadfast conviction, for she missed her father desperately. But, in the years since he'd been gone, she'd taught schoolchildren that two plus two equals four, C-A-T spells cat, Paris is the capital of France. Those facts were as undisputable as Ross Bartlett's acts of treachery and the ruination of her beloved South. Did her mother really expect her to accept the remote possibility that her father had survived the brutality of this awful war? Faith in God's might and power was one thing, but. . .

"Brynne?"

Immediately, she recognized the deep timbre of his voice. *But how did Clay find me here?* she wondered, dabbing her eyes with a corner of her apron. Ever since that day beneath the willow tree, she cared very much what he thought of her. He'd told her, when that first delicious kiss ended, how much he admired her strength of character. What would he think if he saw that she'd given in to self-pitying tears? What would he think if he knew the reason for them?

"Your sister-in-law told me I might find you here," Clay said, settling beside her and sliding an arm over her shoulders. "This is quite a view you have on the world," he said after a moment. "It's easy to see why you've kept it such a well-guarded secret."

"This was my father's favorite place," she said softly. "He came here often, when the trials and tribulations of life beset him."

He lifted her chin on a bent forefinger. "And what trials and tribulations have brought you here, my sweet Brynne?"

Silently, Brynne repeated his endearing words. *If you knew the answer to that question, you wouldn't be looking at me with such care in your eyes,* she told him mentally. *I am here because I'm a faithless follower and a miserable excuse for a daughter. And that's the very least of my sins.*

He pressed a kiss to her temple. "Why is this place called Kismet Hill?"

"My father, like his father-in-law and Grandpa Moore before him, was often drawn to this place. Papa had read in one of his books that, in the far east, kismet means 'God's will.' It was God's will, he believed, that his father-in-law Grandpa Moore settled this land, and God's will that it remained in the family ever since."

Brynne brought Clay's attention to the stubborn little pine, growing from the boulder behind them. "Papa said this was God's will, too." She sighed. "It's been here for as long as I can remember, growing slow and steady, despite the constant wind and the bitter cold and the desolation of this place."

He took her hands in his. "Seems to me if God could make that pitiful little thing grow where nothing else could, He truly can do the impossible."

The impossible, Brynne repeated mentally. Could Clay's simple words be God's answer to her prayer? A hopeful smile lifted the corners of her mouth.

"What're you grinning about?" Clay asked, wiping an errant tear from her cheek.

"Just the fact that you seem to be a mind reader."

"I can't read your mind, Brynne, but I think I know what's in your heart."

The mere thought of it set her pulse to racing. Brynne didn't want him to know the truth about her part in the devastation that befell Fort Fisher....

He kissed each of her eyelids, her chin, the tip of her nose. "You're feeling guilty because you don't share your mother's optimism about your father's safe return. You don't think he survived the prisoners' camp, do you?"

Brynne focused on their hands. "I don't see how he could have." There was venom in her voice when she said, "The sergeant who delivered Papa's last letter described how things were the day the Yankees took my father away."

"You really hate them, don't you?"

She set her jaw. "I've tried not to. I've tried, instead, to hate what they've done. But sometimes it's hard to separate the vicious acts from the men who committed them."

Clay nodded. "I felt the same way for a long time." Unconsciously, he stroked his mangled thigh. "But I'm realizing that God can't come close to me, not when I hold such bitterness in my heart. I've had to let go of my anger and forgive. That's the only way I can feel close to God again. But it's not easy." On a lighter note, he added, "Still, God calls us to have faith."

Brynne harumphed. "In what?"

"Why, in Him of course."

"I have plenty of faith in the Lord." *It's He who has lost faith in me,* she thought dismally. "Death is as much a part of life as birth. I think He also calls us to accept that."

"If you really felt that way, you wouldn't be here."

"How can you possibly know why I'm here?"

"I overheard your prayer. Deep in your heart, you hope your mother is right."

Brynne snatched back her hands. "You couldn't be more wrong! That wasn't why I was praying. It's my fault. All my fault," she spat, then bit her lip to keep back the words that would reveal her guilt. She choked, then continued more calmly, "But that doesn't change the fact that my mother may as well try to hold onto the air, for all the good her hope is doing her."

"She's holding onto the air every time she takes a breath. Seems to be doing a pretty good job, that air, at keeping her alive."

Who do you think you are, Brynne demanded silently, *coming up here, uninvited, telling me what I think and feel?* She leapt to her feet and began pacing a few steps from where he sat.

" 'When the Spirit of truth comes,' " Clay recited, " 'he will guide you...' "

Guide me to what? she demanded silently. *To tell the truth and face the hatred of everyone in Spring Creek who lost a loved one at Fort Fisher? No thank you!* "How is it you can quote the book of John so easily, yet you can barely tolerate sitting through a Sunday service?" she snapped. "I may not believe in the impossible, but I haven't turned my back on God!"

"What makes you think I have?"

She took several steps closer to face him. "You stopped going to church."

Clay sighed. "I only stayed away to give myself time. . ."

"Your leg was healed long before your first visit to the Spring Hill church, Mister Holier-than-thou!"

He chuckled quietly. "I stayed away," he continued as though she'd never interrupted, "to give my head time to clear, so that when folks slathered me with pitying comments and sympathetic stares, I wouldn't respond with anger and resentment. I was angry with church—but that didn't mean I'd given up on God."

She understood only too well what he'd said. Brynne had yet to figure out a way to deal with those well-intended yet hurtful comments that came when people heard what happened to her father. What would they say if they knew the whole truth?

" 'O ye of little faith,' " Clay said, smiling slightly. " 'Do not be anxious. . .for your heavenly Father knows your needs.' "

If she and Clay had been anywhere else, Brynne might have kept a rein on her taut emotions, might have repressed the sob aching in her throat and the grief beating in her heart. But they were not somewhere else. They were high atop Kismet Hill, her father's favorite place. Never again would he enjoy the pristine view as the crisp winds fingered through his hair. Never again would he hear the screech of an eagle overhead, or the rushing river waters below. All because of her!

Brynne slumped onto the rock where the pine grew, and hid her face in her hands. Before the first tear slipped between her fingers, Clay was beside her, engulfing her in a reassuring embrace. She had allowed herself a few tears here and there since the war began. But here, in his arms in this special place, Brynne let herself mourn openly, for Edward, for Moorewood, for Virginia, for her father.

"It's all right," he whispered, stroking her hair. "It's going to be all right."

Too ashamed to admit her horrible sin to Clay and unable to trust herself to make up some other excuse to leave Kismet Hill, Brynne scrambled to her feet and, without a word, ran toward Moorewood.

She didn't get far before Clay caught up to her. "Talk to me, Brynne," he said, gripping her upper arms. "What did you mean when you said it was your fault? What's your fault?"

Too much had happened in too little time, shattering Brynne's control. "If. . .if I, if I tell you," she began haltingly, "will you leave me in peace?"

A faint smile glittered in his eyes. "I doubt it." He gave her a gentle shake. "Let me help you, Brynne."

She bit her lower lip to stanch the tears that burned behind her eyelids. "If you could help me, it would be a miracle," she sighed, her voice foggy with grief and sadness.

For a long moment, Clay didn't speak. "We're on Kismet Hill," he said at last, nodding toward the little pine. "If a miracle can happen anyplace, it's here."

Chapter 8

When she had finished her miserable story, he was silent for a moment, and she could not look at him; she was too afraid of the condemnation she would read in his eyes. "I love you," he said softly, and her eyes flew to his face. "Don't you know that by now?"

In the past few months, as they'd walked hand-in-hand down his magnolia-lined drive or sat side by side on her mother's porch swing, Brynne and Clay had discussed many things, from his brother's problems to world politics. Most of the time, though, he had kept a tight rein on his emotions.

But sometimes, when the breeze was soft and the birds were singing, Clay would hint that he loved her. Several times, she'd caught him staring at her, and she had been warmed all over by what she thought she saw in his dark eyes. If their hands accidentally touched as they exchanged Cullen's schoolwork, she felt the heat of his feelings for her. And every kiss since that first one, beneath the willow tree, had told her how much she had come to mean to him.

Still. . .he'd never said the words aloud.

"I'm a traitorous blabbermouth," she reminded him, "not a mind reader."

Clay held her at arm's length, his hot gaze boring deep into her eyes. "You knew that Bartlett was a double agent?"

Brynne's jaw dropped with shock. "Of course not! I only just found out."

He pressed a silencing finger over her lips. "Mm-hm. But if you had known, would you have told him what was in your father's letter?"

Shaking her head, Brynne's eyes filled with fresh tears. "Absolutely not," she whispered hoarsely.

"So it's just as I said. . .you're not responsible for what happened."

She turned away, unable to continue looking into his confidant gaze. Oh, how she loved this man! While Ross had been courting her, she had thought what she'd felt for him had been love. She couldn't have been more wrong, she realized now.

Sadly, she'd never taken the measure of the man, hadn't called Ross's character into question, hadn't weighed the positives against the negatives in his personality. He'd entered her life when her girlfriends were either married or engaged. It had seemed time to begin planning the future—a husband, children, a home—and so when he'd asked her to marry him, Brynne never considered any answer but yes. If she'd known what kind of man he'd been. . .

Brynne knew what he was made of now, not only by his own words and deeds, but in comparison to Clay, who had willingly gone off to war, prepared to die, if he must, so others might live. Once Clay had returned from battle, his leg damaged beyond repair, he avoided pity at all cost. He had been adamant about taking a stern, heavy-handed tactic to end Cullen's silence—and yet in the end his love for the boy had outshone his desire to have his own way. Because of his patience, Cullen was at last beginning to break free of grief's silence; in the past weeks he had begun to speak again.

Despite all these emotional burdens, Clay worked long, hard hours to keep Adams' Hill afloat—and yet he had put what little free time he had into helping rebuild Spring Creek's church and school. No, Clay was nothing like Ross.

~

The summer rolled by like a steaming locomotive as Brynne fell deeper and deeper in love with Clay. And, he continued to profess his undying love for her, despite her protestations that she was unworthy of it.

On Thanksgiving eve, the old-fashioned young man put on his best coat and tie and knocked on Amelia Carter's front door. To protect her from the clamminess of his palms, he didn't take her hand when Amelia opened it, and he cleared his throat to hide the tremors in his voice.

"There's something we must discuss," he said as Amelia stood back to let him in, "so if you have a moment. . ."

Over tea in her parlor, Clay told Brynne's mother, "Under ordinary circumstances, I would speak with the Colonel about this matter. But these are hardly ordinary circumstances."

Amelia nodded her agreement, her smile telling him that she knew why he'd come to see her. "I'm afraid I'll have to do, then, since you haven't the patience to wait for Richard."

Clay met her eyes—and her statement—with straightforwardness. "I admire you, Mrs. Carter, for your steadfast belief that your husband will return, but there's no point beating around the bush, for as your daughter so aptly put it on the day we met, bush beating is a waste of time that's hard on the shrubbery."

Amelia laughed softly. "That's my Brynne, all right!"

"Then we'll make a good pair, your daughter and I." He leaned both elbows on his knees and laced his fingers together. "This war has taught me that life is fleeting, at best," he began. "Call me foolish, or impetuous, but I haven't the time or the patience to wait for Colonel Carter to give his permission for Brynne to marry me. I'll take very good care of her and. . ."

"I'm sure you'll be an excellent provider, Clay," Amelia injected. She put her hand upon his sleeve. "But how does my daughter feel about this?"

He smiled sheepishly. "I didn't want to discuss marriage with her until I had your blessing."

She gave his arm an affectionate squeeze. "Do you love her?"

His heart beat double-time. "With all my heart."

Nodding, Amelia stood and walked to the French doors. "Have you a date in mind? For the wedding, I mean?"

Clay rose and joined her. "I thought I'd leave the details to you ladies."

Hands clasped at her waist, she focused on some distant spot known only to her. "You must promise me something, Clay."

"Anything."

She faced him, and in the late afternoon light that filtered through the bevelled panes, a silvery tear shimmered on her cheek. Amelia grabbed his hands. "Promise you'll never leave her, no matter what your male pride calls you to do." She blinked tear-clumped lashes. "Promise me you'll never break her heart the way. . ."

"I promise," he said, rescuing her from completing the sentence.

She lifted her chin and threw back her shoulders. "Well, then," Amelia said, "you have my blessing." She whispered conspiratorially, "So tell me, when do you plan to pop the question?"

Clay smiled. "Right now—if you'll be so kind as to tell me where to find her."

Amelia faced the horizon once more. "Where else?" she said on a sigh. "Kismet Hill."

Clay turned to leave, but her hand on his sleeve didn't allow it. "What are you and your brother planning for Thanksgiving?"

"Planning? A quiet meal, I suppose."

"Just the two of you?"

Clay nodded.

"Nonsense!" Amelia closed the curtains, blocking the light—and the view—with one snap of her arm. "You're family now. We eat at three, and we dress for dinner," she tossed over her shoulder, "so I hope you both have neckties."

❧

Later that afternoon, Brynne watched as Clay walked away from her down Kismet Hill, his shoulders slumped with discouragement. Yes, she loved Clay Adams. But Brynne believed he deserved better than the likes of her, a silly woman who didn't know when to keep her mouth shut.

"I know what you're thinking," he had said softly, turning her to face him. "You're worried that if we were to marry, Cullen might have a relapse."

Brynne sighed heavily. That he'd considered his brother in the mix—while she'd focused on her own selfish needs—proved how wrong she was for him. "You deserve someone better than me," she admitted huskily. "That's what I was thinking."

Clay laughed. "Better than you? Darlin', there's no one on this earth more suited for me." He gathered her close and whispered into her hair. "You saved me, Brynne. Like the old song says, 'I once was lost, but now I'm found'. . .because of you. God used you so that I could learn to forgive. . .without you I would never have been able to forgive Cullen for what I thought was his weakness. Without the love I feel for you, I would still be nursing my anger at the Yankees. Your love has helped me to forgive. You're my miracle, Brynne, and I thank God for sending you to me."

Someday, she believed he would realize how wrong he was being. Until then, Brynne had to be strong enough to say no to his proposal. As much as it broke her heart, she couldn't marry him.

༄

"You haven't had much to say since Thanksgiving," Cullen said a month later, on Christmas Eve. "What's wrong—cat got your tongue?"

Clay good-naturedly elbowed his brother. "Look who's talking." He laughed.

"It's Brynne, isn't it? She's the reason you're so sad."

The older brother did not respond.

"If I were you, I'd find her, right now. Tell her how you feel. If she knew how miserable you've been, she'd marry you just to put a smile on your face!"

Clay said nothing.

Cullen frowned. "At least my silence had a good reason."

That brought Clay's head up. "What?"

The boy shrugged. " 'It is good that one should wait quietly for the salvation of the Lord. . .let him sit alone in silence. . .that there may yet be hope.' "

Cullen had quoted the book of Lamentations, Clay acknowledged. "I don't get it."

"Ma and Pa went on down to Petersburg in the middle of a war to do church business, leaving us here to fend for ourselves. And you just home with a terrible wound! God couldn't have been pleased with them. I thought He might even be a little angry with them. So I decided to keep quiet, till I was sure He'd forgiven them. Turned out it was me that needed to forgive them though. I was so angry with them—but once I'd forgiven them, then I knew that God would have forgiven them long ago. Way back when Jesus died on the cross, I guess. Nothing I could do could ever earn the forgiveness they needed for their prideful sin, because Jesus had already taken care of it. When you started taking me to church with you, that's when I figured it all out. And then I could begin to talk again."

"Prideful sin? Our parents? Cullen, you're not making sense."

"Yes I am. They always took risks, without ever making provisions to protect themselves. If the body is His temple, He expects us to take care of it. Besides," Cullen continued, his voice hard-edged with anger, "we didn't need a new pastor right then. And even if we did, why couldn't someone else go and fetch him? Someone with no family obligations? They enjoyed the praises they got when they did good works. It wasn't faith that made them believe they could make that trip safely, it was pride."

"And stubbornness," Clay said dully.

Cullen gave his brother a slight shove. "You inherited it."

Clay frowned. "Which? Stubbornness, or pride?"

"Both."

He read the teasing glint in Cullen's eyes, and smiled. "Why, I oughta tan your hide, you ornery. . ."

"Sticks and stones will break my bones," the boy taunted, fists up as he hopped like a boxer, "but proposals will never harm me."

⌒

Just as he'd suspected, Clay found her at the top of Kismet Hill, bundled up like an Eskimo as she leaned into the biting wind. "What're you doing here in this miserable weather?" he shouted into the howling air currents.

Brynne pointed to the garden spade that lay at her feet. "I wanted to dig up the pine," she said, peeking out from under her fur-trimmed hood. "It would make a lovely Christmas tree, and afterward, we could plant it in the yard, as a memorial to my father."

"But. . .it's growing from a bed of rock."

"I thought I could hack away at it, bit by bit, until I freed the roots, and. . ."

Her voice floated away on a powerful gust as Clay looked at the boulder. She'd whittled away a considerable chunk of the rock. "Let me see your hands, Brynne," he said, taking a step closer.

She held them out. Gently, he slid off her gloves, and grimaced at the red, watery blisters that covered her palms. He wrapped her in a fierce hug. Rubbing her upper arms to warm her, Clay said, "Let's go back to the house and get the tools we need to do the job right."

"It's nearly noon. Do we have time?"

Cupping her face in his hands, he kissed her long and hard. "We're on Kismet Hill, remember. . .the place where miracles happen!"

⌒

They'd been hard at it for hours, Clay hefting the sledgehammer, Brynne holding the chisel steady, when the last bit of stubborn rock finally gave way, exposing the tree's gnarled roots.

Clay was amazed at the way the roots had burrowed into a hollow in the boulder. Over time, he surmised, the constant winds must have blown dust and dirt and leaves into the crevice, and the debris had nestled there, as though waiting for the little seed to float into its nourishing bed.

He stood and faced the valley, flexing his aching hands as Brynne led the horse and buggy as close as the rocky surface would allow. "Praise God that's over," he said, working the kinks from his neck. "I thought we'd need to blast it out, and I'm plum out of dyna. . ."

His voice faded away. The expression on his face made Brynne race to his side. "What is it? What do you see?"

Clay pointed to a form below them, half a mile or so away.

It was a man, walking alone, leaning heavily on a cane and dragging one foot behind him. His *step-slide-clomp, step-slide-clomp* echoed quietly over the rocks and floated to them on blasts of wintry wind. When he stopped and looked up at them, the blood froze in Brynne's veins.

Clay slid a protective arm around her waist and pulled her close. "My rifle is in the wagon," he said through clenched teeth. "I'd hate to have to use it on Christmas Eve."

Her pulse pounded in her ears as the distant stranger made an eerie eye contact with her. Something about him seemed familiar. But what? Brynne held her breath, watching, waiting.

The man raised his left arm, made a fist of the hand, and thrust his forefinger into the air. Only one man had ever waved that way.

"Papa," she whispered.

Clay's gaze swung to Brynne's dazzled face. "Are you sure?"

In place of an answer, she scuttled down the rocks and ran full-out until she stood no more than ten feet from him. Her joyous cry reverberated from every nook and cranny around them as she flung herself into his arms.

᎒

8:00 P.M., *Christmas Eve, 1865*

Richard was surprised that not one of the messages he'd sent by way of returning soldiers had reached his family. When their jubilant welcoming hugs and kisses subsided, he explained that in the seven months since President Johnson issued amnesty to those who'd taken part in the "rebellion," Richard had recuperated in the home of an elderly Yankee widow.

"We can harbor the Northerners no ill will," he warned, "because for every dastardly deed one of them did, another of them did a kindness."

The woman's son, Richard said, had been killed at Gettysburg, yet she'd risked the ire of friends and family to tend Richard's wounds, wash his clothes, feed him healthy meals. When he was able, he left her humble abode, hitching rides with returning Confederate soldiers, pausing in his journey only long enough for meals and rest.

After downing bowls of thick vegetable stew, the family set about decorating the pitiful little Christmas tree, each acknowledging, as they hung the ornaments, what they were thankful for.

Cullen gave thanks that not only could he speak again, but that anger and bitterness and grief no longer filled his heart.

Edward and Julia praised God for the child He'd bring them in the spring, a brother or sister for little Richie.

"I'm thankful for the miracle of having my husband back," Amelia said.

"And I'm thankful to be back," came Richard's reply.

His wife snuggled into the crook of his arm. "I always knew you'd come home."

"Believing in your faith and loyalty was my miracle." He focused on Clay. "What about you, boy? What are you thankful for?"

Clay's gaze sought out Brynne's. "There's so much, I don't know where to begin. Let's just say I'm grateful to have your daughter in my life. She is my miracle." He strode purposefully toward her, and took her hands in his. "If she'd consent to be my wife, I'd think I'd died and gone to heaven."

She met his eyes, and for the moment, they were alone in the universe. *Except,* she thought, *for "God also bearing them witness, both with signs and wonders, and with divers miracles. . .according to his own will."*

She glanced at her mother, whose faith in the miracle of her father's return had never wavered. At her father, who admitted that belief in that faith is what gave him the strength to take each painful step home. At Cullen, who'd finally broken free from his prison of silence. At Clay, who'd called her his miracle. She took a deep breath, and she felt the burden of fear and guilt that she had carried slip off her back.

In the glow of the fire's light, Brynne's eyes misted. "I think we should start the year off right and be married on January first."

Epilogue

June 1866

When they reached the summit, Clay covered her eyes with his neckerchief. "You're sure you can't see anything, now?"

"Positive," Brynne said. "Now, what's all the secrecy about?"

He led her to the highest point on Kismet Hill and helped her sit on the boulder where the little pine had grown. The tree had brightened their Christmas and now thrived on the Carter lawn, where Amelia could see it each time she peered through the parlor's French doors.

"Ready for your surprise?"

Grinning with exasperation, Brynne sighed. "Clay, really. Stop teasing, or I'll..."

He whipped off her blindfold and directed her attention to the hole they'd carved from the big rock.

Clasping both hands under her chin, Brynne gasped. "I don't believe it. How do you explain a thing like this?"

He sat beside her and hugged her to him. "There's only one way to explain it." Gently, he touched the tiny sprig of green that would one day grow into a scrub pine. "It's a miracle." Pulling her into his lap, he said, "I love you, Mrs. Clay Adams."

Tenderly, she laid her right hand against his cheek. "And I love you."

He held her gaze for a silent, intense moment. " 'Thou dost show me the path of life, in thy presence there is fullness of joy, in thy right hand are pleasures for evermore.' I reckon that about describes what the Lord has done for me." He was taken aback when tears filled her eyes. "I had no idea the book of Psalms had such an effect on you," he teased.

Brynne snuggled into the crook of his neck. "It's just that. . .well. . .I have a surprise for you, too."

"No blindfold?" he asked, chuckling. "I'm disappointed."

"I saw the doctor yesterday. . ."

Holding her at arm's length, he frowned. "The doctor? Why? You're. . .you're not ill, are you?"

Smiling serenely, Brynne shook her head. "Of course not, silly." Tilting her head, she said, "It seems we're going to have a baby."

Clay's eyes widened with awe and wonderment. "A. . .a baby?" He leapt up and danced a merry jig. "I'm gonna be a father!" he bellowed. His joyous shout echoed across the valley, and when it bounced back to him, he sat beside her again, and pressed his palm to her belly. "When, Brynne? When will our child be born?"

"Christmas."

"Christmas," he sighed. He gathered her close and whispered into her ear, " 'A man attested to you by God with mighty works and wonders and signs.'"

"Yes, Clay," she agreed. "Another miracle. . .on Kismet Hill."

Yuletide Treasures

Gail Gaymer Martin

Favour is deceitful, and beauty is vain:
but a woman that feareth the Lord,
she shall be praised.
Proverbs 31:30

Chapter 1

A cloud of black smoke curled past the window of the Chesapeake and Ohio locomotive. As the shrill whistle sounded, Livy Schuler snuggled deeper into her travel cloak and studied the changing winter scenery. Scattered buildings stood along the tracks and she sighed, sensing their lengthy journey neared completion.

She gazed at her four-year-old nephew as he lay fast asleep, his blond curls bobbing against the stiff seat cushion as the locomotive swayed through the countryside. "Davy," she murmured, "wake up."

The child shifted against the seat, but did not wake. Her heart ached for the boy. Christmas was no time for a child to be away from his parents, but his mother's illness necessitated the journey. And when her brother, John, asked for her help, she acquiesced. With Ruth's unfortunate stroke, how could she refuse?

The trip from Detroit stretched into hours with stops for passengers and when an occasional cow wandered onto the tracks. She had amused Davy with toy soldiers and storybooks. Later, when he drifted off to sleep, she found a discarded newspaper and read about President Grant's fight against the greenbacks and the resurgence of Queen Victoria's popularity.

"Next stop, Grand Rapids," the conductor called, moving along the aisle.

Opening his weighted eyes, Davy shifted and released a soft whimper.

"We're nearing the station, Davy. We're going to have such fun with your Aunt Helen and Uncle Charles."

Only sadness filled his face, and she hoped Helen and Charles would understand the child's lack of enthusiasm. Ruth's brother, Charles, had been gracious to invite Davy for the holiday. Livy pictured her brother John's somber expression when he had no other choice but to accept their offer.

Livy could only imagine the Mandalay home and life among the wealthy. Charles owned one of the largest furniture-making businesses in Grand Rapids, which, after the war, became the furniture capital of the world. And Charles had found success on the coattails of inventive, skilled craftsmen like George Pullman and William Haldane. Livy shook her head in wonder at the life the Mandalays must lead.

Anticipating their arrival, Livy returned Davy's lead soldiers to her satchel. With the bag open on her lap, she looked at the small package John had asked her to deliver to Helen.

Shameful curiosity overtook her, and she felt through the paper. Wood, perhaps, and a strange shape—rounded on one end, pointed on the other, one side smoothly curved, the other a jagged zigzag. She couldn't determine what lay hidden within the paper. Guilt needled her, so she withdrew her hand from the satchel and latched it. The package didn't belong to her, and as curious as she was, she had no cause to look inside.

A whistle blast jarred her back to the present. The train slowed and came to a shuddering halt. Livy rose, buttoning her dark gray travel cloak, then hooked Davy's coat and, grasping his hand, led him down the aisle.

With the conductor's assistance, she stepped to the platform while soot from the smoke stack showered down in a fine spray of drifting black flakes like ebony snow. Her gaze swept along the station's visitors, looking for Charles's son, Andrew, whom she had never met. Seeing no likely prospect, she turned and lifted Davy to the ground and headed toward the small depot, searching for warmth.

"Hello. Miss Schuler?"

She pivoted, hearing the voice, and looked into a pair of glinting, ice-blue eyes. Her pulse lurched as radically as the chugging locomotive had. "Mr. Mandalay?"

"Yes, but please call me Andrew." He paused, bending at the waist. "And this must be Davy."

The child peered at him and nodded.

"How do you do, Davy? I'm your cousin, Andrew." Straightening, he focused on Livy. "How was your trip? Too long, I'd guess."

Livy drew her gaze from his delightful smile. "Six hours, yes, but tolerable."

"Leaving your friends and family during the holidays is very generous of you. I'm sure Uncle John was grateful."

"Yes, but I had no choice. John and Davy needed me."

"No matter, it was very kind. Well then, it's much too cold on the platform. The carriage is this way." He motioned behind him, then reached for her satchel. "I'll carry that for you, Miss Schuler."

"No need, thank you. It's light, and please call me Livy." She turned, pointing to the two small trunks sitting on the baggage cart. "But those cases are ours, if you don't mind."

"Aah. Then I'll retrieve those," he said. "Wait here for one moment."

As he darted down the platform, admiration rose within her. Besides his dazzling eyes, Andrew had been graced with other handsome features. His fair hair contrasted with his darker skintone, likely the result of his days at the logging camp. John mentioned Andrew had only arrived home for the holidays.

Watching him return with their baggage, she noted his tall stature and broad shoulders, dwarfing her own petite frame. She imagined his muscular arms swinging an ax to fell a pine tree or hoisting a log onto a large logging sled. As he approached, she caught her breath. His firm, square jaw was softened by his deep dimples and generous, captivating smile on his full, sensitive mouth.

"Ready?" he asked, moving to her side. "Follow me."

Tucking Davy's hand in hers, she hurried behind Andrew, following his long strides. He stopped beside a carriage, a claret-colored Dearborn pulled by two matching bays, then opened the door and slid their baggage inside.

"Come, Davy," he said and lifted the boy into the coach. Then he reached for Livy's hand. As she stepped to his side, his gaze swept across her face and heat rose to her cheeks. They stood so close, the scent of his damp woolen coat and peppermint filled her senses. He assisted her into the conveyance and spread a thick robe across their laps.

"That should keep you warm," he said, his dimples glinting with his steady gaze. "The ride is short."

She swallowed, finding her voice. "Thank you."

He grinned again and closed the door. Livy nestled against Davy, her thoughts shifting back to Andrew's earlier comment, "Leaving your friends and family during the holidays is very generous of you." *Leaving my friends? If the situation weren't so pitiful, I would laugh.*

Lately, her life rose before her in a dismal, gray picture like the winter day. At twenty-eight, she was a spinster, a word she detested. Looking in a mirror, she saw no reason for her lack of beaus. Though she would not be considered a beauty by most, her features were pleasant, her figure was trim, and she earned a suitable income as a music teacher. But single, she was.

Though the Bible said God would provide, "ask, and ye shall receive," she had long given up asking God for a husband. The Lord, from all she could comprehend, desired her to remain the detested word—a spinster. But she had other plans.

Recently, Henry Tucker, owner of the neighborhood mercantile, delayed her in the shop with casual, genial conversation. She sensed his interest, and though she had little attraction for him—*none,* if she were honest—he was a likely candidate as a husband. Not God's plan perhaps, but her own.

Sadly, Henry's young wife and baby had died in childbirth. Now at forty, he told her he longed for a wife and family. Each time she entered the shop, he looked at her with yearning, and she had begun to wonder if this were the man for whom she might set her cap.

Heat rose to Livy's face, recalling her deceptive words to John as she boarded the train earlier in the day. She explained a commitment to the church choir influenced her to hurry back to Detroit. But in truth, a different reason motivated her.

Shame filled her at the deception. Telling a lie, no matter what color, was a sin. But she couldn't admit to John that Henry indicated he'd come to call during the Christmas holiday. That was the true reason she needed to be home. Though she hadn't extended an invitation to him directly, Henry was most persistent.

And he was a man of his word.

A chill shivered through her as she felt the icy air and considered her possible future—a loveless marriage. Why? She asked herself the question many times. Why did she long for marriage if it wouldn't be filled with love and contentment? The answer that marched into her head was always the same. She recalled Noah. God guided the animals to the ark two by two. She was a *one*. And besides, if God had a change of heart, her amiable feelings for Henry might grow to love.

Livy pulled the lap robe higher around Davy's shoulders and her own chilled body. The carriage jolted, and she slid sideways as the horses trotted around a corner. Elegant houses stood along the rutted roadway, and she huddled closer to Davy, as much for her own comfort as for his.

Picturing her handsome driver, Livy admired Andrew's splendid frame. A strange sense of longing rose in her chest. She closed her eyelids and wondered what the next days might bring.

Chapter 2

Andrew snapped the bays' reins, and the carriage lurched forward. He adjusted the heavy blanket across his legs and veered the animals onto the rutted roadway. To satisfy his father's wishes, he'd been genial to the guests. More than genial, he'd been pleasant. Yet, he hoped his own plans weren't thwarted by their stay.

Three months at the logging camp left him eager for feminine companionship, and with four more months to follow, he was unwilling to sacrifice his own plans to entertain a child. His memory drifted to a flirtatious young woman he had met at a house gathering in the autumn, and he looked forward to seeing Rosie Parker again.

His mother discouraged such relationships, prompting him to find a suitable young lady from the church, particularly the music director's sister. He'd seen the prim and proper young parish women dressed in their demure, somber gowns but found himself drawn to Rosie. She was so like her name—curly blond hair, crimson dress, musky perfume, and a spirited wit.

He grimaced, recalling the biblical missive ringing in his mind: women should dress modestly and decently, not with gaudy jewels or expensive clothes, but with good deeds. Despite the verse, Rosie's image filled his head. She didn't fit God's description, but he'd live for now with his sinful desire. Rosie beguiled him.

Yet, his mind drifted to his passengers inside the carriage. He recalled the sad, frightened face of his young cousin, Davy. The poor boy had been forced to leave his home at Christmas. Then, Livy—Olivia Schuler, John's unmarried sister. A spinster, they called her. He noted she dressed in somber colors like the young church women he knew. Still, the shy sparkle in her green eyes hung in his memory.

As the house appeared, Andrew slowed the bays. He drew the carriage to a halt beside the long pillared porch and climbed down. After hitching the horses, he opened the coach door. At the same time, his mother, wrapped in a fur-trimmed cape, stepped from the house.

"Here we are," he said, assisting Livy to the ground then swinging Davy beside her. "I hope you were warm enough."

"We were fine." Livy's gaze swept across the wide expanse of house. "Your home is lovely."

"Thank you," he said, grabbing her satchel and guiding them up the steps. "A servant will see to your luggage," he added.

Livy forced her mouth closed after she gaped at the vast structure before her. The lovely home of broad, white clapboards and black shutters was graced by a sprawling porch.

As she headed toward the entrance, John's sister-in-law, Helen, waited for her. They'd met only once, years earlier. Livy had forgotten how lovely she was. It was clear that Andrew, with his fair hair and blue eyes, had inherited his mother's good looks.

As Livy approached, Helen stepped forward, her arms opened wide in greeting. "Davy, Olivia, welcome." She swooped down to wrap Davy in her arms, but he slid behind Livy's cloak and peeked out at the gracious woman.

Livy took the woman's hand with a gentle squeeze. "Thank you, Helen." She motioned to Davy. "He's a bit shy, but he'll adjust with time." Livy caught her nephew's hand and pulled him out from behind her skirts. "Davy, this is your Aunt Helen. Say hello."

A soft greeting fell from his lips, but instead of looking at her, his focus riveted to the expansive dwelling.

"Won't you come in?" Helen moved forward while a servant pushed the heavy door inward and gave them wide berth.

Livy scooted Davy ahead, and they entered the central hall. A broad staircase rose to the second story, and a door stood open on the right where Livy could see a fire burning on the hearth. "Come," Helen said, motioning toward the fireplace. "Warm yourselves. We'll have tea and chocolate."

The word "chocolate" seemed to motivate Davy. He hurried ahead of her, wide-eyed as he took in the scene. After the servant brought in a heavy tray, they sat in the parlor sipping hot chocolate and nibbling on tea cakes.

"We're having a small dinner party this evening in your honor," Helen said. "Our young choirmaster, Mr. Daily, and his sister will join us."

"How nice," Livy said. As she spoke, Andrew's expression drew her attention. He grimaced and his reaction aroused Livy's curiosity.

When teatime ended, Andrew left the room, and shortly thereafter, Helen led them up the stairs to their bedrooms where their baggage had been placed. After unpacking Davy's trunk, Livy left him playing with his toy soldiers and headed for her room next door.

She made quick work of hanging her few garments. As she emptied her smaller satchel, her hand settled upon the keepsake John had given her, and she lifted it from the bag. She recalled John's discomfort as he asked the favor. "Would you. . .slip this trinket to Helen? I'm sorry I can't explain, but it's a keepsake from long ago. She'll understand."

Livy had eyed the package with curiosity and agreed to deliver it safely, but as John slipped her the parcel, he added, "And. . .er, I'd appreciate the utmost discretion. The memento is nothing, really, but. . ." He had faltered without finishing his sentence. With his fervent request for tact, she wondered how she might secretly deliver the gift to Helen.

As if her question were heard, Helen tapped on her open door. "I hope everything is satisfactory."

"The room is lovely," Livy said, admiring the deep rose and delicate blue decor and the elegantly carved bedstead. "Thank you."

"I suppose leaving home during the holiday season was difficult. It's very kind of you to bring Davy here."

"I hope to return to Detroit before Christmas—if Davy seems settled," Livy said, clutching the small package.

"I see. John didn't mention your plans. I'm sure Davy'll be fine after a day or two. We've asked Andrew to spend time with him. I hope that'll help."

Livy smiled. "I imagine Andrew has other plans for his holidays, but I appreciate everyone's kindness. Davy is a good boy, but he's never been away from his parents before."

"How is Ruth?" Helen's face knit with concern.

"It's sad. She can't speak or use her left limbs properly. But praise God, the doctor expects a good recovery."

"I pray that's true," Helen said. "She and I were best friends when we were young."

"Best friends? I didn't know." She hesitated. "You knew my brother, John, then." She ran her finger across the jagged edge of the memento clutched in her hand.

Helen plucked beneath her collar at the pleats of her bodice. "Oh yes, John and Charles were school friends. To Charles, I was only his younger sister's friend. But one day, he noticed me." She paused for a moment. "Your brother and I were dear friends even before Charles."

"I wondered," Livy said, extending the tissue-wrapped parcel toward her. "He asked me to give you this package. He said you'd understand."

Helen stared at the gift without moving. When she took it, her fingers followed the erratic shape beneath the tissue and a faint smile rose to her lips. "Yes. Yes, I believe I do understand. Thank you." Her fingers curled around the tissue, and her shoulders lifted with a sigh. "Well then, I'll get back to the dinner arrangements. Our guests are expected at seven." She turned toward the door. "Please let me know if you need anything," she said, before she disappeared down the hall.

Livy sat on the edge of the carved oak bed, her mind filled with questions. Being twelve years younger than John, she didn't recall his friends. "Dear friends," Helen had said. She chided herself for her blatant curiosity.

Rising from the bed, she opened the chifforobe and rifled through her gowns. Nothing seemed suited for a dinner party. With the holiday season at hand, why hadn't she planned ahead to bring a few party dresses? She chuckled at herself. Party dresses? She really had nothing particularly "festive" in her wardrobe. A spinster's need for party frocks was minimal.

She pulled the garments from the closet one at a time. A tailored, navy wool skirt and brilliantine shirtwaist seemed inappropriate for a dinner party. Livy examined her three dresses and settled on a brown day gown with shoulder piping and deeper brown velvet trim on the sleeves and peplum. She would have to make do.

When she'd finished dressing, Livy went to Davy's room. Earlier in the day, he seemed listless and ate his dinner in the kitchen. Now, when she peeked into his room, Davy had already fallen asleep. She left a small lantern burning in the hall outside his room, for fear he'd waken and be frightened in the strange surroundings.

As Livy descended the stairs, the fireplace glowed through the doorway, and voices drifting from the parlor seemed as warm and inviting as the flames. When she entered the room, Charles stepped forward to greet her, but Livy's attention was drawn to Andrew. Her face warmed with the greeting. She stifled her emotions and focused on Charles. Taller and sturdier than Andrew, his imperious size awed her. "It's been a long time, Charles. Thank you for having us."

"You're entirely welcome, Livy. Anything for Ruth and her family." He brushed his thick mustache with long fingers and turned to the guests. "Livy, this is Mr. Daily and his sister, Miss Daily."

"Roger and Agatha, please," the young man said.

"How do you do? And please call me Livy," she responded, admiring the young woman who greeted her. She was trim and attractive, dressed in a rich brocade gown of deep lilac with a fashionable bustle. Her bowed lips curved slightly in greeting, but her interest was not on Livy.

Dressed in a brown worsted suit, sporting a tan corduroy vest, Andrew looked dashing. Tonight his tall stature and broad chest were more impressive than in the afternoon. He paused in the soft lamplight that brought out red highlights in his golden hair. Livy understood Agatha's gawking on his appearance. A feathering of longing rippled through Livy, and she struggled to keep her admiration hidden.

"You look refreshed, Livy," Andrew said, his gaze sweeping her from head to toe. "Have a seat and let me bring you some warmed cider."

"Thank you," she said, sinking into the sofa cushion across from the two dinner guests. In a moment, Andrew returned and slipped a cup into her hands. She wrapped her cold fingers around the mug, enjoying its warmth and hiding the slight tremor awakened by his touch.

"And how was your trip, Livy?" Roger asked.

"Fine, thank you." Livy studied the pleasant-looking young man, admiring his gentle face and friendly smile.

"I understand you gave up your holiday to bring your nephew here," he added.

"No accolades, please. With Ruth's illness, my brother needed my help with Davy. Besides, I must admit I'm returning to Detroit before Christmas. . .that is, if Davy seems well-adjusted here."

"Ah I see," Roger said.

An unexpected look of disappointment shot across Andrew's face. "But you must stay," he blurted. "Who'll entertain Davy?"

His sudden explosion caught Livy by surprise. When she looked, a pinkish hue crept to his neck. Embarrassment? His first words had sent a ripple of pleasure through her, but the next comment that shot from his mouth dampened her hope. He wasn't anxious for her stay, in particular, only for someone to watch over Davy.

But Roger's next words softened the tension of the moment. "I had hoped to coerce you into joining our choir for the services. I understand you teach music. Singing, I'm told."

"Yes, voice and piano. Though I must admit, piano is really not my strength."

With a sheepish grin, Andrew bounded from his seat to the spinet in the parlor alcove. "Please, play for us, Livy." He raised the cover from the keys and pulled out the bench. "Maybe a carol."

"Yes, do play," Agatha gushed, moving to Andrew's side. Her hand captured his arm. He looked at her fingers gripping his forearm, and a covert frown flew across his face. Unobtrusively, he lifted her hand and stepped back to his chair. Agatha's lips pursed a delicate pout.

Livy grinned inwardly at the silent antics. Though she was unaccustomed to flirting herself, Agatha's pursuit of Andrew was straightforward. When the amorous drama ended, Livy accepted Andrew's invitation to play. She preferred to sing than play, but rather than refuse his request, she stepped to the piano. A collection of sheet music lay on a small cabinet beside the spinet, but she needed none for carols. Livy played them without a musical score. She slid onto the bench, fingered the keys for a moment, then struck the first chord. The rich tones of the instrument drifted through the room, and in her head, she sang the familiar song, "Good Christian Men Rejoice."

As the music ended, Helen swept into the room and graciously announced dinner. When Charles took his wife's arm, Livy's heart thudded as Andrew approached, but before he reached her, Agatha anchored herself to his side. With a lavish bow, Roger smiled and guided Livy to the table.

The scrumptious meal was served on translucent Haviland china in an elegant rose pattern and genuine silver. Livy had never tasted such succulent roasted pork. Helen served the meat with sweet potato pie and apple butter. Genial conversation filled the room, and when they finished, Helen guided them back to the living room for dessert.

"What a fine meal, Helen," Roger said, leaning back and patting his lower vest where the buttons strained against the cloth. She thanked him with a smile and continued to pour coffee from a silver pot. "I'd like to return the invitation.

Perhaps next Friday you could join us for a holiday dinner."

Livy glanced at her hosts, waiting for their response. Though Helen sent Roger a bright smile, Andrew responded before his mother. "Sorry, Roger. I have a previous engagement, but thank you for the invitation. Hopefully, the others can join you."

Livy's heart tumbled with disappointment.

A desperate look on Agatha's face seemed to curb her brother's response. "Let's find a time agreeable to everyone," Roger suggested with haste. "Would Saturday or Sunday accommodate everyone?"

Livy waited. After a quick discussion, Saturday evening was accepted, so she would be included in the dinner. If the train schedule cooperated, she had planned to be on her way home by Sunday afternoon. Now, though, Livy felt differently. She looked at Andrew with masked longing. Why did she allow herself to dream such foolish dreams? Must she spend her entire life yearning for the impossible?

Henry's less-than-perfect frame rose in her mind. Though not handsome, he was a kind man, owned a business, attended church regularly, and wanted a child. *I must stop tormenting myself with wishes. A kind, gentle family man is best. And Henry shows interest in me.*

She chided herself for her wavering emotions. *Use common sense, Livy. If God wants something else for you, He will let you know.*

God? Perhaps it wasn't God who wanted something else for her. She faltered and looked toward Andrew's captivating face, then bit her lip, knowing the truth that tugged at her heart.

Chapter 3

On Thursday morning when Andrew came down the stairs, Helen beckoned him into the morning room. "You know, Andrew, Livy is returning home on Sunday and we'll need help with Davy. He's a good boy, but your father and I can't spend the complete holiday entertaining him."

Andrew clenched his teeth to keep himself from blurting his frustration. Though he always showed respect to his parents, he wanted to remind his mother that he had personal plans, too.

"You do understand?" she added.

He unlatched his tensed jaw. "I understand, Mother. I'll do what I can. . . though I wish we could convince Livy to stay."

"She warned us when she arrived that her intention was to leave before Christmas. She must have a reason."

Andrew looked at his mother, his mind searching for a solution. Would he have the pluck to ask Livy why she wanted to return home? "Maybe she'd change her plans if we entice her to stay."

"Andrew, that would be manipulative. We need to respect her wishes."

Though he heard her, Andrew's mind reeled with schemes. What would keep Livy in Grand Rapids? He examined his own motivation, and his stomach tightened as he pictured Rosie. While he pondered the question, an idea crossed his mind. Could he be a matchmaker? Roger Daily was a good-looking fellow. Yet Andrew had noticed during dinner how she looked past Roger, and afterward in the parlor, she looked everywhere but at him.

"You will cooperate, Andrew?"

His mother's voice brought him back to the present. "Yes, I'll do my best."

"Thank you," she said and left the room.

Playing cupid with his imagination, he envisioned Livy and Roger together, a perfect pair: restrained, quiet, musical. Yet the idea aroused an ominous constriction in his chest. He didn't like the picture. But why? Livy and Roger were perfect for each other.

Livy's pensive face filled his mind. His thoughts drifted back to the family dinner party, and he envisioned Livy in her subdued brown dress. Though she wasn't as colorful as Rosie, Livy had many appealing qualities.

He pictured her dark brown hair and clear, ivory skin. Most of all, her gentle, gracious nature filled his mind. Picturing Livy with Davy, Andrew was touched by her gentle kindness.

Andrew hesitated and his mouth sagged at his recollections. He sounded like a lovesick schoolboy, mooning over a girl. What had gotten into him? Tomorrow he would see Rosie again. Then he'd know the pleasure of a vivacious woman's company.

He struggled to push Rosie's image into his mind. Instead, her blue eyes transformed to large, green emerald ones. Livy. A shudder rifled through him. "Control yourself," he whispered aloud.

"Pardon me."

Andrew jumped at the soft, feminine voice. As if she had stepped from his vision, Livy stood in the doorway, dressed in a white shirtwaist and dark blue skirt.

"Good morning." He forced a lighthearted chuckle. "Apparently, I was talking to myself, but now you're here, so I can talk with you." His mind raced. "Have you eaten?"

Her delicate hands were folded at her waist, and she focused on her intertwined fingers. "No, I was on my way to breakfast when I heard you."

He latched onto the pause in conversation. "Then let's go together." He rested his hand on her arm, feeling the warmth of her skin through the soft airy cloth. As they headed down the hall, his plan gathered momentum, hoping to arouse her interest in staying for the holiday's duration. Inner pleas filled him. He so rarely prayed, and today he was praying for God to manipulate a situation. If he weren't so desperate, he'd be ashamed. Still, he had no interest in spending his vacation playing with soldiers or wooden puzzles.

෨

Walking beside Andrew, a spicy aroma like cloves or bay rum soap filled Livy's senses. The pressure of his hand on her arm sent a warm jolt to her fingertips, and her chest fluttered with the sensation.

In the dining room, a sideboard was spread with sausage, bread, butter, and baked apples. Livy filled her plate, completing her meal with a cup of hot tea, then sat at the table with Andrew across from her. "Would you like to ask the blessing?" Livy inquired.

Andrew bowed his head and murmured a brief prayer. Then without lifting his fork, he leaned back and stared at her. "So you're hoping to return to Detroit for Christmas."

His riveting gaze left her suspended for a moment. Lowering her head, Livy caught her breath. "Yes, I have a commit. . . . I should say, I have an engagement."

"Engagement?" His mouth curved to an appealing grin.

Discomfort bound her. "Well, not an *engagement*, exactly," she said. "A friend is to come calling."

Andrew forked a piece of sausage. "A gentleman?"

His boldness surprised her, and she answered without thinking. "Yes, Mr. Tucker. . .Henry."

"Is he a beau?" A frown flashed across his face before he turned it to a smile.

"No, well. . .Andrew, your questions are rather inappropriate."

"Forgive me, Livy. I wondered what called you back home. Mother would love to have you. . .*we* would love to have you stay for the holiday. New Year will be fun."

Did he mean "we"? And why? His blunt question had confused her. "Won't you be with your friends on New Year?"

"Yes, a few friends."

"And will *you* spend time with a lady?"

He faltered, and a hint of discomfort settled on his face. "I have many friends. . .male and female."

Since he circumvented her question, she suspected he had a special young woman in mind. "Then, the answer is, 'yes.' "

"Perhaps one. A Miss Parker."

Livy blanched at his admission. The woman had a name, and the name made her real. "Then you should understand why I'm anxious to return home."

His jaw tensed, and his full lips compressed without a response. Instead, he focused on the food that remained on his plate.

A sense of loneliness washed over her. She was sorry she had confronted him. The silence echoed in her head until, finally, she cleared her throat. "Besides, I neglected to bring appropriate gowns for the holidays. My dresses are much too plain for holiday dinners and parties. So you see, I need to return anyway."

His face relaxed and a sparkle lit his eye. "I'm sure Mother could solve that problem. She owns a million gowns. With a few nips and tucks, you'd have no worry." He placed his napkin on the table edge and slid back, the chair legs scraping the wooden floor. "Will you excuse me?"

"Certainly. I'm finished, too." She folded her napkin, dropping it on the table, and rose. Without another word, she turned and darted from the room, chastising herself. Why had she tempted herself with dreams again? Shame lifted in her chest. A young Christian woman had no right to lust after a man.

She whispered a prayer of forgiveness for her sin and pushed her attention to Henry. But nothing stirred in her, except memories of his pleasant demeanor and his kindness.

An amazing awareness blossomed in her mind. She understood, now, why God had not given her beaus. She couldn't control her covetous nature. Unbridled passion rose in her when she looked at Andrew. Instead of being angry at God, she thanked Him. The Lord knew she needed restraints and God provided them. Henry Tucker was the answer. She'd hurry home, assured Henry was the Lord's plan for her.

As Livy retraced her steps to her room, Davy filled her with concern. She hadn't seen him yet this morning. She hurried down the hallway. Listening at his door, the room was silent. When she stepped inside, Davy still lay in bed. Livy rushed across the room to his side. His cheeks burned a fiery red, and beads of perspiration ran from his hairline. She placed her hand on his forehead. A fever. Her heart skipped. She'd never nursed a sick child before. What should she do?

Without question, she turned toward Helen's room. Tapping on the door, Livy waited only a moment before Helen answered her knock. "Livy, good morning. Oh dear. Is something wrong?" Helen asked as she set something on the nearby dresser. It was a small wooden heart. A jagged line ran from top to bottom where the two halves were joined together like a jigsaw puzzle, forming a complete, unbroken heart.

"Yes, Davy is ill. He has a fever. Would you come and see?"

"Certainly."

Inside Davy's room, she studied him for a moment, then pressed her cheek against his. "Yes, a high fever, I would say."

Davy's eyelids fluttered and opened. A soft moan left his lips, followed by a deep, rattling cough. Livy pressed her hand against his cheek. "You don't feel well, Davy?"

He shook his head and tried to speak, but he coughed again.

Helen rose. "I made cough elixir not long ago. I'll mix it with warm lemonade." She looked at the child. "You'll like it, Davy. Perhaps I should make a poultice for his cough," she said to Livy. She darted through the doorway.

Livy wet a cloth and cooled Davy's cheeks, then poured a glass of water from the nearby pitcher.

"What's wrong?"

Livy peered over her shoulder. Andrew stood in the doorway.

"Davy's ill. A fever and cough." She lifted the child's head with her hand as he sipped the water.

"Nothing serious, I hope?" He stepped into the room and approached the bed.

"I pray it's nothing serious. Maybe a winter cold." She lowered Davy's head, setting the glass on the table.

"A winter cold. Yes, I'm sure that's it."

Helen hurried into the room, carrying a mug. "Here it is." Steam rose from the cup and the scent of lemon filled the air. She sat on the edge of the bed. "Davy, try some of this drink. It will help your cough."

He sipped, and when he tasted the acrid contents, he puckered his lips, but he drank without complaint. The liquid ran from his chin.

"Livy, you give him a bit more, and I'll prepare a mustard plaster. It'll do wonders to ease the cough."

She did as Helen asked while Andrew stood nearby. Gooseflesh rose on her arms with the sense that he was watching her. She longed to make him stop. . . or, better yet, to halt her rising emotions.

Davy sipped the liquid again. As she eased him to the pillow, his eyes drooped closed. She studied the boy, caressing his cheek while Andrew watched her.

"You look like a mother," Andrew murmured. "The picture fits you."

She looked downward to gain control, then faced Andrew. "Thank you," she whispered, "but I don't think God means for me to be a mother."

He tilted his head. "I think you're wrong, Livy. You're gentle and loving. Look how you care for the boy. You were meant to be a mother." He moved beside her and placed his hand on her shoulder. For a brief moment, his fingers kneaded the tense cords in her neck. Then, he was gone.

A sigh quivered from Livy's chest at his familiarity. She eyed the empty doorway. Resting her hand on Davy's arm, she listened to the raspy breathing and waited.

When Helen returned, she carried a folded cloth. The pungent odor of mustard permeated the air. She peered at the concoction in Helen's hand, two pieces of muslin cloth with a dark ocher paste spread between them.

"It's ground mustard and meal mixed with hot water," Helen said. She pulled down the cover and opened Davy's nightclothes, pressing the poultice to his chest. His eyes fluttered open then closed. "There now, if this doesn't work, we'll send for the doctor."

Livy gazed at the sleeping child then pulled a sturdy rocker to the bedside. "Thank you, Helen."

"You're very welcome, Livy."

"I believe I'll sit here for a while," Livy said, her focus on Davy.

"Remember, worry helps nothing." Helen patted her arm. "If his fever doesn't break, the doctor will come."

As Helen left the room, Livy sank into the rocking chair. While Davy slept, she rested her gaze on the gentle fall and rise of the blanket. *A mother?* Was she meant to be a parent like Andrew said? Her present life was free, unburdened, and—to be honest with herself—self-centered. Would she have patience to care for little ones who needed her totally? The questions tumbled in her head.

Children meant marriage. She sighed, imagining a life with Henry. She would live above the mercantile and, perhaps, work in the store. But she would teach her music lessons as well. A life with Henry? Somehow the idea did not settle well in her mind.

And what about love? Must marriage and love go hand in hand? She was fond of Henry. Were fondness and love the same? *What is love?* Perhaps her fondness for Henry *was* love. Then what was it she felt for Andrew? *Passion?* The dreaded word rose in her mind again.

Suddenly an image appeared. The wooden pieces in Helen's room—two jagged sides pushed together to form a perfect heart. With its peculiar shape, she felt positive that it was half the wooden heart she had carried to Grand Rapids. John called it a keepsake. A keepsake? But why did he return the remembrance to Helen? Her pulse accelerated at her conjecture. What did it mean? Would she ever know?

Chapter 4

Andrew left the carriage with the attendant and mounted the wide porch steps. The music reverberated through the brick exterior. When the door opened, a cacophony of sound billowed out into the quiet night—music, voices, and pandemonium.

Leaving his outer wrap with the servant, he turned to the large parlor. Matthew's parents had stored pieces of their fashionable furniture somewhere. Tonight, chairs and sofas lined the walls, leaving the bare wood floor open for dancing.

Across the hall, friends waved to him. They gathered around a piano, its tinkling notes blending with the music across the way. He stepped toward the smaller parlor as a hand nabbed his arm. "Why, Andrew, how lovely to see you again."

Without looking, he recognized Rosie's voice, and a shiver raced up his arm to his neck. He turned and looked at her. Dressed in a fashionable vibrant purple gown of velvet, her bustle and peplum were designed in a deeper shade like a polished plum. Her neckline scooped to reveal the soft white skin of her neck and shoulders, and for a moment the view startled him.

He had longed to view her lovely feminine frame, yet his subconscious thoughts reminded him of God's Word, *"Favour is deceitful, and beauty is vain: but a woman that feareth the LORD, she shall be praised."* Livy would never wear a gown cut as low. Her dresses were modest.

Rosie smiled at him, and a lilting laugh rose from her throat. All eyes turned from the small parlor to watch them in the hallway. She was a beauty. Her eyes sparkled and her lashes fluttered like a coquette. Yet he liked to think she flirted only with him. He pushed the Bible verse from his mind, assaying the admiring crowd, and she followed him into the small parlor.

Gathering around the piano, the crowd clapped their hands and sang to the merry music. When Rosie tugged on his sleeve to divert him to the dance floor, Andrew took a step forward to follow her; but at that moment, a gentleman slid onto the bench, and instead of the popular songs, he struck a series of introductory chords. The voices around him lifted in a Christmas carol. "Good

Christian men rejoice with heart and soul and voice."

Andrew lingered, turning again to the music. Rosie spoke his name, but he quieted her. His mind soared back to the day Livy arrived and, sitting at the spinet, played the same carol. He had yet to hear her sing, and she said that singing was more her talent than playing. He longed to be with her now, to hear her sweet, sensitive voice raise in song.

He closed his eyes and pictured Livy seated at Davy's bedside. Her dainty hand probably rested on the child's arm. Did she sing him lullabies when no one listened? He shook his head in wonder. God meant her to be a mother. He had no doubt. She had all the attributes: gentleness, compassion, love, generosity, and kindness.

A pressure on his sleeve brought him back, and he turned to gaze into Rosie's pouting face. "I thought you enjoyed my company," she mewled.

"I am sorry, Rosie," he responded. "Would you please me with a dance?"

She nodded and her bright yellow curls bobbed at the fringe of her upswept hair. He took her arm and lead her across the hall to join the dancers in a lively polka, but his thoughts crept back to a quiet room with a sick child and a gentle woman.

﹒‿

As she rubbed the cords in her neck and shoulders, Livy studied the sleeping child. Her eyes drooped as if weighted, and she struggled to dispel sleep. A soft sound through the window alerted her that Andrew had arrived home. She had no idea of the time, though hours earlier, the grandfather clock in the upper hall chimed ten o'clock.

She waited until she speculated Andrew had retired for the evening, then rose. A cup of tea might relax her so she, too, could climb into bed and sleep. For the past two nights, she had keep vigil at the boy's bedside, praying for improvement. Though he had gotten no worse, his cough and fever lingered. Tomorrow she would recommend they send for the doctor.

Her plans to return home seemed thwarted by Davy's illness, but she had not given up hope. She felt it imperative to receive Henry's Christmas call. The visit could be the beginning of their relationship, and though she questioned her motive, she believed that God's will might be done after all.

Stepping quietly through the doorway, she tiptoed down the upper hall, to not awaken those asleep, and edged her way down the darkened staircase. The glow of a softly burning lantern lit the foyer. A bright moon shone through the fanlight above the door as well.

Moving with caution, she made her way to the kitchen. Coals still glowed in the range grate, and to Livy's surprise, a pot of heated milk sat on the top cover. Grace must have warmed a cup for herself. Livy sprinkled sugar and cinnamon into a mug and stirred the warmed liquid. As she turned, her heart leaped to her throat, and her hand flew to the neck of her shirtwaist where she had loosened a button. In the dim hall, a shadowy figure watched her.

"I'm sorry I frightened you." Andrew stepped from the darkened hallway into the kitchen with a mug in his hand. "I didn't hear you come down."

Her speeding pulse slowed as Andrew spoke. "I thought you'd gone to bed. The time sitting with Davy has been stressful, and I hoped to calm myself with a warm drink. But I'm afraid I have taken your milk."

"Please, it's not a problem. I made far more than I wanted."

She lifted the pot from the range. "Would you like the rest?"

He stepped forward, and she drained the simmering milk into his mug. "Let's sit in the keeping room," he suggested.

He turned, and she followed him down the hall to the keeping room.

A warm glow shimmered from the hearth, and she slid into a cozy chair, wrapping her skirt about her legs. "Did you enjoy the party?" Livy asked, sipping the sweet liquid.

"Yes, as party's go, it was jolly. Music, dancing, and singing Christmas carols." He leaned forward, staring into the glowing embers. "I thought of you, Livy."

He lifted his gaze to hers, and her pulse tripped at his directness. "Thought of me? But why, with so many friends around you?"

"The singing, perhaps. I have yet to hear you sing, and I'd like to. I hear it's lovely."

Her heart hammered with confusion, and she was convinced he might hear it in the room's silence. "You embarrass me, Andrew. You've only heard idle chatter."

"Tell me it is not lovely, and I will believe you."

She pondered how to respond. Others told her she sang like an angel, but she was no judge of her own voice. "I cannot answer you. I have never heard my own voice except in my head. I only know what others say."

"And do *they* say it is lovely?"

The heat rose again to her cheeks.

"Then I am correct."

His gaze captured hers until she lowered her head to quell the pounding in her chest. Her vindictive nature sneaked out of hiding. "And how did you find Rosie this evening? As charming as ever?"

His lips pressed together as if in thought, then his mouth curved to a droll smile. "Why yes, she is an alluring woman."

Livy's heart quieted then fell like a weight. "I'm glad. You are a handsome man, Andrew, and I pray God will bless you with an equally handsome wife."

"God? You believe God's working for me, Livy? I'm afraid you are looking in the wrong direction." His dimples deepened with this wily chuckle. "God's Word leads me to a woman pure in *deed*, not one who is flirtatious. No, Miss Parker is not God's choice." He tilted his head, gazing at her. "Nor my mother's."

His mother? Livy struggled with his meaning. And who did Helen choose for him as a wife? Apparently, someone "pure in deed." Her mind shifted to Agatha. Was the dinner invitation as much to bring Agatha and Andrew together as it was "in her honor" as Helen had stated? She smiled at the idea.

"And what makes you smile?"

"Only a private thought."

"Private? Well, my sweet Livy, you should have 'private thoughts' more often. The smile lights your face and puts diamonds in your emerald eyes."

A tremor rushed along her arms to her chest, and her breath escaped in a short gasp. No man had ever said such bold, yet lovely, words to her before. Like the devil, Andrew beguiled her. She needed to be wary. When she caught her breath, she murmured a thank you, having no idea how to respond to his compliment. "I need to go to bed. It's very late."

"Yes, I know. You've had a trying day. How is Davy this evening?" he asked, concern blanketing his usual grin.

"The same, I'm afraid."

"I admire you, Livy. You and your selflessness. You sit at the boy's bedside with rare devotion."

"Me? Thank you, but no, Andrew. I am ashamed at my selfish thoughts. I was resentful coming here with Davy. As a spin. . .an unmarried woman, I have only myself to consider."

"Perhaps, but you have changed. Your concern is for the boy alone."

"I do feel a responsibility. Davy is my brother's only child. I would do everything in my power to keep him safe and healthy."

"You see? What I have said is true."

His words amazed her. Perhaps she had changed for the better. "Though he's no worse, I think we should send for the doctor in the morning. . .to be certain."

"The doctor, yes. Rest, Livy. I'll go for him at sunrise."

She rose. "Thank you, Andrew."

"You are welcome." He stood and, with one stride, stopped beside her. He raised his hand, tilting her chin upward, and his gaze locked to hers. "I'm right. They are emeralds. Beautiful." He brushed her cheek as he lowered his hand. "Time for bed, and I'll rise early as I promised."

He turned and sped from the room with Livy peering at his shadowed form ascending the staircase. When he vanished into the darkness, she brushed her cheek where his hand had rested. A sense of pleasure washed over her, and she lifted her eyes toward the ceiling spangled with light from the hearth. *Dear Lord, guide my path. Clear my mind. Rein my unbridled passion to self-control in Your Son's holy name.*

Chapter 5

Andrew kept his promise, and by nine in the morning, Dr. Browning arrived. Livy rose from the rocker at the sound of the footsteps. When he entered, he greeted Livy and set his bag on the rocker she'd abandoned. Andrew and Helen hovered in the doorway.

"What have we here?" he said, leaning over Davy and peering into his eyes. "How are you, lad?"

Davy stared at the stranger. "I cough," Davy said, his voice raspy from his hacking.

"How is his appetite?" the doctor asked as they hovered near.

"He's taken broth and some bread with apple butter. Little else."

The elderly man nodded, then leaned over his patient. "Open wide, lad."

Davy dropped his jaw, and the doctor peered inside, then pulled a stethoscope from his bag. He pressed the instrument against the boy's chest. "His lungs sound congested, but nothing serious."

He straightened his back, placing the stethoscope in the bag, and looked at Livy. "I'd like you to prepare some alum and honey mixed with sage tea. It's a valuable gargle. Continue with an elixir for his cough, and keep him warm to sweat out the fever."

He turned to Davy. "And lad, you must eat." The doctor pulled the blankets around Davy's shoulders, tucked them in, then grabbed his bag. "I see nothing serious. He'll be fit again in a few days."

"What do I owe you, doctor?" Livy asked, sliding her hand into her pocket where she'd tucked her currency.

"Four dollars," he said.

She pulled the paper money from her pocket and laid bills into his hand. "Thank you for coming."

He looked at the crisp dollars and nodded. When he passed through the doorway, Andrew followed him. Helen hurried into the room. "Olivia, please let us pay for the doctor's expense. You shouldn't use your savings."

Livy shook her head. "Thank you, Helen, but I've paid him this time. If he visits again, I'll let you pay."

Helen acquiesced with a nod. "I'll ask Grace to stay with Davy tonight while we're at the dinner party."

Livy rubbed her temples. "I think I'll excuse myself and stay at home. If he wakes, he may be frightened with a stranger."

"Grace is no stranger, Olivia." She leaned over the child. "Davy, you know Grace, don't you?"

He nodded. "She gives me pudding," he said in his raspy voice.

"You see," Helen said. "I insist you come with us. Tomorrow you'll leave and all you'll remember is sitting in this chair."

"I've enjoyed myself, Helen."

If Helen knew the truth, Livy's heart flew heavenward recalling the time she'd spent with Andrew. Leaving Davy—and Andrew—tomorrow weighed in her mind. And though she longed to stay, she felt driven to leave. "I'll see how Davy is in the morning. I'm not comfortable going unless he's totally well."

Helen pressed her arm. "You know you're welcome to stay, Olivia. More than welcome. We'd be delighted if you changed your mind."

"Yes, delighted," a voice echoed from the doorway.

Livy swung toward the sound of Andrew's voice.

"Please, convince Olivia to join us this evening, Andrew," Helen said. "She says she'd rather stay home to sit with Davy."

"Nonsense. What would a party be without you, Livy? You've had no fun at all. In fact," he volunteered, "I'll stay home, and you go along with mother and father."

Livy drew back in surprise. "You? Thank you, but no. If anyone stays home, it'll be me. Anyway, your mother said Grace would stay with Davy. If he's well enough, I'll join you. I promise."

Helen nodded. "Then let us do as the doctor said." She rested her hand on Davy's arm. "I'll send Grace up with some soup, and I want you to eat. Do you understand?"

"Yes," he said, his head bobbing against the pillow.

"That's a good lad."

Helen swept from the room, but Andrew remained and ambled to the bedside. "Livy, Father suggested I go out this morning and cut the Christmas tree. I'd like you to come along. If you go bundle up, I'll sit with Davy until Grace comes with his soup. What do you say?"

"I'd like to. It sounds nice. I saw the snow falling from the window."

"Good. Dress your warmest. I'll meet you at the side door in a few minutes."

Livy nodded, and Andrew turned to Davy. "Would you like me to tell you a story of the lumber camp? How about a tale of Paul Bunyan and his great blue ox, Babe?"

Davy's face brightened, and he scooted his head upward on the pillow. "Paul Bunyan? Is he a logger man?" His voice grated, but the cough seemed to have vanished.

Andrew chuckled. "Paul Bunyan is the greatest lumberjack around. And his ox, Babe, is so large he measures forty-two ax handles and a plug of chewing tobacco between the horns."

Livy inched her way to the door. Though she was eager for a break, she'd love to stay and hear the tales of the mythological lumberjack. Guilt tugged at her, too, knowing she had little time for the luxury of a sleigh ride; but Andrew asked, and she couldn't refuse.

"One day when Paul Bunyan came to the logging camp," Andrew continued, "he spied a giant tree that. . ."

In the hallway, Livy peered a final time into the room as Andrew sat in the rocker, his animated hands detailing the story of Paul Bunyan. He had captured Davy's interest, and Livy was grateful.

As Livy exited, Andrew's gaze followed her to the doorway. To his amazement, his chest fluttered like an inexperienced oaf when she agreed to the sleigh ride. He forced himself to concentrate on the tale of Paul Bunyan, and when Grace arrived with the soup, he darted from the child's bedside, anxious to meet Livy.

Dressed in his warmest attire, Andrew gazed through the window, watching snow flakes drift to the ground, and outside, he hurried to the stable. When the sleigh was ready, he grabbed the ax and gathered the buffalo robes, then guided the bays to the side door. Livy waited, her face framed by the window, and he bounded up the stairs to meet her.

Settling into the sleigh, he tucked the heavy lap robe around their legs and steered the horses onto the road. The brisk wind whipped across their faces. Gasping in the icy air, Livy laughed at their adventure, chattered about his Paul Bunyan tale, and then asked about being a lumberjack.

Andrew studied her and, realizing she was sincere, told her about the life of a logger.

"That's a long time away from home," Livy said, her voice reflective. "Months."

"Lumberjacks are home from spring to autumn. Many are farmers and come home in time for planting. It's a life we learn to accept."

"But what of the wives?" she murmured, then continued without waiting for his response. "And what do you do for fun in those long evenings?"

Andrew laughed. "Getting up at four in the morning, I'm in bed early; but after dinner in the bunkhouses, they sing endless ballads, share personal stories, and tell folk tales. I hate to tell you about their trips to the nearest town. Some get mighty wild." He glanced at her. "You can rest assured, I'm not one of those."

"Rest assured?" she repeated, returning his grin.

When they reached the evergreens at the edge of the frozen river, Andrew secured the bays and helped Livy from the sleigh. He held her arm as they wandered through the fir trees. "What do you say, Livy? Which one? We need something that'll fit in the alcove of the parlor."

Livy's face glowed, and she pivoted in a circle, gazing at the myriad of trees. "There are too many, Andrew."

"Which do you like? Balsams? Douglas firs? White pines?"

"Which is which? You tell me what tree is best for decorating, and I'll pick the prettiest."

A smile perched on his lips. *Livy* was the prettiest, so pretty, he couldn't drag his attention to the trees. They marched through the snow, slipping and sliding, grasping each other for balance. Each time, he longed to hold her at his side, yet he feared she'd resist. Instead, he forced himself to let her go with each laughable mishap.

Finally, like a young girl, she darted between the trees to a shapely one, circled its branches, and returned to his side. "This one," she said. "Look at its color and shape." She bounced like a happy child while he pointed to the snow-laden limbs.

"Good choice, Livy. It's a blue spruce." The tree stood at least seven feet high with well-shaped branches that would hold the candles safely.

She touched the sleeve of his heavy coat. "It's perfect, Andrew."

He swallowed his heart and lay his hand on hers. "But not as perfect as you. Your size, your color, your fragrance. You're much more lovely."

Her face paled, then a rosy flush heightened her coloring. "Please don't say things you do not mean, Andrew. I'm not a young woman who knows how to handle your teasing." Her eyes pleaded with him. "I'm twenty-eight, not a young woman at all."

His hand slid around her shoulder, and he drew her to him, his emotions swaying like a pendulum. "You're young, Livy. What about me? I'm thirty." He dropped the ax and tilted her face with his thumb beneath her chin. "When I watch you with Davy, I don't know, you're. . .perfect, like an angel."

As she lowered her chin, she turned away. "No one's ever spoken to me like this. I don't know what to say."

He'd embarrassed her, and he admonished himself. Where was his self-control? Still, he doubted her words. He couldn't believe she'd never heard such words before. So many questions filled his mind. Reining himself, Andrew dragged his hand from Livy's shoulder and crouched down to clear the snow from the spruce's base.

When he swung the heavy ax, Livy gasped then cheered him on. No longer flustered, her lighthearted demeanor warmed his heart. Though felling trees was a daily chore at the logging camp, Andrew had never felt such pleasure with each stroke of the ax. Livy clapped her hands as the tree tilted, and for her amusement, he yelled, "Timber."

As the spruce toppled to the ground, Livy bolted to his side, and he nestled her in his arms. Silence wrapped around them, and he held his breath. "I want to kiss you, Livy."

Anxiety filled her face. "Please, Andrew, I'm terribly confused. Your life is so different from mine. I can't respond until I know my mind."

"I'd never do anything against your will. Believe me. But I'll ask you again, Livy. You can be sure." He had dampened her pleasure. For that, he was sorry. Grabbing the ax and hoisting the base of the tree, he pulled it to the sleigh and heaved it onto the back. He tucked Livy beneath the lap robe and joined her.

Before he called to the horses, he paused, turning to Livy. "I assume you think I'm forward. But I want to tell you something. When you first came, I found you attractive, but you seemed like the parish women, prim and proper. Yet I've changed, and now, I see a different side of you."

She lifted her head, and the sunlight glinted in her eyes like the diamonds sparkling in the snow.

"I don't know why you've never married, but you're meant to be a wife and mother. It's clear to me. You belong with a loving husband who'll support you with a good business. One who wants children and loves you with all his heart. I believe that's what God has planned for you."

"I don't know if you're right, Andrew. For the past few years, I believed that God has no husband for me. Some days, I think about taking the matter into my own hands. Then I'm ashamed of my frustration with the Lord."

Andrew couldn't hold back his grin. "Livy, you're not alone. We've all tried to sway God to our thinking. I've done it myself. . .too often, I'm ashamed to say. Wait and see. Put your life in God's hands, and I'll do the same."

"I'll try," she whispered.

He prayed she understood his obscure message and moved the bays back onto the path. He'd say no more.

❧

Livy's mind spun with all that had happened. As if Andrew knew Henry, he'd described him with perfection. A business man eager for children. A Christian man who understood the commitment of marriage. Yet it wasn't Henry, but Andrew, whom she wanted to open his heart and tell her he loved her.

A logger's life didn't seem adapted well to marriage. Lumberjacks were away from their homes for months at a time. Not a welcome life for a new bride. Still, she could imagine keeping a pleasant home and awaiting her husband's arrival. Each time he returned, she pictured how she would open her arms and greet him.

Life would be lonely when he was at camp—as lonely as her present life as a spinster—maybe worse. No, she wouldn't be content, married to a logger. And Andrew was a lumberjack. Better to have a life with a businessman, a man like Henry Tucker.

Livy bowed her head, sensing something was wrong. What would the Lord want her to do? Was a spinster's life what God meant for her? Or maybe a life tending orphaned children? Was safe, faithful Henry Tucker the man for her? Or Andrew? Could she trust him, knowing his taste for alluring, flirtatious women? No, she'd never attract a man like Andrew. Why even think about it?

Chapter 6

Returning home, Andrew dropped Livy off at the door. After leaving the horses and sleigh with the stableboy, he came back to the house and brushed the snow from his boots. When he entered the keeping room, his father sat in his favorite chair, reading the *Grand Rapids Eagle*.

"Good evening, Father."

"Andrew, sit and listen to this," Charles said, motioning to the newspaper. "The newfangled Christian Women's Temperance Union is holding a rally tonight." He released a boisterous chuckle. "I wonder if Governor Bagley will be forced to deal with the issue. Pressure's coming from all over."

"I don't know. Did you read about the lobbyists in yesterday's *Detroit Free Press*? They're fighting for exclusive river rights for running their logs to the sawmill. Now that worries me."

Charles peered over his spectacles. "Could be a serious problem for the small logging camps."

"Like mine," Andrew said, thinking of his young lumber camp. Though his business had grown, he wasn't eager to pay heavy costs to boom logs on the river. He had a distance to go before becoming a lumber baron, but the title was inevitable, and he had to use good judgment. He'd noticed many young women fawning over him, and he guessed it was his future wealth that appealed to them. He hoped that wasn't cause for Rosie or Agatha's obvious attention. Andrew didn't question Livy's friendship, certain that her intentions were pure.

"I suppose, son, you should try to keep a positive attitude." He pulled his gaze from the newspaper to Andrew. "You have mail on the hall table, and there's a letter for Livy, too, I noticed."

"Thank you," Andrew said, returning to the foyer. On the table he found the two envelopes.

He opened the mail addressed to him and scanned the enclosed invitation, a New Year's Eve gathering hosted by Rosie Parker's family. Days earlier he would have smiled with pleasure, but now confusion tugged at his conscience. He wanted Livy to stay for the holiday, and he wouldn't have her sit home while he attended a party.

Yet, if Livy were determined to leave, sitting home on New Year's Eve would be twice as long and lonely, knowing his friends were enjoying the evening. He fingered the card, contemplating his decision. He decided to wait before accepting the invitation, wait until he knew what Livy planned to do.

Holding his invitation, he carried Livy's letter up the stairs. When she opened the door, the scent of ironed linen and soap filled the air. Livy smiled, and he delivered her mail, hoping it was good news from her brother, then went to his room to prepare for the evening.

Inside her room, Livy read John's letter which was filled with satisfactory news. Though Ruth hadn't fully recovered, she'd made progress. He hoped they would bring Davy home within the next two or three weeks. Thrilled with the good news, she was anxious to share it with her nephew.

Placing the letter on her dresser, she peered again into the chifforobe, pondering what she might wear. Tonight, if she attended the dinner party, she'd select her most fancy gown, a light blue dress of voile with embroidered Valenciennes lace. The modest neckline wasn't stylish, but her unassuming personality made it most appropriate.

⌒

That evening, Davy seemed content with Grace's company, so Livy slipped on her pale blue gown, tucked her hair into a chignon ornamented with blue ribbons, and joined the family. When she descended the stairs, Andrew observed her with an admiring smile, causing her heart to flutter like birds' wings.

"You look striking this evening, Livy," he said.

His words nestled into her memory. "Oh, it's nothing special, thank you. It's the most festive gown I have."

Without comment, he grasped her hand and brushed it with his soft lips. As Helen added her own compliments, Livy's heart danced.

With everyone ready, a servant held open Livy's cloak, and after each donned his outerwear, they departed.

A light snow drifted from the sky, sparkling in the brightness of the rising moon. The coachman helped them into the carriage and soon they were rattling down the rutted lane. Livy nestled beneath a heavy lap robe beside Helen. Charles and Andrew sat on the seat across from them. Facing Andrew's broad shoulders covered by his chesterfield, her memory drifted to the sleigh ride earlier in the day. The day's events took her breath away.

In the growing snowfall, the bays halted before an attractive dwelling. Though smaller than the Mandalay home, the house glowed with candles in the windows, and through the panes, firelight flickered on the hearth. Livy climbed from the carriage and followed the others into the foyer with smells of spices and roasted meat filling the air.

"My, my, something smells wonderful," Charles boomed as he pulled off his heavy coat then removed his steam-covered spectacles.

"Cloves and cinnamon," Agatha simpered as she took their wraps and hung them on the hall tree. "You smell my mulled cider." Then, leaning closer to Andrew, Agatha added, "And maybe a bit of lavender."

"Yes," Livy agreed, "lavender is lovely. My favorite is lily of the valley."

Agatha dismissed her with a nod and motioned for them to enter the parlor. Livy sat on the divan, and to her pleasure, Andrew joined her. Agatha took note, evidenced by her frown.

Roger arrived with a tray of steaming mugs and, after greeting his guests, handed each a cup of the warm brew. The heat permeated Livy's hands, and as she sipped, it warm her chilled body.

After dinner, the conversation flitted from one topic to another until Roger slid onto the piano bench. "Now, Livy, won't you sing something for us? A hymn or carol."

Comfortable with singing, Livy rose and stood beside him at the piano. After a brief moment to agree upon a song, Livy looked at her small audience. "I hope you'll enjoy one of the newer carols. Have you heard 'O Little Town of Bethlehem'?" No one had, and they listened with interest as Roger played the introduction.

Livy drew in a deep breath and began the words of the less famous carol. Singing to this intimate group of friends, Livy's knees trembled before she gained courage. From her vantage point, Andrew sat enraptured, his gaze riveted on her.

When she finished the carol they assailed her with compliments. "Sing another," Andrew said. "Anything, please."

"That was lovely," Helen added. "Truly lovely."

"One more," Livy agreed. "This is another new carol telling the story of our recent war, I think you'll like the refrain, and when you catch on, please join in."

Roger played, and Livy sang. "I heard the bells on Christmas Day, their old familiar carols play." As she reached the end of each verse, her spirit lifted as the voices joined hers with the words of hope, "of peace on earth, good will to men."

When the song ended, Livy returned to her chair. Then together they sang familiar carols which ended when Agatha rose to bring in dessert.

"Livy, you must sing in church for Christmas if you decide to stay. Your voice could be enjoyed by the whole congregation, not only the few of us here," Roger said. "Will you stay for the holiday?"

She peered from one to the other, wondering what her answer would be. "I'm still not sure. In the morning, I'll see how Davy is feeling."

"If you do stay through the holiday, I'd enjoy your company on New Year's Eve," Roger said.

Livy's heart sank to her toes. If she extended her stay, she prayed that Andrew would be her escort for the evening. "Davy's health will make the determination," she said again.

"Well then, we'll wait and see," Roger said. "Andrew, are you up for a New Year's Eve celebration?"

"I've received an invitation already, Roger. . .but don't let my plans ruin your own."

"We'll decide later then. If Livy stays, we'll find an agreeable time for everyone to celebrate the New Year."

Hearing Andrew's answer, Livy made an immediate decision. Tired of wishful thinking and useless dreams, she prayed Davy would be well by morning. She refused to stay another minute in Grand Rapids with her uncontrollable, romantic fantasies. She guessed his invitation was from Miss Parker. No matter what Andrew said to Livy in private, his heart seemed tied to the vivacious woman.

No matter what compliments Andrew dropped in her presence, she'd block them from her hearing. Andrew wanted only one thing: for her to care for Davy. She was certain. No matter how many sweet things he said, he had no interest in her whatsoever.

Her mind sent up a silent prayer, asking God, once again, for forgiveness. Andrew's captivating personality and good looks aroused feelings she should never have. God expected chaste thoughts, and Livy assumed that her longing for Andrew's hand on hers and his lips pressing against her mouth could be nothing but sinful.

At twenty-eight, her inexperience embarrassed her. With no older sister, she wished she could garner courage to talk with Helen about love and romance before she returned home. Even though Ruth lived near Livy in Detroit, her illness made her seem an unlikely candidate to discuss romance. John certainly showed his wife affection, but Livy had a difficult time imaging Ruth feeling the strong emotions that wended through Livy's thoughts.

Helen seemed an appropriate counselor. Remembering the wooden heart, Livy was certain the keepsake held a tale of love.

❧

Determined to leave on the next train, Livy packed her bags before the sun had fully risen the following morning. She hurried to the kitchen where Grace was mixing a large pot of oatmeal for the family's breakfast.

When she entered the kitchen, Grace turned. "You're up early, Miss Schuler. Would you like some warm oatmeal?"

"Yes, and tea, Grace, if it's ready."

Livy downed her quick breakfast then returned to the second floor, eager to see Davy. When she entered his room, the boy looked at her with sleepy, reddened eyes. He lifted his head from the pillow, squinting at her traveling gown. "How are you feeling today?" Livy asked, sitting on the edge of his bed. "Did you have fun with Grace?"

"She told me about Joseph and Mary and the baby Jesus. Mama tells me the story sometimes when she's not sick."

"I know. And she's feeling better, according to your papa's letter. You'll be going home in a while."

Davy placed his hand on the sleeve of her traveling dress. "Are you going away?" His mouth pulled downward, and his coloring appeared mottled.

"I'm catching the train this morning."

"With me?"

A pang of regret caught like a knot in her chest. "No, Uncle Charles and Aunt Helen want you to stay for Christmas, but I have reasons to go home."

"I want to go with you."

"No, Davy, your mama isn't well enough yet. In a couple more weeks."

"Please don't leave."

A soft noise from the doorway caused Livy to turn. Andrew leaned against the doorframe, observing them. "You're leaving?"

"I'm ready, yes, but. . ." She tilted her head toward Davy. "I seem to have opposition."

"It doesn't surprise me." He stepped into the room and sat beside her at the foot of the bed. "You want your Aunt Olivia to stay here, Davy?"

The child turned his head back and forth, not sure where to concentrate his attention.

"You're much better now, sweetheart," Livy persisted.

Wide-eyed, he didn't response.

"I have no reason to stay," she said, turning to Andrew. "Would you ask if a servant could drive me to the railroad station? I'm sure a train is scheduled for today sometime. I'm willing to wait."

"You're determined to go?"

"Yes, it's for the best." She rose, patting Davy's arm. "I'll see you before I leave." She paused at the door and spoke to Andrew. "I'll be in my room when the driver's ready."

Andrew watched her bolt through the doorway. His folded hands rested on his knees, and he stared at his boots. Why did she insist upon rushing away? He'd believed for a while that she might change her mind. He eyed Davy, noticing a skin rash. He pulled his nightshirt away from his neck. Not sure of the illness, he knew one thing. Davy's problem wasn't a cold. He stepped to the doorway and called to Livy.

Her door opened, and when she saw him, she rushed into the hallway. "What?" she asked, peering toward Davy's room.

"Take a look. The fever and cough were only symptoms."

"Symptoms? I don't understand." She followed him inside. Andrew pulled back the neck of Davy's nightshirt. Livy eyed the red spots. "Scarlet fever?" she gasped.

"I'm not sure," Andrew said. "Maybe only the measles. I'll call Mother."

Livy nodded, sinking to the edge of the bed. "Please, Andrew. . .there's no need to arrange a ride for the station. I'm staying here with Davy."

Chapter 7

Andrew rose from his bed and ambled across the room to the window seat, his mind on Livy. Two days earlier with the discovery of Davy's scarlet fever, she decided to stay in Grand Rapids. Davy's illness, he thanked God, seemed a light case, according to Doctor Browning, but Livy was nailed to the boy's side.

To his frustration, Livy was with Davy or did all she could to avoid Andrew. Her most direct conversation came when she asked him a favor. He agreed and had gone to Western Union to sent John a telegraphic message, alerting him of her change in plans and alleviating their fears with the doctor's positive prognosis.

Since that day, Andrew's plans had changed, too. Strange visions somersaulted in his mind. Marriage had evaded him for the past years. First, he was busy building his lumber business. Then he avoided women, fearing their interest was in his money. Finally, he'd enjoyed his freedom, the unfettered life of a single man. Now he could think of nothing else but Livy.

Today he opened his Bible and stared at the scripture. The Testament had lain in a drawer for many months. . .years, if he were honest. But since Livy stepped into his life, he'd been driven to God's Word.

He was thirty, no longer prompted by his parents' guidance, yet his mother's teachings clustered like a litany in his mind. *"Marriage is a blessed union, guided by God. A happy man loves his wife, but as important, he must respect her. She instructs and loves his children and supports her husband. A Christian wife is a wonderful gift from God."*

The words his mother uttered for years described Livy. He pictured Rosie, but her allure had vanished. Since her arrival, Livy had, with slow assurance, invaded his mind. . .and more, his heart. He admired her grace and compassion, and she radiated beauty despite her reserved appearance. Her face glowed, and her mouth curved to a warm smile when she looked at him.

Andrew looked down at the scripture verses open on his lap. His fingers had guided him to Proverbs 31, and he lifted the leather volume and stared at the words rising from the page. *"Who can find a virtuous woman? for her price is far above rubies. The heart of her husband doth safely trust in her, so that he shall have no need of spoil. She will do him good and not evil all the days of her life."*

Andrew contemplated Livy's gentleness and intelligence. He returned to the page. *"She riseth also while it is yet night, and giveth meat to her household, and a portion to her maidens. . . . She girdeth her loins with strength, and strengtheneth her arms. She perceiveth that her merchandise is good: her candle goeth not out by night."* He envisioned her sitting at Davy's side, empathy and love shining in her eyes.

"She openeth her mouth with wisdom; and in her tongue is the law of kindness. She looketh well to the ways of her household, and eateth not the bread of idleness. Her children arise up, and call her blessed; her husband also, and he praiseth her." Andrew felt as if God were describing Livy in His Word.

He read further, letting the Lord's lesson take hold. *"Favour is deceitful, and beauty is vain: but a woman that feareth the Lord, she shall be praised."*

Andrew recalled the same verse entering his thoughts at the Christmas party. Was God speaking to him that evening? The question sent gooseflesh galloping along his arms. Though he'd never been a religious man, today his faith pushed against his heart.

He bowed his head, thanking God for the realization that flooded through him. He had to win Livy's love. It wasn't only God's will, but his own.

⌒

For two days since she'd changed her plans, Livy dashed from one task to another. Besides nursing Davy, she had approached Helen about appropriate garments for the holiday.

On Tuesday afternoon, Helen searched her closets for frocks that might fit Livy with simple alterations. Livy was amazed at the number of fashionable gowns hanging in Helen's closet.

"Now, Olivia, this one is ideal for you. A few tucks and it'll fit perfectly. And the shade will look wonderful with your coloring. Look in the glass."

Olivia steered her around, and Livy eyed herself in the mirror. The hunter green taffeta gown cinched her narrow waist and draped in graceful folds to the floor with a wide ruffled hem. Livy agreed, the color brightened her eyes and highlighted her dark hair.

"Well," Helen asked again, "will it do?"

"Do? Helen, it's beautiful. More than I could ever afford. I'm sure it's an expensive Worth gown, isn't it?"

"Yes, but I want you to have it. We'll ask the tailor to take in an inch or two, then it will be ideal. No one would ever recognize the dress. And this orchid gown is lovely, and you'll look so beautiful in it. This is fun!"

Livy's mind raced. After the tailor, she had to visit the local mercantile to purchase Christmas gifts.

Once Helen had collected the gowns, Livy and she headed for town to complete their holiday preparations. While Helen lingered at the shop, Livy visited the general store and selected gifts for each family member: a leather brush set for Charles, a gilt-finished sewing box for Helen, a cashmere scarf for Andrew, and a wooden horse and carriage for Davy. Choosing a black velvet reticule and green ribbons for herself, she returned to the tailor shop to meet Helen.

"Olivia, I can't wait for you to see the gown Mildred finished for me. It'll be delivered with yours tomorrow. And not a minute too soon."

"I waited too long to make my decision, Helen. I'm sorry."

"Don't worry yourself. Everything will fall into place." She rested her hand on Livy's arm. "Now, do you think we have time for tea?"

"Whatever you say," Livy said. "The bells sounded three a few moments ago."

"Then we have time. Come. I'll take you to Birdie's Tea Shop." She beckoned Livy to follow. "She serves the most delicious tea cakes."

Outside in the brisk winter air, Livy struggled to keep up with Helen's brisk pace to the tea shop. Before they were seated, Livy gaped at the elegant display of breads and cakes.

When they were seated, they nibbled and chatted like old friends. Sensing the time pass, Livy struggled to muster her courage. She'd wanted to speak with Helen about many personal concerns, and today, the opportunity seemed perfect. Drawing a deep breath, Livy began, "I have a confession to make, Helen. When I arrived here with Davy, it was really against my wishes. My life is usually my own, but I pushed my plans aside to help my brother and Ruth."

Helen's brow creased. "You were being kind, Livy, but I can understand, though my life hasn't been my own for years." She fingered her teacup, and a gentle grin rose on her face. "I'm not certain I'd have it any other way."

With Helen's admission, Livy's heart lifted. "And that's why I'm confessing, Helen. I've want to talk for so long with someone. . .someone who might offer me advice."

Helen's expression melted to tenderness. She rested her palm on Livy's hand. "Please, treat me as you might a sister. If I can help you I will."

Livy sighed. "I've had so little excitement in my life. For twenty-eight years, I hoped God would lead me to a loving husband, but I'm afraid my hope and God's plan don't match; so earlier this year, I decided to take the matter into my own hands."

Helen's eyes widened. "Your own hands? What do you mean by this?"

Livy sensed disapproval in Helen's expression, and she lowered her head. With careful detail, she described her relationship with Henry Tucker. "Helen, my real wish to go back to Detroit is that I want to be home for Henry's Christmas visit. As I said, I'd longed for a husband who I could cherish. . .one who'd stir my heart. But as you can see, I wasn't meant to be in Detroit for the holiday."

Guilt edged up Livy's neck as Andrew flew to her mind. "I was trying to find someone on my own. Now I wonder if Henry's the husband God has chosen for me."

Helen stroked Livy's arm. "Olivia, we can't force the Lord's will. God's plan for each of us is revealed in His good time, not ours. I understand your eagerness for a home and family. The problem is, we don't see God's full plan."

"But Helen, look how perfect your life is. You and Ruth were childhood friends. . .and her brother fell in love with you. It seems the plan was laid out so carefully. But I don't have a friend with a handsome, loving brother—"

Helen pressed her arm, her face drawn. "Olivia, my story's not that simple. Not that simple at all. Love didn't come as easily as you think. We all must accept God's will and guidance by opening our eyes and our hearts."

Livy searched Helen's face, wanting to understand the message tangled in her words. Questions spilled to Livy's tongue, but she waited for Helen to continue. The only sound was the clerk's voice speaking to a customer.

"You mentioned love," Livy said, after the silence lingered longer than she could bear. "I've asked myself so often, 'What is love?' I have a fondness for Henry. A tender affection, maybe. He's a cordial, kind man who'd be a faithful husband and loving father. Is that love, Helen?"

Helen's tensed mouth relaxed. "I suppose love is different for each of us. . . and remember, Olivia, love can grow. A small spark becomes a flame. A flame can kindle a fire that warms our days." She quieted. Then a flush rose beneath her collar.

Livy's skin heated at her burning questions. "If I'm too direct, Helen, please tell me." Livy leaned toward her and lowered her voice. "Are love and passion the same? Does love ripple through your chest and take your breath away?" Amusement grew on Helen's face, but Livy didn't care. The questions bubbled from her. "Does your heart dance and long to. . . ? I am embarrassed to say it." Her hands knotted against the table, and she lowered her head.

"To be kissed and caressed?"

The words jolted her. "Oh yes. To be kissed. Is that passion or love?"

"I can't answer that, Livy. Marriage is a warm intimate relationship between two committed people—a sharing of mind, body, and spirit. It's a gift from God."

"A gift from God. I've never thought of marriage in that way." Livy's mind raced at her own foolishness. Taking matters into her own hands wouldn't be a gift from God.

"And that's why," Helen added, "you must let God be in charge. Wait for the gift. . .whatever it may be. Be assured, Olivia, if you really listen, God will guide you. He'll show you the way. . .even if it's not the path you'd planned to travel."

"Not the path you'd planned to travel." The words sent a ripple of excitement down Livy's spine. "Like my trip here, Helen. It wasn't my plan to travel. Was it God's?" Her pulse tripped on its rushed path.

"You have to decide that for yourself. I won't second guess God. But I will say we've enjoyed your company beyond words. And maybe your visit has answered *my* prayers."

"Your prayers? In what way, Helen?" Without delay, the wooden heart leapt to her thoughts.

"Time will tell, Olivia. Time will tell."

Chapter 8

"You seem a little better, Davy," Livy said.

"May I watch Aunt Helen decorate the hall?"

"We'll see. Maybe for a while. Would you like to sit in my room and play? We'll see how well you feel then?"

He nodded and swung his legs over the edge of the bed. Livy tugged his heavy stockings over his chilled legs and wrapped a coverlet around his shoulders. "Follow me." Her spirit soared seeing him up and about.

With Davy seated at her desk with a pencil and paper, she sat nearby, wondering what the next days would bring. Celebrating the holiday with the Mandalays had introduced Livy to new customs like cutting the tree. This afternoon, they'd decorate the hall and parlor. Helen promised tomorrow, Christmas Eve, would be filled with surprises.

When Livy rose to admire Davy's artwork, a tap sounded against the door. In a step, she pulled it open, and Andrew peered in at her. "Mother asked me to knock. The servants are bringing in the greens, and she wondered if you'd like to join us."

"Thank you. I'm looking forward to it."

He peered beyond Livy to the desk. "Well look who's out of bed."

Davy turned with a smile, and Livy pulled back the door. Andrew stepped through the doorway and strode to Davy's side. "You don't look like a leopard any longer."

Davy giggled. "Aunt Livy said I might be able to watch Aunt Helen decorate the hall."

"If you do, Davy, you should only come for a little while. You must stay well. Tomorrow evening, we'll open gifts by the tree. You don't want to miss that."

Excitement spread across Davy's face. "Gifts? Are there gifts for me?"

"Certainly." Andrew brandished a smile. "And gifts for Aunt Livy, too."

An unexpected excitement rifled through Livy. "You shouldn't have."

"But why not? Everyone should enjoy the fun." He rested his hand on her shoulder. "Will you be down soon?"

"Yes, I'll help Davy dress and be there shortly."

"I'll see you later." Gently patting her arm, he turned and left the room.

As he closed the door, Livy pressed her hand against her bodice, calming the riot in her heart.

～

Davy sat on the bottom of the staircase, his face flushed.

"I hope Davy's reddened cheeks are from excitement and not a fever." Livy touched his face and laughed at herself. "I sound like an overprotective mother."

"Your cheeks are rosy, too," Andrew said. "Or are the red ribbons throwing a reflection?"

She pressed her palms against her heated skin, hoping to hide the truth. "Too much excitement for both Davy and me. Everything looks so beautiful."

She pivoted around the foyer, admiring the wreaths hanging at the front windows, the garland and ribbons draping the staircase, and the swags of cedar displayed over the doorways. Unable to control her enthusiasm, Livy burst into song. "Deck the halls with bows of holly. . . ."

"Fa-la-la-la-la. . . ," Andrew joined her.

One by one, the others followed. Charles grabbed Helen's hand as she stepped from the keeping room, then Andrew clasped Livy's hand, and forming a ring, they circled in the center of the foyer. Davy jumped up from his perch to join them.

With the unfamiliar words in the second verse, their voices faded except Livy's until they roused again at the end of each line, booming the refrain.

"Follow me in merry measure," Livy sang, twirling them faster and faster. "While I tell of Yuletide treasure." The spirited circle broke rank with laughter as the final refrain died away.

Gasping for breath, Helen fanned her face. "I'm much too old for all of this," she said, "especially since we need our energy to finish the tree." The sound of a playful groan echoed against the high ceiling. "We have a reprieve. I believe it's nearly dinnertime. We'll finish after we eat."

As if hearing Helen's words, Grace announced the meal, and the troupe turned to the dining room.

Davy's presence added a special spark to the family meal. They lingered over dessert until Davy yawned, and Helen offered to take him up to bed. Charles rose, saying he needed to ask the stableboy to bring in a fresh load of logs for the fireplace.

With the others conveniently gone, Andrew faced Livy, knowing the moment had come. Hurrying to her side, he pulled her from chair. "Follow me, Livy. We have one more decoration to hang before the others arrive."

Her face filled with question, but he left her to wonder and headed to the foyer. He heard her brisk footsteps behind him, and he feared to look at her because he'd give himself away. Beneath the parlor archway, he stopped and beckoned. "Come here. I'll lift you up to find the tack."

She frowned but did as he asked. Grasping her small waist in his hands, he swooped her into the air level with the upper doorframe. "Do you see it?"

"Yes," Livy gasped.

With caution, he held her against him with one arm and handed her a sprig of mistletoe bound with a red ribbon. "Hang the string over the tack, please."

She grasped the bright spray of white berries and raised it above his head. "Finished," she called.

His stomach knotted as he lowered her, and when her feet touched the floor, he kept her close in his arms. She faced him and hesitated. What if she resisted him? He swallowed the anxiety that rose to his throat. It tumbled downward, tangling around his heart. As the possibility filled his mind, she tried to step backward, but he kept his grasp firm, binding her to his chest.

His fear faded. She didn't struggle or cry out. Instead, a look of wonder filled her face. "I don't have to tell you what happens now, do I? It's tradition."

Livy's lips parted with a gasp of surprise. As if in suspended motion, he lowered his lips to hers.

At his touch, Livy closed her eyes and savored the sweetness she had only dreamed about. A roar grew in her ears. Her knees weakened. Would she faint? Would she die?

His gentle lips lingered on hers until she sensed she would scream. Warmth spread through her, growing and swelling, until she felt ignited with a dazzling glow. *Sparks. Flame. Fire*. Helen's words burned in her mind.

As tenderly as their lips had met, he drew away, and when she lifted her lids, his looked as weighted as hers felt. A heated flush burned on her cheeks and spilled down her neck, and she released a sigh.

"Oh Livy. Dearest. I've wanted to kiss you for so long. Have I offended you? Please say no."

She stumbled backward, her hands clutching at the folds in her dress. "Only surprised me, Andrew. I've never. . .no man has. . .I'm—" No words expressed her feelings.

"You're beautiful." He tilted her chin upward with his thumb while a finger caressed her lips. "And you're loved."

Loved? But what of Miss Parker and his logging career? And what of Henry Tucker and. . . ? Livy halted her racing mind. "Andrew, please, don't say things you don't mean. I can't bear it."

"I mean every word. I know we've only met, Livy, but sometimes God speaks in ways we never imagine. God's guided me to you. I believe that with all my heart."

"But. . .I'm not sure of my heart. It's beating so fiercely, I think I'll die."

He slid his arm around her shoulder and nestled her against his chest. "You won't die, Livy. You've only begun to live. Me, too. I won't press you, Livy. I only ask you to pray that God's will be done. If you do, I know you'll love me as I love you."

The thundering of her heart drowned his next words, but Livy didn't need to hear more. She'd heard all she ever longed to hear. "*You'll love me as I love you.*"

Chapter 9

Livy avoided Andrew throughout the evening as the family adorned the tree with apples, strings of cranberries, candy, cookie ornaments, paper creations, and candles. Not that she didn't care about him, but that she cared too much. As soon as possible, she took her leave, hurrying to her room to ponder the day's events.

Sleep evaded her, her thoughts rushing and surging throughout the night. If she hadn't kept her wits about her, she would've awakened Helen from a sound sleep to lay her tangled heartstrings before her. Livy cared deeply for Andrew, yet she couldn't forget all the difficulties she'd bear, especially his months away at the logging camp. Trying to push her fears aside, she reminded herself that God would guide her through the difficult times.

Livy felt bleary-eyed when the sun's golden rays sneaked through the window. During the night, the joyful song they had sung lingered in her mind. *"While I tell of Yuletide treasure."* She recalled, again, Helen's treasure, her keepsake, and longed to know its meaning. Finally, Livy pulled herself from the bed and faced the day.

With the holiday at hand, Livy joined Helen, adding the final touches to the decorations, dinner menu, and gifts. The parlor door remained closed, awaiting the evening's festivities. And Davy, feeling stronger, hovered near Livy, not giving her a moment of privacy.

Finally before the dinner hour approached, she coaxed Davy to nap, explaining he'd enjoy the evening more fully. With him safely in bed, Livy knocked on Helen's door. Hearing nothing, Livy turned away, but as she did, the door opened, and Helen freed a soft chuckle.

"It's you, Olivia. Charles and Andrew are like children trying to peek at their gifts. I assumed you were one of them. Come in."

Livy entered, her eyes shifting immediately toward the wooden heart. "I'm sorry to disturb you. I didn't sleep well last night. Since you offered to listen, I'd like to take a few minutes, if I could."

"Please sit, Olivia. I meant what I said. Whatever your worries, my ears are open."

Helen sank into a cozy armchair, and Livy situated herself on an adjacent settee. "So many things are banging in my head, I don't know where to begin. When I spoke to you yesterday, I concealed some of my strongest feelings. . .out of embarrassment, I suppose. Since I arrived, Andrew aroused my interest, and now, I'm very fond of him."

To Livy's astonishment, a smile lit Helen's face.

"I tried not dream about it. He's handsome and fun, and many attractive woman vie for his attention. I'm quiet and restrained, not his type at all. Yesterday he made me blush like a schoolgirl."

Helen frowned. "Nothing inappropriate, Olivia, I pray."

"Oh no, compliments. Lovely things no man has ever said before."

Helen chuckled. "Ah, I feel better."

"But yesterday, Helen, after dinner, he asked me to help hang the mistletoe . . .and he—"

"He kissed you!"

"Yes, the kiss was wonderful, better than I've dreamed, but it was more than a kiss. He said he *loved* me."

Helen bounded from her seat and wrapped her arms around Livy. "This is even better than I dreamed. At tea when I said maybe your visit had answered my prayers, this was my hope—that Andrew and you would fall in love."

Livy's mind spun. She'd been so certain it was the heart that had answered Helen's prayers.

"I saw a spark of interest in Andrew's eyes when you arrived," Helen continued. "I've always hoped he'd find a charming Christian woman, but he had his own mind. And he's an adult. I couldn't sway him. But I prayed that God would. And you see, my prayers are answered." Helen quieted, then peered at Livy. "You do love him, Olivia? I pray you didn't spend the night wondering how to tell him you don't love him."

"No, no, that's not my problem. I'm afraid I love him *too* much. That my feelings are only passion and not real, lasting love. I've imagined his lips on mine and his arms holding me close—emotions that I know God doesn't approve."

Helen sank onto the cushion beside her. "Don't you know that God created both love and passion? He directs a man and wife to share the intimacy of their lives. It's only when we step beyond our marital beds that God becomes angry. Weigh your feelings for Andrew, Olivia. Do you think only of his lips on yours? Or, do you picture a life together, sharing all the joys and sorrows of marriage?"

Livy's clenched hand covered her heart. "I've compared it all: sickness, health, trials, joys, work, play, everything that happens."

Helen patted her hand. "Then if you can accept it all, God's blessed you with both love and passion. Not all marriages are built on both."

Livy released a deep sigh. "I should talk with Andrew. I didn't respond very well to him." She paused, her interest drawn to the dresser top. As the keepsake tugged at her curiosity, a shiver rippled down her arms. "Helen, when you said my visit might be an answer to your prayer, I suspected you referred to the package I brought you from John. It was half the heart on your dresser, wasn't it?"

Livy expected anger or distress, but a tender smile rose to Helen's lips. "Yes, it was the heart, but it wasn't the keepsake that I referred to. My prayer was you and Andrew. The heart's a different story altogether. Would you like to hear it, Livy? It might explain what I was talking about the other day."

"Please, tell me, Helen," Livy said, edging forward, eager to hear her explanation.

"I think it makes a rich closure to our discussion." She settled into the chair. "Your brother, John, and I knew each other *before* I became Ruth's friend. We were neighbors and played together as children. But when we became aware of each other as a man and woman—I should say boy and girl—things changed. We fell in love." She smiled. "Or so we thought."

John and Helen? Livy's pulse raced.

"He was a wonderful woodcarver, like Charles, and maybe that's what brought about their friendship. For a birthday gift when I was fifteen, John carved the heart and divided it in half. We shared each other's heart, he said, and when we married our hearts would become one."

"Helen, I never knew John to be so romantic."

"Oh yes, he was. Very romantic. But the story continues. Around the same time, Ruth came into my life. So she became part of John's life, too. Ruth was frail. She had a weak heart, and John—you know how kind he is—was always around to help her or encourage her on.

"Soon, John spent more time with Ruth than with me. I was angry, I'm ashamed to admit, and wished terrible things on Ruth. But one day, I realized that God guides our walk in life. John, with his patience and quiet gentleness, was a perfect husband for Ruth, not for me. Then I noticed Charles. . .and Charles noticed me."

The story had captured Livy's imagination. "Was he the spark that became a flame?"

"Ah yes, like a match struck to yellowed paper. Our love ignited about as quickly. We were young, but God guided us to marry. And, Olivia, I'll never be sorry. Not for one moment. God's will was best for me. . .and for Ruth and John, too. He's made her a fine husband."

So caught in the story, Livy gasped for air. "But what about the heart? Why did he return it now?"

"Oh, I suppose he found it after all these years, tucked somewhere in his belongings. I don't know, but I was touched when I saw it. Touched because he gave back my heart. He reminded me in the dearest way that we're both whole and complete in our lives as we live them now."

"You don't think he's loved you these past years?" Livy whispered.

"My, my, no, Olivia. He's loved Ruth forever. Your brother is such a gentleman, a good man. He would never be unfaithful, nor would I. God guided us as I believe He's guided you."

Livy flung her arms around Helen's neck. "Like you said, sometimes God sends people on a path they hadn't planned to travel. I think my path was here."

Helen squeezed Livy's hand. "And I can't tell you how happy I am."

～

A tap on Livy's door brought her to her feet. When she opened it, Andrew grinned, holding a large package. "Delivery from the tailor shop," he said, his dimples deepening. "I imagine you've been waiting for this."

"Or I'd be wearing rags this evening," she said. For the first time, she looked at Andrew without a nagging fear or frightening questions.

She moved away from the door, and he stepped inside, placing the large parcel on her bed. As she moved past him, he caught her hand. "Have you been thinking, Livy?"

"I have. A great deal. . .in fact, all night long."

"Me, too," he said, laughing. "And can you tell me your thoughts?"

"I might," she said, "and then I might not."

"Livy, your smile takes my breath away. I'll wait. You'll tell me when you're ready. . .but I know your answer. You can't hide it from me." He strolled from the room, leaving a portion of his happiness lingering behind.

Livy unwrapped her gowns and hung them, choosing the violet frock for the evening. Time was short, and she saw to Davy, and then dressed for the Christmas Eve celebration. Tonight was one to truly celebrate—a night of love, God's gift of love, His Son born to save the world, and her own gift of love for Andrew.

When she'd completed her toilette, she took Davy's hand, and they descended the stairs. As they reached the bottom step, Grace called the family for dinner. Though the meal was tasty, Livy felt like a child, waiting for the moments following dinner.

Finally, Charles stood, offering a Christmas prayer, and they followed him to the hall outside the parlor. In anticipation, Davy jiggled from foot to foot. When Charles swung the French doors open, Livy reveled in the spectacular Christmas tree.

Davy rushed forward while Livy controlled her desire to join him. She marveled at the candles glowing from every branch. She felt childlike as she approached the towering tree that radiated light, reminding her of the star of Bethlehem. Beneath the tree, packages stood wrapped in brown paper, cloth, or lace all tied with ribbons and bows. Nearby a water-filled bucket stood with the rag mop to douse any possible fire.

"Livy, would you lead us tonight? Why don't we sing a carol," Charles suggested, stroking his mustache. "What will it be, Helen?"

" 'Silent Night,' " she said, stepping forward and taking Charles's hand, then Davy's. "It's my favorite."

Livy grasped Davy's free hand, and Andrew stepped to her left and slid his fingers through hers. As they clasped hands around the tree, Livy sang the first notes of the carol, and they joined her. Tears welled in Livy's eyes. She'd never experienced this kind of happiness. Her life seemed complete.

When the song ended Davy was the first to open his presents. From the first wrapper he pulled a strange contraption that Charles explained was a stereopticon. Livy had heard Queen Victoria had taken a fancy to them, but this was the first she'd seen.

"See the cards, Davy," Helen coached. "Put one in the machine and look at the picture."

Livy removed a card from the package and slid it into the brackets. Davy held it to his eyes and let out a squeal. "It flew at me," he said in wonder. "Look, Aunt Livy."

Livy lifted the contraption and gasped while laughter rang around the room.

When Livy finished her last gift, Andrew slipped another into her hand, a small package wrapped in brown paper tied with a lace ribbon. Inside the package lay a hand-carved angel, delicate and detailed. She eyed Charles, but he shook his head and nodded toward Andrew.

"You carved this?" Livy asked, gaping.

He grinned.

"Yourself?" She eyed the exquisite detail again. "I'm impressed. No, amazed. It's beautiful." She pressed the tiny carving to her chest. "Thank you, I'll cherish it."

"You're an angel, Livy. It seemed right."

"I love it. It's my very own Christmas treasure." She looked toward Helen who smiled with understanding.

While they thanked each other for the gifts, Grace appeared at the doorway with a tray of hot chocolate and a plate of Christmas desserts. Livy longed to speak with Andrew, but the family's excitement continued without a break. She knew her talk would wait until Christmas Day.

Chapter 10

Christ Church radiated with candle glow, garland, and wreaths. Following the service, Helen sent Andrew to tell the Dailys what time they should arrive for Christmas dinner. Livy cringed inwardly, wondering how Agatha would react when she learned of her new relationship with Andrew. She hoped to spare the young woman embarrassment.

As they left the building, Roger approached her and murmured in her ear. "Andrew told me the news. I am happy for you, Livy. You deserve a fine man like Andrew."

Embarrassed, she mumbled her thanks, but when she stepped outside, she filled with relief. If Roger knew, then Agatha would be forewarned.

As the bays trotted along the street, snowflakes drifted from the sky like downy feathers. Arriving home, Andrew beckoned Livy to remain in the sleigh. "Mother, Father, I thought I'd take Livy for a short ride."

Charles patted Andrew's arm with a sly grin. "Let me send out a buffalo robe for you."

Helen didn't hide her pleasure. "I'll take Davy inside. We have many more stereopticon cards to view, don't we?"

When he agreed and followed Helen into the house, Livy was grateful. In a moment, the stableboy rushed out with a heavy lap robe, and Andrew took the reins, guiding the horses onto the roadway.

Gliding through the fresh snow, Andrew drew a nervous breath. He gathered the straps in one hand and wrapped his free hand around Livy's. His heart swelled at their nearness. When they reached the river, he turned the bays along the shore until they approached a small grove of trees that blocked the wind, and he reined the horses to a standstill. He marveled at the hazy golden sun making diamonds on the falling snow. Wrapping his arm around Livy, he nestled closer to her side, and she cuddled nearer.

"Could we talk?" His heart thundered in his ears. "I hoped we might be ready to—"

"I wanted to talk with you last evening, but the time never seemed right."

Praying her words were what he longed to hear, he waited, suspended until he could no longer tolerate the silence. "And what do you have to tell me, Livy?"

"I do love you, Andrew."

"Oh Livy, you've made me the happiest man on earth. Then you'll marry me?" He captured her face against his palm.

"Yes."

"Soon?" he asked, awed by her radiant face.

"Soon."

He drew her into the fold of his arms, and Livy embraced him fully. He lowered his mouth to hers, and she yielded to his kiss. Though the cold wind blew past the sleigh, Andrew's body warmed and ignited with love for the cherished woman in his arms. When they withdrew, he faltered, seeing the look of concern on Livy's face.

"We're not free of problems though, Andrew. I know my life will be lonely when you're away at the logging camp, winter after winter. And though I don't know exactly, I'd imagine a lumberjack doesn't make a large income. So I've thought about it and decided I'd move here soon and teach music. I enjoy it very much, so it'll be no problem. By the time we're married, I'll make—"

He couldn't halt the laughter that rose in his throat, and when it escaped, Livy's face blanched, then she glowered. "I don't think you should laugh at me, Andrew. I'm being sincere in my—"

His heart soared at her willingness to share the family responsibilities. "I'm not laughing at you, dearest, dearest Livy. I'm not a lumberjack."

She gaped at his statement.

"I own the logging company, my love. You'll be a wealthy woman one day, I'm certain. But please, teach music if you'd enjoy it. I'll never ask you to give up something you love. I'm not that proud."

She covered her face. "I'm mortified. I didn't know."

"Don't be embarrassed. I thank God for your generosity. And Livy, this will be my last full winter at the camp. Now, with three years experience, I'll hire a competent manager, and most of the cold winter nights I'll be at your side. I love you, Livy."

Livy's face shone with a radiance, he'd never seen before. "We can marry in June," Andrew said. "Would you like that?"

"I'd *love* that." She pulled her warm hand from the furry muff and caressed his icy cheek.

"Then let's hurry home," he said. "Our announcement will be another gift to my parents. 'Olivia Schuler has consented to give me her hand in marriage.'"

With Livy nestled to his side, Andrew cracked the whip, moving the bays back to the roadway and hurrying home to share the news.

Epilogue

On a warm Tuesday evening in early June, the bridal party gathered inside Christ Church. As the organ's rich tones filled the sanctuary, the bridesmaids and groomsmen marched with measured steps down the aisle.

To Livy's great joy, Ruth's recuperation was amazing, and today, in the place of Livy's mother, Ruth followed the attendants on Andrew's arm. Livy caught her breath at his striking appearance in an elegant morning coat and sky-blue cravat.

With her arm linked to John's, Livy waited. Her wedding dress, an exquisite Paris gown of ivory tulle and lace with its fitted bodice, was a gift from Helen and Charles. Behind a fashionable bustle, the skirt draped to an extensive train.

On her dark curls, Livy wore a lace veil belonging to Helen. Earlier as she dressed, Livy had stared in the glass, amazed at the extraordinary woman who peered back at her.

On John's arm, his loving smile echoed her own happiness. As the organ swelled and pealed the bride's processional, she took her first step toward the altar. John pressed her hand covered with a lace glove, and Livy's heart lifted with a joy she knew they both felt.

In her left arm, she carried a lovely bouquet of lilies, stephanotis, and orange blossoms, a gift from Andrew. Inside the bouquet, she had attached the tiny carved angel, the keepsake Andrew had given her at Christmas. As she made her way past family and friends, the flowers' sweet fragrance surrounded her.

On a Sunday before the wedding, Andrew had surprised her with a wedding gift—a lovely teardrop diamond pendant that today hung around her neck on a gold chain. She'd never known such luxury or such love.

When they reached the altar, John presented her to Andrew, then joined Ruth in the front pew. With Andrew's hand on hers, the pastor's words filled her heart with assurance. "'Charity suffereth long, and is kind; charity envieth not; charity vaunteth not itself, is not puffed up, doth not behave itself unseemly, seeketh not her own, is not easily provoked, thinketh no evil; rejoiceth not in iniquity, but rejoiceth in the truth; beareth all things, believeth all things, hopeth all things, endureth all things.'

"'Charity never faileth.'"

Andrew riveted to the pastor's words. "'When I was a child, I spake as a child, I understood as a child, I thought as a child: but when I became a man, I put away childish things.'" He recalled his past foolish behavior and the foolish notion that Livy was plain and demure.

Today, her dark hair, crowned by the fragile veil, highlighted her delicacy. She was a woman of beauty, spirit, and deep affection. She completed his life with joy and love.

The pastor's voice rose, "'And now abideth faith, hope, charity, these three.'" Andrew sought Livy's face, and at that moment, the Word of God wrapped them in complete oneness. "'But the greatest of these is charity.'" Looking into each other's eyes, Andrew desired no other treasure in his life, only their vows of steadfast and undying love.

For the Love of a Child

Sally Laity

Chapter 1

Angelina Matthews closed the back door of Mistress Haversham's Dress Shop behind her and stepped cautiously out onto Front Street. A frigid December wind, fraught with dampness from the Delaware River a stone's throw away, flung icy shards of falling snow mercilessly against her face. Switching her lantern to her other hand, she gave her scarf an extra wrap and buried her nose deeper into its confines. Then she set off through the growing darkness toward her rented house on Elfreth's Alley.

On either side, the shops and warehouses lay dark and silent. *No doubt the other businesses had closed early, at the very onset of the storm,* she surmised with irritation. If only Mistress Haversham afforded her employees the same consideration! But with the Christmas festivities fast approaching, there were endless orders for new party frocks. And unless Angelina and Ruby, the other hired seamstress, toiled until closing time every day, the gowns would never be finished on schedule.

Angelina sought the likeliest route through the gathering drifts, bolstering herself against the pain in her withered leg as she limped over the uneven cobbles. Once she reached home, a grand fire in the hearth and a pot of hot tea would erase the misery of this blizzard from her mind for the night. Tomorrow, thankfully, was Saturday, and she wouldn't have to be at work until noon. If it weren't December, she would have had the entire day free.

The wind howled over the narrow street—an eerie, almost human whine that whistled around the brick and stone buildings, leaving snow in its wake. Angelina shivered and pressed on.

The wind wailed louder—but another sound mixed with the storm's ghostly moan, and she paused to listen. What was that? A cry?

Holding her breath, she raised her lantern high, peering beyond the scant circles of light cast by the gas lamps. Perhaps a kitten had gotten lost, she mused, straining to hear over the fury of the elements.

The sound came again, stronger. . .and almost sounded like a plaintive "Mama. . ." She shook her head. It had to be her imagination.

But as each step brought her closer to the source of the cries, they became all the more recognizable. All the more wrenching. Ahead, Angelina made out a small shape huddled between the bare branches of a shrub and a vacant warehouse. She moved toward it as quickly as her weakened leg would allow and held the light aloft.

Her breath caught in her throat. A child!

She bent to touch the little one's shoulder. "I'll help you, dear," she crooned.

The young girl of about three started and looked up, then let out an ear-shattering wail.

"Shh, shh," Angelina coaxed. The child's threadbare coat looked at least a size too small and did little to protect the spindly arms or legs. Setting down the lantern, Angelina bent down and gathered the shivering form close. "What on earth are you doing out in this storm?" she asked, as much to the heavens themselves as to the child.

"C–c–cold!" the little girl chattered, swallowing a sob.

Angelina removed her scarf and tied it about the short, damp curls, then unbuttoned her long wool coat and picked up the urchin. Tucking her against the warmth of her own body, she wrapped the thin little legs as best she could. She couldn't imagine from whence the youngster had come, or what circumstances might have cast her alone in this dark business district. But she had far more urgent matters to consider, like getting help. Now. But from where?

St. Joseph's Church was known around the city for providing refuge to the downtrodden and dispossessed. . .but even if Angelina left the lantern behind, she could not possibly carry the little girl all the way to Willing's Alley. And Christ Church was also much too far to get to in a blizzard.

Then she recalled a smaller house of worship Ruby had mentioned one day, where occasional homeless souls had been given shelter. On Second, wasn't it? Just the next street over and not really out of her way. Once the little girl had been deposited in the care of the person in charge, Angelina could continue up the street and enter Elfreth's Alley the back way.

Thus decided, she tightened her hold on the little one and started toward the church, the wind whipping her own dark tresses in every direction as she went.

"What's your name, sweetheart?" she asked, trying to keep the child calm as she labored toward Second Street.

"N–Noely." The breathless voice was almost a whisper.

"Noely?" Angelina repeated, and felt the small head nod against her shoulder. "My, that's a pretty name. I'm Angelina." She paused. "Does your mama know you're outside in the dark, Noely?"

A leftover sob racked the tiny frame.

"Well, I'll take you to some nice people who can help you find her, dear."

Noely sniffed.

For such a little thing, she was surprisingly heavy, and Angelina tired by the minute. Surely it couldn't be too much farther.

At last the brick structure loomed into view. With renewed strength she trudged across the intersection separating them. The church sat in darkness, but warm lamplight glowed from the appealing two-story house next door. She hoped it was the parsonage. Shifting Noely's weight to her right arm, Angelina lifted the brass knocker and rapped.

Astounded that anyone could be out on such a night, Gabe Winters laid aside his Bible and sermon notes and hurried to answer the summons, ill-prepared for the arctic blast that stole his breath. On the stoop stood a fragile, dark-haired young woman with the most exquisite features he had ever seen. Her luminous brown eyes peered up at him through a fringe of long lashes. In her arms she carried a young child. . .and both of them were flocked head to toe with snow. Realizing he was gawking, Gabe quickly yanked the door wide and stepped back. "Please come inside. Warm yourselves by the fire."

"Thank you," the woman breathed. She entered, setting the little one down.

As they gravitated to the hearth, Gabe closed the door, then went to the hall. "Aunt Clara," he called up the staircase. "Any of that hot cocoa still left?"

"Sure an' there is," came her reply, the *r*'s rolling smoothly from her Irish brogue. "I'll be fetchin' it right away."

When he returned to the parlor, he found the pair kneeling before the blazing warmth. The little one's wet outerwear had already been shed, and now she extended her hands toward the heat. He switched his attention to the woman. "What might I do for you and your little girl?"

"Oh!" she gasped. "She isn't mine. I only just found her shivering outside in the storm. I thought perhaps you might help her. You are a minister, are you not?"

He nodded. "Gabe Winters. I pastor the Baptist church here. And you're—"

"Forgive me, Reverend," she murmured, rosy patches heightening those the fire had already called forth on her fine cheekbones. "Angelina Matthews. I'm a seamstress on Front Street. And this is Noely," she added, turning the little girl to face him. "But I'm afraid that's all I know."

Gabe had no reason to doubt her word, but even if he had, the uncertainty would have evaporated as he compared her and the child. Noely's complexion was fair, nowhere near the rich olive tones of Miss Matthews. Nor were her huge blue eyes in the slightest way similar to the expressive doe-like ones of her rescuer. The girl's features—far from being delicately feminine—were stark, almost too mature for her little face, yet Gabe had no doubt she would grow into them one day.

On the other hand, he couldn't help wondering why someone as fetching as Angelina Matthews would find necessity to be employed, rather than married and a mother herself.

Her voice cut across his contemplations. "The child hasn't told me about her parents. She cried when I inquired after them."

"Well now, little Noely," he said, sinking to one knee beside her. "Once we've managed to get you all warm and dry, perhaps you'll tell us a few things about yourself."

She tucked her chin and inched shyly against Miss Matthews.

Aunt Clara bustled in just then, bearing a tray. She set it on a lamp table, then passed steaming mugs around. "This has got extra milk, darlin'," she said, giving one to the child, "so it'll not be burnin' your tongue. Are ye hungry?"

Noely gave a slow nod.

"Well then, we'll be settin' that problem to rights. Come see what we can find, will ye now?" She held out a hand.

Huge wary eyes sought those of Miss Matthews for encouragement, then she hesitantly put her small fingers inside the older woman's plump ones. The two of them ambled toward the kitchen, with Noely intent upon not spilling the cocoa she clutched in her other hand.

Gabe caught the furtive glance the youngster cast over her shoulder before exiting the parlor with his motherly aunt. He switched his attention to the dark-haired woman a few feet away. Her long, loose waves, held back at each side in pearl combs, were already beginning to dry. "So the little thing hasn't told you how or why she happened to be caught out in the weather."

"Not a word." She drank the remainder of the warm drink, then rose stiffly to her feet. "And since she'll be in such good hands, there is no reason for me to stay longer. In fact, it might be best if she didn't see me leave. I shall trust her to your care and be on my way. Thank you for your hospitality—and your aunt's of course."

"But the storm—"

The young woman leaned over to retrieve the short cape and the scarf from the braided rug, then she deftly put them on. "I'll be fine. I live not far from here." She hobbled across the room.

Gabe's heart caught at the sight of her ungainly walk. He easily beat her to the door. "I do thank you, Miss Matthews, for bringing the child to us. We'll do our best to discover the whereabouts of her parents. And until then, we'll take very good care of her, be assured of that."

"I have no doubt of it. Goodnight, Reverend."

"God be with you, miss."

෴

Leaving the comfortably furnished brick home behind, Angelina realized her last comment had been made in all honesty. The warmth she had found at the parsonage had every bit as much to do with the loving atmosphere as it did the burning logs in the fireplace. The sandy-haired pastor—she smiled to herself recalling the giant he had seemed, towering over her and Noely—probably had to duck his head to go out the door! But his kindly face had a certain openness about it, a gentle appeal, especially with the merry twinkle radiating from his clear blue eyes.

And something about his aunt Clara reminded Angelina of her own mother. Not so much the woman's stature, but her manner and bearing, her soothing voice. They awakened memories Angelina only remembered in hazy snatches. Noely should be fine there until her parents could be contacted. Thus comforted, she picked her way carefully through the snowdrifts.

Finally turning onto Elfreth, where simple row houses appeared to nestle against one another for warmth, she used the glow from the windows to get her bearing as she made her way to her own residence, the second from the end. It was nowhere near as grand as the homey abode she had so recently left, she conceded, and it would be cold and dark after sitting empty all day, but at least the wind would be kept at bay while a fire took hold. She unlocked the door and entered, lit the lamps, then disposed quickly of her wet clothes. Once she had replaced them with a warm nightgown and flannel wrapper, she padded to the small, plain parlor to start the fire.

Heat from the crackling logs soon eradicated the chill. Angelina unwrapped the heavy blanket with which she had enshrouded herself and poured a cup of tea to have with her bread and cheese. No doubt little Noely had enjoyed a grand feast, but no one could begrudge her that. . .poor little thing. What could her parents have been thinking, to allow such a young child to wander about on her own? She only hoped the Reverend Winters would give them a sound talking-to when he found them.

Angelina's thoughts lingered for a time on the pastor as she contemplated his sensitive manner. *Curious*, she thought, *such a nice-looking man without a wife— or the woman surely would have been home on a night such as this!* But at least his aunt was there to take charge of a child's welfare. Angelina could almost picture the older woman fussing over Noely, tucking her into a feather bed piled with quilts, tending to her every need.

Yes, she surmised with a yawn, the little girl would probably have the time of her life at the parsonage, then be reunited with her own family. In time she wouldn't even remember getting lost in a blizzard. No reason Angelina shouldn't forget the whole affair herself, really.

But warm thoughts of a nice pastor—and even more disturbing ones of a heart-stealing little girl—weren't so easily turned away.

Chapter 2

A shaft of sunlight slanted across Angelina's bed, right into her eyes. Turning her head away, she yawned and stretched, flung the patchwork quilt aside and rose, slipping into her warm wrapper and knitted slippers. Then she padded to the window.

Beneath the clear blue sky, a two-foot blanket of downy snow glistened as if studded with millions of diamonds. It was hard to believe the elements had put on such a wild show last night—or that she had slept until ten. Now long icicles hung from the eaves of every building, dripping in the blazing sun. Most of the goodwives in the neighborhood had already swept their stoops, Angelina noticed, and bundled children frolicked in the snowdrifts. Undoubtedly their white wonderland would diminish with each hour, turning quickly into dreary slush and mud. But in the meanwhile, the little ones would take full advantage.

Angelina smiled. The sight was so like her own sweet childhood. . .until the carriage accident had turned her whole world upside down. Never would she forget waking up in the hospital that awful day, her whole body racked with unspeakable pain from her shattered left leg. But far worse an agony was learning that her mother had died instantly, and her father, who had lingered for several hours, had succumbed as well.

After being transported to the orphan asylum for the remainder of her childhood, Angelina was granted precious few carefree moments to cherish.

Sloughing off memories which could so easily swamp her in bitterness, she hurried downstairs to stoke up the fire in the stove and make porridge and tea. Then she ate slowly, mulling over the previous night's events in her mind.

How had little Noely fared? Angelina had tried in vain to banish the mental image of the sweet face turned fearfully toward her while being ushered to the kitchen. Angelina had hoped to prevent the pain of parting by taking her leave unnoticed. But whether that had been a wise move, she could only wonder.

Noely's parents must have been frantic when they discovered their little girl missing. Hopefully there would be a grand reunion before the day was spent.

Oh well, what was done was done. Perhaps sometime next week she would drop by the parsonage and ask after the little girl. That decided, she filled a pitcher with warm water and ascended the stairs to her bedroom. She had yet to freshen up and dress for the extra half-day's work required each week in December.

An hour later, she arrived at the dress shop. Tucked between that of a candle-maker and a leathercraft store, Mistress Haversham's tiny endeavor had but one big window facing Front Street. Each month it displayed a new and attractive ensemble in current vogue, complete with the latest accessories to show it off to perfection.

The charming main room with its counter, two fitting rooms, and a niche with a velvet settee and round lamp table had already been tidied for the day, she noted upon entering, but all seemed unusually quiet as she went on through to the cramped back room.

In stark contrast to the outer room's neatness, the work room fairly overflowed with dress patterns, fashion catalogs, colorful bolts of fabric, and assorted buttons and fancy trims. Works in progress draped every available spot.

Frail, auburn-haired Ruby Chambers looked up from the emerald velvet sleeve she was pinning to the bodice of a partially finished gown on the dress form. "Hi, Angie."

"Mistress Haversham isn't here?" Angelina asked, hanging her coat on the rack by the back door.

"Came in to open up," the girl mumbled around the straight pins clamped between her lips, "then went to deliver that burnished gold silk frock we finished yesterday to uppity Mrs. Worthingham. Personally."

"I see."

"That lady is nothin' short of a bother." Ruby jabbed the final dress pin into place, then nudged her spectacles higher with a free finger. "Always has Mistress in such a dither, comin' by every day without fail to check on her gown. You'd think hers was the only order to be done before Christmas!"

Angelina nodded. "Has the hem been marked yet?" she asked, indicating the emerald gown.

"Mm-hmm. All pinned and ready. That and the sleeves are all that's left."

"I'll help you, then, and we'll be able to cross one more off the list." Moving to the cluttered worktable, she retrieved a pin cushion and a spool of thread, then eased down onto a stool at the foot of the dress form. She threaded her needle and deftly knotted the end.

"My, that was some tempest blowed through last night," Ruby exclaimed. "Come near to bein' buried in a snowdrift 'fore I made it home. Percy got there five minutes sooner and was just about to come lookin' for me."

Angelina shot her an understanding smile. "I arrived home a little late myself. I had to take a detour."

"In that storm? Whatever for?"

"It's a long story."

"Well, we got half a day, you know, and Mistress won't be back for at least an hour. She'll be wantin' to fit that gown herself to make sure it suits her highness."

"You're right." Angelina took a deep breath, gathering her thoughts as she worked. "It was the most unexpected thing. Partway home I thought I heard what sounded like a cry. When I went to investigate, I found a child—a little girl—stranded outside."

"No!" Ruby's mouth dropped open. She wrinkled her nose twice to nudge her spectacles higher as Angelina gave a solemn nod. "What'd you do? The orphanage is way across town."

"And that's the last place I'd take a child anyway," Angelina stated flatly. "I know firsthand what it's like. I took her to the Baptist church you told me about, on Second."

"I declare." Pulling a basting thread to ease the fullness of the sleeve she was attaching, the painfully thin seamstress peered down at Angelina. "The pastor's decent enough, from what I hear around. He'll find a home for the orphan right quick."

"Actually, I'm not sure she is an orphan. She barely uttered a word. All I found out was her first name." Remembrances of last evening brought a smile. "Noely, she said it was. The little thing's so plain she's really quite endearing."

Ruby grimaced. "Odd way of puttin' it, if I do say so."

"Perhaps. Anyway, I thought I'd go by in a few days and see what became of her. She was on my mind all through the night." Concentrating on her task, Angelina added a few more stitches.

"Why wait so long?"

She met her coworker's green eyes straight on and considered the remark. "Why, indeed! I'll go home that way again tonight. Pastor Winters and his aunt shouldn't mind my concern. . .after all, I did find the child. Naturally I'd be interested in her welfare."

The thought of putting her mind to rest about Noely carried her through the remainder of the day as she and Ruby finished not only the emerald velvet but a cranberry taffeta as well, much to their employer's delight. And to their own delight, they were dismissed half an hour early.

This time the sky wasn't so dark when Angelina reached the redbrick building with its pristine steeple. She admired the black shutters on the charming parsonage and the neat window boxes which, come spring, would surely overflow with flowers, if she were any judge of the minister's aunt. Angelina's pulse accelerated. She hoped her appearance wouldn't seem an intrusion. But no one could object to her merely asking about Noely. Bolstering her courage, she paused on the stoop to rest her leg momentarily before rapping with the brass knocker.

She'd forgotten how tall the minister was until the light from the parlor lamps outlined the sandy-haired giant's form in the doorway. She swallowed.

"Yes?" Then as recognition dawned, Pastor Winters grinned. "Oh! Miss Matthews. Come in, come in."

"Thank you, Reverend." She stepped past him as he held the door. "I've just come to inquire after—"

A childish shriek sounded from the dining room. Noely, seated at the table with the Reverend's aunt, charged toward the entry and flung her arms about Angelina's waist. "Ang'lina! Ang'lina! You came back! I cried and cried when you went away."

Distressed at the sad pronouncement, Angelina found confirmation in the minister's expression. She bent to hug the little girl. "Oh Noely, I'm truly sorry. I was only trying to help. I thought you would be fine with these kind people."

The child's lower lip protruded. "But I wanted you. Don't go away again. Say you won't. Please, please." A slight lisp enhanced her plea, as did a harder hug.

"There, there, sweetheart. I don't live here, you know. I had to go home to my house before there was too much snow to find my way."

Pastor Winters patted the curly head. "How about going back and finishing your supper, Noely? Miss Matthews and I need to talk."

"But then she'll go away again, and I don't want her to." A flood of tears made her doleful eyes swim as she turned her gaze upward and clutched Angelina's hand in both of hers.

"I'll stay for a little while, honey," Angelina promised. "But when it's time, I really must go to my own house. Do be a good girl and mind the minister. For me."

Noely stood firm for several seconds before finally relenting. Her lips in a definite downward tilt, she trudged back to the dining room table, where the pastor's kindly aunt helped her up onto the pillowed chair she'd vacated.

Angelina tipped her head and smiled at the plump older woman, then limped after Gabe Winters, observing things on this visit that she had missed the previous night. She took a seat on a wine-colored settee, whose rich hues were picked up by the multicolored braided rug occupying much of the plank floor.

"I'm glad you came by," he said quietly, lowering his bulk to one of the wing chairs flanking the hearth.

"I do hope Noely wasn't an awful bother," Angelina began.

He raised a large, broad hand. "No, no, not at all. She was fine. She was upset to discover you weren't here, of course, but Aunt Clara managed to get her settled down again. A warm bath and some hot food, and she was asleep before she knew it."

The news was comforting. "Did she say where you might find her parents?"

His countenance sobered. "From what she told us, there are none. Her mother 'got sick and went away' as she put it, some time ago. Then her father became ill also. Noely said when 'some people came and took him away' yesterday, she ran as fast and as far as she could so no one would get her and never bring her back. Then she couldn't remember the way home. She doesn't know of any aunts or uncles or other relatives." He smiled. "Noely thought you were an angel come to save her. In a way, I would have to agree."

Angelina would have smiled if she could. But the information was far more dire than she had hoped. Her heart went out to the little waif. "Please, Reverend . . .don't put her in the asylum," she pleaded in a whisper. "It's no place for—"

"You needn't worry about that," he assured her. "There are any number of families in my congregation who might be in a position to take her in. I'll bring the matter up at service tomorrow and see what transpires."

"But what if—?"

He shook his head. "I'll do everything within my power to find Noely a good home, a loving family. You have my word, Miss Matthews."

"Thank you," Angelina breathed, finally able to relax against the burgundy upholstery.

The minister's aunt came into the parlor just then, a gracious smile crinkling the pleasant features beneath a coronet of salt-and-pepper braids. "We'd love to be havin' ye to supper, miss, if ye've a mind to stay. I'm sure little Noely would like to have ye visit for a while."

Angelina bolted upright. "Oh, thank you. But I mustn't impose. I should get home before it's too dark."

"Stuff and nonsense," she declared with a wave of her hand. "Me nephew would be more than willin' to see ye safely home. Ye wouldn't want to disappoint a wee lassie."

Meeting a pair of huge, hopeful eyes in the next room, Angelina could do nothing but accept. "Well, this time, perhaps, if you're quite certain I'm not putting you out. But I don't intend to make a pest of myself after this."

"There's no danger of that, miss, to be sure. This house could use a few more young faces around from time to time."

Angelina had no sooner nodded her acceptance than the minister stood and offered her a hand. The homey meal did smell delicious. . .something she had tried not to notice in view of having to go to her own cold, dark house in the very near future.

As Reverend Winters seated her at a newly laid place setting, his aunt served a plate heaped with roast beef and mashed potatoes—fare Angelina never troubled to cook for herself.

"I kept yours warm in the oven," the woman said, returning her nephew's partially eaten portion before him. "Now I'd say grace is in fine order again, don't ye think, Noely?"

"Yes!" She lisped, clapping in childlike delight. Then she grew serious and clasped her fingers, her head bowed.

"Our Father," the pastor prayed, "we do thank You most kindly for sending our friend Miss Matthews to visit us this evening. We pray Your gentle hand will be always upon her for her kindness to our little Noely, and ask Your blessing upon this bounty before us. This we ask in the name of Your Son, amen."

The simple, heartfelt prayer warmed Angelina inside in a way she had never before experienced. The man prayed as if the Almighty were his personal friend. And somehow, she believed God truly listened to the requests that came from such a sincere heart as his. Raising her head, she met the minister's merry blue eyes, and she felt a flush heat her face.

"I'm happy you're here, Ang'lina," Noely said, beaming from ear to ear, her upper lip lightly coated with milk from the glass she had just set down.

"I am, too, sweetheart," she heard herself say. . .and lost herself in the delectable tastes of the Irishwoman's cooking and the pleasant company about the table. That was far less awkward than imagining herself being escorted homeward soon by this man she'd barely met. . .who, she had to admit, seemed to possess a refreshing, gentle manner for someone so large. Sensing his gaze on her, she quickly turned to smile at Noely.

Chapter 3

Is Ang'lina coming to church?" Noely asked, her voice echoing in the stillness of the sanctuary. Soft pastel light diffused by the stained glass windows cast irregular patches of color across her blond curls.

Clara O'Malley tugged the child comfortingly nearer on the hard wooden pew. "I've no way of knowin' that, darlin'. She may have her own church, ye know. We can't be makin' her come here."

Noely pouted. "But I miss her."

"I know, dearie. She's a fine, fine friend, to be sure. And she'll be back to visit us, wait and see. But ye must be quiet now in the House of the Lord." Seeing an obedient nod, Clara patted her little charge's knee. Noely looked quite nice in the somber but stylish dress that had turned up in the Poor Box. Gabe had even managed to unearth a fairly new pair of sturdy shoes and a warm coat, so with her meager undergarments washed and mended, the child was very presentable, if Clara did say so herself. Now one could only hope a suitable family would step forward when Gabe presented Noely before the congregation. Clara tamped down her trepidation and waved to the first arrivals trickling in to worship.

As each one took a seat, she felt a resurgence of doubt. The Stuarts did need help with chores, since the mister's heart was weak, but she was sure they'd specified a boy. And the Butterfields certainly couldn't feed another mouth. As Noely fidgeted beside her, Clara gave her a tiny hug.

Gabe took his place in the platform's middle chair as the organist played the opening notes of "Joy to the World," and beefy-shouldered Dell Taylor stepped to the pulpit. "That's a fine song to get us into the season," the jovial man announced. "Let's turn to page forty-nine in the hymnal and join in on the next run-through." He beat the tempo with one hand as he sang. "Joy to the world! The Lord is come. . . ."

Unable to concentrate on the words, Clara only half participated in that carol or the following one. And what was even more disturbing, for the first time in her life, personal concerns precluded her enjoyment of her nephew's sermon. She barely heard the text announced, let alone kept track of the points Gabe made in rendering the account of the Good Samaritan. All she could think about was the needy little girl beside her who so quickly had stolen their hearts. Surely the Lord had a special place in mind for Noely, a family who would love her and care for her as if she were their own. Breathing a prayer on the child's behalf, Clara was surprised when Gabe closed his big black Bible so soon and stepped alongside the pulpit.

"Folks," he began, "before we close the service in prayer, I have a rather important matter to bring to your attention." He turned to her and nodded. "Aunt Clara?"

Her heart beating double-time, she stood, took Noely's hand, and led her to the platform. The tiny fingers gripped hers so tightly they all but cut off the circulation as Noely sagged shyly against her. Clara thought she felt the child tremble.

"This is Noely Carroll," Gabe said, with a warm smile her way. "Sad to say, she has recently suffered the loss of both her parents. And as far as we have ascertained at this point, she has no relatives to take her in."

Scanning the faces in the audience, Clara spotted Lucinda Blackwell, Hortense Witherspoon, and Miranda Keys—the three Old Crows, as she irreverently referred to the black-clad biddies on widow's row—who sooner or later managed to find fault with everything and everyone at the church. The threesome hiked their scant eyebrows and exchanged significant looks. Clara averted her gaze.

"All we ask, dear friends," Gabe continued, "is for you to search your hearts. Perhaps one of you might be willing to make room in your family for this little one. Make it a matter of prayer this week—and come by the parsonage and get to know Noely. You won't be sorry, I assure you."

Several murmurs passed in the ranks, along with shrugs, nods, and shakes of the head.

None of them deterred him. "She is a very mannerly child, even quite helpful," he went on. "I'm sure anyone who would open his heart to her would be extremely thankful the Lord had sent such a dear little girl into his home. Thank you, sweetheart." Patting Noely's shoulder, he smiled at Clara and indicated for her to be seated. "Now let us close in prayer. . ."

᠅

"*Another* story?" Gabe, in feigned shock, adjusted Noely's weight to his other knee.

She nodded sleepily. "Please?"

Never one to resist a girlish lisp, he leafed through the big picture book he'd loved as a child, settling on the story of Noah. "'Once there was a man who loved God,'" he read. "'The people all around him, however, were far too busy to bother with building altars or making the sacrifices the Lord wanted. But they weren't too busy to make fun of Noah and his family. In fact—'" Gabe looked down at Noely, only to discover her eyes had closed. He smiled and laid the book aside.

"Poor tyke's tuckered out," his aunt declared from the rocker across the room, her knitting needles clicking away.

"It's been a long day."

"And not a soul came by to see her *or* us."

Gabe tipped his head in thought. "Well, not every member of the church attended services. I'll take Noely on my visits this week. Something's sure to turn up. In the meantime, I'd best tuck this little gal into bed." Gathering her easily into his arms, he stood and headed for the stairs.

"And I'll be puttin' on some tea," Aunt Clara offered as he passed. "While the water heats, we'll pray for the little dear. She makes a body wish hearts didn't wear out. I'd gladly live me life over again, just to watch her grow up."

Gabe could only agree with his ailing aunt's sentiments. She seemed in her glory around children, and had the clumsy oafishness of his youth not dampened both of the relationships he had hoped might lead to matrimony, Aunt Clara could be showering all that love on his own little daughter by now. But his hopes had been in vain. Oh well, he was approaching thirty already. . . much too old—and apparently *unappealing*, as an outspoken member of the opposite gender had once informed him—to inspire that sort of lasting bond. Now resigned to bachelorhood, he expended his energies in serving the Lord.

Flipping the layers of warm blankets aside, he gently placed Noely on the bed and covered her up. His gaze lingered on the peaceful innocence in her expression, and his heart crimped. She'd been noticeably subdued today, waiting and watching at the window for Angelina Matthews, but the young woman had never come. Granted, the distance was substantial enough for someone with her infirmity to walk unnecessarily. Perhaps she had spent the day resting at home. Tomorrow after work she'd be more likely to come by the parsonage. At least he hoped so. . .for Noely's sake, he quickly assured himself.

❧

Angelina, her leg propped up to keep it from aching, sipped the warm broth from her spoon as best she could in her awkward position, then gingerly tipped the spoon into the bowl of soup again. The wrapped bricks she'd heated at the fireplace usually soothed bouts of reoccurring pain, but this time they hardly made a difference. The slightest movement caused agonizing jabs almost beyond her ability to endure.

Well it was her own fault for being more hasty than cautious in her eagerness to visit Noely. She should have expected icy spots. The hard fall had severely wrenched her twisted leg. But at least it was Sunday, so she could rest.

Tomorrow her leg had to be better. She couldn't afford to miss a day's work, any more than her employer could have her do so. After all, Mistress Haversham had taken her on with the assurance that Angelina would be faithful in coming to work regardless of her withered leg. So far, the promise had been kept.

Today Reverend Winters had planned to present Noely to his congregation.

Angelina couldn't help wondering how the event had gone. She hadn't much use for church herself since childhood circumstances had raised serious doubts regarding a loving God. But all the same, she knew that many folks set a lot of store by their faith. Maybe among his flock of do-gooders someone would step in to provide a home for a destitute little girl. If Noely had a loving family, Angelina's own spirit would find rest.

In any event, she'd get to work tomorrow, then go home by way of Second Street. And she'd do the same every day after that, until the good Reverend or his aunt asked her not to. . .as long as that sweet little orphan child needed her. *If* she still needed her.

Finishing the remainder of the soup, Angelina braced herself for the painful journey upstairs to her bed.

Thankfully, morning brought measurable improvement, though her limb was far from feeling its best. With care, she could manage the long walk to work— and she would, if it was the last thing she ever did. With that determination, she dressed warmly and allowed extra time to hobble the long blocks to Front Street.

The day dragged as she and Ruby labored over the endless stack of party frocks. And her leg, which had seemed improved that morning, began its relentless aching by midday. When at last closing time arrived, Angelina was only too happy to set aside the butternut velvet gown and take down her coat.

Picking her way along the streets, she watched carefully for any icy patches and headed toward the parsonage of Second Street Baptist Church. It would be so good to see Noely again. She rapped on the door. Then rapped again.

Just as she turned to leave, the pastor answered the summons, a grin of vast relief spreading across his lips. "Miss Matthews! Come in, come in. I was about to be pressed into service by Aunt Clara—to help fit Noely with a dress! She'd be far better off with a woman's help. I have some letters to write anyway." He ushered her inside and took her coat.

"Certainly," Angelina said. "I'll do what I can."

He led her into the brightly lit kitchen, then inclined his head and retreated to the parlor.

A wondrous assortment of copper pots glinted from their hooks on the wall next to the big cookstove whose warmth quickly began to wrap itself around her sore limb. Observing a few unfamiliar and curious devices whose purposes she could only surmise, Angelina realized she had never seen such an efficient kitchen. And in the middle of it all was a wooden chair, with Noely standing like a statue on its seat.

"Ang'lina!" The child grinned from ear to ear, and looked on the verge of hopping down, but the older woman kept tight rein on the little one's skirt.

" 'Tis good of ye to come by," she gushed. "Dresses from the Poor Box always seem to need lettin' down or takin' up, I daresay, if not let out. Gabe's come up with three that still have a good bit of wear."

Examining one yet to be altered, Angelina held it up to Noely and nodded approvingly. "This shouldn't take much to fix."

"Not if ye lean toward such talents," the older woman commented, deep dimples appearing with her smile. "Some of us, on the other hand, discover our strengths blossom better before a cookstove. I haven't even started supper."

"Then I'd be only too happy to take over this chore, Mistress O'Malley, while you tend to yours."

Without hesitation, the older woman relinquished her pincushion and moved to the vegetable bin, where she began gathering potatoes to peel.

While Aunt Clara's back was turned, Noely smiled playfully and bent to administer a quick hug to Angelina, then just as swiftly straightened again.

"How have you been, sweetheart?" Angelina asked, assessing the portion of hem already pinned. After making a few minor adjustments, she continued around the remainder.

"You didn't come to church," the child announced flatly.

"And I'm sorry. I, well. . .almost did. It just didn't quite work out." She cut a questioning glance toward the Irishwoman. "Was there—I mean, did anyone—?"

The braided head wagged slowly. "Nary a soul. But Gabe hasn't quit tryin'."

The pronouncement brought mixed reactions of relief and disappointment, each equally strong. What if someone offered to take the child with the intention of putting her to work, instead of providing a loving, happy home? Or what if the couple already had children of their own who would resent a newcomer's usurping attention which rightfully belonged to them? The morose thoughts crowded out the small hope Angelina still harbored for the sweet little one with whom she had so quickly become enamored.

"Are you gonna eat supper here?" the childish voice asked.

" 'Course she is," Aunt Clara piped in before Angelina had time to answer. "She's welcome anytime, and that's a fact."

"Oh good."

"You're much too kind," Angelina told the older woman. Finished pinning the first garment, she eased it carefully over Noely's upraised arms, then turned the second wrong-side out and slipped it over the child's head.

"After supper, Pastor Gabe reads to me," Noely lisped, sliding her arms into the sleeves. "From the Bible book. It has pretty pictures. Will you stay for a story?"

"We'll see." Unbidden scenes flashed to mind of the huge minister with a little girl curled on his lap, his big head bent over hers. Noely's tiny form would be absolutely swallowed in those long arms. The imaginary picture brought a smile.

Angelina caught her breath. Her solitary existence for the past six years had her enjoying the loving atmosphere of this home too much—and becoming far too attached to the charming family she had met mere days ago. These people were fine Christians, certainly, living up to their own code of standards. But once Noely had been placed, there'd be no further reason to return. Still, if she truly felt welcome, an inner voice reasoned, what harm could there be in visiting while she could?

"The more the merrier," came the reverend's booming voice from the doorway.

Having been unaware of his presence, Angelina turned away to hide her blush. Her embarrassment only strengthened her resolve not to expect more from this association than what was on the surface. After all, these visits to the parsonage were for Noely's benefit—and *only* Noely's. She would enjoy whatever friendship might be offered here as long as it lasted, and then let go. . .no matter how much it might hurt when the time came.

"I'll stay."

Chapter 4

Watching Angelina Matthews ease up from the dining table, Gabe was certain he detected new lines of pain around her dark brown eyes. Earlier, when Noely had inadvertently bumped against the young woman on her jump from the chair, he'd even caught a sheen of moisture across her eyes, but she had quickly blinked it away. In an elaborate gesture of chivalry overdone, he made a grand bow and offered her his elbow. "Might I escort your ladyship to the royal parlor?"

"Oh, but I should help clean up."

"Fiddle-faddle!" his aunt said. "You young folks go on ahead. I'll see to the supper things. Off with ye now."

The seamstress actually grinned, a dazzling smile which somehow made Gabe even more sure she was expending excessive effort to appear natural. With the merest hint of a curtsey she accepted his help. "'Twould be my pleasure, milord."

He felt a rush of gratification when she joined in with the game. . .but then, she *was* trying to help entertain Noely. The little girl giggled and skipped alongside them, then made a beeline for the picture book.

Gabe settled their guest on one end of the settee. Then taking the other end, he drew the curlyhead onto his lap. "What will it be, princess?"

She scrunched her girlish face in thought.

"Well," he coaxed, "there's a very special day coming. How about the story of the first Christmas?"

"Oh, I like that one!"

Opening to the proper page, Gabe cleared his throat. "'Once there lived a Prince who ruled the whole world. Many of His people didn't know Him, and that made Him very sad. They were forever muddling things up, going here and there like sheep without a shepherd. They did many bad things, and He knew that one day every one of them would have to stand before His Father, the Mighty King, and be judged. The Prince knew the only way He could help them was to become one of them Himself, so that's exactly what He did. . .'"

Even as he went on to the simple account of the Babe being born in a manger in Bethlehem, Gabe was aware of Miss Matthews' intense interest. She had never spoken of her personal beliefs, and yet she neither interrupted his reading nor reacted scornfully to the story. Once he glanced at her and saw she appeared faraway, as though lost in a memory. His heart breathed a prayer that whatever her needs, the Lord would meet them.

" '. . .and now we remember the birth of the Christ Child once a year,' " he read, " 'on Christmas. And in giving each other gifts, we demonstrate how God gave His very best Gift to all of us, in His beloved Son.' "

Noely smiled and laid her head back on his shoulder. "I really, really like that story, Pastor Gabe. It's my favorite."

"Mine, too, pumpkin. Christmas is the most special time there is. But it's getting late now. Time to dress for bed."

"Can Ang'lina tuck me in, this time?" she pleaded.

"Don't see why not—unless she doesn't like stairs," he added quickly, looking for her response.

"I can manage. . .but I've never tucked a child in for the night, sweetheart. You'll have to tell me what to do, so I can get it right."

"It's easy," she lisped, sliding off Gabe's knee. "I'll show you." All smiles, she held out a tiny hand.

Gabe watched after them, and tried not to notice the halting, careful steps Miss Matthews took with each rise. Though she hadn't complained, her limp was much more pronounced today. His heart went out to her.

∽

"And now I kneel and say my prayers," Noely advised as Angelina fastened the last button on the castoff man's shirt the child slept in. "But big people usually just sit on the bed."

"Fine." Relieved she didn't have to try and kneel, Angelina took her place as the youngster sank to her knees at the bedside. Noely laced her fingers and reverently bowed her head. "Dear Lord, thank You for bringing Ang'lina today. I miss her when she doesn't come. And thank You for Jesus and the Christmas story. Please take care of my mommy and daddy, and bless Pastor Gabe and Aunt Clara, and help me to be a good girl. Amen." Opening her eyes, she scrambled into bed. "Now you cover me up and kiss my cheek."

"Is that everything?" Angelina asked, following instructions to the letter.

"Mm-hmm. And I hug you, like this." With a surprisingly strong squeeze, she smiled. "Good night. I love you."

The unexpected remark made Angelina's eyes sting. When had anyone last said those words to her? Brushing a curl from the child's forehead, she straightened. "Good night, sweetheart." Tiptoeing to the door, she stole one more look at the little girl, then slowly made her way downstairs.

Seated in a wing chair with his open Bible, the minister glanced up on her approach.

"I shall be going home now. Thank you for supper."

"Wait, please," he said. "No need to hurry off." He gestured toward the settee.

"I thought we might talk."

"About what?" Nerve endings in her spine tingled as she lowered herself to the upholstered seat and perched stiffly on the edge, wondering what was coming.

"Nothing," he said. "Everything. Anything. It's been rather a pleasure getting to know you, that's all. May I get you a cup of tea?"

"Yes, that would be nice, thank you." She knew the pastor and his aunt were merely extending the hand of friendship to her as they would anyone else. The assurance helped her to relax as homey sounds drifted from the kitchen.

He returned moments later with the refreshment. "Noely sure is happy whenever you come," he said, handing her one of the two cups he carried. He settled back in his chair with the other.

"She's a dear little thing," Angelina admitted. "I haven't been able to get her off my mind since the night of the blizzard." With a shake of her head, she went on. "In a scant few days that little child has captured a large part of my heart."

"And ours. It is a wonder." He sampled his tea. "We all expected you to come yesterday."

"I. . .nearly did. Then I could not."

He gave a nod. "You're in pain, aren't you?"

Angelina blinked at the blunt question. "I'm always in pain."

"But not like today."

"How would you know that?"

"I read people."

It was a peculiar remark. She averted her eyes from his and took a sip of the hot liquid in lieu of replying.

"Sorry. I don't normally pry into my friends' lives." His voice were husky, as though he were embarrassed.

"Are we friends?" she couldn't help asking.

He grinned. "We're approaching it. And what my aunt told Noely happens to be true. You *are* welcome here—whether Noely continues to live with us or not."

Hesitant to linger over the ramifications of that particular statement, she centered on the important part. "Have you found someone who'll take her?" she murmured.

"Not yet. But I haven't exhausted all my resources."

Angelina nibbled the inside corner of her lip. "I only hope someone will want her. Will love her." Memories of visiting days at the orphanage cut into her consciousness. She recalled so many endless partings as, one by one, her friends were adopted. . .and she recalled her own hopeless waiting, the people shaking their heads, turning away. She didn't want that for Noely.

"I won't rest until Noely becomes part of a loving family," the minister vowed. "If I have to move heaven and earth to accomplish that, I will."

His sincerity made Angelina smile. "Were you ever an orphan?" she finally asked.

He shook his head. "I grew up with my parents, lived with them until I graduated from theological school. The last outbreak of cholera took them both within days of each other. It's what they'd have wanted. Now they're with the Lord."

"That's something I'm quite curious about," Angelina confessed. "That some people aren't afraid to die. . .yet how can they believe God is so loving when He'll take parents away from a little girl?"

"As He did yours?"

She frowned. "Am I so very transparent?"

"Not at all. I just got that impression from the plea you made regarding not sending Noely to an orphan asylum."

Finishing the last of her tea, Angelina rose carefully to her feet. "Well I really must get home. I have work tomorrow."

"Of course." Having stood at the same time as she, the pastor retrieved her coat from the hall tree and assisted her into it. Then he reached for his own and pulled it on.

Angelina peered up at him in puzzlement.

"Thought you could use some assistance this evening."

She flushed. "That's not necessary. I'm used to getting about on my own."

"I'm sure you are. But this once you won't have to. You have a friend to help. Aunt Clara," he called, "be back shortly." With that, he opened the door.

Angelina preceded him into the starry night, and he closed the door behind them. But before she took a step she felt herself being whisked off her feet and into his strong arms. "What do you think you are doing?" she railed, mortified at the situation and the informality of it all. She hadn't known the man but a few days!

"Helping a friend," he said evenly.

"A friend who can walk on her own," she countered, craning her neck to make sure they weren't being observed.

"If she had to—which she does not. Besides, I haven't done my good deed for the day."

Unsure whether to laugh or cry, Angelina settled for the former—not that she had much choice in the matter. "Surely you don't intend to carry me all the way home! I'm too heavy, and it's too far."

"Heavy!" he snickered. "I've carried sacks of coal heavier than you!"

"Really, Reverend," she began.

"Do you think you could possibly call me by my Christian name, as my other friends do?" he teased.

"Certainly not! It isn't. . .proper."

A chuckle rumbled from his chest. "You actually prefer that sort of stilted friendship?" he asked, not even winded as he strode over the cobbled street. "My forever calling you Miss Matthews, and your referring to me as Reverend Winters? Times *are* changing, you know. Honestly, little Noely's the only one who's got the whole thing in perspective."

Angelina laughed again. It had never entered her mind to be so familiar she'd resort to using his Christian name. *Gabe.* Gabriel. It did suit the man—he was so much bigger than life.

She hadn't had a true friend for many years. Ruby, though chummy to a certain extent, had a husband, a life of her own. Gabe Winters was the first person in a long time who offered real friendship. What harm could there be in accepting it—at least while they both shared a concern for Noely?

Sooner than she'd have expected, the minister set her down on her stoop. "Friends, then. . .Angelina?"

She almost couldn't breathe. "I—I suppose."

"Good. We really do want you to come by the parsonage every day—or whenever you can. I've had my fill of stuffy church business, starched deacons and elders, proper protocol. You and Noely have been like a breath of spring to Aunt Clara and me."

"That's nice to hear."

He nodded, and his gaze remained fixed on hers. "Look, it's bound to be dark and cold in there," he said in all seriousness, motioning with his head toward her house. "Would you like me to get your fire going? Bring in extra wood or coal?"

"Certainly not!" she gasped. "We've probably caused scandal enough as it is. And anyway, aren't you forgetting? You've done your good deed for the day."

He grinned. "So I have."

"And I can manage. Truly. But thank you for offering."

"Gabe," he prompted.

"Gabe," she whispered, waiting for lightning to strike her dead. When it did not, she expelled a pent-up breath and dug into her pocket for her key.

He took it from her and unlocked the door, nudging it open. "Well, take care, then. Will we see you tomorrow?"

"Most likely. Your aunt told me you'll be taking Noely around to some of your parishioners this week?"

"That's right. We'll see that she gets a good home, I promise. Good night."

"Good night, my friend. Thanks for seeing me home."

With a nod, he backed away, and Angelina stepped inside, closed the door, and leaned against the jamb. How many people in the world could boast of having an angel for a friend. . .for if ever one walked the earth, he had to be a lot like Gabriel Winters. Her heart felt strangely warmed with the knowledge. And she had no trouble at all *thinking* of him by his given name. Reaching for the box of matches, she lit the parlor lamp and then the wood she'd laid earlier.

An indescribable peace flowed through her regarding Noely. Gabe would keep his promise. . .to both of them. Could she help it if a tiny part of her hoped he wouldn't find a home for the child too soon?

◠

Gabe rolled over and punched his pillow, trying to get comfortable. He hoped he hadn't been too forward with Angelina. Overfriendliness had always been his greatest fault and rarely endeared him to the fairer gender—in fact, one or two refined lasses had proclaimed him an oaf to his face! Well at least he'd finally managed to overcome the tendency to trip over his own big feet or bump his head going through low doorways, but maintaining proper protocol would forever be a trial.

The trouble was, the profound loneliness in Angelina's dark eyes reminded him of his own, and he desperately wanted to ease her heartache. He knew someone so beautiful as she would never look twice at a big ox like himself— and after the way he'd pushed her tonight, he should count himself fortunate that she even agreed to be his friend!

Then a darker thought surfaced. Once Noely was out of the picture, would Angelina take her leave as well? Releasing a slow breath, he rolled onto his back and laced his fingers beneath his head, staring up at the ceiling.

Chapter 5

H er arms full of fabric scraps, Clara entered the back door of the church. Gabe had already stoked up the furnace for today's gathering of the mission society, and the pervading warmth helped erase the chill. If all the women showed up, the many nimble fingers would easily finish another quilt by day's end. Never fond of stitching, much less possessed of such talent herself, Clara contributed by tearing donated materials into strips or cutting needed shapes for the various quilt patterns, an arrangement which seemed to suit everyone.

She descended the stairs to the basement supply room and piled her burden into a large basket, together with needles, thread, and several pairs of scissors. Then she took the items up to the side room where the activity was held. To her surprise, she heard voices. Some of the ladies had come early.

"You can't tell me there's not something scandalous going on," came Lucinda Blackwell's distinctive high-pitched pronouncement. "And under our very noses, no less."

Clara stopped in her tracks. The Old Crows' Society. Not one to eavesdrop, she nevertheless paused and waited for an opportune moment to enter.

"Saw it with my own eyes, I did," Miranda Keys affirmed. "Pretty as you please, him carrying that hussy in his arms, right past my house for all the world to see! Near brought me to heart failure right then and there, I daresay. That woman's at the parsonage every single night and stays till past dark. And not even a member of the church, at that! I suppose the rest of us are expected to believe she goes there to see that urchin. Hmph! It's downright sinful, if you ask me. Mark my words."

Hortense Witherspoon went into her usual fit of coughing. Clara could just picture the other biddies thumping her back with their scrawny fists. "Why, it's a sheer disgrace," she croaked after the coughs subsided. "That's what."

"Never did approve of calling such a young preacher to our church," Widow Blackwell told the others. "I let the board know my opinion in no uncertain terms, as if it mattered—they voted him in anyway. Well, if you ask me, it's high time a special meeting was called. We'll see what the high and mighty elders think of these goings-on."

"True, true," Mistress Keys said. Clara could envision the old gal's nod of assent. Miranda had little backbone of her own, and usually went along with anything her cronies said.

Tucking a strand of stray hair into her coronet, Clara reached for the latch.

"Wait, girls," came the annoying nasal voice again.

There were far worse sins than listening in, Clara reasoned, detecting a sinister change in Lucinda Blackwell's tone. She settled back onto her heels.

"Maybe we shouldn't stop with the Board of Trustees," the widow went on.

"What are you saying?" the others asked as one.

"Just this. I've never approved of that child-placement sideline of his. Philadelphia isn't a fledgling colony anymore. The city has institutions to handle that sort of thing. People paid to deal with riffraff. I'll wager the authorities would be mighty interested to hear of the preacher's dabbling in affairs beyond his calling. That orphan brat belongs in a proper asylum, and I intend to see she gets there."

Clara's hand flew to her throat. In the pregnant silence that followed, she could almost see the sly conspiratorial smiles spreading from one self-righteous face to the next. Determined to squelch this nonsense before it went any farther, she opened the door and entered.

The maleficent expressions became amazingly guileless as the three bony women turned. "Why, good day, Clara," Widow Blackwell gushed. "You're looking spry. I was just remarking to the girls about how well our little church is functioning under the fine hand of your nephew."

"Indeed." The outright lie stole any more deprecating response Clara might have made. Moving stiffly to the storage closet, she took down the folded in-progress quilts and spread each out on the long tables with precise deliberation.

Hortense Witherspoon broke into another spasm of coughs.

Clara, still searching for the exact words to put the presumptuous busybodies in their place, opened her mouth, but the arrival of two more members stayed her tongue. She knew it was for the best, seeing as how it spared her from having to repent afterward. But all the same, Gabe should know about this. And know he would, as soon as she got home.

"Don't tell me you took that folderol seriously!" Gabe looked incredulously at his aunt over pie and tea as Noely played with clothespins and buttons on the parlor rug.

"Of course I did. And so should you."

He forked a chunk of the dessert and stabbed at the air with the utensil to punctuate his words. "Those meddlesome widows have been nitpicking ever since we got here, Aunt Clara. If it isn't about one thing, it'd be another— whatever their idle imaginations can conjure up and pass on to itching ears. It's not worth losing sleep over."

"But ye didn't hear them, Gabe. They won't stop until they've done as much damage to your ministry as they possibly can, to say nothing of—" She glanced in Noely's direction. "It was all I could do not to be tellin' those troublesome biddies off, and in no uncertain terms."

"And what would that have accomplished?" he asked quietly. "We're all equally capable of wounding another person with the sharpness of our tongues. Only through His grace can those women's cruelty be tamed, and our words tempered and used to praise rather than crush. I'm glad you remained quiet."

"I'm not sure I am, to be quite truthful." She crossed her arms and rested them on the table.

He gave a comforting pat to her worn hand. "You and I both know there'll never be a perfect church until the Lord Himself comes to establish His. No matter how hard His servants labor for the kingdom, or how selfless and faithful their service, there's bound to be some devil's advocate right in the thick of things, stirring up trouble. All I can do is my best to remain faithful and continue to seek and do God's will. Meanwhile, He will handle those *Old Crows*—as you so aptly termed them."

"I only pray He will," she said quietly.

"What crows, Pastor Gabe?" Noely asked, coming to the table and draining the last drops of milk from her glass.

"We're just talking about some grownup matters, pumpkin," he said gently. "Nothing for your little head to worry about." He studied the young child as she returned to her play, then exhaled deeply. "I have more pressing matters to occupy my mind, Aunt Clara. No point worrying about idle threats. Dress Noely up real pretty this afternoon. I've a few calls to make."

Angelina often noticed a slight improvement in her weak limb during milder weather, and even more so after having been spared a long walk in the night chill.

She hardly felt the smile that crossed her lips as she thought back on it. Never would she have imagined she could relax and be herself in the presence of a virile, compelling man like Gabe Winters. Of course, having established the boundaries in her mind, she would never presume anything beyond friendship.

Besides, she had resolved years ago never to set herself up for another heartbreak. She had learned that particular lesson well on the first try, when a young man she thought loved her took her home to meet his parents. Nothing matched the cruel sting of that humiliation. . .the raised brows, the faces beginning to redden slightly, the oh-so-polite stammered excuses which rendered swift death to the blossoming romance.

And no one needed to point out that for all the interested first glances she received from young bachelors who crossed her path, there rarely came a second. But she had come to terms with her solitary destiny. Yes, Angelina resolved inwardly, friendship was blessing enough, for a cripple.

"Any news about that homeless tyke?" Ruby's query interrupted Angelina's musings. Removing her eyeglasses, the willowy girl wiped them on her work apron, then resumed stitching a ruffled gown of sapphire taffeta.

"No. Nothing's turned up for Noely as yet, I'm afraid. But Reverend Winters is still trying to find her a home. At this moment she's probably accompanying him on his pastoral calls so folks can meet her." Angelina clipped a little extra trim for the remainder of the neckline on the coffee satin frock, then turned the raw edge under and tacked it. She snipped the thread.

"Then she shouldn't be on her own much longer, I'd expect."

"No." The sad reality disturbed Angelina greatly.

"Well," her coworker mused, "with Christmas comin', she should have a nice new family to call her own. Case she doesn't, though, will you be givin' her a present?"

"I hadn't thought about it," Angelina admitted in dismay. "I really should get her something to remember me by, I suppose."

"Or make her somethin'. A doll, mebbe."

"Do you think there's time, Ruby? Oh, I should have thought of it myself, only I've been so busy!"

Ruby gestured toward the remnant bin in the corner. "Dig through that when we're done. Might be Mistress would let you have whatever you need. It don't take much to do a doll."

For the first time in years, Angelina felt a measure of joy at the thought of the approaching holiday barely a week away. She'd been contemplating the story Gabe had read to Noely regarding the significance of the event, and as she lay in bed, long-buried childhood memories had surfaced. She could recall taking part in pageants, being filled with the wonder of the birth of the Holy Child, the One destined to suffer a cruel death on a cross so that all who believed on Him would one day live with Him in Heaven. And she recalled uttering a simple girlish prayer that He might come to dwell within her own heart. So long ago that had been. She wondered if God still remembered her.

"Will you look at that!" Ruby declared suddenly. "It's the last one! We've finished them all!"

"Why, so we have." Angelina laughed. "At least, those needing to be done for the holidays. Tomorrow we'll start back to work on the more ordinary garments."

"Yes, those." Grimacing, the auburn-haired girl hung the newly completed gowns, then began tidying the work table in readiness for going home. "Don't forget to look through the remnants, Angie."

But Angelina had already started rooting through the various fabrics in her eagerness, absolutely astounded that there were so many to choose from. Wouldn't Noely be surprised!

Her feet fairly floated over the cobbles that evening, limp and all. Her employer had been wonderfully generous. Patting the soft bundle of materials in her pocket, Angelina visualized them made into a Christmas doll. A shorter visit might be prudent this evening to allow time at home to work on the project.

Though she felt surprisingly at ease when Gabe welcomed her at the parsonage, she found the mood there somewhat subdued. Several peculiar glances passed between the minister and his aunt during supper, and Noely, overtired from her long day, fell fast asleep at the table and was whisked off to bed.

"I take it you were unsuccessful," Angelina remarked when Gabe returned from tucking the little one in.

"That's an understatement." He sank wearily into a parlor chair. "My three best possibilities, and not one was the least bit interested in taking on a three-year-old."

"Well, she can't remain three forever," Angelina said, trying to raise his spirits. "In fact, do you even know her birthdate?"

He raked his fingers through his hair. "Actually, yes. I came across it when I checked the birth and death records of the only Carrolls known to be in Philadelphia. Noely will turn four on April tenth."

"Would either of ye be wantin' more tea?" Aunt Clara asked, stacking supper dishes on a tray.

"Not just now," Gabe answered.

Angelina rose. "Nor I, thanks. I'd best be on my way."

"Already?" he asked, getting up also. "You've only just gotten here."

"Yes, but I have something urgent to do at home."

"Need my assistance?"

She barely stayed her blush. "Actually, I'm much better this evening. But if you could spare the time to walk with me part of the way, I really would like to talk with you."

"As you wish." Fetching her coat, he helped her into it, then put on his own, and they took their leave.

The night was chilly, with blue-white clouds drifting across a velvet sky and a partial moon. The arm he offered aided her greatly as they strolled toward Elfreth's Alley.

Gabe broke the silence. "What did you want to discuss?"

Not quite certain how to put her thoughts into words, Angelina peered up at the minister, feeling quite at ease with him, drawing strength from his presence. "It's. . .well, it's about the story last night. The Christmas one."

"And? What bothers you about it?"

She shrugged. "Nothing, really. It's just—" Pausing, she drew a deep breath and released it. "It's been ages since I'd been reminded of the significance of Jesus' birth. After you read the account last night it brought back long-forgotten experiences from my own childhood. And I was wondering. . .that is, do you think—" Angelina swallowed.

Gabe gave an encouraging pat to her gloved hand in the crook of his arm.

"Do you think God would still remember me?" she finished in a near whisper.

He stopped and smiled down at her. "Of course He remembers you, little friend. He sees you when you lie down and rise up again. He knows the number of hairs on your head and everything else there is to know about you. And He loves you as He does all His children."

"Even if I haven't spoken to Him in years?"

"Even then."

They had reached the end of her street. Angelina was almost too overcome to speak as she gazed up at him. "Thank you. That's what I wanted to know. I can go the rest of the way home on my own."

Somehow, as she left him behind, she knew he wasn't merely counting stars when he lifted his face to the sky.

Chapter 6

Angelina stitched far into the night on the surprise doll for Noely. Though she had never attempted making anything in the nature of a child's toy, her basic sewing talents made the project much easier than she had dared to hope. In a burst of inspiration she decided to use straw-colored yarn for the hair and embroider eyes of blue, so the little plaything would resemble its new mama. That would make it all the more special.

However, as she assembled the front and back sections of an indigo muslin dress similar to one Noely wore, the thoughts which meandered to the parsonage on Second Street did not always remain on the young orphan.

The new friendship she shared with Gabe Winters seemed truly precious. For the first time in ages, she felt free to be herself, so much of her loneliness was fading away. The minister possessed the ability to put her completely at ease and never treated her like a cripple. . .nor had he belittled her for what must have sounded like a childish question.

Angelina tried to picture the sandy-haired pastor standing behind the pulpit of his church, encouraging his little flock to be faithful to Almighty God. Did he read his sermons, as had the few ministers who had come to give services at the orphanage, or merely speak from his heart? And did all his prayers fall as naturally from his lips as those she had heard at the table?

Somehow she imagined his messages—no matter how deep their subject—would be delivered in the simplest of ways, so that anyone who heard them would be able to understand. To someone with as big a heart as Gabe Winters's, that would be of the utmost importance.

It was still a struggle for her to call him by his Christian name, but perhaps as time passed it would become easier to be casual about such things. After all, as he'd said, times were changing. People were turning from the old stiff rules to more relaxed ones.

A deep sigh evolved into a yawn. Glancing at the clock, Angelina discovered it was half-past midnight. She'd best put away the Christmas doll and get whatever sleep remained before time came to go to work.

⌒

Gabe knelt at his nightly prayers, lingering longer than usual as he upheld his church members before the Lord, along with the various concerns of the church itself. On visitation rounds he always accumulated a growing number of requests for prayer, and he did his best to remember them all.

Then there was Angelina. He'd felt compelled to pray fervently for the beautiful seamstress since she had appeared on his doorstep the night of the blizzard. He pleaded ceaselessly that God would allay the suffering she endured from her frail leg and lighten any other cares she might have. He was intensely gratified that she'd felt free to discuss personal spiritual concerns with him, and he hoped her mind had been put to rest. *And Father,* he added, shifting position on the braided mat at his bedside, *I ask You to keep my thoughts and motives pure regarding her. Never let me take advantage of the friendship we've only just begun. You know my tendency to rush and bungle things, the many relationships I've managed to sour single-handedly. Please restrain me from doing anything that would make Angelina take flight. If I can just be a true friend to her, I will not presume to ask any more.*

And then there was Noely, who barely resembled the timid, ragged urchin who had arrived at the parsonage in Angelina's arms. *Dear Lord, the little one is becoming more attached to Angelina, Aunt Clara, and me with each passing day—as we are to her. You know this could make her adjustment into yet another family every bit as painful and devastating as the loss of her own parents such a short time ago. Please help me to find a solution to this problem. Soon.*

Gabe rubbed his temples as he sorted through his jumbled thoughts. It galled him to admit that Noely had some very definite points against her. She wasn't a newborn baby, and folks tended to look more favorably on an infant of either gender than a child of nearly four. She wasn't a boy, and the latter remained much more in demand after the long years of the Civil War had exacted such a high toll among the male population. And she wasn't heart-stoppingly pretty or possessed of delicate features, but rather plain and sturdy instead. That particular prejudice was hardest of all to justify.

His mind went over the sweet charm Noely had about her. Once past her initial shyness, she tugged at a person's heartstrings and moved right in to take over the whole heart. She seemed, in some uncanny way, able to sense when to be quiet—or when a jubilant hug might be in order. Her musical giggle never failed to bring a smile. And anyone could see that the dear face which now seemed so grownup for such a young child would one day blossom into a lasting and stately beauty which would not quickly fade, but become all the more handsome with the passing years.

Oh Lord, what will become of this little one? Why hasn't there been even one ray of hope for her? If Aunt Clara weren't prone to recurring heart seizures, we could try to seek permanent custody ourselves. But You know she's much more frail than she lets on. Were something to happen to her, I wouldn't have an inkling about how to nurture a little girl on my own. I don't know where else to turn. Or what else to pray. I cast this burden at Your feet and ask You to do with it what You will. Provide an answer which will bring glory to Your Son, in whose name I pray.

At the end of himself, Gabe climbed into bed and pulled the blankets and quilts snugly about his neck. . .but sleep eluded him for some time.

A summons at the door rendered an end to the peace of mid-morning. With Aunt Clara bathing Noely in a tub in the kitchen, Gabe answered the knock.

Dell Taylor, turning his hat around and around in his work-hardened hands, stood on the stoop, along with two other deacons from the church. "Reverend," Dell mumbled, shifting uneasily from one foot to the other.

"Gentlemen," Gabe replied with a nod, already beginning to suspect why they were here. A niggle of dread coursed through him. "Come in."

The beefy tradesman shook his head. "Might be best if we could speak over at the church office."

"If you don't mind," rawboned Harris Thresher quickly added, appearing every bit as ill at ease as Mr. Taylor.

Small, highbrow Randall Bent had yet to meet Gabe's eyes as he hunkered into the collar of his dark wool coat.

"Certainly," Gabe replied, plucking his own wrap from the hall tree. He led the others to the house of worship next door and ushered them into his tidy, book-lined study. He motioned toward three chairs and took his place behind the worn mahogany desk, trying to ignore the signs that an ax was about to fall.

The deacons exchanged furtive glances before Dell spoke up. "We, er, that is, a rather disturbing matter has been brought to our attention—one that's probably just so much rumor and gossip. But anyways, we thought we'd best lay it all out on the table right here, before it grows into something more serious, requiring a meeting of the whole board."

Thresher and Bent gave nods of assent.

"What is it?" Gabe asked, glancing from one grim face to the next, finally settling on Dell Taylor.

Dell flicked an imaginary speck of lint from a trouser leg, then met Gabe's gaze. "It concerns a certain young woman who's been frequenting the parsonage of an evening." He reddened and averted his attention to the floor.

Gabe relaxed a bit. "Is that all? Well, allow me to put your minds at ease. Miss Matthews happens to be the person who found Noely freezing on the street and brought her to us. She's been coming by to visit the child—who, by the way, formed a singular attachment to her rescuer. There's nothing more to the matter, I assure you."

Thresher cleared his throat.

"I'm afraid there is, Reverend," Taylor went on. "It's been reported that, er, you've been seen—" His color deepening, he tugged at his starched collar, then managed to continue. "You've been seen conducting yourself in a fashion most ...unseemly, in public." That said, he exhaled a long breath as if greatly relieved to have the problem off his chest.

For a moment Gabe stared, dumbfounded. Then the evening he had escorted Angelina home in his arms popped anew in his memory. He felt his ire start to rise and fought to keep his tone even. "I don't suppose it was also reported that the young woman suffers from a serious infirmity which renders walking quite difficult. Or that sometimes she is in such pain she requires assistance."

"No sir, it wasn't." Some of the color left Dell's face.

"Well then, you can see the charges are erroneous. I can tell you here and now, my conscience is entirely clear before the Lord and before my church. I hope this sets the record straight."

"Only on one of the charges, Reverend," Thresher announced, gesturing for Mr. Taylor to elaborate further.

Dell swallowed. "About the orphan. . ."

Completely baffled, Gabe didn't respond.

"Certain folks in the church think," the deacon went on, "that your concern for her is taking up time which might be better spent in matters directly related to your ministry."

"Is that a fact?" Gabe responded, his anger barely contained. "And does the Bible not tell us it is the duty of every Christian—minister or layman alike—to aid a person who comes seeking need? Someone who cannot lift a finger to help herself?"

"There are institutions for that very purpose," meek Mr. Bent finally piped in.

"I see. Let someone else do it? Well, I have reasons not to agree with that particular conviction, and the primary one has to do with love. Noely is a dear, sensitive little child who happens to be in dire need of a family to love her, not an institution where she'll be one of a throng of homeless children in her same position. . .though I'm sure her continued presence at church probably inflicts a measure of guilt upon people who have refused to help her. But if she happened to be your grandchild, would you not be a lot more concerned about what becomes of her and feel as strongly about her as I do?"

The man had the grace to nod in agreement, and as the other deacons did the same, the tension lightened noticeably.

Gabe softened his tone. "I have every reason to believe I'll be successful in placing her in a Christian home in the very near future—perhaps among the congregations of other churches. And until that time I intend to continue striving toward that end. . .as I believe God would have me do."

"Yes," Dell conceded. "Put that way, I would share your feelings." He stood, and the other men joined him. "We'll be on our way, then, and pass on the results of this meeting to the wom—I mean, folks who brought it all up. We hope you won't hold this against us, Reverend."

"Not at all. I know people like to be sure things are being handled in a manner which behooves a minister of God. And," he could not restrain himself from adding, "you might advise them their added prayers would be of greater benefit in all of this than their criticism."

"I heartily agree." With a sheepish grin, Dell Taylor extended his hand.

Gabe shook it warmly, and did the same with the others, then showed them to the door. "God be with you, gentlemen."

As they exited the study, Gabe returned to his chair and bowed his head in a prayer of thankfulness. Aunt Clara would be glad to hear that nothing came of the hornet's nest stirred up by the widows who perched ever so piously on the more prominent church pews. He smiled inwardly and headed home.

When he related the discussion he'd had in the church office, his aunt placed a hand over her heart as if to quiet the agitation the news had caused. "I knew those biddies wouldn't quit until they started trouble for ye."

Gabe touched her shoulder. "Oh now, I wouldn't worry over it, Aunt Clara. As I told you, I managed to put the minds of the deacons at rest, so I can't see anything else coming of the accusations." But he could see she was clearly disturbed about it and retained considerable doubts.

The better part of that day and the following one were spent in what had quickly become routine, calling upon church members who for one reason or another had not been attending services regularly. Not one to give up hope easily, Gabe resorted to asking these parishioners for the names of any other prospects they might know who might be interested in taking in Noely. But even those efforts failed to pan out.

On the third afternoon a purposeful rap sounded on the door. Gabe set aside his Bible and commentary and went to answer. This time he found two unsmiling strangers attired in crisp black suits and felt hats. "Good day, gentlemen. How may I be of service?"

"You're the Reverend Gabriel Winters?" the taller of them inquired, peering at him through a gold-rimmed monocle.

"That's correct."

"I'm Harland Smeade, of the Agency for Displaced Persons. This is Mr. Townsend, of the Nesbitt Orphan Asylum."

A jolt of alarm slithered up Gabe's spine. Glancing over his shoulder at Noely at play with the button box, he stepped out on the stoop and closed the door behind him.

"We have been informed that you are presently providing sanctuary to a dispossessed minor, one Noely Carroll."

"That is correct. But—"

Before Gabe could finish, Smeade reached into an inside pocket of his waistcoat and drew out some folded documents and presented them. "You are hereby ordered to deliver said minor into Mr. Townsend's custody within forty-eight hours. If you do not comply with this order, we have been authorized to remove the child from these premises. Good day." With a curt bow of the head, the two turned and departed.

A suffocating heaviness deprived Gabe's lungs of air as he stared after the officials. He leaned back against the door, his eyes searching the heavens. *Dear Lord, why this? Why now, when I've been trying day after day to find little Noely a Christian family and get her settled in before Christmas?* But no answers blazed across the brilliant December sky.

He had let them down. All of them. Noely. Aunt Clara. And most of all, Angelina. How would he ever find courage enough to tell her he had failed?

Chapter 7

Forty-eight hours! Two days. Oblivious to the winter cold, Gabe slumped despondently against the parsonage door. Never in his life had he felt so utterly inadequate or powerless. All the effort he had expended. . .was it all for naught? He could parade Noely before his flock again tomorrow at service, but should that action prove fruitless, there would be only one final morning to find the orphan a home.

How insanely cruel to uproot a youngster right before the holiday! Gabe couldn't bear to dwell upon the memory of an unsmiling, fearful little girl who huddled by herself in the corner, or of her wrenching sobs that first night at the parsonage. . .and now to think of her being torn from this home, too, and cast away with more strangers. There had to be some way to keep it from happening. Maybe he could obtain a few days' extension from the authorities, precious time to place her himself. . .or at least postpone the inevitable until after Christmas. Surely they would see the benefit of that, wouldn't they? *Please, Father,* he pleaded. *For Noely.*

Expelling a ragged breath, he shored himself up and went back inside. . .where the sound of a little girl's giggles ripped at his heart.

❧

Angelina relaxed over her morning tea. Out the window she could see gathering clouds dulling the Philadelphia sky, and the draft seeping around the window frames and doorjamb gave evidence of a quickly dropping temperature. Thank heaven there was no longer a need to report to the shop on Saturdays. It was a little early to call at the parsonage yet, but perhaps after her noon meal she'd go to visit Noely. In the meantime she would continue working on the child's gift.

The doll was adorable, Angelina had to admit, assessing the toy at arm's length. She didn't know when was the last time she had derived such joy from making something—and she'd finished the project with days to spare! With Christmas still four days off, there was no reason the dolly shouldn't have an entire wardrobe. It was easy to envision an array of sweet dresses, undergarments, a tiny flannel sleeping gown, even a wool cape. Smiling, she spread out a remnant of apple green calico and began cutting out a second dress.

The first huge feathery snowflakes began swirling to the ground on a gusty wind in mid-morning, a sight Angelina found particularly depressing. She could nearly always manage to get where she needed to go, as long as she allowed extra time for caution. But watching the snow gradually increasing in density and the layer of white beginning to smooth out the uneven cobbles in the street, she emitted a sad sigh. And she was all too aware that the worst of winter still lay ahead. It might be prudent to stay inside until the storm abated. Well, she would make the best of it. Squaring her shoulders, she eyed the remaining materials, then set to work.

Thoughts of what she would miss at the parsonage—one more treasured visit with Noely, a lively conversation with Gabe and his aunt, and that over another scrumptious supper—were made bearable as a small stack of doll clothes began to accumulate.

But one disappointment could not completely be dismissed. Angelina knew slippery conditions would keep her away from services at Second Street Baptist Church on the morrow. She had planned to start attending worship each week and become part of what surely must be a wonderful and loving Christian family. As she'd lain in bed the night before, she had tried to imagine Gabe's expression when he stepped to the pulpit, surveyed his congregation, and discovered she was there. Just thinking of surprising him had brought a smile that refused to go away. Oh well, the worst that could happen would be a postponement of her plans until next Sunday. But that seemed a month away.

⌒

"Ye seem a bit off your feed," Aunt Clara remarked, helping herself to a small second portion of roasted chicken.

"Hm?" Gabe let go of the fork he'd been turning absently in his fingers and swung his gaze to his aunt.

"Not hungry?" she asked.

He hadn't realized his meal sat untouched before him. "I have a lot on my mind is all. Would you care if I save this for later?"

"Not a bit."

"I finished everything on my plate, Pastor Gabe," Noely boasted with her light lisp. She rested her forearm on the table, the fork in her fist standing straight up.

"I'm real proud of you, pumpkin," he told her, giving her wrist a squeeze.

"Do I hafta go see more people again today?" she asked, blue eyes wide.

He shook his head. "I have an errand to run by myself. You can keep Aunt Clara company."

"Oh, goodie! Then I can help make gingerbread cookies, huh, Auntie?" A pretty little grin disclosed her anticipation.

"That ye may, darlin'. 'Tis much more fun with two of us doin' it, to be sure." The older woman lifted a questioning glance to Gabe.

Preferring not to dump extra worries on his aunt's shoulders, he offered as much of a smile as he could work up, then blotted his mouth on his napkin and stood. "I'll be at my study for about an hour, after which I must pay a call on someone," he told her, then ruffled Noely's curls. "Just thinking about fresh-baked gingerbread makes my mouth water. Sure hope it'll be done before I get back."

She giggled. "Me, too."

The bright expectation in her eyes made him all the more aware that his own hopes were diminishing like sand through an hourglass.

In the solitude of the church office, Gabe fell to his knees before his leather chair, needing to pour out his heart to God, yet finding no words. He dared not imagine tomorrow morning's appeal to his congregation would be unsuccessful, nor could he allow himself to think past it. He had to believe God had things under control and was working out His purpose in the very best way for all concerned. Hadn't he preached those lofty ideals often enough? Well, if the promises in the Bible were true for one person, they were true for everyone, and if that were the case, then they'd work for a little defenseless girl like Noely, too. And right now, he would do everything within his power to be sure they did.

Gabe hadn't managed to acquire many influential friends in the city during his years at Second Street, but God had mercifully provided him with one man who had offered wise counsel on several occasions. Rising from his knees, he pulled on his coat and strode purposefully out the door into the falling snow.

Harrison Lawrence, an aged justice of the peace, now retired from most civic duties, had befriended Gabe when he'd arrived in Philadelphia and sought directions to his first pastorate. Evenings spent with the elderly man and his gracious wife during the first several months in the city were among some of his most treasured memories. Though the aging pair were affiliated with one of the more prosperous churches in Philadelphia, they had nevertheless welcomed Gabe into their stately home and treated him like the son they had never had. He regretted allowing the visits to taper off to almost nil.

Reaching the four-story mansion fronting Fourth Street, its fountains and well-maintained gardens now dormant and covered with snow, Gabe inhaled a fortifying breath and rapped on the door.

A soft-spoken butler ushered him across a marbled entrance hall flanked by huge urns of fragrant evergreen boughs and into an immense library, where books of every size and color lined floor to ceiling shelves on three walls. There the white-haired gentleman sat in a wheelchair behind the elaborate carved oak desk, a plaid woolen shawl draped about his stooped shoulders.

"Gabe, my dear boy," he said, extending a blue-veined hand. "I was just thinking of you the other day. How are you, lad?"

"Fine, sir. Just fine." Almost speechless at the toll taken on the once hearty man since his last visit some months ago, Gabe tried his hardest not to crush the feeble hand in his own grip. "I'm afraid I've neglected you far too long. But that was unintentional," he added, trying not to be obvious about his surprise at seeing the wheeled conveyance.

The keen hazel eyes astutely read his expression. "Don't let this contraption get to you, son. I took a tumble down the stairs a few weeks ago and broke my leg. The doctor—tough old sawbones that he is—insists I stay off it till he says different."

Relieved that the man retained his sense of humor and still spoke with surprising vigor, Gabe grinned. "Well I hope your recovery is speedy, sir, and that you'll be up and around very soon."

He nodded his thanks. "How's that church of yours coming along these days?"

"Very nicely, actually. It's grown quite a bit over the last year or so."

"I'm glad to hear that. I pray for you and your ministry every day." The white head tipped slightly. "What brings you by?"

Gabe released a nervous breath. "Some of that insightful counsel of yours, actually. I've always been thankful for the friendship and encouragement you and your dear wife, rest her soul, gave me when I first came to Philadelphia. Welcoming me into your home, praying with me, helped me over some of the rough spots. Not every minister fresh from his theological studies is fortunate enough to have such wonderful mentors."

"Yes, those were grand times. Margaret thought the world of you."

With a smile, Gabe continued. "I only wish I'd kept in better touch. I might have been able to help after your accident."

"Oh, pshaw!" he exclaimed with a wave of one hand. "I've got servants a'plenty, lad. I know a growing church keeps its pastor occupied. I'm just glad you came by today. Now, how can I help you?" His snow-white brows flared wide.

Gabe shook his head. "I don't know where to start. What I need most is an ear to confide in, a shoulder to lean on. And I thought the two of us might pray about a matter that's weighing heavily upon me just now."

"Always a wise step, seeking the Lord's intervention. I'm more than glad to offer my support."

Pausing, Gabe grouped his thoughts. "Not long ago—in that last blizzard we had, to be precise—a young woman brought an orphan to the parsonage, hoping we could find the little girl a new home. It seemed of considerable importance to her that the child not be sent to the asylum."

"I see."

"I've turned all my efforts since then into trying to fulfill that request and find a family willing to take the girl in. But so far, no one has come forward. Meanwhile, someone at church reported the matter to the authorities, and they've swooped in like vultures, intent upon following proper legal procedure to the very letter. They want to take the child away. Day after tomorrow, in fact. Today being Saturday, there's nobody I can go to and slow things down."

Mr. Lawrence kneaded his thin jaw in thought. "I can see your concern. Once those sharp-nosed authorities get wind of something, they latch onto it like English bulldogs. If I know those buzzards right, they're more interested in the fee they'll get paid to house one more orphan than they are in the child's welfare." He frowned. "Pity you've never taken a wife."

Gabe shook his head. "Not that I haven't considered it, mind you," he admitted sheepishly. "I do have my widowed aunt still living with me, but her health has been failing. She had quite a bad spell this past fall. So needless to say, I'm not in a position to take legal custody of Noely myself, no matter how much I wish I were."

"Hm. That's too bad. If you only had a wife, they'd have no reason to bother anybody."

With a lopsided smile, Gabe shrugged.

"Well, I'm sure none of this catches Almighty God by surprise," the older man said, his eyes glinting. "But His ways are far above ours, and sometimes what seems wrong in our own judgment turns out to be wise beyond our ability to understand. Let's lay the matter at His feet and let Him work out His will."

As the white-haired gentleman bowed his head, Gabe knelt by the desk.

"Our Gracious Father," Mr. Lawrence prayed, "we thank You for Your constant and abiding presence in our lives, for the unceasing blessings You shower upon us every day. We praise You that through Your Son we can come boldly into Your presence at any time, knowing You are concerned with all our circumstances. And now, Lord, we bring before You this little orphan and her needs. We ask You to stay the hands that might carelessly bring harm to her. Grant wisdom to young Gabe as he deals with this matter, and show Him Your perfect will. This we ask in the name above all names, Jesus Christ. Amen."

As always, Gabe found himself drawing immense and immediate strength as much from his mentor's unshakable faith as from the man's fervent prayer. Renewed peace began to flow through him as he smiled and stood. He reached for the man's gnarled hand and held it warmly in his own, trying not to acknowledge its almost transparent papery skin. "I do thank you, sir, for listening to me. Somehow, though I can't explain it, I always feel better after coming to you."

"I trust things will turn out for you."

"I'm sure they will. I must get back now, spend whatever time is left with Noely and Aunt Clara."

"Well don't be a stranger, son. Let me know what happens. Meanwhile, I'll continue to keep all of you in my prayers."

Gabe felt a new spring in his step as he headed home after the visit. The city always looked so pretty with a new blanket of snow, especially at times like this, with the clouds drifting away and the sunshine adding its glory.

And hearing one of his own convictions reinforced by Mr. Lawrence somehow revived his spirit. If Noely had parents to look after her, the authorities would have no reason to bother anybody. And an almost outlandish idea began to take root.

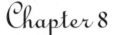

Chapter 8

Angelina was ecstatic when sunshine flooded her parlor in the middle of the afternoon. A glance outside revealed almost two inches of new snow, but at this time of day she could manage walking through it easily enough without fear of slipping. Putting aside her sewing, she limped upstairs to freshen her face to go visiting. Shortly after, in an emerald gabardine nicer than her typical work attire, her hair brushed and shining in its soft waves, she made her way up Elfreth's Alley toward Second Street.

The world glistened anew in white splendor as huge cloud puffs in the brilliant sky reflected blue-violet shadows across the snow. Angelina could not restrain a thankful prayer that she hadn't been confined at home for long. Reaching the parsonage, she tapped lightly with the knocker.

The door opened within seconds.

"Angelina." A curious spark in Gabe's blue eyes made her heart trip over itself as he stepped aside to allow her in. "I was hoping you'd come by." He took her coat and scarf and hung them while she removed her boots.

"It's lovely outside, isn't it?" she remarked casually, certain that the curious tension in the air had to be her imagination. "I was lonesome for Noely." She glanced around, becoming aware of an abnormal quiet in the parsonage.

"Aunt Clara took her out to frolic in the snow for a little while. They'll be back shortly. Come sit down." Gabe gestured toward the settee. "We need to talk."

A prickle of apprehension fluttered up Angelina's spine.

"By the way, there's fresh tea. I was just about to have some. Join me?"

She nodded. "Thanks."

In moments he returned and handed her one of two cups he carried. "Sugar? Cream?"

"Black is fine, thanks." She sipped some of the soothing warmth as she watched him lower himself to the wing chair he seemed to prefer. Without even a hint of childish laughter anywhere in the vicinity, the ticking of a grandfather clock was the most prominent sound in the house. How far away had Gabe's aunt taken Noely? "Any new developments?" she finally asked.

He cocked his head. "I have gone to every possible home I could think of—and to a few where I had never met the people before."

"And no one wanted her?"

"Well, actually, there is someone quite interested."

Angelina felt a lump rise in her throat at the announcement. The familiar combination of relief and sadness flooded her. "Is—is it someplace where Noely will be happy, do you think?" Schooling both her expression and her emotions to remain even, she took another sip of tea.

"I sure hope so. It took me a lot of prayer to even find this solution, and if it's going to work, it will probably continue to require prayer for a while. But something tells me this may be God's will."

There is no way to argue against that, she told herself. If God had found a home for dear little Noely, it had to be the best one for her. But it was hard to think of her being passed on to strangers after all she had been through. . .and even harder to imagine never coming back here to visit again, never seeing the child who had become such a part of the three of them. She surmised Aunt Clara and Gabe would battle a similar attachment when they had to let go. Noely was such a presence, such a sparkle. The reality of how much she herself would miss the little girl made Angelina's spirit deflate.

Trying to breathe over the heaviness, she became aware that Gabe was staring at her. She raised her lashes and met his gaze.

"Of course," he said quietly, "I haven't had the nerve to approach the party as yet and bring up the matter."

Something in his voice made Angelina's cup rattle slightly in its saucer. She tightened her grip, then carefully set the cup on the lamp table beside her as the sandy-haired giant rose to his feet and crossed to the settee.

He sat down next to her, and his huge hands captured one of hers. Her heart stopped. She could not draw away. . .nor was she certain she would have, had she the strength. Her pulse picked up again, making it increasingly difficult to breathe as the rush of it throbbed in her ears.

"Please look at me, Angelina," he pleaded softly.

Knowing exactly how much she wanted to do just that made it all the more difficult. But she slowly obeyed, and warmth flooded her cheeks.

Gabe's eyes held hers. He didn't speak for a moment, and she saw him swallow. She thought she detected the hint of a tremor in his touch. "I've. . .exhausted every other possibility. I haven't mentioned this to Aunt Clara yet, but unless Noely is placed in a home immediately, the authorities are going to take custody of her. On Monday."

"Oh Gabe!" she gasped. "Right before Christmas? But I thought you said—"

"That someone wants her," he finished. "It's true."

"Well, then, I—I don't understand."

A muscle worked in his jaw, and then he smiled. "Noely needs a home. She has one here. She needs love, and she has that here, too. And she needs parents. A man and a woman who love her as if she were their own. . ." He paused, and his face turned a dark red. "I think she. . ." He cleared his throat. "I think she has a man and woman who love her right here, too."

Angelina's lips parted at the implication she could read in his eyes.

"I know this is sudden, Angelina, but there's nothing I can do about that. If only there were more time, I could court you properly." His forehead wrinkled. "Heaven knows a beautiful woman like you could do far better than a big ox like me."

To her dismay, Angelina felt tears well up in her eyes and spill over her lashes. She fought to stem the tide.

Gabe's head bowed and his shoulders slumped. "I knew you'd find the very suggestion repulsive. Forgive me." He released her hand and turned away. "You were my last hope. I thought that since we're friends—good friends who can be honest and open with one another—maybe we could have a chance. Could make a home for Noely somehow." He grimaced and shook his head. "I guess that was stupid of me. I'm sorry."

Mustering all her resources, Angelina touched his forearm. "Sorry?" she whispered. "You think I'm repulsed by you?"

"Well, you're crying. . ." His voice was hoarse.

"Only because I thought *I* would be unattractive to someone like you. Someone. . .perfect."

He lifted his head and stared at her, amazement filling his face. Then slowly he began to smile. "Believe me, sweet Angelina, I am far from that, I assure you." He cupped her face in his palm, and his thumb gently brushed away a tear. "And there is nothing about you I would ever consider less than beautiful, not even that weak leg of yours. I'm sorry that it pains you—but it does nothing to mar your beauty. You will never have to hide it from me, I promise you that."

Angelina could not speak past the ache in her throat.

His gaze never wavered as he searched her soul. "But with Noely's welfare to consider, we can't afford to take the time to do this properly. I must ask you now." He paused, as if choosing his words very carefully, and she thought she heard a tremor in his voice when he continued, "Could you find it in your heart to marry a humble pastor? I vow I will spend the rest of my life courting you. But I have to tell you, we must do this today. Tomorrow at the latest."

Today! Angelina thought in shock. *Tomorrow at the latest!* There wasn't time to list advantages and disadvantages, to reason things out, to find another— perhaps better—solution. A little girl needed them, needed them both, and needed them now. And Christmas was coming. Could either of them bear to break her heart on that day of all days?

"Yes," she heard herself murmur. "I'll marry you."

His strong arms enveloped her and ever so tenderly drew her near.

Any second thoughts Angelina might have expected vanished as Gabe's heart pounded against hers. She knew they were rushing things, that a lifetime commitment such as marriage should be entered into after great deliberation—yet she was consumed by the greatest peace she had ever felt in her life. She had felt drawn to him and to Noely since the first time their paths had crossed. Surely God had brought them all together. . .and He wanted them to stay together always.

❧

Gabe never imagined the world could contain this much joy. He had no idea how on earth he had gathered courage enough to propose to this enchanting young woman who had so recently become such a part of his life. He had tried to ignore the attraction he had felt for her from the first, had tried to deny it even as it grew stronger with each meeting. Somehow she seemed to have always been there, just beyond his dreams, part of himself that he had never hoped to find—and yet she was reality.

Angelina's courage in suffering had touched him more deeply than anything else about her, even more than the loneliness lurking in her beautiful eyes. Everything about her made him want to protect her and keep her safe from anything that might bring her further pain. And to think she had actually accepted his offer of marriage! He grinned to himself and shook his head. Mr. Lawrence was surely a mighty man of prayer.

Of course, Gabe's own prayers had been no less fervent, he had to admit. Both Angelina and Noely desperately needed someone to look after them. To love them. Maybe they needed him just as desperately as he needed them and their love.

Love. Dare he speak that word aloud again after having had it thrown back in his face by someone else he had once thought he loved? Looking back, he could see the feelings he had known then paled in comparison to what filled him now. Letting his gaze devour Angelina's features, he decided to take the chance.

With the edge of his finger, he tipped her face upward. "I—" He swallowed and sucked in a breath. "I know you love Noely. You want to do what's best for her, and so do I. But I wanted you to know that this isn't just about Noely. I know it's too soon to expect you to— Well, what I mean is. . . " He rubbed a big hand across his face and then said in a rush, his voice barely louder than a whisper, "I just wanted you to know—I love you, Angelina. With all of my heart. More with every passing day."

He hardly dared to look at her, but when he did, he saw that her tears had come again. . .but this time, with a sense of wonder, he recognized them for what they were.

"And I love you," she whispered with a misty smile.

❧

Clara, with Noely in hand, stood beside Angelina and Gabe as the pair faced Mr. Lawrence in the gentleman's parlor later that evening. Having returned home from an hour's play with the exuberant child, the news of an impending wedding was almost more than Clara's old heart could contain. But observing the couple, seeing the breathless smiles and exchanges of expression, she could do naught but thank the Lord for His wondrous working—and for the influential justice of the peace's abilities to make swift arrangements.

Her nephew had seemed much more settled since these two dear ones had shown up on the doorstep. Noely had provided a new avenue for his attention, one that was separate from his ministry, one far more personal which put his faith into action. And Angelina, precious soul that she was, had brought to the fore a gentle, caring side of him which Clara knew he had buried deep inside long ago. They would be good for each other. All of them.

"You may kiss your bride," she heard Mr. Lawrence say.

Gabe smiled down at Angelina with heart-stopping tenderness, and she, with shining eyes, melted into his embrace. Their lips met. . .tentatively at first, then again with the greatest of joy, and they embraced for a long moment.

Noely leaned against Clara with a big grin, and Clara gave the child's tiny hand an encouraging squeeze.

Who would have thought this foundling would bring together two people who once considered themselves undesirable? Strange what love could do—and right before Christmas, too.

Christmas. Ever so special. . .ever so precious. From the very beginning the most wondrous of days.

And all for the love of a Child.

Paper Roses

JoAnn A. Grote

Chapter 1

Minneapolis, Minnesota, 1893

*H*ow can life have gone from perfect to perfectly awful in only two weeks? Vernetta Larson wondered, seating herself at the luxuriously appointed Thanksgiving dinner table. The crystal and china glinting in the light of the gas chandelier seemed to mock her with their reminder of the life of wealth she'd taken for granted for so long.

Her tall, broad-shouldered Swedish father took his usual seat at the head of the table and bowed his head. His voice rumbled out with the same humble gratitude to the Lord as always.

How can he sound so sincere? Vernetta asked herself. *Is he truly thankful, even now?* In all her nineteen years, she'd not found it this difficult to be thankful, and things must seem worse to him.

"Hmph!" Her mother snapped her lace-edged napkin open with a plump, well-manicured hand and laid the napkin across the lap of her ice-blue satin gown. "Thanking God, indeed! We should demand to know why He let this happen instead."

No need to ask what her mother meant by "this." The financial depression, commonly known as the Panic, had finally reached its tentacles into their home. The bank Vernetta's father had started twenty-five years ago had failed two weeks earlier. Hundreds of other banks across the country had failed, but Vernetta hadn't expected her father's bank to fail.

The gray color of her father's face cut her to the quick. He'd looked poorly since the bank collapsed. Must her mother grind salt into his wounds? She bit her bottom lip hard to keep from expressing her thoughts. Her father wouldn't tolerate criticism of her mother, even in his defense.

"Now, Lena," he was saying in the strong Swedish accent that lingered even after twenty-five years in America, "I know you don't mean that. It isn't our Lord's fault that I and the other bank officers invested our depositors' money unwisely."

Her mother's blue eyes snapped. "And how were you to know railroads were a bad investment, I'd like to know, with tracks being laid from here to yon and back again?"

A grin spread across her father's broad face and twinkled in the blue eyes beneath his graying blond hair. "Now that's the woman I married, defending her man against the world."

A delicate flush swept over Mother's round face beneath the heavy, dark hair that was piled in a loose bun. "Anton, honestly!" Her lashes swept her suddenly rosy cheeks.

Father had often told Vernetta she looked like her mother had at her age. She'd never been able to see the resemblance between herself and the portrait of her mother at eighteen that hung above the parlor fireplace. Vernetta's long hair, which she wore up with a fashionable fringe of curly bangs, was not-quite-brown and not-quite-blond, certainly not the rich brown of her mother's. Her eyes weren't blue like her parents, but a striking, unusual violet. She had the traditional wide Scandinavian face but had a narrow chin instead of the rounded, broader chin of her mother.

Mother was fingering the fluted edge of the bud vase that held a single red rose. Father had given her that rose. There was one by each of their plates. They were beautiful, but Vernetta knew it was hard for her parents, seeing the single roses. For as long as Vernetta could remember, her father had bought two dozen red and white roses for the Thanksgiving table and for the Christmas table also. It was a tradition he'd started the first year he'd made enough money to more than meet the young couple's expenses.

Vernetta smiled at her mother's flustered attitude. *She looks like a young bride, very much in love,* she thought. She couldn't recall ever seeing her mother look that way. It was sweet but cut into her heart with fresh pain.

Would her own face ever fill with love for another that way? Love had walked out of her own life last evening. She pushed down the pain that had filled her chest since she awoke. She'd thought she might receive an engagement ring from Andrew Reed for Christmas. He'd been courting her for six months and had profusely proclaimed his affection for her.

Last night he'd made it clear that he wouldn't be escorting her in the future. He'd actually told her that his parents wouldn't allow him to see a young woman whose father had embarrassed himself by losing his business and his family fortune. *I'm better off without him if his love is based on my father's money and position,* she told herself for the twentieth time since he'd spoken the awful words. The thought helped her hold her head up in pride but didn't help her wounded heart.

She hadn't told her mother of Andrew's decision yet. Mother had been thrilled that a future lawyer, the son of a state senator, was courting her daughter. "The best marriage prospect in the state," she'd said. Vernetta sighed.

The swinging door between the kitchen and formal dining room opened, and a maid entered with a large china soup tureen. Along with her came a welcome drift of warmth from the large cookstove and the smell of wood smoke mixed with the mouth-watering odors of pumpkin pie and roast turkey.

Dora was the only servant left in the household. She wouldn't be here, Vernetta remembered, if she hadn't offered to work for room and board. Jobs were almost impossible to find in these days of high unemployment.

Dora moved smartly as always. The white apron covering her black dress was crisp, as was the small white hat she wore pinned behind the blond braid that circled her head. She set the tureen in the middle of the lace-covered, mahogany table and served the three Larsons.

Vernetta accepted a steaming bowl of rich oyster stew, the usual first course in their Thanksgiving meal. "Thank you, Dora."

The front-door chimes sung through the house, and Dora hurried to answer them. She was back in a minute with a calling card on a small silver tray.

Father took the card and frowned. Vernetta thought his face grew grayer. His broad shoulders drooped beneath his fine jacket. "A newspaper man?" he growled. "Haven't they torn me apart enough? Must they also invade my home and family on Thanksgiving?"

Vernetta's heart felt like it was being squeezed. She pushed back her chair and stood in one smooth motion. "I'll ask him to leave."

"The gentleman said he wishes to speak with you about boarding, Mr. Larson." Dora's quick, softly spoken clarification stopped Vernetta before she reached the door to the hallway. She swung around, staring at her father.

Mother slapped her napkin onto the table beside her plate. "He is no gentleman if he interrupts us on Thanksgiving, Dora."

"Yes ma'am," Dora murmured, retreating to the kitchen.

Mother leaned forward, glaring at Vernetta's father. "Anton, I told you I won't have my home turned into a boardinghouse!"

Father's huge chest lifted in a sigh. He looked so tired that Vernetta's chest clinched in pain for him. "Lena, I cannot possibly afford to keep this house without some kind of income. I didn't think the ad would be in the newspaper until tomorrow. I apologize for this intrusion." He handed Vernetta the gentleman's calling card. "Please ask him to come back tomorrow."

Hurrying down the walnut-paneled hall, the sound of her footsteps hidden in the depths of the carpet runners, Vernetta could hear her mother's angry voice through the closed door. Her cheeks grew hot. Could the possible boarder hear the tirade?

She set her thin lips firmly and lifted her chin. *No matter how bad things become, I won't allow myself to become bitter like Mother,* she promised herself. She barely knew the woman her mother had become since the bank failure. *Starting tonight, each evening I will find something for which to be thankful, no matter how trivial, and write it down in my diary. I won't allow my soul to become warped.*

The man, who had been seated on the upholstered mahogany chaise near the door, almost leaped to his feet when he saw her, his brown derby in his hands. A few snowflakes still sat on the camel-colored wool coat covering his brown, high-buttoned business suit. His black hair was a tumble of curls he'd obviously tried and failed to repress.

Vernetta found herself responding immediately to his friendly brown eyes and quick smile. Remembering their roles, she suppressed the smile that had come to her lips in answer to his own. She glanced at the card. "Thank you for your interest in our ad, Mr.—"

"Thomas Michael McNally." He bowed from the waist with a flourish of his derby that brought back her smile.

"Yes, so your card states. It is Thanksgiving, Mr. McNally. Could you please return tomorrow?"

"Unfortunately, I can't, Miss Larson. I have to catch a train for an out-of-town assignment in an hour. I won't be back until midnight tomorrow."

Was this true, she wondered, *or was it Irish blarney?* In spite of his Irish last name, there was no hint of an accent. His people must have been in America for a long time.

"One of the men who works in the advertising department at the *Tribune* knows I'm looking for a room," he continued. "He knew from the address this would be a fine place to stay and, that is. . ." His fingers played with the edge of his derby, and he stumbled over his words.

Vernetta felt blood seep from her face. *He recognized Father's name as the one placing the ad,* she realized. Once it would have been a sign of the station her father had achieved. Now it was a sign of his failure. Mr. McNally's knowledge of her father's business affairs was likely also the reason he knew she was Miss, not Mrs., Larson.

She lifted her chin, folded her hands together at her waist, and watched him. She wasn't about to offer him a way out of his predicament. The newspapers hadn't been kind to her father. *I'd have thought when they reported his bank's failure to the world, they'd have also remembered all he's done for this city through the years.*

Their gazes met. She thought his eyes surprisingly honest—for a newspaperman. He spread his arms slightly and lifted his thick, dark eyebrows. "I didn't want to miss the opportunity to stay in such a fine home. Most boardinghouses aren't anywhere near this nice, though I expect a lady like yourself wouldn't know that firsthand. I realize it's inexcusable, intruding on your family at Thanksgiving, but—"

"But you aren't above offering an excuse, just the same," she ended for him, unable to control her grin at the obvious.

His laugh filled the hall. She decided she quite liked the sound of it and the way his eyes almost shut in a mass of crinkles when he laughed. "You're quite right, Miss Larson. Ungentlemanly behavior, at the very least. I most humbly apologize."

"Let me show you a room."

"That won't be necessary. I'm sure the room will be more than adequate. However, I would prefer the quiet of a room at the back, if you have one, after the noise of the news office."

She told him the rental amount in the most businesslike voice she could muster. Her father had decided to charge more than most places, knowing the value of their location.

He nodded without hesitation at the price, as if agreeing it was fair, and she breathed a quiet sigh of relief. With greater confidence, she explained the boarders would be eating in the kitchen and would have the use of the family living room. Father knew Mother wouldn't allow the invasion of their formal dining room and parlor.

Vernetta showed the young man to the living room, which was across the broad hall from the dining room. The living room was comfortable, with wallpaper striped in shades of mauve and pearl, mauve plush-covered furniture, and a welcoming fireplace. "You may wait here while I ask my father if we might accept you as a boarder, Mr. McNally."

He seemed a pleasant young man. Crossing the hall, she whispered to the Lord, "Perhaps his cheerful spirit would be contagious, Father. Our home could use a little cheer!"

Entering the formal dining room, she avoided looking at her mother, whose disapproval seemed to fill the room. Mother had not been able to change Father's mind about renting.

"I'll trust your judgment," he assured Vernetta. "If you believe him to be a man of high character, rent him a room."

Mother's voice rang in disapproval as Vernetta left the room. Vernetta couldn't remember ever before hearing her mother's voice raised so high in anger. Would nice Mr. McNally hear those derogatory comments about the class of people from whom boarders came and about newspapermen in particular?

Upon entering the family room, Vernetta realized immediately that he could not help but hear. He looked almost as embarrassed as she felt. His brown eyes were filled with sympathy. His dark brows lifted. "Your mother?"

She nodded, trying to swallow her embarrassment. Her fingertips played with her rose-colored gown's silk skirt. "Her manners aren't usually so. . .so unacceptable. It's difficult for her, opening our home to strangers."

"Change is always frightening. We often react with bitterness or anger to the things that frighten us, don't you think?"

His words surprised her as much as the gentleness in his voice. He'd never met her mother, yet in only a moment he'd helped her understand her mother better. She smiled slightly. "Yes, we do."

He cleared his throat. "You, um, haven't said yet whether your father gave his approval."

"Oh! Yes, he did."

Mr. McNally's smile filled his face. "That's grand! I'll move in Saturday, if that's acceptable."

She assured him it was and walked him to the door. Snow was still falling in large, drifting flakes. *A nice start to the holiday season,* she thought.

Mr. McNally shifted his derby in his hands and cleared his throat. "I want you to know, Miss Larson, that you needn't fear I'll invade your family's privacy because I'm a newspaperman. I won't print anything derogatory about your family. I wouldn't print anything about your family at all without your father's approval."

Rather than reassure her, his comments sent chills along her arms while she watched him hurry down the snow-covered walk. She hadn't for a moment considered that danger! Could he be trusted? Or had she betrayed her father's trust in her judgment?

She was still worrying about it when she slipped onto her chair in the dining room.

"You'll have to eat quickly, Vernetta," her mother said. "You won't have much time to prepare for tonight's party. Wait until Andrew sees you in your new green satin with the black velvet trim! He'll likely propose to you on the spot."

"Lena!" Father's protest wasn't loud or even very serious. Vernetta suspected he made it because Mother expected it of him.

Mother waved a hand at him in dismissal. "We all know Andrew is smitten with her. Manners may prohibit our discussing it with others, but why not mention the obvious within the family?" She picked up her crystal goblet. "When is Andrew stopping for you, Vernetta?"

Vernetta's stomach clenched. She took a deep breath, trying to release the tightness. This was the moment she'd dreaded. Facing her mother with the news was almost harder than hearing it from Andrew.

She lifted her head, forced a smile, and looked into her mother's expectant eyes. "Andrew isn't coming, not tonight, not ever again."

Chapter 2

Mother slowly set the crystal goblet back on the table. "What do you mean, not ever again?"

Vernetta's hands clenched the linen napkin in her lap. The anger and apprehension in her mother's eyes made her want to steal away and pretend everything was as usual between herself and Andrew, but that wouldn't change the facts. Her smile trembled. She tried to keep her voice light. "Andrew has decided he doesn't care to escort me any longer."

"Nonsense! He dotes on you!" Mother snorted and shook her head. "I suppose you said something foolish and hurt his pride. You must be careful of men's pride, you know. Men like to think they are strong, but their pride is their weak point. A wise woman is careful to build it up."

Vernetta caught her bottom lip between her teeth. Mother certainly hadn't been building up Father's pride lately!

"What foolish thing did you do to raise Andrew's ire?" Disgust dripped from her mother's voice.

Anger heated Vernetta's cheeks. "I did nothing foolish. He. . ." She caught back the revealing truth just in time. She glanced at her father's puzzled expression. It would tear him apart if he knew Andrew was no longer seeing her because her father had lost his fortune. Father would be sure to think her broken heart was his fault. She swallowed hard. "Andrew simply discovered his feelings for me weren't what he thought."

"Nonsense! Of course they are the same." Mother wagged a finger in Vernetta's direction. "I want you to apologize to him at the first opportunity for whatever it is you have done."

Vernetta drew an angry breath. "Mother! I—"

Father threw his napkin down beside his plate. "Lena, that's enough of this. If Andrew has so little sense that he would walk away from our daughter, then he isn't good enough for her."

Tears heated Vernetta's eyes at her father's defense, his love warming her heart.

"We must think of our daughter's future, Mr. Larson," Mother reminded him indignantly. "Her social standing may be hurt irretrievably if she doesn't apologize to Andrew."

"No one worth their salt will think less of Vernetta because that young man is no longer escorting her."

"But—"

Father cut off Mother's comment with a sharp wave of his hand and a scowl. "I'm sure any number of respectable young men will gladly take Andrew's place, if she's willing to allow them to do so."

"Mr. Larson—"

Angry lights darted in his eyes, but his voice didn't raise a note. "The subject is closed. Let's remember this is a *Thanksgiving* meal."

Vernetta kept her gaze on her plate as she started eating. She was grateful for her father's reprieve. *But I've no doubt Mother will reopen the subject as soon as we're alone.* Her stomach tightened at the thought.

⌒

Two days later, Vernetta stood patiently in the mirrored fitting room of the most exclusive shop in a downtown emporium. The woman who was fitting her elegant party gown and the clerk who had waited on her were as familiar as old friends. She had purchased her tailor-made gowns here for years.

In the past, the visits had been times of anticipation. Now the reflection of herself in the satin and lace gown enveloped her in sadness. *I feel like a thief,* she thought, *as though I'm stealing from Father, ordering gowns I know he can't afford.*

She'd argued with her mother over the dresses. "My gowns from last year will be adequate. Surely no one has bothered to remember what I wore last year."

Mother's eyes had flashed. "Do you want to advertise that your father is putting us into the poorhouse? No, your image must defy those awful newspaper tales. Besides, since you've chased away Mr. Reed, you must be especially careful of your appearance if we wish you to attract another worthy suitor."

The look her mother flashed assured Vernetta that Mother believed "we" did indeed wish to attract another "worthy suitor."

Thomas Michael McNally's smiling face, entirely lacking Andrew's pretentious facade, flashed in her mind. She saw her reflection smile in response to the cheerful Irish eyes that filled her imagination. The regret that flashed through her at the realization that such a man would never be considered a worthy suitor surprised her.

"I think we're done for today, Miss Larson," the clerk said from the floor, where she'd been seated while pinning a piece of the lace insert to the gown's skirt. "What do you think of it?"

Vernetta's gaze swept unenthusiastically over the gown's reflection. "It's lovely."

With the clerk's assistance, she removed the pinned garment and dressed in her simple but elegant gray cashmere suit, which was trimmed with black embroidery. As she entered the main shop, the head clerk hurried over, her face wreathed in smiles. Vernetta responded to the clerk's thanks for her orders even as her mind was elsewhere.

The daring thought blazed through her mind, taking her breath. *Maybe I could find a position here.* A picture of her mother's face, filled with horror at the idea of her daughter being a mere store clerk, came immediately to mind. Vernetta pushed it away. *Mother's fragile pride isn't as important now as Father's money problems.*

"Mrs. Drew," she interrupted the head clerk before she could lose her courage, "I would like to apply for a position here."

Mrs. Drew's straight brows met above her thin nose. Her eyes grew a bit glassy, but she didn't lose her smile. "A position? What type of work are you seeking?"

Vernetta was glad for the years of social training that kept her voice low and pleasant, without a trace of the tremors she felt in her spirit. "Why, I don't know exactly. A sales clerk, perhaps. I do know your line of clothing well after all the years I've purchased here."

Mrs. Drew pressed her lips together and shook her head. "I'm sorry, but we've no positions available. The store's owner is keeping on more employees than the work justifies already." Pity filled her eyes. "It would have been delightful working with you, I'm certain." She spread her hands slightly. "Perhaps when the current financial troubles have passed. . ."

"Of course. Thank you." Vernetta tried to keep her chin up and her walk casually graceful as she left the room, but inside she felt like running out the door in tears, like a small girl.

She pushed through the emporium's heavy front doors onto the sidewalk. Tall buildings on either side of the downtown street tunneled the December wind in shrieking gusts that whipped a pedestrian's clothing. Vernetta's warm, magenta muffler blew over the shoulders of her gray coat. She tucked her chin into the muffler's soft folds.

The cold, stinging wind brought the tears to her eyes she had managed to repress since the conversation with Mrs. Drew. The bustling Christmas shoppers filling the walk were blurred to her. The scent of roasted chestnuts from the nearby street vendor didn't warm the air.

Her long, heavy wool skirt brushed against something. "Excuse me," she murmured, barely glancing in the direction of the child her skirt had touched.

"Flowers, miss?"

"No, thank you, I—" She focused her gaze on the child. The sight stopped the words in her throat.

The girl hunkered inside a worn brown corduroy coat. It was woefully short. From beneath it stuck slender legs encased in once-white woolen stockings with holes in the knees. Attempts had been made to darn the holes, but even the darning was wearing through.

Isn't her skirt even long enough to cover her knees? Vernetta wondered.

The girl held up a homemade satin flower, clutched in a glove as holey as her stockings. With the other hand, she brushed her hair from her face. Wind-whisked, golden-brown waves tangled about her red ears. Snowflakes hung like miniature stars on her lashes.

Vernetta's heart crimped. *The child must be freezing!*

"Flowers, miss?" the girl repeated between chattering teeth.

"What a lovely idea!" Vernetta smiled at her, opening her purse. Her smile died. She had no money with her. She'd forgotten that she'd given her last coins to the maid for the marketing that morning. Her father's financial worries had caused her many disappointments, but none so painful as this. To think she didn't even have a few pennies for a purchase from a flower girl!

The wind tossed the end of her muffler into her face. She brushed it aside impatiently, then noticed the girl's gaze resting on the muffler. Vernetta hesitated only a moment. She pulled the strings of her purse shut and smiled again. "I'm sorry. I haven't any money with me today, but perhaps we can work out a trade."

The girl's brows met in a puzzled frown above huge gray eyes.

"I'd truly love some of your beautiful flowers. Would you accept my muffler in exchange? It's new. This is the first time I've worn it."

The girl stared at the muffler as if unable to believe such good fortune could be hers. "I. . .I don't know."

Clearly the child wasn't accustomed to bartering. Was she afraid her parents wouldn't want her to bring home a scarf instead of money? *But it's worth far more than the pennies her entire supply of flowers would bring,* Vernetta assured herself.

Quickly, she removed it from her neck. Icy air struck her exposed throat. She winced at the sharp pain of it but didn't change her mind. The girl had no hat or muffler. *She must feel like an ice sculpture!* Vernetta thought, holding out the muffler.

The girl reached her worn gloves to touch it. A soft gasp came from her chapped lips when her fingers closed around the luxurious thickness.

Vernetta knelt before her and wrapped the muffler over the girl's head and ears, then around her neck. "How is that?"

"Oh! It's wonderful!" The girl's words were barely a whisper.

Vernetta beamed at her. "I'm glad you like it."

"How many flowers do you want?" the girl asked cautiously.

Vernetta looked over the flowers in the oak basket. Her muffler was worth many more flowers than the basket held, but she couldn't take all of the girl's wares. Silk and satin flowers mixed with crepe paper roses. Surely the crepe paper were the least costly to make. The observation decided Vernetta immediately. But how many to request? To ask for too few would belittle the girl's creations. "Let's see, do you think a dozen paper roses would be a fair trade?"

The girl's eyes sparkled. Her mouth spread in a grin above her pointed chin. "Oh, that would be a fine trade, miss." She held out the basket. "Would you like to choose them?"

Vernetta chose a selection of pink, red, and white paper roses.

"You'd best let me wrap them in one of these old newspapers, miss, so's the wind won't wreck them." The girl pulled a newspaper page from the bottom of the basket and deftly rolled the flowers in it. "Here you are, miss."

"Thank you. I'm Miss Vernetta Larson. What is your name?"

The girl looked suddenly shy. Her winter-whisked cheeks couldn't possibly grow redder, so they didn't betray whether she blushed. Her voice was low, and Vernetta leaned forward to catch her words before the wind snatched them away. "Lily, miss. Lily Mills."

"What a pretty name! How old are you, Lily?"

"Eight."

Only eight years old and trying to make her living on a cold Minneapolis street! "I shall enjoy your flowers, Lily. I'll think of you each time I look at them. They've brightened my day."

Her own problems did seem lighter as she hurried down the street, the bundle of flowers held close against her coat. *But, Lord, how can You allow poverty to put children into such a position?* her heart cried.

Chapter 3

Vernetta's troublesome thoughts about the flower girl evaporated when she walked through the walnut and etched glass door into her home. Round-topped trunks and worn valises, some of tapestry and some of leather, were piled about the large entrance hall. Two tall women with white-gray hair in large buns were giving contradictory directions at the same time to a smiling Thomas Michael McNally.

Vernetta recognized the women as Cora and Cornelia Wibbey, unmarried sisters in their sixties. They'd rented the bedroom at the front of the house, the one with large windows overlooking the front walk.

Mr. McNally's gaze met Vernetta's, and they shared an amused smile over the sisters' vocal disagreement. The shared amusement sent happy warmth through Vernetta's chest. *I was right about him*, she thought, setting her newspaper-wrapped bouquet on the marble-topped hall table. *His cheerful spirit will be good for our home.*

He tucked one valise under an arm, grabbed a valise handle in each hand, and started up the stairs. The sisters followed, holding their skirts out of their way, neither sister missing a syllable of instruction to Mr. McNally, urging him to handle the valises with care and telling him where each was to be placed, though he could not even see the door to their room as yet.

How kind of him to help them carry their things upstairs, she thought. Dora, as the only remaining servant, would be hard-pressed to provide all the service the guests needed. Father was at the bank, and Vernetta could not see her mother waiting on the boarders. She reached for one of the smaller valises, intent on helping.

"There you are!" Mother bustled toward her, the sound of her footsteps hidden in the thick oriental carpet. "I thought you'd never get back from the dressmaker's."

"Is something wrong?"

"Everything is wrong! All these extra people in the house are making me addlepated."

More likely you are making them addlepated, Vernetta thought. She turned toward the hall closet, removing her coat and hiding her smile from her mother.

"What have they done?"

Mother's arm swept through the air, indicating the pile of luggage remaining in the entryway. "Look at all this. . .this. . .*rubbish* they are moving into our home! First that newspaperman arrived—"

"Mr. McNally?" Vernetta asked, keeping her tone innocent, trying to establish delicately the fact that "that newspaperman" had a name.

"I think that's his name." Mother made a small dismissing motion with her hand. "Anyway, he came with his paraphernalia right after you left. The women arrived right on his heels, and Captain Rogers arrived before the busman had carried in all the women's luggage. Goodness! The busman was opening and closing the door, letting in the wind and cold, as though we'd nothing better to do than heat all of Minneapolis!"

Vernetta patted her mother's shoulder. "It's over now, dear. Surely all the boarders' belongings have been delivered."

"I should hope so! It took Dora and me all day yesterday to find places to store our personal belongings in order to make the rooms available for the boarders."

As Vernetta remembered it, Dora had been the one to pack the belongings and carry them to the attic. "I haven't met Captain Rogers yet. Is he in his room?"

"Yes. He said he needed a nap." She wiped the back of one hand across her forehead. "*I'm* the one who could use a nap! I do hope he won't be sickly or expect us to nurse him."

"I'm sure he's only tired, Mother. He must be quite elderly. Wasn't he a captain in the Civil War?"

"So he says." She sighed deeply. "I'd best check to see that Dora has everything in hand for luncheon." She swept down the hall in a rustle of skirts and with an air of important haste.

Vernetta reached for the paper roses, shaking her head. Her mother's attitude would be amusing—if it weren't so sad.

From the china closet that filled most of one dining room wall, Vernetta selected three porcelain vases. She filled them with the roses, then set the cheerful bouquets on a silver tray and carried them up the stairs. Maybe the flower girl's roses would brighten the boarders' rooms.

∽

After dinner, Vernetta stopped in the kitchen. "Did you remember to serve coffee and dessert to the boarders in the living room, Dora?"

"I'm preparing it, miss, as you asked me to do." Dora indicated the silver tray on the table. Delicate rose-sprinkled china cups and saucers sat beside a matching cream pitcher and sugar bowl. Scalloped sugar cookies rested daintily upon an etched crystal plate. Linen napkins with small pink roses embroidered in the corners lay to one side.

The silver coffee service was on another silver tray. Vernetta knew Dora would be using it to serve after-dinner coffee to her parents in the parlor, as usual. Her mother didn't know Vernetta had instructed Dora to serve the boarders in the living room. She was sure her mother wouldn't approve. "They are boarders, not guests," she had repeatedly informed Vernetta throughout the day.

What did the flower girl have for dinner tonight? Vernetta wondered, gazing at the simple dessert trays. *Did she have something warm and filling after the day spent in the cold Minneapolis wind and snow?*

Dora set the coffee-filled silver teakettle, which matched the coffeepot with which she would serve Vernetta's parents, on the tray for the boarders. Vernetta reached for it and smiled at Dora. "I'll serve the boarders."

Dora's eyes grew large. "Oh no, miss, you mustn't! Your mother would never approve."

"Nonsense. It is the boarders' first evening in our home. It wouldn't be proper not to welcome them. Besides, Mother and Father are waiting for you in the parlor."

⌒

With a brass poker, Thomas pushed at the bottom log in the fire grate. It broke quickly with crackling sounds into charred pieces that glowed a cheerful orange.

The Wibbey sisters were seated on the plush mauve sofa on the other side of the room. Old Captain Rogers was reading the Minneapolis newspaper in the matching stuffed chair.

"Tell us about your war adventures, Captain Rogers," Cornelia was urging in a sugary voice that didn't match her lined, narrow face.

"Maybe the captain doesn't care to discuss the war," Cora reprimanded. "Might be his memories are too gruesome for women's delicate natures. Isn't that so, Captain?" She smiled at him in a manner Thomas thought oozed "understanding female."

Thomas thought he caught a sigh as the captain lowered the paper to show gentlemanly politeness to the women. "Some memories might be, some might not. The war was a long time ago. I prefer to live in the present."

Cornelia straightened her shoulders beneath her crocheted shawl and darted a "see, I was right" look at her sister, who ignored her.

Thomas's gaze dropped to the captain's right leg. There was something wrong with it, something that caused the captain to walk with a cane. Had he injured it in the war? Was that one of the reasons he preferred to live in the present instead of rehashing old war stories with other veterans as so many of the veterans of the War between the States liked to do?

He set the poker back in its brass holder and shifted his shoulders. His brown sack jacket was almost too warm to wear inside this evening, with the fire going. At the last place he'd rented, he would have removed his jacket without a thought while he relaxed after dinner.

A smile tugged at his lips. *Miss Vernetta Larson didn't live at my last boardinghouse. Not that she'd give me a second look.* A woman of Miss Larson's stature wouldn't have anything to do with a mere newspaper reporter. He likely wouldn't even see her this evening. Mrs. Larson had made it clear the boarders were to eat in the kitchen, relax in the living room, and generally stay as far from the Larson family members as possible. He understood Mrs. Larson's feelings, but he didn't like the unworthy way they made him feel.

He glanced up as Vernetta entered. "Let me help you with that." He quickly replaced the poker and hurried across the cabbage rose carpet. "Those cookies look mighty tempting."

"Thank you," she murmured as he took her tray. "You may set it here." She indicated the marble-topped table in front of the couch.

Settling herself in a delicate chair, she reached for the teapot and smiled at the Wibbey sisters. "Do you take cream or sugar in your coffee?"

"Both, please." Cornelia's gentle smile shone through her wrinkles.

Cora's back straightened. "You needn't be serving us, deary. You should be visiting with your family not us boarders."

Thomas could see, however, that Cora was pleased at Miss Larson's service. So was he. He'd thought from the moment he met her that Miss Vernetta Larson was a young woman with a large heart. He liked the way she treated himself and the other boarders as guests. *Especially the others,* he hurriedly assured himself. It gave his heart a warm glow to see Miss Larson welcoming them as friends.

Thomas had just taken his cup from her when the door chimes rang. A couple minutes later, the maid entered. To his surprise, she handed him a small envelope.

He noticed the notepaper's fine quality as he removed the note with "Mrs. Jonathan Johanson" written in script across the front. Quickly he scanned the contents. His heart sank.

Vernetta's sweet voice cut through his disturbed thoughts. "I hope it's not bad news."

"Nothing irreparable," he assured her, "but it is a problem. I work with a newsboys' Sunday school each week. As part of the program, we supply a lunch for the children. It's an important part of the ministry, as many of the children aren't adequately fed at home, especially during these hard times."

He lifted the note slightly. "The woman who was to supply the lunch tomorrow informs me she is down with the grippe." He tried to smile. "I won-der if any of you has a suggestion as to how I might arrange lunch for a bunch of hungry youngsters on short notice?"

"Why, how thoughtless of the woman!" Cora's eyes flashed. "Surely she would have made arrangements for the food before the last minute. Perhaps she only means that she'll not be able to be there to serve the food. You can surely find a way to transport it from her home to the mission."

He shook his head. "I'm afraid that isn't the case."

Vernetta's face looked troubled. "The children mustn't go without lunch. Dora," she addressed the maid, who was leaning over the tray, "do we have anything we can prepare for the children?"

Dora hesitated. "I could probably find something, miss, if Mrs. Larson would allow it."

Thomas's hopes disintegrated. Mrs. Larson didn't appear the type of woman whose heart would be touched by the children's plight.

Determination fixed itself upon Vernetta's features. "I will speak with Mother about it. Perhaps it would be best if we had a menu in mind when I do so. Mr. McNally, how many children do you expect?"

"There's usually about forty, all together."

He saw the surprise and concern flash across her eyes, but her training didn't allow it to show in her manners, words, or tone. "Dora, what do we have to feed forty hungry youngsters?"

Dora rubbed the palms of her hands over her starched white apron. "We haven't enough meat to serve so many. I could make a hearty stew or soup though. And maybe doughnuts. Doughnuts are always popular with children and filling, too. The cost wouldn't be too great," she assured.

"Thank you, Dora. I'll speak with Mother immediately." Vernetta rose gracefully.

Thomas stood, too. "I don't wish to cause trouble. If you think your mother wouldn't approve—"

"Not approve of feeding hungry children? Nonsense."

He wasn't as certain of Vernetta's mother's generosity as he was of hers. "I'll be glad to pay for the food. It's the preparing of it that's beyond my abilities."

Her laughing eyes lit his heart. "I'm sure that can be remedied with Dora's help."

Dora blinked in surprise, then fell in with Vernetta's spirit. "To be certain, miss."

Thomas's cheeks heated as the Wibbey sisters chuckled their approval of Vernetta's plan to educate him in the art of cooking, but he only grinned at Vernetta. "I'll be grateful for the lesson."

It wasn't long before the large, modern kitchen was bustling with activity. The shining black stove with its fancy grillwork poured forth welcome heat. While Dora prepared the doughnut batter and heated oil, Thomas and Vernetta washed and dried the dinner dishes, and the Wibbey sisters browned meat and cut vegetables for the soup.

For Thomas, the most fun was watching the doughnuts plump up crispy brown and fat in the hot oil. The doughnut making had just begun when Mrs. Larson called Dora away to prepare the family's Sunday clothes for church the next day, brushing and pressing outfits and polishing shoes and boots. The remaining ladies and Thomas took turns retrieving the bobbing golden circles, rolling some in powdered sugar.

"Don't you be eating the young ones' dinner!" Cornelia slapped lightly at Thomas's hand when he reached for a cooled doughnut. Her eyes were laughing like those of a grandmother teasing a hungry grandson.

Thomas winked at her. "I'll share it with you. Just one, to make sure they are fit for the newsies." The women laughed at him as he split the doughnut four ways.

"Tell us about the newsboys' club," Vernetta urged.

He glanced at her. Powdered sugar dappled one cheek, flushed red from the heat of the stove, and the tip of her chin. Her eyes sparkled with the fun of cooking with the others. *She looks delectable,* he thought.

"Well," he started, "the club was started by the church I attend. The church-men were concerned for the newsboys' welfare and souls. Most of them come from poor homes. Many don't have families, and their entire support comes from selling newspapers."

The women nodded. Sympathy replaced the sparkle in Vernetta's eyes.

"We struck on the idea of starting a Sunday school for the boys. We were afraid they wouldn't attend with the other children. We were right. They wouldn't even come to the church for a class. Then one of the churchwomen, who has a store downtown, offered the use of the store basement. We jumped at the opportunity. It was right in the boys' neighborhood, and they started coming. It didn't take long to find out a lot of them don't get enough to eat, especially in these hard times, so to sweeten the draw, we added the lunch. We also give away books for those who attend regularly."

"What a wonderful ministry," Vernetta said.

The Wibbey sisters murmured their agreement.

"Perhaps. . ." Thomas hesitated. Would Vernetta think him bold or ungen-tlemanly in his request? Surely she would take it in the manner he offered it. "With the woman who was in charge of the lunch ill, we could use another volunteer tomorrow. Would you care to assist us, Miss Larson?"

"I should be glad to." Vernetta's immediate response and the warmth in her eyes assured him of her sincerity.

He smiled at her across the hot stove, but it was her generous heart that warmed him.

Chapter 4

Vernetta was glad her father hadn't yet sold all of their horses and carriages. She didn't know how they would have managed if they'd had to transport the soup and doughnuts downtown by streetcar. Though her father gave permission to use the carriage, her mother did not agree to Vernetta's request that Dora be allowed to help at the mission. "She is needed here. Surely you don't expect me to prepare and serve the boarders' Sunday meal?"

In front of the mission storefront, Thomas lifted a large basket and handed it to Vernetta. She could smell the fresh, yeasty scent of the doughnuts hidden beneath the large oatmeal linen towel. She followed him as he carried the heavy soup kettle.

"Watch your step," he warned. "The snow has mostly been cleared, but there are a few icy patches left."

They went down the steps that were protected from the sidewalk by a cast-iron railing and entered the basement of a millinery shop. Immediately Thomas was surrounded by noisy boys, ranging in age from ten to sixteen.

"Hi, Mr. McNally!"

"Need some help there?"

"Thought ya mighta got lost in a snowdrift! What took ya so long?"

They greeted Thomas with friendly pats on the back or slaps on his shoulders, in the manner men and boys have that is so incomprehensible to women.

Vernetta smiled at the boys, who swarmed between her and Thomas. They came in every size and shape, but their clothes were the same: hip-length coats over vests, cotton shirts, corduroy trousers—all ragged.

One boy, taller than the others and with broader shoulders, bumped his shoulder against Thomas's. "Who's the new lady?" He whisked his hat off politely, but his brown eyes met hers boldly, in a manner to which she wasn't accustomed. Vernetta swallowed a gasp and took a small step backward.

Thomas introduced her. "Miss Vernetta Larson. Miss Larson, this is Erik Johansen, leader of the newsboys in this part of the city."

Vernetta could tell he hadn't noticed the boy's ungentlemanly gaze. She nodded cautiously. "How do you do, Erik?"

The boy reached for her basket. "Let me help ya with that, Miss Larson."

Vernetta allowed him to take it from her. "Thank you."

She followed Erik and Thomas into another room. It was small, with wooden barrels and crates piled along the cold walls. An old wood-burning cookstove was already giving off heat. Thomas set the soup on it. Erik set the basket of doughnuts down on a long, well-worn wooden table, then slid his hat back on.

Thomas slid it off in one smooth move. "You forgot, it stays off while you're inside."

Erik flushed, and Vernetta turned away, glancing over the bare kitchen, not wanting to embarrass the proud lad further. "Will you get a couple of the other boys together and see that the classrooms are set up, Erik?" she heard Thomas ask. Then Erik shuffled out of the room.

Vernetta was glad to discover that there were other women at the mission to help serve the lunch. Thomas introduced her to them, then invited her to join him in looking over the rest of the Sunday school.

Children were milling about everywhere: not only boys, but girls, too. They looked like feminine versions of the boys with their tattered, misfitting clothing and dirty faces and hair.

"I thought this was a newsboys' Sunday school," she whispered to Thomas. "What are the girls doing here?"

Thomas turned surprised eyes to her. "Didn't I mention the flower girls? Not long after the school for the newsies started, it was expanded to include the girls."

He shook his head, sadness filling the lines of his face. "They're as bad off as the boys, working the streets with their wares, some of them living on the streets as well."

"Surely not!" Her whisper burned her throat. She looked at the ill-clad, ill-cared-for children, laughing and running about while they waited for class to begin.

He took her elbow and bent toward her to say in a low voice that wouldn't carry to the children, "They have a rough lot in life. We do all we can for them." His touch urged her forward.

The tour didn't take long. Thomas explained how the part of the large basement room that wasn't used for storage for the millinery was divided into classrooms with screens and with blankets hung over wires. Simple oak chairs were set in each classroom. Easels with slates stood at the front of the rooms. A few pictures on construction paper, obviously the work of the children, were pinned to the blanket walls.

All along the tour, boys stopped Thomas. He introduced many of them to Vernetta. She was relieved that most of the boys did not look at her in Erik's insolent manner but was dismayed by the tough way they spoke and acted. *Like men in boys' bodies,* she thought.

Thomas stopped to speak to a boy, and Vernetta walked slowly back toward the public portion of the basement.

"No! Give it back!" a young girl's voice cried out from the middle of a circle of boys. Vernetta stopped, looking to see what was the matter.

A cloth doll appeared in a boy's hand, held above his head. The doll was passed from one high-held hand to another, amid boyish laughter and the girl's repeated pleas.

Vernetta took a step toward them. Before she could reach the circle, someone brushed by her.

Erik reached above the smaller boys with ease and grabbed the doll. "Quit actin' like slobs! Don'cha have anything better to do than tease girls?"

The younger boys bit their lips and backed away. Erik handed the doll to the girl. "Here ya are, Lily. Don't mind them."

Large, water-drenched gray eyes looked up at him. "Thanks, Erik."

Surprise made Vernetta's heart skip a beat. "Lily!" It was the flower girl from whom she'd bought the paper roses. Vernetta hurried forward.

Erik frowned at her and moved so he half-blocked the girl from Vernetta. "We don't need you. I can look after her."

Vernetta glanced at him in surprise. "I'm sure you can." She smiled and leaned forward. "We met the other day when I bought some of your beautiful flowers, remember?"

Lily only nodded. She leaned against Erik's leg. Her gaze didn't leave Vernetta's. One small hand reached up to clutch the soft muffler about her neck.

Does she think I'll ask her to return it? Vernetta wondered, shocked at the thought. "It's so nice to see you again. Is this your doll? What is her name?"

"Amy." Lily continued her hold on the muffler.

A whistle cut through the air. It was Thomas, calling everyone together for prayer and hymn singing.

"Come on, Lily." Erik started toward the group. Lily, her hand tucked safely in his, hurried along with him.

Thomas stopped beside Vernetta. "The grippe must be taking a lot of victims. We're short on teachers today. Would you mind helping out by teaching one of the Sunday schools for the flower girls?"

Vernetta agreed and was rewarded by Thomas's huge smile. She was glad to find Lily among her students. By the end of the class, the shy girl even smiled at her and had removed her grip on the muffler.

⌒

The sound of the horse's hooves were muffled by the snow and slush on the road as Thomas and Vernetta drove home in the carriage. As they passed through a residential area, the laughter of children danced through the crisp, nose-biting air.

Thomas laughed and pointed to children playing Fox and Geese on a large front yard. "They are so bundled in winter clothing that they run like penguins!"

Vernetta laughed with him. Remembering the children they'd been with earlier, her laughter died. "The newsboys and flower girls should be playing like this— lighthearted, enjoying the snow—not trying to earn a living on cold, dirty sidewalks."

"Yes, they should be able to live like the children they are." Thomas touched the gloved hands in her lap with one of his own. The touch lasted only a moment, but the intimacy of it surprised her. Her gaze darted to his face. His brown-eyed gaze met hers. "I knew you'd be like this—good and kind." His voice was quiet and rich, and the simple compliment seemed very personal.

Vernetta's breath seemed to stop. Her heart hammered in her chest.

Thomas broke their locked gazes to guide the horse as they met another carriage. "Mrs. Pilgrim said she was going to ask you to teach regularly."

Vernetta took a deep breath, trying to regain her equilibrium. "She did ask, and I agreed. I think it will be fun."

Thomas's grin split his face again. "I'm glad. Mrs. Pilgrim said the girls like you."

"I like them." Two boys in a snowball battle caught her eye. "It seems whenever I'm downtown, there is a newsboy on every corner. It's humbling to realize I wouldn't have been able to tell one from another before today. As though they were as interchangeable as. . .as the marbles with which they play!"

She knew Thomas must hear the shame in her voice, but she didn't know how to hide it. She *was* ashamed she hadn't paid more attention to these brave boys.

"Many of the boys, like Erik, and the flower girls are orphans." Thomas spoke quietly. "Others are runaways or have been abandoned by their parents. Right now with the Panic, more than the normal number of newsies and flower girls live with parents who are out of work."

"And I felt sorry for myself because Father lost his fortune." Her whisper sounded strained, even to her own ears. "We still have so much compared to those children."

"I don't know that we can always measure loss in that manner. Every loss requires healing and adjustment. Your father lost more than money. He acquired his fortune by his dedication to serving people. When the bank failed, he must have believed he'd failed those people. I'm sure believing that is a greater measure of failure to him than losing his fortune."

Vernetta stared at him, gratitude for his insight filling her with wonder. "Yes, that is exactly how he feels."

Neither spoke while Thomas guided the horse across the trolley tracks, the carriage jerking. Then Vernetta said, "The offering this morning surprised me. I would think the children would need the little money they make so badly that they wouldn't have anything to give. Yet every child put something in the plate."

"We encourage tithing. We also encourage saving. Most of the children have started savings accounts because of the Sunday school and add to their accounts regularly, though it might be only a few pennies. We don't force either tithing or savings. We believe the decision is between the children and God and their families, if they have families."

"I'm surprised their parents allow them to give money away during these hard times."

Thomas held the reins loosely. He had a thoughtful look on his wide, handsome face beneath his gray bowler. "I believe tithing and saving are ways of expressing their faith in our God of hope, don't you?" He guided the carriage to the horse stoop in front of Vernetta's home.

She recalled the verse from the fifteenth chapter of Romans that he'd read to the assembled classes that morning: *"Now the God of hope fill you with all joy and peace in believing, that you may abound in hope, through the power of the Holy Ghost."* She nodded slowly. "Don't you find it difficult to hope when you see the poverty the children live in?"

He sat looking out over the snow-covered lawns. "I think it is the work with the children that *gives* me hope." She watched his face as he struggled for the right words. "I know that no one person can solve all the children's problems, but if we each do what is put in front of us—what we are able to do financially, physically, and emotionally—how can things help but get better, even if bit by bit?"

Warmth spread through her chest at his words. "I guess they can't."

His answer to her question reminded her of when he first came to her home to ask about a room. She'd hoped he would become a boarder, for she'd felt they needed his cheerful spirit. *It was his spirit of hope we needed,* she thought. *My family needs that, the way the entire country needs the God of Hope now, in the midst of the Panic of 1893.*

Chapter 5

Vernetta bit her bottom lip and frowned, bending over the gown she was mending. She'd caught the hem with the heel of her shoe. Sewing had never been her strong suit, and it took all her concentration to keep her stitches even and small. She shifted slightly, so the light from the painted parlor lamp fell more strongly on her work.

She looked up at the quiet rap on the parlor door. Her mother, seated across the room on a delicate upholstered rocker, muttered, "What can those boarders want now," before raising her voice. "Come in."

Cora and Cornelia Wibbey bustled into the room, smiles filling their wrinkled faces. "Mrs. Larson, may we use your kitchen to make cookies?" Cora asked.

"For the men at the Veteran's Home," Cornelia elaborated.

"We'll pay for the ingredients of course," Cora added in a breathless tone.

Vernetta smiled. The ladies' attitude reminded her of ten-year-old girls who might ask the same favor. She found the manner with which they approached life delightful.

Mother held her needlework in one hand and made a shooing motion with the other. "Yes, yes, of course. But see that you clean up the kitchen after yourselves. Dora hasn't the time."

"Thank you, Mrs. Larson." Cornelia turned to leave.

Cora stood where she was, glancing about the parlor. "What a lovely room, Mrs. Larson! You've created a charming atmosphere. No wonder you spend so much time in here."

"Thank you, Miss Wibbey."

Cornelia grasped her sister's hand. "Come along, Cora. We must get started if we want to get those cookies baked this evening."

The door swung shut behind them silently. Mother gave a deep sigh and returned to her Swedish tatting. "Honestly, the boarders have become such a bother. I told your father they would, but he didn't listen to me. He said if they used the living room and kitchen, they wouldn't be under foot." She dropped both hands into her lap and glared across the room at Vernetta. "As though we could keep from running into them coming and going! The Wibbey sisters are the worst of the lot."

"How do you mean?"

"They are talkative and inquisitive. Why, they act as though they wish to be *friends* with us, and with Dora." Mother pinched her lips together and picked up her needlework again. "They should know their place."

Vernetta concentrated on her stitches, trying to quiet the indignation filling her chest. What was it Thomas had said the day they'd met? Oh yes. That people often react with bitterness or anger to change and the fears change brings in its wake. "Do you know what Miss Cornelia meant by saying the cookies were for the men at the Veteran's Home? Do they have friends there?"

"Not that I know of. I expect they mean to send the cookies with your father and Captain Rogers. The captain has friends at the home at Minnehaha Park. That young newspaperman has convinced your father to go with the captain to visit some Civil War veterans tomorrow."

"What a wonderful idea! It will be good for Father."

"Hmph! I'm not so sure of that. It would be better if he spent his time among men of his own class."

Vernetta bit back an angry retort.

"I expect the Wibbey sisters aren't baking those cookies for the veterans out of the goodness of their hearts," Mother added. "They've set their caps for the captain, or I'm not Swedish."

Laughter bubbled up inside Vernetta. "Both of them?"

"Of course, both of them." Her mother's eyebrows rose in surprise. "Isn't it obvious?"

"Now that you mention it, I guess it is. It's rather cute, isn't it? But I hope their hearts aren't truly involved. Wouldn't it be awful if one of the sisters won his affection and the other was left alone?"

"They should know better at their age." Mother straightened her shoulders. "Speaking of knowing better, I hope you aren't letting your heart get away from your head."

The smile the Wibbey sisters had brought to Vernetta's lips froze. "What do you mean?"

"You are friendlier than necessary with that young newspaperman. I think it would be better if you gave up the notion of working with the newsboys' Sunday school."

"Why would you object to my working with the children?"

"Don't put words in my mouth, child. I condone mission work, but I don't like you working so closely with that newspaperman. Your pride is bound to be a bit battered after losing Andrew. It would be only natural if you encouraged Mr. McNally's attentions."

"Mother, I have not—"

"I understand why you want to show Andrew that other young men find you attractive. However, a newspaperman will not make a man of Andrew's stature jealous. Such a friendship might chase away not only Andrew but other young men of our social standing."

Taking a deep breath to settle the indignation rising within her, Vernetta set the gown on the sofa beside her and stood. "I'd like to speak with Father. Is he in?"

Mother snorted inelegantly, her gaze still on her fancywork. "I expect you'll find him in the living room with Captain Rogers and that newspaperman. I can't imagine why he neglects our presence to spend time with them!" She looked up. "Now, don't you forget what I said about encouraging Mr. McNally's attentions."

"I won't forget, Mother." Vernetta slipped into the hallway, glad to leave her mother's acid remarks behind.

As her mother predicted, she found her father in the living room talking with Thomas. Captain Rogers was not with them. Yellow flames danced and crackled merrily in the fireplace in front of which the two men sat in wing chairs.

Vernetta was glad for the friendship her father was finding with Thomas and the captain, glad he was going to the Veteran's Home. It would do him good to center his attention on something besides his financial problems.

He still went to the bank daily. It was closed, but there was much to do to pass the bank into receivership. Vernetta knew from what he'd said that the work was depressing. He was no longer receiving an income for the work, either, and because of the time spent at the bank, he had no time to seek employment elsewhere.

"Who would hire a man whose bank has failed anyway?" he'd asked Vernetta one day. The memory sliced at her heart.

"The work you are doing with the newsboys is a good thing, Thomas," Father was saying. "They need young men to learn from, men they can look up to."

Thomas leaned forward, his elbows on his knees, his hands linked loosely. "I love the work, sir. From the first time I heard of the Sunday school, I've wanted to be part of it. I guess working at the newspaper makes the newsboys special to me."

Father wagged an index finger in Thomas's direction. "The time you give to those children is an investment in their lives. It will pay rewards in the future, the same as money that is invested earns interest."

"I hope the investment earns a good interest rate on each and every life." Thomas's voice was lower than usual. Vernetta heard the crack in it and knew he spoke his heart.

"There are no guarantees," Father warned. "We can't make choices for others, even when we can see their own choices are leading them into dangerous and unhappy places. There will be boys in whose lives you won't be able to tell you've made a difference. That will not lessen the importance of the lives your investment will change."

Thomas stared into the dancing flames. Vernetta could hear nothing but the crackle and pop from the fireplace as he considered her father's words. Then Thomas shifted his gaze to Father's face.

"You're right, sir." His voice was still low and quiet. "If I might be so bold, I hope you take your own advice to heart. You should not judge yourself and your career only by the investments that failed. You made many wise investments in the past that benefitted the people you served."

Sudden tears burned Vernetta's eyes and blurred her view of the two men.

Father cleared his throat. Still, his voice sounded thick. "Thank you, my boy."

Thank You for Thomas, she prayed silently. *He has been such a gift to our family.*

She blinked suddenly, staring at Thomas through her tears. No wonder her mother's implications about Thomas and herself had made her so angry. Her mother's perceptions had been far clearer than her own. *I think I am falling in love with him!*

A strange mixture of wonder and dread filled her. Her mother would be furious if she discovered Vernetta's feelings for Thomas. Likely she would think her daughter had fallen for "that young newspaperman" simply to upset her.

No need to worry about that yet, silly goose. Thomas Michael McNally has shown no signs of falling in love with me!

Sadness touched the edges of wonder that had filled her only moments before, like the brown wilt at the edges of a rose's petals.

Chapter 6

The next Sunday Vernetta waited for Thomas in the sleigh after Sunday school. He stood nearby on the sidewalk, talking with Erik. Watching them, she remembered the discussion between her father and Thomas. The memory warmed her more thoroughly than the thick buffalo lap robe Thomas had tucked about her.

A minute later he climbed up beside her and they started home. There had been a snowfall the night before, and the sleigh schussed along smoothly on its runners. The street was filled with others enjoying the sleighing. People greeted each other noisily as sleighs met and passed in the street. Sleigh bells lent melody to the crisp air, which carried the smell of wood smoke from numerous chimneys and stung Vernetta's nose.

"Hey McNally!" a young man called from a sleigh that drew alongside them. "Looks like you have a good sleigh and horse there. Come to the lake and let's race!" It was common for young people to race their sleighs on roads along the city's lakes.

Thomas laughed and waved him away. "Not with the lady with me!"

Vernetta saw his friend's gaze sweep over her face. "Don't blame you!" he called. He urged his horse on and in a minute left them behind.

Vernetta glanced at Thomas from the corner of her eye. She was learning to cherish this time traveling between the downtown Sunday school and home with Thomas. There were so few times they were alone. She found it easy to confide in Thomas during these times. Perhaps his concentration on driving helped; she knew every expression in her eyes and face were not open to his gaze.

"Every time I'm around the newsboys and flower girls I feel more useless," she confided now. "I've tried to find employment to help with the family finances, but with no success. I don't know how to do anything for which anyone will pay. Even the flower girls have more skills than me!"

"You're too hard on yourself. You forget that many of the children's out-of-work fathers have experience working and still can't find jobs. It's the hard times that are the cause, not your lack of skill."

"Your words are kind, but I'm not sure they are accurate in my case."

"Look at the impression you've had on the flower girls. Surely you don't consider that useless?"

"What do you mean?"

"Haven't you noticed they've begun imitating you? The way you carry yourself, your manner of speech, the way they are trying to be more careful of their appearance?" He flashed a smile at her. "They are imitating a most lovely example, if I may be so bold."

She turned her gaze quickly to the beaver fur muff that warmed her hands. She couldn't stop her smile at the unexpected compliment. *He finds me attractive!* Her heart swelled with joy.

His attention back on the horse and street, he said, "It was a great idea you had, bringing soft towels and soap for the kids to wash up with before dinner. Good training for them. And the flower girls liked the fragrant soap you brought."

Indeed, the hall had smelled like lavender when the girls were done washing their hands and faces. Vernetta remembered the way Lily had held the lavender-scented soap to her nose and breathed deeply before washing. "Now I'll smell like you, Miss Larson," she'd said in a timid voice.

A greeting called from another sleigh brought her back to the present. She waved and smiled at her friend, but her mind was still on Lily. "Sometimes," she told Thomas, "when I think of Lily, the story of the little match girl comes to mind. I don't want Lily to end up like the match girl. Remember how the match girl lit the matches she was to sell, burning up her only way to make a living, and then died during the cold winter's night?"

His brown eyes went almost black with emotion. His jaw was tight. "That won't happen to Lily."

She met his gaze steadily. "Thanks to you and people like you who started that Sunday school—investing in children, as Father said."

He flicked the reins lightly, his attention apparently back on his driving. She sensed he was uncomfortable with her obvious admiration of his heart's work and changed the subject. "I've been trying to think of something I could do to make money. At the very least I would like to make enough to pay for the—"

She stopped abruptly. She'd almost said she wanted to pay for the holiday gowns her mother insisted she have. Even though she felt her mother was wrong, she had no intention of insulting her to anyone else, even Thomas. "Do you think. . .I might be able to write articles for a newspaper?"

Thomas jerked up straight, almost causing the horse to stop. "A reporter? I'm sure you are a capable writer, but it isn't so easy as it apparently seems to research a news story, write it in the number of words the editor wants, and get it done before the presses roll."

I hurt his feelings! The realization tightened her chest. "I didn't mean to imply that it doesn't take skill to do your work. It's only. . .I'm trying to find something I can do."

"Maybe you could submit some short pieces for the social page." His voice sounded as though he was somewhat mollified by her apology.

His answer was dissatisfying. Small social pieces weren't likely to pay much, but his advice made sense. She decided she would keep her eyes and ears open at the next of the season's many parties.

⌒

Thomas looked up over the top of the evening paper as Cora Wibbey's voice drifted into the living room from the hall. "Don't be modest, dear. Everyone will want to see how lovely you look before you leave for the party."

Cora entered the room. Vernetta, her cheeks bright red, protested quietly but followed along. What else could she do with Cora's hand clamped tightly about hers? Thomas stifled his grin with difficulty, laid aside the paper, and stood up. Captain Rogers rose also, leaning on his cane.

Cora stopped in the middle of the room. "Miss Vernetta is going to a Christmas party. I knew you'd all want to see how pretty she looks."

Cornelia pushed herself from the sofa and hurried across the room. "What a beautiful gown!" Her fingers caught the edge of the material that stood out over the top of the puffed sleeves. "Such a perfect shade of brocaded silk. Petunia it's called, isn't that right?"

"Yes," Vernetta admitted quietly. "Thank you."

Cornelia stood back, admiring the gown. "That deep purple gore of velvet with the lace trim in the middle of the skirt adds so much."

"Turn around," Cora insisted.

Vernetta obediently turned, careful to lift her train.

The captain cleared his throat. "Lovely, my dear. Simply lovely."

Vernetta stepped quickly to his side and pressed a kiss to his cheek.

Cornelia waved a hand toward Thomas. "Well, aren't you going to tell her what you think?"

"Perfect. You are perfect, Miss Larson." The words came out almost a whisper. He was surprised they made it out at all past the painful lump in his throat.

Her unusual violet eyes widened slightly, and his gaze tangled in hers. All he could hear was his heart pounding in his ears.

"I like the paper rose you've pinned in your hair," Cora said.

Vernetta's fingers touched the edge of the white rose, and Thomas's gaze followed. "Lily made it," she told them.

"Perhaps your escort will want you to wear the flowers he brings instead," Cornelia suggested.

Vernetta's smile looked a little tight. "No escort tonight. I'm attending with friends."

Thomas's heart clenched. He pressed his lips together firmly and caught his hands behind his back. He wished he were of her social class. If he were, he could escort her to the party and see that she had real roses to rest in her beautiful hair. The paper rose was a fine example of where her heart lay, but would her friends look down on it?

He watched out the front door's etched glass window as Vernetta and her friends left, but what he saw was her eyes when he told her she was perfect. *I'm falling in love with her.* The thought caught him by surprise, but he recognized the truth of it immediately. *Forget it, McNally. She's out of your league, even with her father's present financial situation. Besides, she's still nursing a broken heart over Andrew.* Dora had told him all about Andrew, the family's expectation that he and Vernetta would marry, and the breakup. He couldn't imagine any man walking away from Vernetta.

He heard Dora's step in the hall behind him and turned, forcing a grin. "How about going ice-skating with me, Dora? It's a fine evening for it."

"My young man is taking me skating, but you're welcome to join us."

"I think I will, if you don't mind a third party." Thomas started up the stairs to get his skate blades, wishing Vernetta would be joining them at the pond, her gaze lingering in his mind.

Chapter 7

Thomas was in the living room when Vernetta returned from the party. Unable to sleep, he'd taken a volume of Dickens from Mr. Larson's library shelves and settled in a wing chair before a dying fire. His efforts to read had been futile; his mind was filled with Vernetta.

He hurried to the hall when he heard the front door close. He knew there would be no one else to greet her; her parents and Dora had been in bed for hours.

She jumped slightly, startled, when she saw him, but recovered quickly and smiled. "Hello."

"Hello. Let me help you with your cape." She turned her back to him, and he lifted the soft black velvet from her shoulders. The smooth ivory curve of her neck tempted him. What would it feel like to press his lips to her neck? He pushed the thought away. "Did you have a good time?"

"Oh yes! It was such fun!" Her eyes sparkled up at him in the light from the opal gas lamps on the walnut walls. "When my friends asked about the paper rose in my hair, I put on my best surprised face and said, 'Why, paper roses are all the rage for Christmas this year, haven't you heard?'" Her laugh rang out.

Thomas grinned. "How did your friends respond to that?"

"Skeptical at first. Then I explained that during the financial troubles, using paper roses was a way to decorate themselves and their homes, be fashionable, be thrifty, and be charitable all at the same time." She laughed again. "I was so convincing that a girl who is hosting a party next week asked my assistance in buying the flowers she will need to decorate. I can't wait to place the order when I see the flower girls at Sunday school!"

"They'll be thrilled. Perhaps you should write a newspaper article about this current rage for paper roses. That would ensure your friends that you are telling the truth! Of course, you wouldn't want to use your real name for the byline."

She clapped her hands. "What a wonderful idea! Do you think your editor would print it?"

"I'll try to convince him to use it." It was fun acting the conspirators. "I was telling Dora tonight at the skating pond that—"

"You and Dora went ice-skating?"

"Yes, I—" Something in her eyes made him lose his train of thought. Why was she looking at him that way?

"I love ice-skating." Her voice was quiet, and the light had left her eyes. "It was a beautiful night for it. If you'll excuse me, I'll retire. I'm awfully tired."

"Of course." He watched her climb the stairs. What had he said to take the life out of her that way?

⌒

Vernetta slipped into bed. She piled the pillows between her and the ornately carved headboard, then leaned back against them and picked up her journal. She pulled the pale pink satin comforter over her knees and opened the journal. It was her usual bedtime ritual. Normally she began writing as soon as she opened the book. She should have had a lot to write about tonight, after the Christmas party, but the only thing in her mind was a picture of Dora and Thomas skating together.

"Likely Mother was very happy to see them go off for an evening together," she whispered. Her heart burned at the thought of Dora and Thomas skating hand-in-hand, laughing together in the moonlight, enjoying hot cider and popcorn, standing around the fire that was always kept going for the evening skaters.

Every night she made it a practice to record one thing for which she was grateful. Usually she couldn't stop at one! Tonight, she couldn't remember anything for which to be thankful.

"Lately, Father," she spoke quietly into the softly lit room, "it seemed life was beginning to turn around. Working with the flower girls has been so rewarding. The boarders have brought in a little money and also added cheer and fun to our house. Thomas has befriended Father. And. . ." Her voice dropped to a whisper, and her throat ached. "I thought Thomas was beginning to care for me."

She drew her knees up to her chest and hugged them, letting the pain wash over her. Finally she swallowed hard and took a deep breath. Things no longer seemed to be improving. Tonight the difficult things seemed harder than ever to bear: Her parents were still dealing with the pain of the bank failure, the newsboys and flower girls lived in poverty's gray depths from which there appeared little hope of escape, the entire country remained in the middle of financial chaos.

"On top of everything else, I'm falling in love with a man whose romantic interests lie not with me, but with my maid!" A tiny smile tugged at the edge of her lip and caught the hot, salty tear that rolled over her cheek. She couldn't help seeing the irony in her situation. Never in her wildest imaginations had she ever thought she would be jealous of her maid!

With a sigh, she put out the light in the lamp beside her bed, too preoccupied to notice the pretty roses painted on the china shade. She slid down between the sheets and pulled the comforter about her shoulders.

"I'm trying to trust You, God," she whispered into the shadows, "but I don't understand how You can allow so many hard things." Guilt wrapped around her fears and questions like a fog. If her faith and that of other Christians in the country were strong enough, wouldn't it have meant an end to the hard times?

◦～

The next morning, Vernetta spent hours at the delicate writing desk beside the window in her bedroom, working on the article Thomas had recommended that she write. When he came home for lunch, she handed it to him. Fear swamped her as she watched him read the short article. *What if he thinks I'm a terrible writer?* She wanted to snatch back the paper over which she'd labored so diligently.

He looked up from the page with a grin. "This is great! I'll show it to the editor this afternoon."

All afternoon, she tried to find things to occupy her mind and stop worrying what the editor would think, but she was unsuccessful. When the hour neared for Thomas to return home, she pretended to do needlework in a chair by the parlor window. She dropped the needlework and hurried to the front door when she saw him coming up the walk. If it was bad news, she didn't want to hear it in front of others.

Thomas laughed when he walked in the front door and found her standing just inside. From the sympathetic twinkle in his eyes, she guessed that he could read the hope and dread that filled her as she waited for his report.

He rested a hand on her shoulder. "The editor liked your article. It will be in the Sunday paper."

Vernetta rose to her toes and clapped both hands over her mouth. Excitement and pleasure coursed through her. She slid her fingers down just enough to ask, "Oh Thomas, truly? This isn't Irish blarney?"

She saw his expression soften and the laughter in his brown eyes quieted to a tender glimmer. Even his voice softened. "No, my lo. . . No, lass. No blarney." His hand moved from her shoulder to touch her cheek. The touch warmed her in spite of the cold that lingered on his fingers from the outdoors. Her breath caught in her throat and her emotions tumbled about in her chest in wild and wonderful confusion.

He dropped his hand and began unbuttoning his coat. Was he as flustered as she by his touch? she wondered.

Thomas opened the door to the hall closet. "The editor said if you wish to write other articles for the society and home pages, he'll be glad to consider them."

Joy flooded her. She clapped her hands lightly. "It seems too good to be true!"

"I almost forgot the best part!" Thomas reached into his coat pocket, withdrew some coins, and held them out to her. "Your pay."

The coins tinkled as they fell into her palm. Dismay mingled with awe. It wasn't very much money, but it was something. No matter how little it was, she knew God was answering her prayer in providing a way in which she could contribute, however slightly, to the family income.

She knew her eyes were shining when she looked up at him. "My father has given me an allowance to spend upon myself for years, but this is the first money I've ever earned."

"You earned it well. It was a good article."

She felt wrapped in the smile that shone in his eyes, and she was glad that he was the person who was sharing this special moment with her.

⌒

At the next Sunday school, Vernetta placed orders with the flower girls for flowers for some of her friends. The girls beamed with delight at the size of the orders. They assured Vernetta they would have no trouble making enough flowers to meet her friends' requests.

Thomas's eyes glowed as he caught Vernetta's gaze. "I knew God had a special purpose in your work with the flower girls. All the volunteers here are special, but you've touched the children's lives in so many ways in which they've not been touched before."

A warm glow enwrapped her heart at his words. She was growing to love the children and her work with them. She didn't need Thomas's approval, or anyone else's approval, to be happy that she was here. It wasn't his approval of her that touched her so. Rather, his words only added to her belief in his goodness and to her growing love for him.

Vernetta had convinced the other volunteers at the Sunday school to put on a Christmas pageant with the children. Some of the volunteers had been reluctant at first. "The children's parents and families will never come," said the woman who had been working with the mission the longest.

"It's important to do it anyway," Vernetta insisted. "Recreating the Christmas story will make it more real to the children."

To Vernetta's utter amazement, Thomas convinced her mother to play the piano for the Christmas program. "I still can't believe you talked her into this," she whispered to Thomas as Mother played "Silent Night" at the first practice. "However did you do it?"

He shrugged. "I told her the children seldom heard music played by someone of her talent and that by playing she would be giving a great gift to the children." He smiled down at her. "I didn't tell her what a gift the children's appreciation would be to her."

Vernetta watched the children singing the well-known hymn. Most of them, she was sure, noticed no difference between her mother's playing and that of the woman who usually played for the hymn singing, but Lily was entranced by the playing. In spite of the song leader's attempts to move Lily back with the other singers, the little girl stood beside Vernetta's mother, her fingers curled over the wood in front of the keys. Her gaze followed the woman's long, lean fingers with something akin to hunger. The sight caught at Vernetta's heart.

"You were right," Vernetta whispered. "Mother is a gift to the children."

The Christmas play practice went better than Vernetta had dared hope. The volunteers appeared to have forgotten their misgivings and put all their energy into teaching the children their parts and places.

When Thomas, Vernetta, and her mother were walking out to the carriage afterward, Thomas shook his head. "Looks pretty hopeless to me. The children couldn't seem to remember when to do anything or where to do it."

The two women laughed. "Practices for children's Christmas pageants are always like that," Vernetta's mother told him. "They will do beautifully the night of the play."

Vernetta's and Thomas's laughing gazes met over her mother's head as he helped the older woman into the carriage's backseat. It certainly appeared Mother was well on the way to being won over by the children!

Vernetta missed the usual comfortable visit with Thomas on the way home while she sat in the backseat with her mother.

When he helped her out of the carriage in front of their home, Vernetta said, "Mrs. Pilgrim is one of the leading society women in this part of the city. Do you think the editor would like an article on her work with the flower girls' Sunday school?"

"I think that's a wonderful idea!" Thomas agreed heartily.

Mother frowned. "An article? What do you mean, Vernetta?"

Vernetta's face burned. She'd forgotten she hadn't told her mother about the article on the paper roses, which was to come out that day. She'd been afraid her mother would disapprove of her daughter being a "newspaperman." Thomas, whose hand still lingered on her arm after helping her from the carriage, gave her arm a slight, encouraging squeeze before removing it. In halting words, Vernetta told her mother about the paper flowers article.

Mother's lips pursed. She straightened her shoulders beneath her fur-trimmed cape. "Well, if you are going to write articles, they may as well be about worthy causes and not the unsavory topics newspapermen are apt to call news."

Vernetta stared at her in surprise. She heard Thomas cough to cover a chuckle and fought to control her own grin.

"I think you have a good idea," Mother continued. "Showing Mrs. Pilgrim's involvement with the mission might encourage other women to give more of their time to needy causes."

Still dumbstruck, Vernetta followed her mother up the walk. They'd only gone a few feet when the front door was flung open. Dora raced across the porch and down the walk. "Thank the Lord you're home! It's Mr. Larson! He has great pains in his chest. The doctor says it's his heart!"

Chapter 8

Vernetta's own heart felt as though it would burst from fear and pain. She and her mother hurried to her father's bedroom, not stopping to remove their coats. The doctor intercepted them at the door and ushered them back into the wide upstairs hall, shutting the door behind them. He held his finger warningly to his lips.

Mother clutched the doctor's hands, her gaze searching his face. "How bad is it, Dr. Brown?" she whispered. "Will I. . ." Her voice broke. "Will I lose Anton?"

"Heart situations are always difficult to predict, Mrs. Larson. For the moment, he seems to be improving. His heart rate is decreasing, and the pain is easing. He will have to remain in bed for a few days and take things easy once he's up and about again." He held up a finger in a warning manner. "Mind, he's not to do any work."

It was the sympathy in his eyes rather than his words that cut through Vernetta's chest. She knew the doctor couldn't guarantee her father's heart wouldn't yet take his life.

"May I see him?" Mother asked with tears in her eyes.

Dr. Brown patted her hands. "For a couple minutes. Then you must let him rest."

But Mother refused to leave his room. She pulled a chair close to his bed and told the doctor, "I won't disturb him, I promise. I'll just sit right here, where he can see me when he wakes up, and so I'll be here if. . .if he needs anything."

At her mother's orders, Vernetta arranged for a nurse, recommended by Dr. Brown, to stay with them and care for Father. Vernetta didn't dare bring up the subject of how they would pay the nurse. She was relieved when Mother brought it up herself. "We'll ask her to take part of her payment in room and board. Have Dora prepare a room for her. For the rest of the fee. . ." Mother paused and sighed deeply. "Perhaps I can sell some of my jewelry or some of our artwork. Anton must have a nurse, in case. . ."

Vernetta knew the meaning of the words her mother did not speak: "In case your father has another episode with his heart." A nurse would recognize the symptoms before she or her mother and would know the best thing to do for him until the doctor arrived. *Thank the Lord for the telephone*, she thought. *We'll be able to reach the doctor quickly.*

❧

Later that evening, Thomas had a few moments alone with Vernetta in the living room while Mrs. Larson was introducing the nurse to Mr. Larson. He listened as she explained her mother's decision.

"I'm so relieved she's willing to part with her prized personal possessions," she said. "When the bank collapsed, Mother revolted at the suggestion of selling anything."

Thomas stood in front of the parlor fireplace, one elbow resting on the mantel. His chest seemed too small for the sympathy he felt as he looked down at the young woman sitting in the nearby wing chair. If only he could spare her the pain of fearing for her father's life!

"When our loved ones face serious illness, we often find our values change, or perhaps more accurately, we become more clear about them," he said gently.

"Yes, I suppose that's true. I hope Father won't need to pay the cost of a stronger lesson for us." A tear lingered at the edge of one of her beautiful eyes, catching the light from the table lamp beside her.

The sight crushed him. Thomas wished he could put his arms about her, draw her to his chest, and comfort her. But all he could do was lift a prayer for her and her father.

Dora bustled into the room. "I may be speaking beyond my station, miss, but I was thinking—" She paused, then rushed on. "I was thinking that it's time to begin the Christmas baking. The missus always likes lots of baked goods about for guests who drop in. The stove is still warm from dinner, so it wouldn't take much to heat it back up. Baking cookies always makes me feel better. I thought it might cheer you up a bit to help. It won't change your father's awful sickness, but—"

"What a thoughtful idea," Vernetta interrupted her, rising. "It will be nice to have something to keep my mind from despondent thoughts."

Thomas watched the women leave the room together. Dora's offer had been unconventional and perhaps, as she had said, beyond her station, but it had been offered with love. He was glad Vernetta had accepted it as such. He didn't imagine many women would accept such an offer from their maid with the grace with which Vernetta had accepted Dora's offer.

There was no longer any doubt in his mind that he loved Vernetta, but as wonderful as he believed her to be, he couldn't believe she would ever agree to marry a man of modest means such as himself.

❧

As the days passed, Father obeyed the doctor's orders and kept to his bed, but Vernetta was worried. *Has he lost his will to live?* she wondered.

Whenever she spent time with him, he spoke of the bank failure. "I don't mind so much for myself that I lost my money," he repeated again and again, "but I hate that I've lost Lena's respect and that I've failed the depositors' trust, lost the life savings of so many."

It did not matter how many times she and her mother assured him that he was not a failure and that he hadn't lost their love and respect. He would not be convinced.

After one such session, Vernetta joined her mother in the parlor. Mother was pacing back and forth, wringing her hands. When she saw Vernetta, she burst out, "How could I have been such a fool? When. . .how did I allow my values to become so. . .so misplaced? When did money and other people's opinions become more important to me than my husband?"

Vernetta reached out to her impulsively, but her mother kept pacing. "Mother, I know those things have never been more important to you than Father."

Her mother nodded furiously in disagreement. "Oh yes, I'm afraid they were." She stopped in front of Vernetta. "Why didn't I let him know as soon as the bank failed that I was willing to make whatever financial and social sacrifices necessary to help him get back on his feet financially? Why didn't I let him know I love and admire him and will continue to do so even if he *never* regains his former status? It's what I would have done as a young bride."

Vernetta took her mother's hands. "It's not too late to tell him now."

Mother's shoulders slumped. "I have told him. I asked his forgiveness. It's too late. All he can see is how he thinks he's failed me. Failed me! I'm the one who has failed him."

Vernetta squeezed her mother's fingers. "You haven't failed." Yet inside, she felt her mother's despair and understood it.

◠

Thomas passed the store windows, filled with Christmas displays and enticing gifts and decorated with pine roping and brightly painted Christmas tree decorations. It was snowing, so the sidewalks were white and hard to maneuver.

He stopped in front of an especially interesting display of a village of small houses in winter, but he barely noticed them. *I wish I could make Christmas a happier time for Vernetta,* he thought. Things had been hard enough for her before Mr. Larson's heart had frightened them all so. *With her added fear for her father's health, both physical and mental*— Thomas shook his head.

A pretty silver vanity set caught his eye. He'd like to give Vernetta a Christmas gift, something beautiful like this set. Of course, it was inappropriate for their friendship, and even if it weren't, she likely had a fine vanity set. Until recently, her father had always given her everything she needed and, Thomas suspected, everything material that she desired. It was a wonder she had grown up so sweet and unspoiled.

No, the vanity table set was definitely out. Besides, hadn't the article in the *Tribune* delineating popular Christmas gifts said that it was considered an outrage if a man, even a relative, gave a woman something as personal as manicure sets or toilet articles?

He stopped to say hello to Lily, who was selling her wares in front of a photographer's studio. He spoke with her for a few minutes, then left with a paper rose tucked in the lapel of his coat. He tried to push aside the familiar aching in his chest at the sight of a child working on the cold streets. There were too many of them. A man couldn't walk a block without passing more than one. Maybe one day such things would not be allowed. Progress with child labor laws was slow, but Minnesota had passed a law recently that would cut the number of hours children could work for merchants. The law didn't apply to children who sold their own wares on the streets though.

When he'd crossed the street, Thomas turned and looked back at Lily. In her dark coat and muffler, she was silhouetted against the photographer's window. A grin slid across his face. "Ah yes," he said aloud. "That will be the perfect gift for Vernetta."

After dinner, Thomas visited with Mr. Larson. As usual, the older man was deep in self-pity, mourning in his Swedish accent that he'd lost his depositors' money. Thomas gathered up his courage, took a deep breath, and said, "Perhaps there's something you can do for the people who were hurt by the bank failure."

Mr. Larson grunted in surprise. "What could I possibly do? I've lost my fortune, too, you know."

"Only your financial fortune. You haven't lost your hard-earned knowledge and wisdom."

Mr. Larson waved a hand in impatience. "Knowledge and wisdom! I'm a man whose bank failed! People don't pay for knowledge that leads to failure."

Thomas leaned forward, elbows on his knees. He hadn't thought the idea through before he mentioned it, but now he knew it was sound. "You could write a book and maybe speak about bank failures. Put in writing why your bank and others failed. Interview banking friends whose banks didn't fail and ask what they believe they are doing right. That would help other bankers and the depositors who put their faith in them."

For a moment, he thought he saw a glimmer of excitement in Mr. Larson's eyes. Then the man slumped even deeper into his pillows. "I was a banker, not a writer."

Thomas grinned. "I'm a writer. I'll be glad to edit your work and help you find a publisher."

Mr. Larson stared at him for a long moment. Then a smile began to tug at one corner of his mouth. His eyes began to glimmer again. *"Uff da!* You are a persistent man, Thomas McNally. Maybe—only maybe, mind you—your idea will work."

He rubbed a large hand across his chin. "There are some friends who might even allow a failure an interview." He listed a few powerful men whose names

Thomas knew the public would certainly respect. By the time Mr. Larson was through, Thomas could see the man was excited about the idea.

Mr. Larson sat up, no longer leaning against the bed pillows. "If this works out, if I make money from this, maybe one day I can pay back my depositors." His voice was thick with emotion and brought a lump to Thomas's throat. "It might take the rest of my life," he continued, "but I can try. When the Panic subsides and the real estate market is better, perhaps I can sell this house and move to a smaller place. That would give me more money to use to pay the depositors." He smiled and met Thomas's gaze. "I think Mrs. Larson will support me in this now."

Thomas swallowed hard. "I'm sure you're right, sir. She's a fine, strong woman."

Mr. Larson grinned. "She is, isn't she? She's had a lot to put up with, too, with me for a husband."

Thomas laughed and rose. "Truer words were never spoken. I've stayed longer than I should have. The nurse will accuse me of overtiring you."

"Tell the nurse to bring me writing paper, pen, and ink," Mr. Larson ordered. "I have work to do!"

"I'll tell her, but I don't expect she'll bring them before morning."

When Thomas stepped into the hall, he was surprised to see Vernetta standing to one side of the doorway. It was obvious she had no intention of entering the room, so he closed the door.

Vernetta grasped his hands. Her eyes shone with joy. "Thank you, Thomas!"

"For what?" He tightened his fingers about hers, enjoying the rare intimate touch.

"I overheard your discussion with Father. I was going to visit him, but when I heard you two talking, I hesitated in the hallway. I heard you suggest to him that he write a book about the banks. I know he can do it."

"Of course he can," Thomas assured her, still reveling in her touch, in the glory in her eyes.

"I was afraid he'd lost his will to live. If I was right, you've given it back to him. You've helped everyone in our family regain hope."

"Me?"

"Yes, you. You introduced Mother and me to the flower girls and newsboys, giving us a reason to think of someone beyond ourselves. You've helped me get newspaper articles published, to bring in a little more money. Most important, you've given Father a reason to live, a way to make something good come out of the worst experience of his life."

Thomas shifted his shoulders uncomfortably. "I hardly think I did all that."

Her laugh sounded like music to him. "Oh yes, you did. The Bible tells us we may entertain angels unaware, but I must admit"—she glanced up at him coquettishly from beneath her lashes—"I never thought an angel would come to us with a name like Thomas Michael McNally."

Thomas laughed. The idea was absurd! "I'm no angel. I'm a man, and I'll thank you to remember it, Vernetta Larson."

Vernetta shook her head. "To me, you will never be a mere man." She squeezed his fingers quickly and started toward the stairway.

Thomas watched her, his heart pounding, wanting to believe her comments meant she would welcome him as a suitor. "Don't be foolish, McNally," he admonished himself in a harsh whisper. "She may consider you an angel, but women don't often fall in love with angels."

Chapter 9

The evening of the Christmas program, the basement mission Sunday school was alive with activity. The reporters at the *Tribune* had taken up a fund to contribute a Christmas tree for the pageant. It was so large that the trunk had to be cut off so the tree didn't hit the ceiling.

"The children will love it!" Vernetta cried. "How wonderful of your reporter friends to provide it."

"You're one of my reporter friends now." Thomas stood beside her, admiring the tree.

A reporter! She hadn't thought of the title in relation to herself. A thrill ran along her arms at the thought. "You didn't ask me to contribute to the tree fund."

"I thought you were contributing enough with your time." He shook his head. "Afraid the reporters' donation didn't include decorations."

"I have the perfect decorations." She turned toward the kitchen, where Cora and Cornelia were busy unloading baskets. "Miss Cora, Miss Cornelia, please come here."

Thomas watched their approach, puzzled.

"What would you think of decorating the tree with your mittens?" Vernetta asked them.

Cora clapped her hands in delight. "A mitten tree! What a wonderful idea!"

Thomas crossed his arms over his chest and leaned forward. "Mittens?"

Cora's soft, wrinkled face lit up. "We wanted to do something for the children. . ."

"So we asked our knitting group to help us make mittens," Cornelia finished.

"They have enough to give each child a pair." Vernetta smiled at Thomas, but he looked blurry through her tears. The Wibbey sisters had told her of their project only that morning, and their generosity warmed her heart.

The Wibbeys, Mother, Vernetta, and Thomas hung the mittens on the tree. They covered the tree so thoroughly that the branches were almost hidden. Then Vernetta and Thomas attached small beeswax candles in tin holders to the edges of the branches, where the flames wouldn't catch the branches above on fire.

"We'd best give out the mittens before lighting the tree," Thomas said, setting a large pail of water beside the tree in case of fire.

When they were done, Captain Rogers set a small wooden fence around the bottom of the tree. He laid moss within the fence and then placed wooden animals he'd carved and Mother's nativity. Vernetta, Lena, Thomas, the Wibbeys, and the other volunteers raved over the captain's work. Thomas grinned at Vernetta. "I see this has become a family affair."

Her heart leaped at his words: a family affair. What a wonderful thought, that he and she would be part of the same family. She tried to shush her thoughts. Didn't he and Dora have a special relationship? It would serve her well not to forget.

"It's too bad Dora couldn't be here with us," she said carefully, "but she did help us bake cookies for the lunch."

Thomas leaned close. "Don't tell your mother, but I think Dora is planning to spend the evening at the skating rink with her beau."

Vernetta felt her jaw drop. "Her. . .her beau?"

Thomas nodded. "Didn't she tell you about him?"

Vernetta could only shake her head.

"He's a nice chap, recently arrived from Sweden. Dora's head over heels for him."

"You. . .know him?"

"They let me join them ice-skating a few times." He turned as the door opened and a bunch of newsies came in noisily.

I thought he *had taken Dora skating!* Vernetta's heart leaped with joy. *Thomas doesn't love Dora!* With an effort, she turned her attention to the newsies.

Their arms were filled with pine roping and wreaths, and their faces were filled with grins. "What do ya think?" Erik asked, stopping in front of Thomas and Vernetta and lifting his laden arms. "We went ta parks and down along the river and gathered the pine ta make these ropes and wreaths ta decorate the mission."

"They are beautiful!" Vernetta assured him. She and Erik had grown to know and respect each other since she began working at the mission.

"Great job, boys," Thomas chimed in.

"Wow!" Erik started toward the Christmas tree, almost forgetting his usual swagger. "Check out this, newsies!"

The boys flocked around it, loud in their praise of the tree's size and beauty.

Soon the boys were stringing the rope along the top of the piano, the top of the picture that hung over the piano, and from the corners of the room to the light that hung from the middle of the ceiling.

They were barely done when the flower girls arrived in a group. Lily was clutching a bouquet of tissue paper roses so huge that it hid her drab, ill-fitting coat. Lily's gaze quickly searched the room, then lit up when she saw Vernetta. The girl hurried over, followed by the others. Bright, expectant smiles filled the girls' too-thin faces.

Lily held out the bouquet. "These are for you, Miss Larson." Her voice was almost as soft as real rose petals.

"*All* of these?" Vernetta struggled to stop the laughter that filled her throat. It was such a huge bouquet! Surely Lily's family couldn't afford to give away so many flowers. *I'll have to find a way to give them back and still spare Lily's feelings,* she thought. The roses crackled when she gathered them in her arms.

"They're from all of us," Lily told her. "We each made one, just for you."

Tears sprang to Vernetta's eyes. She couldn't dash them away with her arms filled with roses. Her gaze swept the faces turned toward her as trustingly as flowers turn toward the sun. Every face held a smile, but Vernetta recognized a trace of fear as well, and realized the girls were afraid she wouldn't value their gift.

She dropped her gaze to the flowers. A tear fell upon a tissue petal, leaving a wrinkle as a permanent memory. Vernetta lifted the bouquet to her face. It seemed she could almost smell the fragrance of roses. *It isn't the roses,* a voice in her heart said, *it's the fragrance of love.*

Vernetta swallowed hard. She smiled shakily and tasted a tear on the edge of her lips. "It's a magnificent gift. The most beautiful gift I've ever received."

She shifted the roses clumsily to one arm, which was barely able to contain them. Then she knelt and held out her free arm. Lily slipped into it. Vernetta's heart swelled until her chest hurt when Lily's arms tightened about her neck. One after another, each girl received a hug and thank you.

As the last girl slid her arms around Vernetta's neck, Vernetta glanced up. Thomas leaned against the wall, his arms crossed over his chest, his Irish smile not as jolly as usual. Was it tears she saw glistening in his eyes as he watched her and the flower girls? Or were they only a reflection of her own tears?

Lily touched a delicate, red-and-white tissue paper rose. "This is the one I made."

"It's the prettiest one of all," Vernetta whispered in her ear. Gently, she pulled it out of the bouquet. While Lily held the other flowers, Vernetta fastened Lily's rose to her gown with the dainty silver bar pin she was wearing. Lily's huge smile showed her pleasure.

Vernetta heard a man greeting Thomas loudly and looked up to see who was behind the unfamiliar voice. A man was setting down a tripod and a large camera.

Thomas introduced the man to Vernetta. "I've asked him to take pictures of the children tonight. Why don't we begin with one of you with the flower girls?"

"Oh, I would like that!" How nice it would be to have a picture of the girls she was growing to love.

The children's program went well. More of their parents and families showed up than the volunteers had dared hope, and the children outdid themselves in their efforts to impress them. They succeeded.

Standing to one side in the crowded basement, Vernetta watched the children's happy, proud faces and the proud, loving faces of their families. Children's voices rang with the music of "O Little Town of Bethlehem": "The hopes and fears of all the years, are met in thee tonight."

Her heart skipped a beat. She tensed, suddenly alert to the words of the beloved hymn. Hope meeting fear. Hope in the form of God's Son, Jesus Christ, meeting humanity's fears.

I didn't understand! she thought. *I thought hope meant the elimination of fear, the elimination of the evils that cause fear, or at least knowing the answers to eliminating fears and evils.* For the first time, she saw they existed together, that hope was God's presence in the midst of fears, His promise that the fears wouldn't win in the end. She relaxed against the wall. A serenity she'd never known filled her chest.

After the program, Cora and Cornelia distributed the mittens to the children and other volunteers handed out small bags of peanuts supplied by the church. At first, Erik and some of his followers hung back, telling Thomas they weren't charity cases and didn't need the mittens.

Vernetta held her breath, her arms clutched tightly over her chest, watching Thomas anxiously. What would he say? Many of the children had chapped, raw hands from going without mittens or gloves.

Thomas listened attentively to the boys, nodding, his hands in his trouser pockets. "It's your decision," he finally said quietly. "Many of the women who made these have no families of their own to give gifts to, no children of their own to love. I don't think knitting these mittens was an act of pity but an act of love." He shrugged. "Of course, I may be mistaken. You must each do what you feel in your own hearts is right."

Erik shifted his feet uncomfortably. The other boys watched him. Vernetta knew whatever Erik decided for himself, he decided for them all.

After what seemed many minutes to Vernetta, Erik lifted his chin. "Guess it would be rude not ta take the mittens when the old women worked so hard on 'em."

Vernetta let out a soft sigh of relief.

When the boys started forward to accept their gifts, Thomas sidled over to Vernetta. He nodded toward the piano. "See that?"

Vernetta's mother was still seated on the piano stool, one arm about Lily's shoulders. Lily leaned against her, looking as comfortable as though they'd known each other all of Lily's short life. Vernetta's heart contracted in a sweet pain at the sight. She pulled a lace-edged handkerchief from the wrist of her gown and dabbed at her eyes. "Everything seems to bring tears to my eyes tonight," she told Thomas in a jerky voice.

He smiled down at her. "Christmas is a time for miracles of the heart."

"Yes," she agreed, wondering at and thrilling to this man's sensitivity, as she had so often since he'd come into her home and life.

Lap robes and happy memories of the evening kept everyone warm on the way home. The Wibbey sisters chatted merrily about the program and mitten tree. Mother revealed that she'd decided to offer free piano lessons to any of the flower girls who wished them. "Little Lily wants *so* to learn to play, and surely others will want to learn, don't you think?"

Shocked and delighted, Vernetta could only nod.

"Will there be any objection to my using the hall and the piano?" Mother asked Thomas.

He assured her that he would arrange it, and she settled back contentedly against the thick leather carriage seat.

Vernetta was the last to be helped from the carriage by Thomas. "Would you like to go walking after I've put away the carriage and looked after the horse?" he asked, with her gloved hands clasped in his.

"That sounds lovely."

The home was filled with the smell of pine from the fir tree that stood in the bay window in the parlor and the pine roping that decorated the tops of the doorways in the broad hallway. With Dora's help, she found some vases and filled them with her treasure of paper roses while waiting for Thomas, her heart racing with anticipation.

Was it wishful thinking, or had his glances and touches been more intimate than usual tonight? She tried to quiet her heart. Perhaps it was only the knowledge that he was not in love with Dora that encouraged her to believe he was romantically interested in her.

It was snowing when they went out. Large, soft flakes drifted lightly down, making a gentle hissing sound as they slid through the bare trees. Mellow light from the gas streetlights spread blue shadows on the snow-covered yards, walks, and street.

A rabbit peeked out at them from beneath the spreading branches of a fir tree. They laughed together at it, and in their shared laughter, Thomas slipped his arm about her waist and drew her close to his side.

Vernetta almost stopped breathing. It was so special, walking together that way. She heard him clear his throat.

"I hope the pictures the photographer took tonight turn out well," he said.

"I'm so glad you thought of having photographs taken."

"I'm glad you feel that way, because. . ." He hesitated.

She looked up at him, curious, waiting. Her cheek brushed the wool of his coat, and her awareness of his nearness cleared everything but Thomas from her mind.

He cleared his throat again and looked away from her gaze. "I hired him to take a picture of you with the flower girls. I hope you won't think it presumptuous of me, but. . .I. . .the picture is my Christmas gift to you."

Vernetta stopped, and Thomas stopped, too. His arm slipped from her waist. He stared at her, his brown eyes unusually anxious. *Surely he cannot think I find his gift unwelcome!* She held out both hands. "It is the loveliest gift you could have given me. How is it that you know my heart so well, Thomas Michael McNally?"

He took her hands. "I have a suspicion about that."

She wasn't certain she was ready to hear his suspicion! She gently pulled her hands from his and began walking again, her heart beating like a child's Christmas drum. She changed the subject and told him about her revelation during the Christmas program, her new view of hope.

"Since Father's bank failed, there have been many times I was afraid hope was as unreal as the flower girls' paper roses, but I tried to cling to hope, to God's promises, anyway." She stopped beneath a streetlight, snowflakes falling softly about them, and looked into the face that had become so dear to her. "You helped me do that. In many ways, it's due to you that I've discovered the God of Hope is real."

"I can't believe I'm responsible. I saw the strength and courage in you the first day I came to your home. You accused me once of being an angel. I warned you then that I am only a man." He rested his hands on her shoulders. "Dora told me about Andrew."

She blinked. It took her a moment to realize he was speaking of the man she'd thought only weeks ago that she would marry.

"I realize it may take a long time for your heart to heal from losing him," Thomas was saying, "but I give you fair warning that my hope is for your love, and I don't intend to give up hoping until I win it."

The suddenness of his declaration took her breath. Then happiness swept over her like a winter wind sweeps down a hillside, filling her with joy and delight and amazement. "I haven't thought of Andrew in weeks."

She saw hope flash in his eyes. Dropping her gaze in shyness, she made herself continue. It was forward and inappropriate to express her feelings this way, she knew, but it was so important that he understand. "Andrew can't measure up to the man you are, Thomas Michael McNally."

His fingers tightened on her shoulders. "Are you sure of that, Vernetta?" His voice was husky.

"Completely," she whispered. "I could never love Andrew after knowing you."

He pulled her into his embrace with a deep sigh. "Oh Vernetta!"

She leaned against his chest. She'd never experienced the contentment that filled her now, the knowing that this was the place she was meant to be for the rest of her life.

She felt his lips touch her hair, the edge of her eyebrow, the corner of her lips. His breath was warm against her ear as he whispered, "And if I should ask if there's any hope I will win your heart, Vernetta?"

She slid her arms around his neck. "It is already yours, my love."

His arms tightened in a bear hug. Then he released her just enough to bend his head to hers and claim her lips. Vernetta melted into his embrace as simply and naturally as the snowflakes melted against their cheeks.

Dreams

Peggy Darty

Chapter 1

August 15, 1894
Pine Ridge, Alabama

Caroline Cushman sat on the board seat of the one-mule wagon as her grandmother gripped the worn reins and guided Ol' Bill down the red clay road.

"Granny, how many times do you reckon you've driven this road?" Caroline smiled tenderly at her grandmother.

"Oh child, I can't count that high. Spent my life here at Pine Ridge and only left a few times. Never could wait to get back."

Caroline sighed. "I know I'm going to be homesick. But I want to make you proud."

"I'm already proud of you, Caroline!"

Caroline was a slim, five feet, six inches with hair as dark as a raven's wing, pulled back from her oval face in a neat bun and secured with the black satin bow she had made the night before. Her deep blue eyes were large and wide-set, fringed with dark lashes. The round nose and mouth contrasted to her square chin, a determined chin—just like her father's, Granny often boasted. Her cheeks were smooth hollows, her cheekbones soft ridges. Her complexion, normally a smooth ivory, was still tanned from the summer sun, for she had worked many long hours out in the vegetable garden beside her grandmother. Selling vegetables was their main source of income, and Caroline had planted, hoed, gathered vegetables, and sold or canned them with Granny for most of her life.

Suddenly, all their years together blended into one sweet memory as Caroline glanced again at her grandmother. A tower of strength resided in the seventy-year-old body, and although her hair was white and her tanned face deeply lined, there was still a joy for life that gleamed in her bright blue eyes and quick smile.

Caroline reached across to touch her grandmother's hand. "Thanks for all you've done for me," she said, her throat tight.

"I think we're about even," Belle said, squinting down the road. "You've been a blessing from God after so much tragedy. First my beloved Clarence, then your parents. . . ." She broke off for only a second, then continued bravely. "I'd 'ave shriveled up and died with them if I hadn't the gift of you to raise."

Caroline's blue eyes swept the Alabama hills, and for one anxious moment, she wondered if she could bear to leave the only home she had ever known. Well there *had* been another home, but she was too young to remember it. As a child she often had nightmares of flames and smoke; she would wake up screaming. Then Granny would be at her bed, hugging her, assuring Caroline she was safe.

The wagon rattled on, making the last turn into Pine Ridge. The Nashville-Birmingham train ran along the tracks opposite the storefronts once a day at twelve o'clock. If a red flag hung from the pole beside the platform, the train stopped to pick up a passenger or some cargo going into Birmingham. If there was no flag, the train never slowed down.

Her eyes flew to the pole. The red flag was flying. "I'm glad Mr. Willingham didn't forget to put up the flag."

"He wouldn't dare!"

The front door of the general store opened and Frank Willingham lumbered out, hands thrust in the pockets of his overalls.

"Morning, Belle. Caroline." He angled down the front steps to wait as Ol' Bill trudged into the vacant spot at the hitching rail. Then he reached into the wagon and removed Caroline's suitcase. "Young lady, you're the only person from the ridge ever to go off to college."

"To Davis University," Granny spoke the words proudly. "The good Lord blessed my child with a real sharp mind," Belle stated, braking the wagon and hopping down as spryly as a teenager.

Caroline lifted the long skirt of her blue cotton dress and planted her black ankle boots firmly on the ground. The boots had been a gift from the Women's Missionary Society, and everything else she owned had been sewn by her and her grandmother during many a long night at the treadle sewing machine.

"Train's on time," Frank said, crossing the street with her little suitcase as Granny and Caroline hurried after him.

In the distance, the *chug-chug* of the approaching train filled the summer day, and both Caroline and her grandmother looked north until they spotted the train, like a giant cockroach, lurching toward them.

Suddenly, a feeling of panic clutched at Caroline's stomach. Could she really do this? Could she really go off to a world of strangers?

She whirled to her grandmother and met a glow of pride in the blue eyes that looked Caroline up and down. "You look mighty pretty, Caroline. Just don't go forgetting any of the morals you've been taught."

Caroline shook her head, close to tears. "I won't. I couldn't."

Her arms flew around her grandmother, who was shorter by several inches and weighed no more than a hundred pounds. The scent of lilac engulfed Caroline, and she knew that whenever she thought of Granny, she would always recall the pleasant sachet she wore. Despite her efforts, Caroline couldn't hold back the tears.

"Now don't do that or I'll start blubberin'," Granny scolded, turning pale. "We already talked about this. You're gonna write and it ain't that long till Christmas."

Caroline sniffed. "I know."

The train's whistle and then a screech of brakes ended their conversation. Caroline turned, squaring her shoulders, as a little man rushed down the train steps and reached for her suitcase and ticket.

"Good-bye, Mr. Willingham," she called.

"Good-bye, Caroline. You do your granny proud, now. You hear?"

She nodded, blinking. "I'll do my best."

"All aboard," the little man said, interrupting their emotional good-byes.

Belle's arms flew around her in a tight hug, then with an even mightier strength pushed Caroline forward. "Go now."

Taking a deep breath, Caroline lifted her skirt and climbed the steps to enter the train. She located a seat near the window and looked out at Mr. Willingham and Granny. Caroline waved again, trying to memorize every feature of the little woman she loved so much.

Then the train was speeding off and tiny Pine Ridge gave way to rolling green hills. She pressed her head against the seat and closed her eyes, praying for courage and guidance in the coming days. Comfortable and warm, Caroline soon forgot everything as her eyelids grew heavy after a sleepless night.

Sometime later the conductor's voice jolted her awake.

"Bir-ming-ham," he announced, walking down the aisle.

She sat up, staring wide-eyed through the window. The train was puffing into the station and her eyes flew over the waiting crowd. In her last letter from Davis University, she had been informed that a Miss Agnes Miller, Dean of Students, would meet her train. She smoothed her hair in place, straightened her dress, and summoned her courage.

When she stepped tentatively onto the platform and scanned the sea of strangers, she spotted a small, handmade sign that bore her name. A blond woman in a gray taffeta dress and matching hat held the sign. She had a slim face with sharp features and clear hazel eyes, now sweeping Caroline as she approached.

"I'm Caroline Cushman," she said, smiling at the woman who was slightly shorter but at least ten pounds heavier than she.

"I'm Agnes Miller, Dean of Students. Welcome to Birmingham." Her gloved hands lowered the sign. "William," she said over her shoulder to a tall man emerging from the crowd. "You'll need to pick up Miss Cushman's trunks." She turned to Caroline. "How many do you have?"

Caroline swallowed. "Just one suitcase." She described her cardboard suitcase to the man, certain he would have no trouble spotting it among the trunks.

"This way," Dean Miller said, lifting her skirt and walking ahead of Caroline. "You're going to like Davis."

"I'm real excited." Caroline trailed after her to an elegant carriage.

William had caught up with them, her suitcase swinging lightly from his hand. He opened the carriage door and withdrew a small rail that enclosed three steps.

As Dean Miller preceded Caroline into the carriage, a lace-edged petticoat peeped from beneath her flowing skirts. Caroline followed, knowing there would be no dainty rustle of her skirts as she settled into the butter-soft seat.

"Thank you for coming to pick me up," Caroline said, smoothing out the folds of her skirt. In the process, her fingers brushed a fold of the taffeta skirt Dean Miller wore. She had never felt anything so soft and fine in a garment, and she wished she could touch it again.

"My pleasure," Dean Miller replied, peering out the window as William climbed into the driver's seat. "Was the train ride comfortable?"

"Yes ma'am, it was."

Caroline stole another glance at the elegant woman beside her. Her face was rather plain beneath the jaunty little hat. Caroline guessed her to be at least middle-aged, and although she was much younger than Granny, her eyes lacked the sparkle that danced in her grandmother's eyes.

Silence fell, and Caroline looked out the window. She didn't know how to talk to a woman like this, so instead she concentrated on the fine-looking shops along the boulevard. *Riding in a fine carriage pulled by sleek black horses was quite different from bumping over country roads in a wagon,* she thought to herself. In less than an hour, she had dropped out of one world into another, one so starkly different that it had taken her breath away. There were fancy buggies and carriages everywhere, and the women wore dresses with yards and yards of fabric, giving them the look of floating rather than walking. Their hats, all sizes and shapes, matched their dresses. Men departed the shops in black suits and hats, looking distinguished and quite busy and in a hurry to get wherever they were going.

"We were quite impressed with your entrance score," Dean Miller spoke up.

"Thank you," Caroline replied. "I studied real hard, but then I have what Granny calls a passion for books. I never get tired of reading." She wondered what Dean Miller was thinking as her eyes lingered on Caroline's face. She felt nervous and uncomfortable and turned back to the window as an escape.

❧

Dean Miller was thinking about the beautiful girl beside her and wondering how she would fit in with the students at Davis. Caroline Cushman would say exactly what she thought. She had dealt with all sorts of girls, but she knew from having studied this student's background that this girl would have a lot to learn in the social graces. Still, she had made one of the highest entrance scores in the history of Davis. Upon receiving Caroline's records from Oak Grove, the community school near Pine Ridge, she had been astonished at what she read. This bright student had made straight A's from first through eighth grade, in the one-room schoolhouse. Then, upon entering high school, she had traveled with a neighbor in a wagon to Oak Grove, five miles each way, to finish school. During all those years, she had missed only three days of school, and she had graduated at sixteen. She was barely seventeen now, and yet she seemed older and wiser than most of the girls at Davis.

Dean Miller stole a quick glance at her pitiful little dress. Davis maintained a reputation of high standards both academically and socially. She had a feeling this beautiful young woman with the alert blue eyes would have no trouble making her grades, but she was concerned about how the other students would react to her clothes and her country twang.

The carriage turned into the campus driveway, sweeping past manicured lawns where boys and girls strolled, laughing and talking. She tried to see the campus through Caroline Cushman's eyes, and in doing so, suddenly felt younger.

"Dean Miller," Caroline whirled on the seat, "this is the most beautiful place I've ever seen in my life! What kind of bushes are those?" she pointed.

"We have several types of *shrubs* here, Caroline. I'm not sure just what those are."

"They're so *pretty*," Caroline replied. "Do they stay green like that all year?"

Dean Miller frowned. Did they? "Yes, I believe so. Actually I don't notice them that much. You're very observant, aren't you?" She looked at Caroline, noting the way her eyes glowed as she stared at her new world. Suddenly, Dean Miller felt sorry for this young woman, who was so. . .fresh, so untainted by the sophistication of city life.

〜

Caroline felt the woman's hazel eyes boring through her face. She bit her lip and turned back to look out the window. She was talking too much; Granny had warned her about that.

Shrubs, she thought, *I must remember to call them shrubs.* She was still curious, however, about their beauty. "I reckon it makes the place more cheerful to have green things growing in the dead of winter, doesn't it?" She bit her lip, wondering why she couldn't just shut up.

Dean Miller nodded and her gray hat slipped lower on her forehead. She reached up to adjust her hat pin. "Yes it does."

The carriage rocked gently to a halt and Dean Miller lifted her gloved hand to point at yet another brick building. "This is Brunswick Hall, the dormitory where you'll be staying."

"It's beautiful," Caroline sighed, admiring the way the ivy made a dainty crisscross pattern up the side of the dark redbrick wall.

The man named William had jumped down from his seat and was opening the door of the carriage. Caroline studied the way Dean Miller gave him her hand and gracefully descended the fancy little steps. Caroline followed, trying to hold her skirt the way Dean Miller did.

Once her feet touched ground, her eyes flew around, absorbing every inch of her new setting. She felt as though she had just stepped into the pages of one of the classics. Her eyes drank in the surroundings, admiring the stately buildings and the rows of *shrubs* and the brick walls surrounding everything.

She turned to the right, studying another handsome brick building. Through a large window, she could see a boy and girl sitting at a table.

"That's the library," Dean Miller explained. "I imagine you'll be spending plenty of time there."

"Oh yes," Caroline nodded. "I can't wait!"

෬

Ryan Blankenship sat in the library with Amelia Gardner, trying not to look bored as she chattered on about the garden party her family was hosting. His eyes strayed to the window and halted suddenly on a young woman getting out of the school carriage. He could see that she was a new student for the driver was unloading her suitcase.

She was dressed a bit differently; was that what had caught his eye? She turned her face and looked toward the window and he caught his breath. What an exquisite face! He sat upright in his chair, feeling the boredom lift. Who was she? Where had she come from? And the eyes, wide-set and bright blue, were looking everything over carefully. She seemed to have a keen interest in everything around her. He couldn't help wondering if a conversation with her would be more enlightening than this one he was struggling through with Amelia.

It occurred to him that Amelia had finally stopped talking. He glanced at her.

". . .What did you think about it?" She tilted her blond head and batted her eyelashes.

Ryan blinked and wondered what she had asked. "I'm sorry. What did you say?"

"What did you think about the Wilfords' party?"

He shrugged. "It was fine."

"Oh. Well. . . ," she rambled on, unaware that she no longer held his interest.

It was amazing how girls thought he cared about social events and fashion. He wanted to socialize with them, but he would enjoy discussing something else, like politics or world news or nature. He really enjoyed discussing anything pertaining to nature. And of course, medicine, which was his field of study. He couldn't expect girls to be interested in that however.

He sneaked a glance back to the window, and as usual, Amelia hardly noticed. He spotted the new girl, who was turning toward the front steps of Brunswick. Her clothes were obviously plain, but she had a nice figure and excellent posture. He watched her disappear into the building, disappointed that she was gone.

෬

Dean Miller pointed out the parlor with its gleaming furniture, thick drapes, and nice carpet. She then led the way down the hall and Caroline glanced right to left, absorbing the gleaming wooden floor, the creamy walls, the *electricity*. At the ridge, not one single family had electricity.

Dean Miller greeted two girls in the hall who gave her a wide smile, then turned surprised faces to Caroline, particularly her dress. She and Granny had worked long into the night for weeks, trying to copy the dresses they had seen in the mail-order catalogs. And she had felt so good about her clothes; but now she realized that while they had copied the style of dresses, they could not duplicate the fine fabric. Even by scrimping and saving, the best they could purchase was quality cotton. She had never owned silk or taffeta or any of the fine fabrics she saw floating past her.

"You're in number eleven, halfway down." Dean Miller pointed, hurrying ahead.

"Oh, hello! You must be Emily Ellison," Dean Miller was saying as she swept into a large room where a girl with brown hair and green eyes turned from the dresser and faced them.

Emily was an inch taller than Caroline and at least five pounds heavier. She was wearing a taffeta dress that was the palest shade of gold, like fading sunlight in late November.

"Yes ma'am. I'm from Atlanta," the girl replied in a smooth, rich voice.

"Nice to meet you. I'm Dean Miller and this is Caroline Cushman."

"Hello," Emily said, staring at Caroline.

"Hello, Emily," she responded and smiled. She wished her stomach wouldn't hurt and that she wasn't so nervous and self-conscious.

"Caroline is on *scholarship*, Emily," Dean Miller continued smoothly. "She'll be a good roommate."

"A scholarship?" Emily's green eyes suddenly lit up.

"Yes, now I'll leave you two to get acquainted."

"I'm glad you're smart," Emily said, still looking Caroline over. "I barely sneaked by on my entrance exams. And to be perfectly honest, I'm not fond of studying."

"I'll be glad to help you if I can. I really like to study," Caroline replied.

"You do? Not me. I wouldn't even be here if my parents hadn't forced me to come."

"Forced you?" Caroline placed her cardboard suitcase in the empty closet as soon as she spotted the handsome trunk near Emily's bed.

Emily shrugged. "Let's just say they gave me no choice. Does it matter which bed you take?"

Caroline glanced at the twin bed by the window where Emily's clothes were haphazardly dumped. "This one's fine," she said, turning to the bed by the door. She saw the bare mattress and wondered if she was required to bring bed covers. She thought she had memorized every word in her letters from Davis.

"What's wrong?" Emily asked, watching her.

"I didn't bring. . . ," her voice trailed away as she stared at the bed and felt the blood rush to her cheeks.

Emily tossed a set of sheets and matching pillowcase onto the bare mattress. "Mother must have bought me a dozen."

Caroline reached down and trailed her fingers over the creamy linen. "Oh, I couldn't. . .I mean. . ."

"Don't worry about it," Emily replied indifferently.

Caroline hesitated, wondering how to respond. "That's very nice of you," she answered slowly. "Maybe I can do something for you."

"Maybe. You found your closet." Emily inclined her head toward the one Caroline had chosen. "They're much too small. I can't get half my clothes in there."

Caroline peered in. She could get her clothes in with space left over.

"At least we're near the central bath," Emily continued. "It's only a few doors down. Father was disappointed that there aren't more bathrooms, but then he owns a hotel and is accustomed to having plenty of baths." She studied Caroline. "What does your father do?"

Caroline's back stiffened, though she kept her smile in place. "He's dead."

"Oh, I'm sorry."

"Thank you." Caroline looked from the mahogany twin beds and nightstands to the small matching dressers. "I think we'll like it here, don't you?"

Emily slumped on her bed. "No, I'll be miserable. I left a boyfriend over in Atlanta, and already I miss him so much I could just die." Tears filled her eyes. "They think Tommy isn't good enough for me. He has a good job, but he didn't go to college." She studied her emerald ring and sighed. "What my parents won't accept is that I'm not smart enough to make it at Davis."

"Oh, I'm sure—"

"No, I struggle with school." She looked at Caroline. "Do you have a boyfriend?"

"No," Caroline replied. She was burning with dreams and ambition and she hadn't time to think of boys. Besides, who would she have chosen for a boy-friend? The only boy she'd ever liked was Billy Joe Whitaker, who had gotten himself killed in a horse race.

"Well at least you didn't have to leave anyone. Where is your home, anyway?"

"Pine Ridge. It's a little place over in Blount County, an hour by train. Well I guess I'd better get unpacked."

With Emily's eyes following her every move, Caroline stood up and went to the closet to open her suitcase. She shook out the five good dresses she had brought and hung them in the closet. Then she took her box of toiletries to the dresser drawer, along with her undergarments. When she glanced at Emily, she noticed her green eyes were huge, as though she didn't believe what she was seeing.

Caroline imagined that Emily was probably amazed at how little her new roommate owned. Well, it couldn't be helped. She was Caroline Cushman from Pine Ridge. She wasn't going to put on airs or pretend to be something different.

Still, Caroline knew that life here was not going to be easy.

She returned to her suitcase and withdrew her Bible. The black leather cover was worn from years of use, but she treasured it, and as long as she could hold it, she didn't feel quite so frightened or alone. She laid it on the nightstand and smiled across at Emily. "Are you a Christian?" she asked.

Again, the girl's brows rose in twin peaks. "I guess so."

Caroline averted her eyes, wondering how you could guess about something so important. Unlike Emily, she wasn't worried about her studies; she was worried about adjusting to these people and their lifestyle. Until she did, she had to remember to think before she spoke. And that would be the hardest thing of all.

Chapter 2

In the coming days, Caroline became totally absorbed in her classes. She had chosen English as her major, and her mind was fertile soil begging for seeds of wisdom. Books and their interpreters were gifts, challenging and exhilarating her, explaining the restlessness of adolescence, the boredom. Davis was the answer to her prayers. There was one problem however; she knew she looked and sounded different from her classmates.

She tried to limit her conversations until she learned to pronounce her words more clearly. When called upon to answer a question, her answer was always correct, no matter how challenging the question. An occasional snicker reached her, but those around her soon conceded that even though she didn't talk or dress like they did, she was smarter.

She was a model student, poised on the edge of her seat, her blue eyes keen with interest, her pen quickly filling her tablet. She devoured every word her instructors spoke, even lingered after class to ask questions. At night, she haunted the library.

On the second week in October, Emily reluctantly joined her at the library. "I have to find a dumb old reference book," she complained. "Have you noticed how musty this place smells?"

"Old books," Caroline replied. She didn't mind a musty book; she respected its age. Her eyes swept the tall ceilings and rows of books that brought a surge of excitement to her. She loved exploring the priceless treasures at her fingertips. "What are you looking for?" she asked helpfully.

Emily related her assignment and Caroline located the specific reference area. "Just decide what you want. Give me your satchel, and I'll find a table."

Caroline entered the adjoining room, where students sat at desks, absorbed in books. She hardly noticed anyone in her haste to get to the nearest table to deposit her load. She took a seat and opened her English book. Suddenly someone bumped her chair. She jumped, and the book tumbled from her hand to the floor.

"Oh I'm sorry."

She turned and looked at the dark head beside her, kneeling to retrieve the English book.

"Here you are," he said, placing the book on her desk.

"Thanks," she replied as he straightened and faced her.

She had noticed him in English class. He was very handsome and he dressed well. Looking up at him, she realized he was five ten or eleven, with a nice physique. Friendly brown eyes were set in an oval face with a high brow, slim nose, and strong chin.

"I'm Ryan Blankenship," he said. "I'm in your English class." He slipped into the adjoining chair.

"I'm Caroline Cushman."

"You look awfully busy," he said, glancing at all the books.

"I am." She felt nervous just looking at him, so she fidgeted with a book.

"Have you finished the theme Mrs. Stockton assigned us?"

She glanced at him, smiled, then looked back at her book. "No. I don't know what to write about."

"She mentioned a special vacation," he said.

"I've never been on a vacation."

"I think Mrs. Stockton was just making suggestions when she mentioned a vacation. I believe the important thing is to write about something we care about. What about the area you come from?"

Her gaze inched back to him. "I do care about Pine Ridge. When I graduate from Davis, I plan to go back there and teach school and write." She bit her lip, wishing she hadn't told him the part about *writing*. Why was she talking so freely to this stranger? Still, her eyes lingered on his face; she sensed a kindness there, and he had a nice, friendly smile. He acted as though he really cared about what she was saying.

"Tell me about Pine Ridge."

"Pine Ridge is over in Blount County. It's only an hour by train, but it seems like another world compared to here."

"How is that?"

"Pine Ridge is a quaint little community where only a few people have running water and nobody has electricity. In fact, most folks there have never even been to Birmingham. And yet. . . ," her voice trailed. She didn't want to offend him.

"And yet what?" He leaned closer, his dark eyes wide, as though he really wanted to know what she had to say.

"Well the community is like one big family. Everyone helps everyone else. If someone's house burns down, we all pitch in and help rebuild. We have quilting bees and shivarees—"

"Shivarees?" he repeated curiously.

"It's an all-night get-together for newlyweds where we bring gifts and food, and Clarence Johnson plays the fiddle and Uncle Mack and Aunt Jenny clog and the Robertson kids play the spoons."

"Play the spoons?" he repeated, smiling at her. It was a kind smile, she decided; he wasn't making fun.

"Sure? Haven't you ever heard of playing the spoons?"

He shook his head, but he was still smiling. She liked the way his brown eyes crinkled when he smiled. In fact, she liked almost everything about him. He was nicer to her than nearly anyone she had met at Davis.

"Tell me more about Pine Ridge," he said, propping his elbow on the table and staring deeply into her eyes. "It's obviously a special place for you. Why?"

She hesitated, trying to form her words in her mind before speaking. As she glanced back at him, she decided to lower her defenses a bit. "Promise you won't laugh?"

His dark eyes widened. "Of course I won't laugh! Why would you even ask?"

Caroline shook her head. "I don't know." She glanced nervously around the crowded library where everyone seemed to be buried in their books, paying no attention to her. She looked back at the gentle boy beside her and swallowed. "Sometimes people snicker when I say things."

He blinked, looked away for a moment, then back again. "I promise you," he said emphatically, "I will never laugh at anything you say."

She took a deep breath and began. "It's the little things in life that have meaning for me: seeing a baby chick break out of its shell, watching the ducks follow their mothers across the lake in a perfect line, catchin' fireflies on Saturday night and holding them in the palm of your hand to study their magic, feelin' the night silence surround me. . ." She stopped. She was forgetting to pronounce her *ing*s.

"There's the subject for your English theme, Caroline. What you just said to me was very special."

She tilted her head and looked at him. "Why was it special?"

"Because it's real. So many people I know fill their lives with things that are superficial. You're talking about the beauties of nature and how a person can enjoy them. I think that's wonderful."

"You think so?"

"Sure!"

Footsteps approached and Emily stood before them, wide-eyed.

"Hi, I'm Ryan Blankenship." He stood and smiled.

Emily stumbled through her name, then stared at Caroline.

"Did you find your book?" Caroline asked.

"I found one I can check out. Do you want to stay longer?"

"No." Caroline stood, gathering her books.

"I'll see you in English class tomorrow," Ryan said. "Good luck with your theme."

"Thanks. You, too."

She walked quickly out of the library with Emily's eyes on her. Once they were outside, Emily spoke.

"Caroline, do you know who he is?"

"Ryan Blankenship. He's in my English class. Why? Don't you like him?"

Emily rolled her eyes. "Of course I like him. There isn't a girl on this campus who doesn't like him. What were you discussing?"

"We were talking about our English themes," Caroline said, looking up at the moonlight filtering down through the oaks.

"And what did you say?"

They had passed under a big oak, and Emily's face was shaded in darkness, but Caroline heard the concern in her tone. "Don't worry, Emily," Caroline said with a sigh. "I didn't say *ain't*."

"Ouch. Aren't you being a bit sensitive?"

Caroline sighed. "Maybe. I'm different from the students here, and I know it," she added quietly as they stepped back into the lights of Brunswick Hall.

Emily touched her hand. "I didn't mean to offend you, Caroline. You're the kindest person I've ever met."

"Thanks." She smiled at Emily as they entered the dorm and walked to their room.

⌒

Ryan had inspired Caroline to begin her theme. She sat at her desk, writing furiously, pouring onto a blank sheet of paper her lifelong knowledge of Pine Ridge.

"Caroline," Emily wailed, "how can you keep at it for hours?" She was lounging on her bed, her dress wrinkled, her books scattered.

Caroline shrugged. "I don't know. Mrs. Stockton may not like my theme; it probably won't be as good as the others."

"Will you stop that?" Emily cried. "Don't you know how bright you are? If not for you, I'd have failed both tests this week." Her eyes dropped to Caroline's dress. "I've been thinking." She got up and went to her closet. "I have some dresses I'll never wear. I want you to have them in return for helping me."

"Emily, you don't have to do that! I've helped you because I wanted to, because it's the Christian thing to do."

"Then let me do the Christian thing and give you something in return." She opened her closet door. "Mother chose these dresses for me, and I don't care for bright colors. I'm more comfortable in soft, muted shades." She pulled out three dresses of vivid green, purple, and blue. "These should fit you because I was thinner when she bought them. I started eating more out of frustration. They might be a bit too long." She frowned, glancing back at Caroline's dress.

"Oh, I can hem them," Caroline blurted, then bit her lip. "If you really feel it's the Christian thing to do."

"I do." Emily handed the dresses to Caroline and smiled. "You know, Caroline, you'll probably have lots of pretty dresses someday. You're pretty enough to snag a rich man and smart enough to keep him." She grinned. "I saw the way Ryan Blankenship was looking at you tonight."

She thought about her conversation with Ryan. He was kind and intelligent and seemed to enjoy talking with her, as she did with him. But. . .she knew he lived in a different world. She didn't belong there, nor did she want to.

"No," she shook her head, pushing Ryan from her thoughts, "I'm not interested in a rich man, as you put it. I'm going back to Pine Ridge to teach and write. It's my dream."

Emily shook her head in despair. "I just don't understand you."

❧

Later, after Emily had closed her books and gone to bed, Caroline threaded a needle and studied the beautiful dresses Emily had given her. Her heart danced with joy as she tenderly touched the soft green taffeta she planned to wear tomorrow. Mrs. Stockton had said she would ask a few students to read their themes aloud. Caroline sighed. She knew she wouldn't sound right, but she had been praying about that, too. Maybe God would answer her prayers about talking, the way He had answered her prayers about clothes.

She had big dreams, but sometimes those dreams brought her heartache. The snickers and stares had been difficult, but she prayed folks would adjust to her, just as she must adjust to them.

Ryan Blankenship sneaked back into her thoughts and her heart lifted. Emily thought he liked her, but Caroline doubted that. She sensed he was the kind of person who was nice to everyone. She was grateful he had encouraged her to write about Pine Ridge. She missed home something fierce, but she would be going back for Christmas; still, that seemed a long time away.

Suddenly a wave of longing for Pine Ridge rolled over her. She swallowed hard and tried to concentrate on what she was doing; but a tear slipped down her cheek as she painstakingly hemmed the dress that Emily had given her.

Chapter 3

Caroline hurried into English class, hugging her books against her chest. She loved the way the green taffeta swirled about her ankles; she felt good about herself today. The theme she'd spent half the night composing was folded carefully inside her English book, and even though she had dressed well, she still hoped Mrs. Stockton wouldn't call on her.

She sank into the middle chair of the first row. It was the best seat in the classroom, although most students seemed to prefer seats in other rows behind her.

A slim blond passed, staring at her. She had seen this girl at the dormitory and tried to be friendly, but the girl turned her head. *Probably homesick,* she thought, glancing at Mrs. Stockton. She was an attractive, middle-aged woman who wore bright floral dresses and smiled with her eyes, unlike Dean Miller.

"We're going to read our themes aloud today," she said, taking her seat. "We'll start with you, William." Her eyes lit on a boy in the back row.

The tall, lanky boy ambled to the front of the room, unfolded his paper, and mumbled about Eli Whitney, the inventor. The subject was interesting, but Caroline thought he could have done better. Mrs. Stockton thanked him for reading. He grinned and ambled back to his seat.

"Amelia, would you like to read your theme?"

The blond girl who had snubbed Caroline strolled up to the front of the room. She wore a beautiful blue silk dress with lace on the collar and cuffs and a wide ruffle around the hem. Caroline admired her dress and the nice cameo at her throat, and she listened with interest as Amelia read about a family vacation in New York. Her voice was filled with confidence, and her grammar was excellent, but her theme had no beginning, middle, or end. She just rambled. Caroline looked down at her book, embarrassed for her.

When Amelia had returned to her seat, Mrs. Stockton's eyes moved slowly to Caroline. Caroline dropped her eyes, praying she wouldn't call on her.

"Caroline, let's hear your theme," Mrs. Stockton said in a gentle voice.

Caroline's eyes shot to Mrs. Stockton in horror. Didn't she know that sometimes the students laughed at her? She bit her lip, trying to think of a reason not to read.

Nervously, she uncrossed her ankles and her new green taffeta rustled. Maybe this was why God gave her the dress. She got up and walked to the front, facing two dozen curious faces.

Ryan smiled at her, encouraging her. She took a deep breath and looked down at her meticulous handwriting. She had revealed the absolute truth about herself and her home, and now she wondered if that were a mistake. The paper was beginning to rattle in her fingers. Someone snickered.

God, help me, she silently prayed. And then, a new strength seemed to flow through her. She realized it didn't really matter what these people thought; what mattered was that she was reading about the most special place in the world. And she knew that Mrs. Stockton and Ryan Blankenship weren't going to laugh.

"'My name is Caroline Cushman,'" she began shakily, "'and I come from Pine Ridge. Pine Ridge is a small community and to me it is a very special corner of the world, fashioned by God's hands and nestled deep in the forest. In the winter, when the lake freezes over, we make skates and sleds out of farm machinery. Everyone goes ice-skating, from the children to the old people. In the winter, we have all-night singings and taffy pullings and hoedowns and quilting parties.'"

She paused to draw a breath.

"At Pine Ridge we make our own musical instruments and on Saturday nights we have parties. Grandpa Sam, who's not really anybody's grandpa, is good with the Jew's harp. Willie Mayberry is a natural on his drums, and Pearline Jones is pretty good with her guitar. Our music brings a smile to the saddest face and warms the hearts of those who have lost loved ones. When little Angela Jones was dying, her mother bundled her up and brought her to our Christmas party. Everyone made special gifts for her, things she never had because her family is poor. Angela played the part of the Christmas angel, and on that snowy Christmas eve, God decided it was time to take His angel home. Everyone had gathered around her to sing "Silent Night"; when the carol ended, we looked and little Angela had gone to be with the Lord.'"

She paused, swallowed hard, and continued.

"'There is a special kind of love at Pine Ridge, a love for God and our fellow man. I miss the people of Pine Ridge, but I also miss the special things of nature that were a fascination to me when I was growing up.'" She glanced up from her paper, meeting Ryan's glowing brown eyes.

She looked back at the paper and read the verbal picture of baby chicks breaking out of their shells, ducks on the lake, and the beauty of a winter morning when ice sculpted the trees and icicles glittered like diamonds. She read the sentences quickly, never looking up again.

Without risking a glance, she hurried to her seat and busied herself folding her paper. Mrs. Stockton's voice broke the silence around her.

"That was excellent, Caroline. We enjoyed it very much. Thank you for sharing Pine Ridge with us."

When Mrs. Stockton dismissed class for the day, she asked Caroline to remain. Caroline's heart thundered in her chest. What was she going to say to her? She was so nervous she could hardly thank Ryan when he stopped to compliment her theme. From the corner of her eye, she saw Amelia. This time Amelia was glaring at her.

Then when everyone had left, Mrs. Stockton looked across at Caroline and smiled.

"I was very touched by your theme," she said warmly. "I wonder if you're really aware of what a unique place you come from or of your knack for telling about it. The students were fascinated and I think other people would be."

Caroline's eyes widened. "You mean I should write more about Pine Ridge?"

"I do. I don't often say this to students, but I think you have a good chance of getting published."

"Getting published?" Caroline asked, wondering if it were possible to achieve one of her dreams this soon.

"Yes. I have a friend who is an editor for a journal that features the best writing of college students. As the year progresses, and you learn more about writing, I think we might want to send her something."

Caroline was dizzied by the prospect. For once, she was at a loss for words. She wanted to throw herself in Mrs. Stockton's arms and give her a big hug, but she knew folks in the city were more formal. So, instead, she looked at Mrs. Stockton with all the gratitude that was overflowing her heart.

"Thank you," she said, trying hard not to cry.

⌒

"Don't forget we're having that get-together in the parlor," Caroline reminded Emily when she returned to her room and found Emily sulking on her bed.

"I don't want to go," Emily complained.

"Why not?"

"I don't see any fun in standing around with the girls in the dorm, sipping punch and pretending to like one another."

Caroline laughed. "Maybe we do like each other."

Emily said nothing as she looked Caroline over.

"Come on, let's go. You just might enjoy yourself," she coaxed.

With Emily halfheartedly joining her, they walked down the hall and entered the parlor. An enormous chandelier poured soft light over the marble-topped tables, the Duncan Phyfe sofas and matching chairs, and thick gold drapes.

Caroline's stomach tightened as they crossed the gleaming floors and stepped onto the lush Oriental carpet. A group of girls stood at the serving table, with Amelia in the center. Caroline had decided to compliment Amelia's theme, and perhaps she could make friends with her—or at least figure out why she acted so unfriendly.

"Hi, Caroline," a small voice spoke up from behind her.

"Oh hi, Claire." Caroline smiled.

Claire was tiny and frail, looking even more so because she was partially crippled on her right side. On Tuesday, Caroline had seen Claire struggling with a load of books and helped carry them to her room. Like Caroline, Claire often seemed to be alone.

"Here." Emily joined them, handing Caroline a dainty crystal cup filled with punch.

"Thanks. Emily, do you know Claire?"

Just as Caroline was introducing Claire to Emily, someone jostled against her back. The punch she had been holding against her chest, sloshed onto her green bodice, leaving an ugly red stain in the center. Horrified, she turned to see what was happening behind her, and Amelia stood glaring at her.

"You bumped into me," Amelia cried.

Caroline awkwardly took a step back from her and as she did, the girl moved as well. The sound of cloth ripping cut across the quiet room as everyone stared.

"Now look what you've done." Amelia played to her audience. "You've torn my dress!"

Caroline's eyes shot to the floor, and she saw an edge of pale blue ruffle lying on the carpet.

"I. . .I'm sorry," Caroline stammered.

"What's wrong?" Dean Miller had rushed over.

"She bumped right into me," Amelia cried, glaring at Caroline. "And now my dress is ruined."

"I'd say Caroline's dress is in worse shape than yours, Amelia," Emily spoke up, moving closer to Caroline.

"Well it's her own fault," Amelia lashed back. "Some people just don't know how to conduct themselves in social situations." She flung the words at Caroline, then daintily lifted her skirt with its trailing ruffle and swept out of the room. Her circle of friends followed, tossing one last disgusted glance in Caroline's direction.

Humiliation scalded Caroline's cheeks as she looked at Dean Miller. "I'm so sorry," she said shakily.

"Dean Miller," Emily spoke up, "Amelia bumped into Caroline. If anyone was to blame it was Amelia."

Dean Miller lifted a dainty shoulder of her black silk dress. "Either way, do try to be careful, Caroline," she said with a little smile before she turned and strolled back to chat with the housemother.

"Here, let me take that cup," Claire offered, reaching for Caroline's empty cup and placing it on the nearest table.

"Let's go!" Emily rasped in her ear.

"I'm leaving, too," Claire said, looking sadly at the group who watched them.

As soon as they reached the hall, Emily huffed an angry sigh. "I'm getting more disgusted with this dorm every day. They're just a bunch of snobs."

"Do you really think Amelia bumped Caroline on purpose?" Claire asked in her weak little voice.

"Of course she did," Emily said as they entered the room. Emily closed the door and faced Claire and Caroline. "Amelia has a crush on Ryan Blankenship, and I don't know why the girls here can't see through her little act."

"Act?" Caroline repeated. "What do you mean?"

"I hear Amelia is really hurt that he's quit courting her. If he ever was. Surely you can see that he's completely taken with you, Caroline. He speaks to you every chance he gets and stares at you as though you're a goddess—"

"Oh, I don't think—" Caroline interrupted.

"No, you don't think so because you're too modest, but it's true. I see the way he looks at you, and I know that look, believe me." She sank onto the bed and tears filled her eyes for a moment. "I miss Tommy so much I could just die."

Claire looked from Emily back to Caroline, her little face bleak. "I'm so sorry about everything."

Caroline shook her head. "It doesn't matter."

But it did, and she felt heartsick when her eyes dropped to the ugly red smear on her bodice. It was the most flattering dress she owned, and if what Emily had said about Amelia was true, she had picked the right dress to ruin.

"Why don't you take the dress off and let me have it?" Claire suggested. "My father owns a shop here that specializes in cleaning garments. Maybe he can get that stain out."

"I hate to put your father to any trouble."

"My father will be glad to help anyone who has helped me. And you have," she said, touching her hand gently.

Grateful for those words, Caroline changed into one of her old dresses, glancing intermittently at Emily, who had stretched out on the bed, her face to the wall.

After Claire left, Caroline thought of how Emily had defended her. She wanted to tell her she appreciated it, but she didn't seem to be in the mood for conversation.

She cleared her throat. "Emily, why don't you write a letter to Tommy? Maybe that would make you feel better."

"I won't feel better until I see him again," she wailed.

Caroline's eyes drifted to her Bible on the nightstand. She sat down on her bed and picked it up, trying to think of a chapter to read to calm her nerves. Was it true what Emily had said? That Ryan really liked her? Was that why Amelia had behaved as she did?

Caroline glanced across at Emily. "Do you think Ryan likes Amelia?"

Emily rolled over and looked at Caroline. "No, of course not. And Amelia is humiliated because she's made a fool of herself over him."

"I guess that would be humiliating," Caroline said. "Feeling an ache in your heart is much worse than getting a stain on your best dress. The dress someone very nice gave me." She smiled sadly.

"Well Amelia has a heartache *and* a torn dress, which was her fault, by the way."

Caroline frowned. "How? I stepped on her dress."

"That dress was so long it spilled over her feet. She was standing so close that if you took a step, it would be on her dress. And didn't you notice the way she suddenly backed up?"

Caroline frowned. "It was my fault."

Emily shook her head. "I still say Amelia is a little schemer, particularly when she dislikes someone."

"And she dislikes me," Caroline said with a sigh, looking down at her Bible. She remembered a verse Granny had taught her. *"Love your enemies, do good to all which hate you. . . ."*

Did Amelia really despise her? And if so, what could be done to change that?

She had been a seamstress all of her life; Granny had taught her well. In her mind's eye, she saw again the bit of torn fabric. It could easily be reattached to the skirt at the edge of the ruffle. She could do it by hand. Probably tonight.

She glanced at Emily, who had taken up her pen and stationery, still ignoring her books. It would do no good for Caroline to remind her she needed to study; she knew that. If she chose to write a letter to Tommy—and Caroline had no doubt he was the inspiration for the letter—then that was Emily's business.

She got up from the bed. There was no point in telling Emily her intentions. Emily would only argue with her.

"I'll be back in a few minutes," Caroline said, but Emily scarcely heard her.

In the hall, Caroline tried to remember where Amelia's room was. When they had met in the hall, Amelia had snubbed her, then turned and entered a room. Which room?

Caroline wandered down the hall, noting the numbers on the left side. It had been a door on the left. Halfway down, one door was ajar and she could hear voices coming from inside.

She stopped at the open door. Inside, two girls lounged on their beds while another leaned against a dresser.

"She comes from some—" All three had spotted Caroline and were staring wide-eyed at her.

Caroline focused her attention on Amelia, wearing a beautiful pink lounging gown as she propped against her pillows, munching chocolate candy.

"Excuse me," she called from the open door.

No one spoke. They just stared at her.

"I came to apologize to you, Amelia. I'm sorry about your dress, and I would like to mend it for you."

Amelia glanced from Caroline to the other girls. Then her lips curled and her blue eyes shot sparks. "No thanks. I don't think you would know how to mend a fine garment."

Caroline had never met anyone so cruel, but rather than be embarrassed now, she was proud of herself for not stooping to Amelia's level.

"I know how to forgive," she said slowly, making her point, "and I know how to be polite." She lifted her chin and turned from the door.

"Isn't she pathetic?" Amelia's voice rang out. But no one answered.

Chapter 4

The next day Caroline took a different route to class. During the past week, Ryan had begun waiting for her near the science building. From there, they walked to English class, but not today, not anymore, she had decided. Furthermore, Mary Elizabeth, whose room was next door to her, had informed Caroline that she often saw Ryan and Amelia together. At that, Caroline decided Mary Elizabeth knew more about Amelia and Ryan than Emily, and she must not interfere.

As she traveled the rear path, she glanced toward the front walkway and saw Ryan through the trees. He was standing with his back to her as he looked down the walk toward the approaching girls. She bit her lip, feeling guilty. She had to do this, she told herself, walking faster, forcing her eyes straight ahead.

"I missed you somehow," Ryan said, pausing at her desk when he entered the room.

She glanced briefly at him and felt her heart wrench. "Sorry," she said, busily opening her book and searching for a pen.

"Me, too," he added, then turned and walked away.

She avoided Amelia, but she could feel her eyes upon her at times. As soon as Mrs. Stockton dismissed class, Caroline grabbed her books and was out the door. If Ryan wondered what was wrong with her, perhaps Amelia could explain.

❦

Ryan spent the next week trying to figure out what he had done to offend Caroline. At first, he thought she was only preoccupied with her studies, but now he was certain she was avoiding him. He wanted to ask her why, but he never got the chance. She was always gone before he could catch up with her.

He sat in the library, staring through the window to Brunswick Hall. Why couldn't he get her out of his mind? She was like a breath of fresh air in his stifled world. Sometimes, after his eyes were dazed from studying, he would think about her and the way she had read her theme on Pine Ridge. To him, she was the most beautiful girl on campus, for there was something radiant and pure flowing from her soul. He longed to get to know her better; he even had a crazy desire to go to Pine Ridge and see that way of life firsthand. But she continued to ignore him, day after day. He stayed busy with schoolwork, poring over his books long into the night, determined to make his family proud as he followed the family profession of medicine.

"Why didn't you come to the Addison party?" The voice pulled him back to reality as he shifted against the library table and focused on Amelia. She had slipped into the chair opposite him. He noticed that she was a pretty girl, but she just didn't appeal to him.

"I've been busy with schoolwork. And besides," he added more truthfully, "I'm tired of parties." He was flattered that she liked him, and he could tell that she did; but they had nothing in common, other than family background. They had none of the same interests, and he suspected Amelia did not take her studies seriously, which bothered him even more.

"Oh. Well I never see you anywhere," she said, starting to pout.

"I never go anywhere," he said, sounding more abrupt than he intended.

Silence lengthened between them as her eyes dropped to his open book. "I'll let you get back to studying since you seem to enjoy it so much."

A wry grin tilted his lips as he took the verbal jab with no offense. "See you," he said, turning back to his anatomy book.

&

The days grew shorter with the approach of November. The sun's rays softened as autumn's cooling breezes settled over the campus. The oaks, maples, and hickories turned to brilliant hues, but Caroline thought that city trees didn't compare to those out in the country, where there was more room for the branches to spread wide. Still, she appreciated the color and shape and texture, and she was always stopping to pick up an exceptionally pretty leaf to press between the pages of her book. She collected so many they often fell from her books, and most instructors, upon finding another stray leaf on the floor, knew the source.

During the second week of November, she had stopped to capture one last dying leaf when she heard a familiar voice over her shoulder.

"This one is prettier."

She was kneeling on the grass, reaching for the leaf, when she heard his voice. She turned and looked up. Ryan was holding a huge maple leaf, the most beautiful shade of scarlet she had ever seen.

She gasped. "I thought all the pretty leaves had died. Where did you get that one?"

"In the backyard of my parents' home." He helped her to her feet and handed the leaf to her. "I know you collect leaves, so I brought this one back for you."

Her eyes met his, and her wall of reserve toppled. "That was awfully nice of you," she said, dropping her gaze to the leaf. It hurt to look into his friendly brown eyes and recall how many times she had avoided and even ignored him.

"There's a catch," he said, as she reached for it.

Her hand paused in midair, as her blue eyes widened questioningly.

"You have to have lunch with me."

"Oh," she said, dropping her hand.

He tilted his head and stared down at her with shocked eyes. "Is it that painful?"

She laughed softly, seeing the humor. "Of course not. It's just that. . .I'm awfully busy these days."

"I'm sure you are," he nodded patiently, "but I assume you do take time out to eat." His eyes swept down the dark taffeta dress she had worn at least once each week. "Still, you look as though you eat like a sparrow."

She laughed again and allowed herself to look directly into his eyes. Their gazes locked as she stared into his and thought of warm chocolate. "I don't know why I do that," she said, blinking and looking away.

"Do what?"

"Compare colors to favorite things." She shook her head. "I'm battin' the breeze," she bit her lip, trying to shut off more country talk.

"Are you comparing this leaf to a place in Pine Ridge?" he asked, trying to catch up with her thoughts.

Her blue eyes danced as she looked at him. She wasn't about to tell him what she was really thinking. She took the leaf from his hand and placed it in her book. "Thanks."

He didn't seem to mind that she hadn't answered him, and they fell into step along the walkway leading back to the dorm.

"You didn't answer my question about lunch. Tomorrow. Or any day next week. We'll go someplace different."

She took a deep breath, staring at the brick walls of Brunswick Hall. It would be rude to say no, for she couldn't make excuses for every day of the week. Besides, Amelia was still just as rude as ever, so Caroline had begun to wonder if avoiding Ryan really made a difference after all.

"Tomorrow?" she asked shyly.

Tomorrow was Saturday and she would welcome a chance for a nice lunch, especially with Ryan. Her scholarship covered meals in the dining hall, but she was beginning to get tired of looking at the same walls every day.

"Great." A wide smile stretched over even white teeth as he looked down at her. "How about a picnic lunch?"

She stopped walking and turned suddenly. "A picnic? I've been wantin' to go on a picnic, but nobody. . ." Her voice trailed as she glanced toward the dorm then back again. "Where would we go?"

"There's a park not far from here. . .and a lake," he added. "Maybe we'll see some ducks."

She smiled at him. "You remembered what I said in my theme about ducks."

"I remember every word of your theme." They had reached the steps of the dorm and were gazing into each other's eyes, oblivious to everything else.

"Hi, Caroline," Claire called with a smile.

"Hi, Claire. Do you know Ryan Blankenship?" Of course she knew of him, everyone did, but she wanted Ryan to meet Claire. Ever since Claire had returned her dress with most of the stain gone, she had been indebted to her. Claire had even given her a locket on a long chain, measuring it carefully so that the locket covered the small stain on her bodice.

"Hello, Claire," Ryan was saying. "I'm glad to meet you."

"Nice to meet you." Claire blushed, smiled quickly at Caroline, then slipped away.

It always touched Caroline to see how Claire carried herself with great dignity, despite her crippled side.

"She's nice," he said as his eyes followed Claire briefly before he turned back to Caroline. "I'll call for you here at noon tomorrow. Will that be okay?"

She nodded, hugging her books. "I'll be looking forward to it. And thanks for the leaf," she added, smiling at him.

⌒

When Ryan called for her the next day, Caroline wore the green taffeta dress with her locket and a black knit shawl that arrived in the mail for her the day before. She knew Granny had spent weeks knitting it, and as she wrapped the shawl around her, it was as though Granny's loving arms enveloped her as well.

Ryan was dressed in casual slacks and a long-sleeved white shirt. As she signed out of the dormitory, he opened the front door and she spotted a sleek buggy and black horse waiting at the curb.

She held her tongue, having begun to practice that art now, as they walked to the buggy and Ryan talked about the weather. It was a beautiful fall day with just enough crispness in the air to bring a glow to one's cheeks and spark a sense of adventure.

When Ryan assisted her into the seat of the buggy, she spotted the picnic basket on the floor.

"Mmm. Something smells good," she said, smiling at Ryan as he got into the buggy.

"Aretha fried chicken." He stopped suddenly, as though he had revealed an important secret.

"What's wrong?" she asked.

"Nothing." He lifted the reins and clucked to the horse.

"Who is Aretha?" she asked, suspecting he was embarrassed over having a cook.

Ryan hesitated. "Aretha helps Mother in the kitchen."

Caroline nodded. "Then I'll look forward to the chicken."

She had heard that his family was wealthy, and now the carriage and his reference to "help" confirmed it. She turned and looked out across the campus as the horse trotted smoothly up the street. Ryan couldn't help being born into wealth, just as she couldn't help being born at Pine Ridge, which she considered a blessing.

Her thoughts turned quickly to the scenery around them. Beyond the campus the boulevard was lined with all kinds of shops—a dry goods store, a meat market, another clothing store—with nice buggies and carriages parked in front of them.

"Are you liking Davis?" Ryan asked.

She turned and looked at him. "Yes. By the way, I've been wondering about your field of study." She had wondered *a lot*, in fact, and had intended to ask before their campus walks got interrupted.

"I'm in premedical studies. I want to be a doctor."

"That's wonderful. What made you choose that profession?"

He hesitated as he steered the horse down a side street. "My father is a doctor, and my uncle as well."

"Here in Birmingham?" she asked.

"Yes. They have a private practice downtown. Here we are."

Caroline turned and looked out at the park. "This is beautiful. Do you come here often?"

"As often as I can," he said, getting out of the buggy and coming around to her side. "When school starts to wear on my nerves, I come here and walk around the lake."

"I reckon it makes you feel better."

"It does." He handed her down and then reached for the picnic basket. "I've thought of inviting you, but you haven't been too friendly lately," he said, pressing her hand into the crook of his arm, with the picnic basket swinging from his other arm.

She turned her face away from him and looked at the lake. "Do you think we'll see any ducks?" she asked.

He chuckled. "You know how to dodge subjects, don't you? Yes," he looked at the lake, "we may see a duck or two."

They located a small wooden table beside the lake and opened the picnic basket. Spreading a cloth over the planks of the table, Ryan lifted out containers of chicken, potato salad, and chocolate cake.

"Ryan, this is so thoughtful," she said, smoothing her skirt as she settled onto the narrow bench. "I really appreciate it."

"I know you do." He smiled across at her as he sat down. "That's why I wanted to bring you here."

She looked out across the lake as it rippled in the slight breeze. An occasional leaf floated there, reminding her of the maple leaf he had given her. Smelling the food, absorbing the lovely autumn day, and feeling the glow of his attention, Caroline thought her heart would burst with joy.

"Aren't you going to eat?" he asked, indicating the plate he had prepared for her.

She hesitated. "Could we say a prayer first?"

He looked startled for a second, then his eyes twinkled. "My mother would love you, Caroline."

Would she? Caroline wondered. *Is she like you, or is she more like Dean Miller?*

But she merely smiled and lowered her head and offered a brief prayer of thanks.

"You're a Christian?"

She nodded.

"So am I. Maybe we could go to church sometime."

"I'd like that."

"When are you leaving for Thanksgiving holidays?"

"I won't be going home," she said, trying not to feel homesick.

"Why not?" he asked, surprised.

She sighed. "I'm waiting until Christmas."

He was silent for a moment, munching his chicken. "Why don't you have Thanksgiving dinner with my family and me?" he asked suddenly.

The question took her completely by surprise. She touched the napkin to her lips, thinking about an answer. "It's nice of you to ask, but I already promised to spend Thanksgiving with some of the other girls in the dorm who aren't going home."

"All of Thanksgiving? Can't you join us for one meal?"

She shook her head, hoping he wouldn't press her. She just wasn't ready to go to his home and meet his family. Her memory darted back to the spilled punch and the nightmare of her one social event, and she lowered her eyes to the food.

"If you won't come Thanksgiving, let me put in a reservation with you now for the Christmas holidays."

She looked up, wondering what he meant.

"We have an annual Christmas party the first week in December at my house. I think it'll be around the fifth this year. That's about the time everyone is leaving to go home." He frowned. "You won't leave before then, will you?"

"No." She looked out across the lake, thinking. "When I first came to Davis, Christmas holidays seemed to be years away. The time is going pretty fast though."

He was watching her thoughtfully. "Caroline, how would you feel about my driving you home for Christmas? I'd get the carriage and our driver so you wouldn't be cold."

She smiled at him, keeping her thoughts to herself. She could imagine the responses in Pine Ridge if she returned in a fancy carriage. "I appreciate your offer, but I've already purchased the ticket. I got a round trip when I came here." And then her return to Birmingham would have to be scraped together over the holidays.

"Too bad. But I do want to see Pine Ridge sometime. I've been fascinated ever since you read your theme."

She studied him for a moment. "You'd probably find it boring compared to Birmingham."

"No, I've been here all of my life, and frankly I'm tired of Birmingham. I'll probably practice medicine somewhere else, even though my father and uncle want me to remain here."

"If you don't stay here, where would you go?"

"I haven't decided. I have another uncle in Montgomery who wants me there."

"You have a lot to decide, don't you? I'm relieved that I don't. It's always been my dream to get a good education and then return home to share what I've learned."

"That's a nice dream," he said quietly.

She held his gaze for a second and then looked away. Her heart was bumping around in her chest, irritating her, and now fresh doubts were creeping into her mind. She enjoyed being with him; in fact, she liked him too much. She had her dreams and he had his, and they certainly could never mix.

"Want to take a walk?" he asked lightly, as if sensing her mood.

She nodded and returned the empty containers to the picnic basket. Then they spent the next hour strolling around the lake, enjoying the view, saying little.

"It's nice to be with someone who doesn't have to talk all the time," he said after one of their silences.

She laughed softly. "Granny says I talk too much."

"You have your times of being quiet and thinking, and I like that about you."

"Thank you," she said. He looked deeply into her eyes and the nervousness that had disappeared during their walk came lurching back. "It's time for me to go back to the dorm," she said.

"So soon?" he asked, obviously disappointed.

"Yes." She didn't bother to explain why, and he didn't ask. They returned to the picnic table and he lifted the basket.

"Thanks for coming," he said, offering her his arm again as they headed for the buggy.

"This is the best time I've had since I've been at Davis," she admitted.

It had been a perfect fall day with a beautiful view and delicious food and the company of the nicest man she had ever known. It was a golden memory to keep and treasure.

Chapter 5

T hanksgiving holiday dragged for Caroline. She helped Emily pack and listened to Emily's plans for the holiday. When Emily's parents came for her, they were a nice, older couple who seemed to dote on their only child.

"Emily has written us about how kind you've been to her," Mrs. Ellison said, looking at Caroline with the same green eyes of her daughter.

"Oh, she's the one who's been kind," Caroline said. "I'm going to miss her."

The girls had hugged as Emily left with her parents, and after Emily, the others began to leave. Caroline waved good-bye to all the girls, then walked alone to her room, hearing the hollow echo of her shoes in the quiet hallway.

Sadness engulfed her then, and she missed Pine Ridge so much she could hardly stand it. Since coming to Davis, she had written to Granny twice a week, painting vivid pictures of her life here. While Granny could read, her handwriting was poor, so letters from Pine Ridge were scarce and usually written by Miss Wallace, the visiting schoolmarm.

Since their picnic, Caroline had spoken with Ryan only twice. They had taken a long walk around the campus and discussed how busy they were, studying for exams. Ryan had neglected his health and come down with a severe cold, which resulted in his missing several days of school. He had told her he was planning to relax over the holidays, enjoy his mother's pampering, and tease his little sister.

⌒

"Caroline, are you eating with us?" Jenny Winslow broke through her thoughts. Jenny was a pleasant girl from New York who was staying at school over Thanksgiving.

"Yes, I'll be right there," Caroline called.

She tried to remain cheerful during Thanksgiving while she and six other girls occupied the dorm with a lonely housemother. She took long walks across the campus making plans, dreaming dreams. But Ryan kept sneaking back into those dreams. Even though Ryan seemed to like her, she knew there was no future with him. Because of that, she tried not to get serious about him.

On Sunday the girls and their housemother attended church near the campus. When they returned to the dorm, Caroline saw the carriages and buggies returning girls to the dorm.

She hurried around, looking for Emily, but she had not returned. Claire had arrived with stories of Christmas shopping. Caroline and Claire waited on Emily until someone reminded them that lunchtime at the dining hall would soon be over.

When Caroline returned, she was surprised to see Emily on her bed, crying softly.

"Emily, when did you get back? And where are your parents?"

Emily sat up, sobbing.

"What's wrong?" Caroline asked, hugging her.

"I had a fuss with my father," Emily said, her voice muffled as she sobbed against Caroline's sleeve.

"Tell me about it," Caroline said gently.

Emily pulled back and dabbed a handkerchief against her wet eyes. "Father forbade me from seeing Tommy and I refused, so he offered Tommy a menial job. Tommy said no. Finally, Tommy told me Father has tried to bribe him to leave Atlanta. Tommy refused his bribe, and I love him more than ever for it." She broke into another sob.

"Oh," Caroline said, staring into space. She didn't know how to comfort Emily. She wanted to tell her how often she had longed for her dead parents. Caroline thought about how she would feel if she and Ryan could have a future together, and suddenly she understood Emily's tears. "I'm so sorry," she finally said.

"I don't care if I flunk out of school," Emily wailed, sobbing harder.

"Yes you do," Caroline said, gripping her shoulders. "Don't you see, now you *have* to show your parents you're mature enough to make responsible decisions. In time, they may give in to you about Tommy."

With those words of encouragement, Emily's tears ceased momentarily, but the bleak look still filled her wet eyes. "I don't know if they'll ever do that."

"We'll pray about it, Emily, if this is your dream. I believe if we do the right thing and ask God, believing that He hears, He honors our prayers—and our dreams," she added, thinking of Ryan suddenly.

She had not asked God for Ryan, but she prayed for him to get over his bad cold, do well on his exams, and succeed in being a great doctor. She had never mixed their futures, for she felt they could not change directions in their life. She had to be true to herself, and she knew where she wanted to spend her life. Ryan, meanwhile, would be in Montgomery. She had to live with that.

"Maybe when you have your morning prayers, we can start praying together," Emily offered, startling Caroline. "I never was very religious, but you're the kindest, most genuine person I've ever known. If being a Christian makes you that way, I want to be like you. I want to start reading your Bible."

"You read my Bible anytime you want," she said, hugging her again.

The next morning, Emily sleepily listened as Caroline read aloud from her Bible. Then they prayed together, hurriedly dressed, and rushed to class.

The following week Ryan seemed to have recovered from his cold, and his eyes were glowing again. "You look rested from the holiday," she said.

"I am." He reached out, clasping her hand as they walked to class together. "I was tempted to bring you a plate of food on Thanksgiving Day, but Mother said you were probably with friends."

Caroline wondered how his mother felt about her, or what she knew. She looked at Ryan. "What did you tell her about me?"

"Everything." He grinned.

"What exactly is *everything*? And had she ever heard of Pine Ridge?" she asked casually as they entered the brick building that housed their English class.

"No, but my father has."

"And what does he think?" she asked guardedly.

"They both think it's wonderful that you're going back there to teach."

"Oh." Maybe she could look forward to his Christmas party after all.

Chapter 6

Emily insisted on giving Caroline a red velvet dress with a lace sash and flowing skirt. "I want you to wear it to Ryan's party," Emily insisted.

Emily was much happier since a letter from her mother indicated her parents were going to give Tommy a fair chance.

"Emily, this is the most beautiful thing I've ever seen!" Caroline trailed her fingers over the soft velvet. "I can't—"

"It's Christmas and I can do whatever I want! I've had that dress a year and have never worn it. Fortunately, the style is still in fashion."

Caroline hugged Emily, unable to say more as she hung the dress in her closet and began to dream about Ryan's Christmas party.

The campus held glowing candles in all the windows, and the girls in the dorm had spent a wonderful weekend decorating the parlor Christmas tree. Caroline donated a small angel doll to sit on top, one she had been sewing on for weeks. Although Amelia and her friends sneered, everyone else was impressed.

The Blankenships' Christmas party was scheduled for three o'clock Friday afternoon in order to give everyone time to return to their dorms to prepare for a Saturday departure. When Caroline made her train reservation, however, the last one available was the five o'clock train Friday afternoon.

Ryan assured her he could get her to the station in time, since his home was only fifteen minutes away.

The last exam was on Thursday, and Caroline was happy as she walked back to the dorm. Her exams had been easy, and she had straight A's for the semester. Emily's parents had come for Emily, and they appeared to be in a good mood. Emily hugged Caroline and wished her a merry Christmas, and Caroline stood outside and waved as they departed.

On Friday she took extra care in dressing, styling her hair in a thick chignon at her nape, securing it with a red velvet ribbon. Then she went to the parlor to wait for Ryan.

He was more handsome than ever in his black frock coat and pants with a white shirt and red cravat that set off his dark hair and eyes. She could feel the envious stares of the other girls as he draped Claire's borrowed cape around Caroline and they walked to his carriage.

A handsome carriage complete with driver awaited them, and he glanced at Caroline, looking sheepish.

She smiled at him, aware of what he was thinking. "Be proud of what you have, Ryan. It hasn't turned your head one bit. And besides," she said, her blue eyes twinkling, "I'm going to enjoy the ride."

They laughed together over things that had happened during the week, and soon she was gazing out at sprawling estates with enormous front lawns.

"My goodness," she said, turning to Ryan, "what do these people do for a living?"

"Some own large businesses downtown. Some are doctors," he added quietly.

"Doctors?" She smiled at him. "Then I imagine we must be in your neighborhood."

"Caroline—"

The carriage made a wide turn and she gripped the armrest and stared through the window. Gas lanterns topped brick posts at the entrance to the driveway. A huge lawn held marble statues and even a miniature Christmas tree had been decorated for outside.

Her eyes widened. Ryan was saying something, but she didn't hear. She had never seen such a grand estate in all of her life; she had never even imagined one like this existed. The drive curved again, ending before a three-story stone house with gabled roof. Candles glowed in every window, dozens of windows, and the front porch was covered with holly and velvet bows and bright tinsel.

She felt Ryan's fingers pressing her arm through her cloak. "It's my home, and I want you to feel welcome."

"It's beautiful," she said, then swallowed hard, dreading going inside.

The driver opened the carriage door and unfolded the steps while Ryan got out to assist her. Carefully, she descended and with her fingers gripping his arm, they climbed the crescent steps of the impressive house; then Ryan opened the front door.

A dozen wonderful smells greeted her—food, spices, perfume. He escorted her into the parlor, which was already filled with beautifully dressed people. She recognized a few faces from school interspersed among adults who talked in rich voices and laughed softly, oozing the kind of sophistication she read about in novels. She felt like a creature from the forest that had been plucked up and set down on a foreign beach. Her eyes moved to a Christmas tree at the far end of the room, and she could only stare. It was a perfectly shaped evergreen that reached all the way to the ceiling and was decorated with garland and ornaments in all sizes, shapes, and colors. Beneath the tree there must have been a hundred gifts.

"Let me take your cloak," Ryan said.

She untied the strings and felt it lift from her shoulders although her eyes never left the room that held oil paintings, antique furnishings, and fancy little sculptures on marble-topped tables.

"Hello."

Caroline turned to see a middle-aged woman wearing a lovely green gown; she had dark hair and eyes and resembled Ryan.

"Hello. I'm Caroline Cushman," she said, offering her hand.

"And I'm Ann Blankenship. We're so glad you could come."

"Oh, you two have met," Ryan said, joining them.

"Yes, and she's even prettier than you told us." Mrs. Blankenship smiled at her son.

"Now get her some refreshments, dear."

Ryan and Caroline walked out of the parlor into the dining room, where a long table was covered with silver trays of food, candles in silver candleholders, and a cut glass crystal punch bowl and matching cups. Caroline stared at the punch; *red again.*

One maid served their food; another ladled out punch. Caroline took a firm grip on the plate and cup.

Voices filled the house as more people arrived. Glancing back, she saw Amelia enter the dining room. Caroline's back stiffened, but she held her smile, determined to be polite. Behind them, other young people mingled, although she didn't recognize anyone.

"Merry Christmas, Ryan!" Amelia linked her arm through his. She looked stunning in a white velvet dress with an ermine collar. Diamonds glittered on her earlobes, and her cheeks and lips were painted a soft, delicate pink. Her hair was swept up in a crown of blond curls.

"Merry Christmas," Ryan said, smiling down at her. Caroline watched his face and felt her heart sink. He was staring at her as though entranced by her beauty.

Caroline heard the clink of glass and realized, with horror, that her fingers were starting to tremble. The sight of Amelia was a challenge to Caroline's nerves.

"Amelia, good to see you," a man's voice boomed across the room.

"You, too, Dr. Blankenship." She released Ryan's arm and extended a dainty gloved hand.

"I had lunch with your father at the club last week. I understand we're all getting together for dinner."

"Yes, Ryan suggested it," she said, giving Ryan a radiant smile before her eyes slipped to Caroline.

Caroline realized the trembling had moved up her fingers to her palms. Desperately, her eyes flew to the table, and she quickly set down the plate and cup in an empty space—before she could drop or spill anything.

Ryan was turning toward her. "Father, I'd like you to meet a friend."

Caroline turned to face a tall, gray-haired man.

"This is Caroline Cushman," he said.

"How do you do?" Cool blue eyes swept her. "You're the young lady from Pine Ridge?"

Caroline felt her stomach tighten even more. "Yes, I am."

"I'm sure your community is proud of you." He glanced over her shoulder. "Oh, excuse me, please. I see someone I must speak with. Nice meeting you." He smiled briefly, then rushed off.

Caroline couldn't decide if he was reserved or if he disliked her. She tried to keep her smile in place as Ryan took her elbow and escorted her into the living room.

Her stomach was now balled as tight as a fist as Amelia's words echoed in her mind. Ryan had suggested their families get together. He *did* like Amelia. Why else would he suggest that? She glanced over the strangers. She had never seen so much jewelry, smelled so much perfume, or felt so drastically out of place.

Ryan introduced her to a gracious older couple who peppered Ryan with questions about school. Half listening, she let her eyes sweep the room. She spotted Amelia chatting with Ryan's mother and a young girl who was dressed in a beautiful blue dress. Suddenly, the girl turned and looked directly at Caroline. What were they saying?

Caroline's stomach lurched. She had to find a lavatory. She was going to be sick. The nervous stomachache that had been troubling her for months increased to severe stomach cramps when she got nervous. She knew, in just a matter of minutes, she would be throwing up.

Before Ryan finished his conversation, she tapped his arm. "Excuse me," she said, lowering her voice. "Could you point me to the lavatory, please?"

"Oh of course." He detached himself from the older couple and directed her down the hall to the first door on the right.

She rushed in that direction, relieved to see it was a large room and that the two ladies present were primping before a gold-framed mirror. She smiled briefly and rushed into the toilet, which, to her enormous relief, had a door to close. The women's voices floated away as the outer door opened and closed.

Enormously relieved to be alone, she gripped the wall and gave way to the heaving nausea. In the midst of her spasms, she heard the door open again. She tried to muffle the sound, but how could you be quietly sick?

"What is that?" a younger voice asked.

"Sounds as though someone drank too much of that special punch your father stashed in the kitchen."

If she felt sick before, it was even worse now. For the voice was Amelia's and Caroline knew she would rather die than go out and face her.

Fear had ended her spasms, and at least she was no longer heaving, but now she felt cold to the bone and dizzy with apprehension.

"Could you please hurry up in there?" a younger voice pleaded.

Taking a deep breath, running a hand over her face, and checking her dress, Caroline opened the door and stepped out.

Amelia stood beside the young girl studying Caroline curiously.

"Oh Caroline," Amelia said patronizingly, "you know you shouldn't start drinking this early in the day."

Caroline's mouth fell open, and for a moment she was too startled to reply.

"Eugenia, this is Caroline Cushman. Caroline, this is Eugenia, Ryan's sister."

The girl's pale blue eyes were filled with scorn as she looked Caroline up and down.

Then she struck the worst blow of all. "How dare you get drunk at my parents' party. I think you're disgusting." She turned and entered the toilet.

Amelia was eyeing herself in the mirror, adjusting a curl. Caroline walked over to the faucet to rinse her hands. She dried them carefully, then turned to Amelia.

"I do not drink, and you have no reason to slander me," she said to Amelia, who was trying to ignore her.

Amelia had turned to face her, her chin lifted, her blue eyes cold. She said nothing.

"You've done your best to make me feel inferior since that day at the dorm when you deliberately bumped me so I would spill my punch," Caroline continued, "but you've only made me more determined to succeed. And I'm proud of where I come from and the people there; we are good, hard-working people who try never to hurt another human being."

She heard the door open behind her and realized that Eugenia was walking around to face her.

"You're mistaken, Caroline." Amelia pushed a little smile onto her lips while Eugenia stared. "It wasn't my fault you spilled the punch. I think you're just upset because Ryan is seeing me again. In fact, I would have been his date today if he hadn't invited you. He gave me a special invitation to come anyway, didn't he, Eugenia?"

The girl nodded, looking from Amelia to Caroline.

"And for your information, we're having dinner together tomorrow night. He told me he felt sorry for you, knowing you had nothing to do."

"I *do* have something to do," she said calmly, looking back at Eugenia. "I am glad to have met you," she said. Then she lifted her chin and left the room.

Yes, she had something to do. She had a train to catch and she wanted no part of this social world ever again. She practically bumped into Ryan's mother as she turned a corner, looking for the coat closet.

"I hope you are having a good time," the woman smiled.

Caroline nodded. "Yes ma'am. I've enjoyed your party, Mrs. Blankenship, but I have a train to catch. Could you please tell Ryan I had to leave?"

She hurried past her to the next room. She had no trouble locating her simple cape among the others as the grandfather clock in the hall struck four. She remembered Ryan had said they could get to the train station in fifteen minutes from his house. With an hour, she would have no trouble getting there on her own. She cast one last glance across the room, seeing Ryan with his father and an older man. He wasn't even looking her way; he seemed to have forgotten her completely. She turned and opened the door, stepping out into the cold gray day.

Carriages filled the drive, but she knew she could easily locate the

Blankenship carriage; it would be the only one with a battered cardboard suitcase on the seat. Soon she had her suitcase and was hurrying down the driveway. Fueled by anger, she walked fast and hard. She glanced around her, trying to forget what had happened. On the contrary, the opulent estates merely reminded her of the Blankenships. And Amelia. The pain of Amelia's insults, Eugenia's scorn, and Mr. Blankenship's subtle indifference was mild compared to the raw ache of Ryan's deception. Or was it deception? He had never said he liked her, but she had assumed. . .

Was it true he felt sorry for her, thought she needed a friend? He was kind to everyone, and he had been fascinated by Pine Ridge. Maybe that was why he had been nice. Emily thought he was crazy about her and Caroline had wanted to believe that; but now she knew they were both wrong. She had seen for herself that Amelia was really his girl. She fit perfectly into his world. And now she had no one but herself to blame for her broken heart.

The wind picked up, making the day feel even colder. On the street corner, carolers huddled together, their breath making tiny circles of fog as they sang.

Her eyes watered and tears trickled down her cold cheeks. Lowering her head, she hurried on, forcing her thoughts toward home. It was the only way she could survive the terrible hurt inside. She thought of the community church on Christmas Eve, with homemade candles in every window, the handmade gifts folks passed out, more precious than those fancy ones under the Blankenship tree.

Deep in thought, she had walked for blocks and blocks until she suddenly stopped and looked around. Nothing was familiar. She thought if she merely headed straight back, she would pass the train station. With a sinking heart, she realized there must have been another street that led to the station, and somehow she had missed it.

With lips trembling from the cold, she stopped a passerby.

"Could you please tell me how to get to the train station?" she asked.

"Miss, you're ten blocks too far north."

She gasped. Ten blocks! Had she walked ten blocks out of the way?

"Thank you," she said, whirling around.

"When you get to Fifth, you have to take a right and go straight west four blocks."

She nodded, wondering about the time. She regretted not taking her father's watch out of its safe place in the bureau as Granny suggested. Walking faster now, reading the street signs, she regretted her impulsiveness. Why hadn't she asked directions before rushing off? *I will find it on my own,* she told herself. She didn't need anyone's help.

Gripping her suitcase tighter, she was practically running by the time she reached Fifth. She made the turn, stopping beside an old man selling newspapers. "What time is it, please?"

Stiff fingered, he fumbled in his pocket for his watch. "Twenty till five."

I can make it, she told herself. With one hand, she lifted her skirt and began to run the four blocks. The frigid air poured through her open mouth as she panted for breath. She could feel her hair slipping out of the chignon, tumbling about her face. *How could four blocks take so long?* she wondered, gasping for breath. Just when she thought she would pass out, she saw the outline of the train station and she tried to calm herself. The dull pain in her side had become a searing ache that warned her to slow down or fall flat; still, the whistle of a departing train quickened her steps again. *More than one train left the station,* she reminded herself as she entered the station.

She could hardly bend her cold fingers, but she managed to open her purse and find her ticket. "Pine Ridge," she gasped to the little man taking up tickets.

He looked up in surprise. "Just left. Sorry."

She stared at him. "Are you sure?"

"Yes'm, I'm sure."

"Then can I trade my ticket for a later—"

"Every train seat is booked for the rest of the holidays."

His words were blows to her frozen ears.

"Hurry up, miss," someone nudged her.

Dazed, she stepped out of line and collapsed on the nearest bench. Her bottom lip began to tremble. She wouldn't be going home for Christmas! She sat there, hugging her useless ticket, as voices rose and fell in harsh cadence. She looked bleakly at the crowd and shivered into her cape.

There had been times when she had thought she was lonely, sitting alone on a creek bank, tossing pebbles in the pond. But *this* was loneliness—surrounded by strangers at Christmas, with nowhere to go and no one who cared.

Then she felt a hand on her shoulder, suddenly aware that someone stood behind her.

"Tell me what happened." She lifted her tear-stained face and looked into Ryan's troubled eyes.

Chapter 7

I missed the train," she said.

He glanced quickly toward the ticket counter, then sank into the seat beside her.

"That's not a problem. What caused you to leave my house?" He pushed a trailing strand of hair back from her face. "Your face is frozen. Surely you didn't—did you walk?" he asked, looking horrified.

"What difference does it make? You had more important guests."

"That's not fair," he said, reaching for her hand.

She tried to hold back, but his touch was gentle, yet insistent.

"When Mother told me you had left, I was puzzled, but I thought you must have left with friends from school. Father saw you leaving and found me; I couldn't believe you would leave like that. I knew something had gone wrong. As I was getting my coat, Eugenia rushed up and told me about Amelia. That explained everything," he said, his voice edged with anger.

He paused, shaking his head. "Amelia has misled you and everyone else into thinking I care for her. We have been friends since childhood because our parents are close friends. Naturally, I asked her if she was coming to their annual dinner party of close friends. As for today's gathering, Mother insisted I invite her to the party, but my friendship with Amelia has ended. She lied to you."

Caroline stared at him, not wanting to hope, and yet she could feel something deep inside warming, just as he was warming her hand with his own.

She stared at him, considering his words. If his family didn't like her, why would they help clear up the misunderstanding? And if Ryan didn't care, why didn't he stay with Amelia? Why had he come here for her?

"Look, there's plenty of time to explain. The carriage and Felix are waiting outside. I was going to insist on taking you home; now you have no choice."

His warm smile reached out to her, and she felt her reserve topple. "Guess I can't say no," she replied.

Later, after they were settled in the carriage with a blanket wrapped around her, Caroline thought she must be dreaming. Was Ryan really saying these things to *her*?

"I have liked you since the first day I saw you. And now I think I've gone beyond the liking stage and—"

"Ryan," she sighed, "I don't fit into your world."

"Who said so? My mother adored you, my father liked you—if you understand that he's always a bit preoccupied, even with me. And once Eugenia's eyes were opened to the truth, she liked you, too. My parents and sister are good Christian people; they are not snobs."

"No, they were very nice to me," she said, regretting her rude departure.

He reached across and pressed her head against his shoulder. "You look exhausted. Why don't you rest until we get there?"

"I am tired," she admitted. The warmth and the gentle rocking of the carriage had worked its magic as she nestled against Ryan and felt the sweetest peace she had ever known.

A gentle hand on her shoulder brought Caroline out of an exhausted sleep. She opened her eyes and looked around. The curtain was drawn back on the carriage window, admitting a soft, yellow light from the candlelit shops in Pine Ridge. Ryan's face was profiled against the light, and he was smiling down at her.

"We're here," he said, turning toward the window.

Caroline looked out at the place she loved and had dreamed of for months.

A full moon streamed pure silver over the small shops and log cabins where homemade candles twinkled in the windows. Wreaths made from pine cones adorned the doors, and in the soft night she could hear the peal of the church bell.

"They're having a service tonight, Ryan. Could we stop?" she asked eagerly.

"Of course." He looked out at the sleepy little community and sighed. "Caroline, I feel like I've landed in a Dickens novel. This is the most beautiful little place I've ever seen."

The carriage slowed to a stop. Felix got down and came to open the door. "Where are we going, Mr. Blankenship?"

He looked at Caroline. "Which church?"

She smiled. "There's only one. The little church straight ahead."

Felix nodded. "Thank you." He closed the door, and Caroline looked back at Ryan.

"Ryan, I can't thank you enough." Her eyes filled with tears.

"The opportunity to come here is my thanks. Where is the doctor's clinic?"

She frowned. "Dr. Felts? Why, he has a clinic in his home. In fact, we'll be passing his house in just a minute. He lives across from the church."

Her heart jumped at the question. Why had Ryan asked? Was it possible—?

"There. That's his house," she pointed. "Dr. Felts wanted to blend into Pine Ridge, and so he built a log cabin as well. His, of course, is larger and nicer."

Tonight, dozens of candles twinkled in the windows, giving Pine Ridge the kind of storybook beauty Ryan had mentioned earlier.

"I can't believe anyone can live like this," he said, staring at the house.

Caroline's heart sank. "I guess it does seem remote and—"

"Stop it." His hand squeezed hers. "I can't believe anyone could have such a peaceful, beautiful life."

Caroline stared at him for a moment, seeing the fascination in his face. He meant what he was saying, but why had she ever doubted him?

The pealing of the church bell was closer now, and she looked out on the cemetery across from the church as the carriage rolled to a halt.

Eyes of the Heart

Rosey Dow

Dedication

In memory of Miriam Dow,
my mother-in-law, mentor,
confidante, and friend.
I still miss you, Mom.

Chapter 1

I was sitting in the library in my favorite oversized chair when I felt a blast of cold wind. Someone had thrown open the front door. My heart lurched. I was afraid that this Christmas of 1925 would be one I'd never forget.

Eighteen-year-old Millie Box squeezed into the chair with me so she could peek around its high back and spy into the foyer.

"Is it them?" I asked.

One glance and she whispered, "It's them all right, Julie. All of 'em red and chapped with cold." She giggled. "I wonder which one is Honey's beau."

"Sh-h-h! They'll hear you."

"Help me off with this coat, Bob," a shrill voice whined, "so's I can go in by the fireplace. My toes are icicles."

I stiffened. Would they choose the library or the parlor across the hall? Both had blazing fires.

"I'll help you, Lucy," boomed a mellow male voice. "Bob's busy with his own coat." He sang off-key, "Oh, you beautiful doll. . ."

"Cut it out, Tubby," the girl said, exasperated. "We've listened to you for three hours straight. You should be on the radio. . . ."

"Then we could turn you off." A tenor male stole the punch line. Several people groaned.

Millie giggled. I jabbed a forefinger toward her middle. "You'll give us away, goosey."

Just then I heard Mother's heels clacking on the oak floor as she bustled down the central hall. Short and wide with a sensible manner, she might have been a matron from a girls' school. "Honey dear!" she cried.

Millie whispered to me, "She's hugging Honey and snifflin'. Say, Julie, Honey got her hair bobbed. She's got bangs and red lipstick."

In a moment, Mother said, "Come into the parlor and get warm." She called loudly, "Millie!"

Millie scooted away, leaving me to eavesdrop alone. Millie was more of a little sister to me than Honey was, though they were the same age. When Millie's mother, our cook, died eight years ago, Mother kept orphaned Millie and trained her as a housemaid. Millie and I were pals. Honey and Millie had never been close.

Honey had just arrived home for her first Christmas holiday since she'd entered the University of Vermont. Being Honey, she'd organized a house party at the last minute. With five friends in tow, she phoned a message to Shegog's Grocery, telling Mother and Dad of her plans. Shegog had the only telephone in the village. Lucky for us, it was a five-minute walk away.

Honey's message arrived with the meat delivery. Mother threw up her hands and scolded, but an hour later she was making lists and chattering about gifts and activities.

Our cook, Esther Quin, grumbled through the menu planning, the pie baking, and the cookie cutting. But that was nothing new. Esther was forever grouching about something.

Dad took the news in stride. A family crisis rarely rattled him. He spent most of his time at his sawmill across the road from our house. He left most things to Mother—especially Honey.

I wished I could overlook Honey's shenanigans, too. I should be used to her scheming by now. When she was ten and I was twelve, she got inspired to start a glee club in Athens, our tiny village. Worst of all, she made her big sister sing "Snookey Ookums."

I hated every note. I still sang of course. I was dying inside, but I sang with all my might. Maybe that's why the glee club dissolved after its first performance.

The next day Honey apologized for embarrassing me. Then she started planning a backyard rendition of *Romeo and Juliet*. Guess who got to be Juliet?

I pressed my head against the upholstery and closed my eyes as Honey said, "Mother, meet Lucy McDowell and Alice Stuart."

Then a deep, resonant voice said, "Good evening, Mrs. Simmons. I'm Jim Clarke."

"I'm Tubby. . .uhm. . .Michael Adams." The singer.

"Bob Barton," said the tenor, sounding younger than the others. He spoke like he'd practiced every word in front of a mirror.

"Honey," Mother said, "after your friends warm up, take them upstairs to their rooms—the boys in the back and the girls in your old room. You'll be in with Julie."

Her voice faded as she called, "We'll have dinner in an hour."

I chewed my lip. An hour till dinner wasn't nearly long enough. If only I could get upstairs to my room. Too late now. Someone would surely meet me on the stairs or in the upper hall. So I held my breath, dreading the inevitable.

The farmhouse smelled rich with mingled scents of linseed oil, the giant fir tree in the parlor, wood smoke from two fireplaces, and tantalizing aromas wafting from the kitchen.

Twenty minutes later, a man's expensive cologne touched my sensitive nose. I tensed.

"Pardon me. I didn't know anyone was here." It was the gent with the deep voice. "Mind if I sit near the fire? This cold gets into one's bones."

"The blue armchair is comfortable," I said, gulping, "and it's near the hearth."

Across from me, the chair made a faint scrishing sound. "I'm Jim Clarke. You must be Honey's sister, Julie."

I wet my lips. "Yes."

"She told me about you. I'm glad to know you."

I scraped together my manners and asked, "What are you studying at the university, Mr. Clarke?"

"Please call me Jim. I'm a senior at pre-law. My father wants me to join his firm. My brother Peter is a partner, and it looks like my younger brother Ron will be one, too." His words tightened. "I'm supposed to make it a happy foursome."

"You don't want to?"

He chuckled. "You have your sister's knack for cutting to the quick."

The dinner bell tinkled, and the chair creaked. "May I escort you to dinner?"

"Why. . .surely. Thank you." His warm hand gently lifted my fingers and placed them on the sleeve of his dinner jacket. It was then that I knew that he knew. . .that I was blind.

⌒

I knew the big farmhouse inside and out, every inch of polished walnut flooring, every piece of antique furniture, every shrub and tree in the yard. Five years ago, I was an average girl in every way. Then a skating accident left me in a coma for days. On my fifteenth birthday, I awoke to a dark world. Only the brilliance of sun on snow could turn my eternal midnight into dense gray fog.

Three years at Perkins Institute for the Blind had taught me how to cope with everything, except strangers. Strangers seemed to think my injury had also dulled my ears and my mind. Strangers my own age were the worst. Why had Honey brought so many of them home for Christmas?

I'd much rather have a house full of rollicking village children. Their spontaneous questions and loving touches warmed my heart. That's why I taught Sunday school for grades four through six.

As Jim led me through the parlor into the dining room, his sleeve felt rough under my hand. His palm lightly covered my fingers.

I pulled in my lower lip. Had my brown curls gone wild while I hid in the chair? My hair was bobbed above my collar with clips at each temple to keep it controlled, but sometimes it felt like a lion's mane. I was afraid to reach up and find out.

"There you are, Jim," Honey called from behind us. "I was looking for you."

"I found Julie in the library," he answered easily.

"Hi, sis," she said, giving me a short squeeze. "I've got tons to tell you later."

Mother broke in with instructions. "Julie sits there next to you, Jim, with Honey on your other side." She seated the other guests opposite us, with Mother and Dad at each end of the table.

After Dad ground out thanks for the food, Millie served my plate and cut my meat. She leaned over me from behind to whisper, "Roast beef at ten o'clock, potatoes at two, peas and carrots at five."

Afraid of who might be watching, I lifted my fork, found a cube of meat, and jabbed it. Success.

A *clink* and a gasp next to me. "Oh no. It slipped out of my hand," Jim said. "Pardon me, Mrs. Simmons. I'm clumsy tonight."

"Esther, get a cloth," Mother ordered calmly. "And another plate for Jim."

He chuckled. "My beef's swimming in grape juice. A new delicacy."

Tubby sang, "I'm forever blowing bubbles. . ."

"Tubby, please!" Alice stage-whispered.

"Oops, sorry, Mrs. Simmons. I forgot myself."

"Michael," Mother said, a smile in her voice, "after dinner you can sing to your heart's content. . .in the parlor."

Honey added, "Julie can play the piano for you!"

My face grew warm as I reached for my glass. My fingers bumped it over. I felt Jim lurch back.

"Jim, your white shirt!" Honey cried.

Esther *tsk*ed. "And I just brought you a new plate, Mr. Jim."

"It's no worse than what I did," he said.

I couldn't breathe. I dropped my napkin on my plate. "Excuse me, please. I'm not feeling hungry." I scraped back my chair and aimed for the kitchen door to make a quick escape.

Millie was at my heels when I reached the hall. "Julie, don't run away. It was just a little accident."

"Please, finish your dinner, Millie. I want to be alone."

Running my hand up the wide banister, feeling the pine garland tied there, I climbed the stairs and shut myself into my bedroom. If only I could stay here until they went away.

I sat on my bed and felt the texture of the quilt. Of all the awful things that could happen, spilling something on a guest had to top the list. My stomach clamped down until I felt sick.

A few minutes later, the door softly opened and Millie's shoes scuffled in. "Julie? You okay?"

"I'm perfectly fine."

She sat in the chair without saying more. She knew how I hated to be fussed over.

I thumped my pillow and pulled it into my lap. "What are they like, Millie?"

"They're silly college kids."

"But what do they look like?"

She moved next to me, her voice warming. "Lucy is a pudgy girl with a shingled bob that makes her look like a boy. She wears red lipstick and orange-colored rouge. She'd be cute if her mouth wasn't always in a pout. She constantly whines at the fellows. I wonder how they put up with her.

"Alice is thin as a bean stalk with frizzy red hair and lots of freckles. Her clothes are from *Vogue*, her face is from Max Factor, and she talks like her head's full of air."

I smiled. "What about the fellows? Is Tubby as big as he sounds?"

"Bigger. He's got a round face and teeth like a picket fence. He needs a haircut, too. The other boy reminds me of a soda jerk in Stowe. He'd steal the shirt off his ailing grandfather."

"Millie! You don't even know Bob."

"He has shifty eyes, Julie. And he's got a sort of pasted-on smile, too."

"What about Jim Clarke?"

"Honey's beau?" Millie's voice became dreamy. "Six feet tall, sandy-brown hair, and eyes that look right through ya. And Honey looks at him like a cat sizing up a fat trout."

I laughed. "Millie, you're the limit."

The door opened, and Honey skipped in. "We're going to listen to the Happiness Boys on the radio and play some games. Come and join us, Julie."

"I need to practice my offertory for Sunday." I hugged my pillow hard. "Maybe another time."

"Suit yourself." She went to the dresser and sprayed L'Heure Bleue until it filled the room. "I see you met Jim. He's a sheik. And rich as Croesus." She laughed softly.

"Did he give you a ring?" I asked.

"Not yet. But he will soon." Her heels tapped across the floorboards. "See you later."

"Why do you have to practice?" Millie demanded as soon as Honey left.

"Because I don't want to play with them."

"I never knew you were such a spoilsport, Julie Simmons." She stood. "I've got to help Esther wash up." She banged the door behind her.

I picked up a brush and dragged it through my curls. Alice and Lucy were in their room. The connecting door was shut, but I could hear their muffled voices, their laughter.

Soon they shuffled downstairs, and the second floor felt like a tomb. Why not play mah-jongg? Dad had carved me a set so I could distinguish the pieces. I loved to play with Millie. But with strangers?

When I couldn't bear the quiet any longer, I slipped down to the library where my baby grand sat in the corner. The smooth bench felt good. My feet automatically found the pedals. My fingers skipped across the keys, playing "The Skater's Waltz" without conscious effort, the tune so familiar that my mind wandered to happier days full of light and laughter.

Chapter 2

Jim, would you like to play mah-jongg?" Honey asked me, leaning over my chair. Light from the parlor fire danced off her golden hair, which hung forward onto her cheeks. Her wide blue eyes looked deeply into mine. Honey had style. She was a unique person who could follow the latest fashions without the gaudy extremes of the flapper.

I was a lucky man. She could have chosen any fellow she wanted. She'd even charmed my father when I took her home for Thanksgiving. Before we left, he told me she was a perfect match for a rising young lawyer—vivacious, beautiful, and not above a daring, inviting look now and then. The better to charm stuffed shirts and politicians. He told me to give her a ring—the sooner, the better, like it or not.

I didn't mind. She sure was beautiful.

"Mah-jongg or charades?" she asked, raising a shapely eyebrow.

"You choose," I said. I didn't feel like playing anything. After driving most of the afternoon, I'd much rather put my feet up and relax.

"I'm turning in," Lucy said. "My head's killing me."

Tubby hooted. "It's hurting me, too."

She threw a small pillow at him on her way out.

On the sofa, Alice snapped her chewing gum. "Not charades. We won't be able to hear the radio." Her red hair billowed around a gold cord she'd tied across her forehead, its ends dangling by her left ear. Cute, if you liked the type. I didn't.

Bob Barton pressed his ear to the radio cabinet, fiddling with knobs. Static hissed into the room as Honey moved to a corner cupboard and pulled out a flat mahogany box.

"This mah-jongg game is the only one of its kind. Dad made it." She set the box on a long, low table in front of the sofa.

"Partners," Tubby called, sliding closer to Alice.

"Without Lucy there are only five of us," Honey said, kneeling on the rug to set out the tiles. "We can't play partners."

"I'll sit out this time," I said, ignoring Honey's surprised, hurt look. "I'm tired from driving all day. I'll catch forty winks in the library."

The moment I crossed the hall, the fireplace lured me back to the blue armchair. I slid down until my neck rested on the back cushion. Warmth seeped into my cold joints until my eyes felt deliciously heavy.

A few minutes later, light fingers playing "The Skater's Waltz" made me blink. I sat up and saw Julie at the piano, a soft smile on her lips. I studied her eyes, so clear and liquid brown. How could those beautiful, perfect eyes be useless?

I didn't move. She was just as lovely as her sister, but what a contrast. Honey knew she was beautiful. Julie didn't. Were there other differences beneath the surface? Intriguing.

At the end of the song, I couldn't keep from clapping. She played wonderfully, effortlessly.

She froze like a frightened bunny.

"That was marvelous," I said, trying to put her at ease. "One of my favorite pieces."

"I—I thought everyone was in the parlor."

I wracked my brain for an answer that would keep her from bolting. "Do you play mah-jongg?" It sounded lame even to me.

"A little." She absently stroked the black keys.

"Why don't we join the game? We'd make a third team."

Her cheeks turned pink. "I'd rather not, thank you."

"Why not? The gang is in fine fettle tonight. We'll have a blast." A burst of laughter came from the parlor, proving my point. I waited, fully expecting her to refuse, but she surprised me.

"Well. . ." She sighed, and a look—half hope, half fear—flitted across her features. "Maybe one game."

"That's the spirit. Let's show 'em how it's done."

Chapter 3

W ake up, Julie!" Millie shook me the next morning, excitement in her words and urgency in her hands. "The kids are going skating. I'm going, too. Will you come? You had such a lovely time with them last night. Please say you'll go."

I pushed away her tugging fingers and sat up, rubbing hair from my face. "I can't, Millie. Go ahead without me."

"But why not? I'll skate with you. It'll be the cat's pajamas."

My skates were hanging in the back of the closet. Five years they'd hung there. The leather had probably cracked by now. I used to be a champion, but the accident had changed all that. Last year I'd slipped them on, but they brought up such painful memories that I'd put them away.

"Ask Esther to bring me a tray, Millie. I'll stay upstairs this morning."

"I wish I could change your mind."

As I slid deeper under the covers, I could hear Honey's friends in the front hall.

Tubby sang loud and long until Lucy made him stop. His booming laugh filled the house.

"Let's take a rope and play windmill," Honey cried. "Millie, can you find one for us?"

"There's one hanging by the back stoop," she called from the top of the stairs.

I pulled the pillow over my ears to block out their voices.

Last night Jim and I had won two games. He was a sharpshooter. I smiled. I wasn't a slouch at memory games either. We made such a good team I forgot to be shy.

A few minutes later, Esther huffed, "Here's your breakfast, Miss Julie. You'd best come down for lunch. My poor legs can't take those stairs twice in a day."

With a murmur of thanks at her retreating back, I bit into a warm blueberry muffin soaked in melted butter.

I finished off the last crumb and drained my teacup. Setting the tray on the floor, I reached under the bed for a shoe box carefully tied with a red ribbon. Inside lay a stack of letters written on crackling paper. I couldn't read them, but I still loved to hold them and smell them, remembering the boy who wrote them to me more than five years ago.

Puppy love, Father had called my feelings for Tom. I guess he'd been right. After twenty-three letters describing my charms and declaring his devotion, darling Tom visited me twice after my accident, then faded away. I never heard what happened to him. I only knew he hadn't really cared.

In spite of that, I loved to remember that he'd found me appealing. Since my blindness, I was so clumsy. My curly hair felt like a tangle. My face seemed so stiff. What man would ever look at me twice?

I fingered the letters, remembering the look in Tom's eyes when he told me he loved me.

The click of an opening door jerked me to reality.

"You're not dressed yet?" Mother asked. "If you don't want to go skating, at least you can come downstairs and help poor Esther roll out the biscuits."

I threw back the covers. "Sorry, Mother. I was daydreaming."

"What's that box?"

I shoved it under the bed. "Just some old letters. It's nothing important."

"Here's your plum-colored dress." She spread it on the bed beside me. "Please hurry. Esther's in a dither. I'd best get back to the stove before my creamed onions burn." She trundled away.

How could I manage my hair without Millie? I wanted to clip it back with the pearl barrettes Dad had given me last Christmas.

Twenty minutes later, the aroma of sugar-cured ham from our smokehouse made my mouth water. Esther greeted me with a sniff. "I could swat that Millie for running off this morning and leaving me with all the work. Here's the biscuit dough, Miss Julie. I floured the board for you, and the rolling pin's beside the bowl."

Mother wrapped a wide apron around my middle. I felt the floured board, used a wooden spoon to scrape out the dough, and sprinkled more flour on top. "Don't blame Millie, Esther," I told her. "Millie doesn't have much time for fun."

"Seems to me that's all she does have time for." The cook thumped a pan to the worktable. My fingers found the biscuit cutter, and I punched it into the dough with practiced rhythm.

The front door groaned.

"I wonder who that is," Mother said, heading for the hall. "The young people aren't due until lunchtime." Her voice drifted back. "Why, Jim, are you hurt? You're limping."

"It's nothing, Mrs. Simmons. I broke my ankle while playing tennis last summer, and it's still weak. I'm afraid I tried to do too much today. Don't worry. A little rest and I'll be good as new."

"Here, come into the library. I'll pull an ottoman near the fire for you."

"That's very kind."

I dropped the last limp circle to the pan and dusted my hands as Mother hustled into the kitchen and straight to me. "Julie, go and entertain Jim. He's hurt his ankle."

"Me? What will I say?"

"He's a polite young man. Ask him questions, and let him do the talking." She untied my apron. "It's the least we can do for Honey's young man." She sighed. "I wonder why Honey didn't come back with him."

"It's her party, Mother," I said, washing my hands at the sink. "She has to stay with the group to keep everything organized."

"You have a flour smudge." A soft towel touched my cheek. "There. It's gone."

"Is my hair okay?"

"You look fine," she said quickly. Had she checked?

I walked the ten steps down the hall, trying to think of an interesting question. I'd already asked about his schooling. It wasn't polite to ask too many personal questions, was it? My brain filled up with limp cotton.

"Good morning, Julie," Jim said when I reached the door. "Do you feel like playing something with a poor cripple?"

Suddenly I was glad I'd agreed to spend time with him. "Do you mean a game or music?"

"You choose."

I stepped inside the library door. "I play a mean game of checkers."

"You're on. Where's the board?"

"In the cupboard under the window seat. I'll get it." I knelt before the cupboard and reached inside. "My father carved these for me. One side is domed, and the other is flat. The pieces have the bottoms indented so they can hold a king, and the board has wooden strips between the squares to hold the pieces secure."

Holding the game, I crossed the room to a square table against the wall near the piano. "We'll have to play here. Can you walk over?"

"Sure. I'm not an invalid. I just need to rest the old ankle for a while. Most likely I'll be able to skate again before we leave, if I take it slow." He paused. "It's not easy to accept one's limitations, is it?"

I turned toward his voice. "No. It's not."

In a moment, I felt his presence across from me. It's strange the sixth sense God gives to those who need it most.

His chair scraped the floor. "Which set would you like?"

"The flat ones. I always win when I play with them."

He chuckled. "Quite the competitive type, aren't you?"

"It's in my blood, I guess." I set my pieces on the board. "I used to enter tons of sporting events: tennis, gymnastics, figure skating."

The pain must have shown in my face. His voice changed to a soft pitch that made me want to answer his next question. "Why didn't you accompany us this morning?"

"The last time. . ." I drew in a breath. "Last time I skated on the river, I had a dreadful accident. I can't bear to go out there again." He didn't speak, and wanting to explain, I hurried on. "The last thing I ever saw was gray sky and a white snowbank as my feet flew out from under me." I shivered. "The very thought of going back there makes me shaky."

I felt the gentle drumming of his fingertips on the table. Without missing a beat, he said, "You get the first move."

We played until we had three pieces left on the board—two of mine and one of his, all kings.

"You must play frequently," he said while I studied out my next attack.

"Millie and I play most evenings. But it's Dad who taught me all the good moves. He's the only one I can't beat." I set the left king forward three spaces. "I don't like to pry, but. . ."

"But you're going to anyway."

He was laughing at me. I hesitated.

"I was teasing, Julie. Ask me anything you like."

I plunged ahead. "If you don't want to be a lawyer, what do you want to be?"

"You'll laugh. Honey does."

"I'm not Honey."

"I knew that the first time I met you." He moved his lonely king, and my hand reached out to find it.

He said, "I want to work with city children. To lead them to Christ and give them hope for the future. With proper encouragement they can become useful citizens. Without help, they'll almost certainly end up in trouble. I've spent the past two summers volunteering at a Brooklyn YMCA. I love it."

"You're a Christian." It was a statement, but a surprised one.

"Dave Yancy, one of my roommates, made a big impression on me. He had a gentle strength that I'd never seen before. And he wasn't afraid to talk about God. Dave had me primed when William Jennings Bryan spoke at the university. I asked God to save me right there in my seat at the end of Bryan's speech." He paused as I made my move. "Dave went to seminary last year. I miss him. My life's been sort of unfocused ever since."

Wood bumped wood. "Your turn," he said.

"I received Christ in the same Sunday school class I'm teaching now. When dear old Miss Susan went to heaven three years ago I took her place. I don't know how I'd get through a day if I didn't know the Lord. . .especially now."

"What about Honey?" he asked.

"Honey's a Christian, but she doesn't think much about it."

He said wryly, "She calls my YMCA work slumming."

I made a sweeping move. "Got you. I win!"

"Well, what do you know? Beat by a girl." He chuckled. "Don't tell the fellows. I'll never live it down."

"Don't tell the fellows what?" Tubby boomed from the hall. The cold from the open door reached the back of my neck. I drew my arms closer to my body.

Tubby went on without waiting for an answer. "Look at you, Jim. We're out there turning into blocks of ice while you're roasting your toes by the fire and playing checkers with a pretty girl." He stamped and called, "Hurry up, slowpokes, or I'll shut the door on you."

The hall filled with gasps and groans about the cold. Millie called over the noise, "I'll bring hot cocoa to the parlor. Esther has some ready for us, I'm sure."

Honey swept into the library, out of breath with exercise and excitement. "Jim, Julie, I have some wonderful news. The parson stopped me on the way home and asked me to organize a Christmas pageant. It's sort of last minute, but he said we can practice with the children Sunday afternoon and—since school is out—several times next week. We'll perform it at the church on Christmas Eve."

"That's great," Jim said. He seemed pleased.

I froze, dreadfully certain that her next statement would involve me.

"We're doing *The Byrd's Christmas Carol.* Julie, you can be Carol Byrd. All you'll have to do is sit in bed and look adorable. It's perfect!"

Chapter 4

Honey's announcement confirmed my worst fears. How could she do this to me?

Full of plans and brilliant ideas about props and costumes, Honey scurried to the parlor, where the others had gathered around the fire. My heart beat heavily against my ribs as I dropped the checkers into their box.

"What is it, Julie?" Jim asked.

I didn't say a word. I couldn't or I'd burst into tears. I shook my head and didn't answer.

Mother used to read the old classic about Carol Byrd every Christmas Eve until we got old enough to read for ourselves. It was about an invalid girl who tried to help a poor family have a merry Christmas. I always cried when she died at the end. I loved the story, but I did not want to play the part of Carol Byrd.

Since we had only one copy of the play, the girls spent the evening taking turns typing extra copies of the short script while the others played mah-jongg and talked about the pageant. I heard them from my room, where I lay with my cheek on the goose down pillow.

"Well what's this?" Millie demanded. "I missed you after dinner so I came to see what's up. You sick or something?"

"I'm fine," I lied.

"Oh, pouting, huh? You should be down there playing mah-jongg and beatin' the socks off them, Julie."

I turned my face away.

When the chair creaked, I said, "You don't have to babysit me, Millie. Go down and have a good time."

"Not with you in a fret. I want to know what's wrong."

"If you must know, it's the pageant."

"Is that all? I looked over the script. You only have a dozen lines. You'll be the first to memorize them, Julie dear. I think you'll make a lovely Carol Byrd."

"With everyone staring at me like some sort of wax museum figure? I hate to be on display like that, Millie. And I can't even read the script myself."

Honey called up the stairs. "Millie, Julie, we're ready to get started. Come on down."

"Come on, love," Millie encouraged with a resigned sigh. "Let's go face the lions."

"I'm not going."

"Well suit yourself, but your mother will have something to say about that. She's always talking about how you hide away too much." She went out with her usual flounce and bounce.

I gnawed my lower lip. Was a ten-minute delay worth a fifteen-minute lecture from Mother?

Taking my good old time, I eased downstairs.

"Sit on the sofa by me, Julie," Mother said. "I was just about to come for you."

Honey stood in front of the fireplace. "I'm going to assign parts tonight," she said, "so everyone has time to look over their lines before practice tomorrow morning.

"Alice is Mrs. Byrd; Jim, Mr. Byrd; and Millie is the cook. Tubby can be Uncle Jack. Bob is Peter Ruggles."

"What about me?" Lucy asked. "I don't want a long part. My head aches if I have to memorize too much."

"You'll be Mrs. Ruggles."

Jim spoke from the window seat. "That accounts for everyone except you, Honey."

She laughed. "I'm the narrator, silly." Her papers rustled. "Besides playing Mr. Byrd, Jim, you'll lead the children's choir. Julie will play for you."

She spoke louder. "The pastor will make an announcement Sunday morning, and we'll have our first full practice Sunday afternoon. Tomorrow we'll practice here. On Sunday, I'll recruit children to play the rest of the Ruggles family. They won't have much to memorize."

"What about costuming?" Mother asked. "That could turn into quite a job."

"I'll dig through Grammy's trunk in the attic," Honey said, her pencil scratching as she made a note. She shoved some pages into my hands. "Here's the script, Julie. Get Millie to go over it with you tonight so you can be ready for practice tomorrow."

"Honey, I can't learn my lines in one night. It's already eight o'clock."

She waved aside my protest. "Millie will help you tomorrow."

"Now that the play's all settled," said Bob, "how about another game of mah-jongg? The night's young."

"You're on," Tubby said. They moved to the game table; Alice and Lucy joined them.

A few minutes later, I escaped upstairs and dropped the script to the floor. With angry fingers I tore at my buttons. I was wriggling into my nightgown when Millie came in.

"Don't get yourself in a stew, Julie," she scolded. "Honey gave you the best part. I've got to borrow one of Esther's dresses and stuff it with pillows." She giggled. "I'll be a sight."

"I don't appreciate the way she manages me. Like I'm a checker piece." My voice grew shrill. "Julie will play piano for you."

Millie sat beside me on the edge of my bed. "She thought she was being nice by including you. I wish you wouldn't take on so."

I didn't sleep well that night. I knew I was being stubborn and unkind, but I couldn't shake my grumpy mood. By morning I had a headache.

Honey was in high spirits. She woke me with cheerful singing that made me want to stuff my handkerchief in her mouth. She buzzed between the adjoining rooms, chattering like a spring blue jay. As soon as she finished dressing, she and Alice scampered upstairs to dig around in the attic.

Lucy strolled in to borrow Honey's lipstick and stayed to chat about her boyfriend. I didn't want to socialize. Finally, she climbed the attic stairs to find the girls.

I didn't feel like eating breakfast, but I went to the table anyway to keep Mother from fussing over me. When Honey clattered down the stairs, I could hardly swallow my eggs.

She swept into the dining room and cried, "Guess what! There's an iron bedstead in the attic that will be perfect for the pageant. You fellows must haul it down. We'll make it up, and Julie can sit in it for practice this morning."

I stiffened. "Can't we put some pillows on the sofa and pretend?"

Honey bore down on me. "C'mon, be a good sport, Julie. The bed will give atmosphere to the whole room."

Her tone told me arguing was useless. If I called attention to myself, she might get inspired and make me go upstairs and change into my nightgown for "atmosphere." Millie squeezed my hand beneath the table. I couldn't tell if she wanted me to keep quiet or if she was sympathizing with me.

Play practice was agony. Millie read my lines for me while I sat in the middle of the library on a lumpy cotton mattress with a quilt over my legs. Worse, I started thinking about the thousands of spiders living in the attic. What if one had gotten on the mattress? I'd always been terrified of them, but since my accident the idea of a creepy thing crawling on me was unbearable. Somehow I held on and didn't make a fool of myself.

I was tired enough to cry by the time Mother called us for lunch. Afterward, I took a nap and woke up to a quiet house. The gang had gone out for another skate-fest.

I dragged a brush through my hair and went down to the library for some time alone with my piano.

"There you are," Jim called, when I reached the bottom step. "I've been waiting for you."

I touched my curls, wishing I'd taken more time with them. "You didn't go skating?"

"You forgot my bad ankle. I'm afraid you'll have to endure my company again this afternoon."

I went to the piano and flicked fingers along the keys. "Would you like to hear anything in particular?"

"Play the one you did before."

" 'The Skater's Waltz'? It's my favorite piece." As I swept through the melody,

I said, "You haven't told me where you're from. Do you live in Vermont?"

"Connecticut. Just outside New York City. My father's practice is in New York, but Mother always hated the city. Ten years ago, we moved to a hundred-acre estate named Thornton's Hill." He leaned against the baby grand. I could almost feel his breath when he spoke. "It's a rambling place with wide fields on each side of the house and white fences dividing the horses' paddocks. Two tennis courts. A small lake on the west side. The house is a three-story Victorian with massive pillars in front."

"Sounds frightening."

He chuckled. "It's a museum, not a home. Especially since my mother died. To be honest, I'd rather be at our bungalow on Long Island. No stress, no neighbors, no telephone for miles. It's lovely, especially in the fall."

I struck the last notes of the song.

"Say," he said, "would you like to practice your lines with me? It's a shame to waste this quiet while the gang's outside. A person can hardly put two thoughts together with Tubby's singing and the girls' chattering."

"If I translated my lines into Braille, I could read them during practice."

"That's a great idea."

"I'll get the slate from my room." My heart felt curiously light as I came back down, the metal rectangle and stylus in one hand, two sheets of stiff paper in the other.

I sat at the table. "Please read me the words, and I'll punch them."

" 'I want to tell you all about my plans for Christmas this year, Uncle Jack,' " he read, pausing every few words until I got them down.

Before I knew it, the gang was back and we were drinking cocoa in the parlor. Honey could talk of nothing but the pageant. As usual, her enthusiasm wore everyone else to a frazzle, and she was still going.

That evening, practice went much better. I still felt stupid sitting in the bed, but the covers hid my hands, and I didn't miss a word.

Sunday morning, Millie helped me into my navy dress with a white sailor collar and red tie. Except for Jim, all of Honey's guests wanted to sleep in.

The weather was clear with an icy breeze when we left the house. Of course, Jim escorted Honey. I was close behind them, holding Dad's arm with Mother on his other side. Millie stayed behind to help Esther.

We headed down the lane to the gravel road. Ahead on the left lay Shegog's Grocery, a squat building with gray shingled siding. When I was six, it already looked as old as Moses. On the other side of the road the clapboard church had a spire but no bell.

The ice-covered river ran parallel to the road until it veered east just before the church, leaving enough space between the road and the river for the church property.

"You're looking smart this morning, Mr. Clarke," Honey said, a lilt in her voice.

Jim chuckled. "Are you fishing for a compliment?"

Usually I smiled at my sister's flirtatious nature, but today I didn't feel like smiling. Once we reached the church, I went straight to my classroom. "Good morning, girls," I said brightly when I reached my room. "Have you heard about the pageant?" My scholars peppered me with so many questions, I could hardly get through my shepherds-and-wisemen lesson.

The day was full with an afternoon of play practice—squirming kids everywhere—followed by the evening service. That night I fell into bed too tired to stay up for the Will Rogers radio program, the family's favorite ending to a Sunday night.

On Monday after lunch, the gang suited up to go skating again. I was looking forward to a quiet afternoon in the library with Jim and his sore ankle. Today, I'd ask him to read my favorite passage from *Jane Eyre*. Instead, he made a suggestion that gave me a shock.

Chapter 5

When Julie came downstairs with her head tilted in that charming way, listening to find out who was there, an idea flashed through my mind. It probably wouldn't work, but I had to try.

I waited until she sat on the piano bench so no one else could hear. Then I knelt beside her and spoke softly. "Julie, won't you come with us to the river?"

Her chin jerked. Her face turned pale. She didn't answer.

I leaned closer. "My ankle won't let me do any fancy footwork today, but it has improved enough so I can do some simple skating with the others. Won't you come out with me? I'll stay beside you every minute. Please come."

She wet her lips. "I can't," she whispered.

"I won't let you bump your nose. Promise." I gulped some air and pushed harder. "You've got to face your fears someday, you know. If you don't, you'll grow old in this cocoon of a house and never know true happiness. I know it's painful, but please try."

She pressed her tiny teeth into her bottom lip until I feared I'd see blood. Her chest rose and fell. I waited, hardly daring to breathe, praying like I hadn't done in months.

"I'll have to change," she whispered.

I touched her hand. "I'll wait for you."

With new starch in her backbone, she climbed the stairs like a queen. I cheered every upward step.

Honey touched my arm. I looked at her, startled to see the others had already gone. "Are you coming, Jim?"

"Julie's coming with me to the river."

Her eyes widened. "You must be a miracle worker. She hasn't set foot near the river since. . ."

"I know. It took some persuading, but I talked her into it."

She lifted a plaid scarf over her chin. "There's no sense in my waiting, too. I'll see you there." She strode through the door, skates dangling over her shoulder. Her green ski hat and that blonde hair made me wish for my Brownie camera and a wide-angle lens.

Fifteen minutes later I was still waiting. Had Julie lost her nerve? Finally she stood in the hall holding out her skates. "Are these still wearable? It's been so long, I'm afraid the leather is cracked through."

I took them from her and turned them over. "They're sound enough. I'll carry them with mine. Which coat is yours?"

"The black wool with a sheepskin lining."

Buttoned up to her chin with her curls bobbing beneath a black cloche hat, she looked like a pixie. I grasped her mittened hand and placed it inside my bent elbow. "Miss Simmons, let's cut some ice."

She smiled, but I could feel her tremble.

When we stepped onto the porch, the sun glaring on the mill's tin roof made me squint and turn away. We crossed the gravel road and reached the river in two minutes.

The gang had vanished by the time we changed into our skates. I could hear Tubby shouting and Alice squealing. Bob called Honey's name as their voices faded on the faint breeze.

"I feel so wobbly," Julie said, clinging to my shoulder as she stood. "Maybe I've forgotten how. I never used to skate with my eyes closed."

"Give yourself a chance to get a feel for the skates. Here, let's get set. Cross your hands and hold on to me." I put my right arm around her waist. My left hand clasped her right and my right hand held her left. She fit into my shoulder like she'd been carved to match. Her hair tickled my cheek. She smelled like a summer meadow.

"Now let's get in stride. Lead with your left." Slowly, jerkily at first, we headed for the center of the ice. After ten strides, she found her rhythm and seemed to anticipate my moves. We picked up a little speed.

"I can't believe I'm doing this." She blinked hard. "The sun is so bright I can almost see it." Energy swelled inside her until she glowed. "The sawmill is on our left, isn't it?"

"Yes. Another river branches off to the west just ahead."

"Let's take the branch, Jim. I used to love to go that way. Some days I'd skate all the way to Nebraska Valley." Her feet moved with natural grace.

"Say, you're pretty good."

A gleam of pride shone in her smile. "I won first at state figure skating two years running. Where are we now?"

"Just beyond the sawmill. I can see a wall of mountains in front of us. They're splotchy with bare trees and evergreens and patches of white."

She nodded. "We haven't had much snow this year. I hope we get some soon or tourist season will be a washout. Dad depends on tourism in the winter." She tilted her head. "There's a cardinal in the woods over there."

I listened. The birdcall came from the pine forest rising on our left. I hadn't noticed it before. The river ran between the mill and Shegog's store, giving me a splendid view of their backyards. Further on, the woods surrounded us.

"Maybe we ought to turn back," I said. "I don't want to tire you out the first day."

"But I don't want to go back yet. I'm having too much fun."

"Why don't we sit and rest awhile, then. My ankle is starting to talk to me."

She turned her face toward my cheek. "I forgot about your ankle! Let's go back."

"All it needs is a little rest. There's a ledge ahead. We'll sit down." A piece of gray slate, about three feet wide and a foot deep, extended out from under an old spruce. We reached it in two glides.

"Whew! I'm warm," Julie said, puffing, as she pulled off her hat. "That was great fun." She tilted her face toward the sky. "I love the crisp feel of a winter breeze."

A masculine shout came from the east.

Julie turned to me. "You'd rather be with Honey. I'm beginning to feel terribly selfish."

"Don't give it a second thought. There'll be plenty of time for me to be with the others. It's your turn, Julie. You deserve it."

She relaxed against my side, contented. The trouble was, I was feeling pretty contented myself.

"Too bad we can't stay here," I said. "It's so peaceful. No problems or worries."

"Like law school?"

"How'd you guess? My father is a good man by most standards. He cares about his sons. He just has his own ideas about what's good for them."

She shifted positions, and her hair brushed my ear. "What are you going to do?"

"Go to law school, I guess." I drew in a slow breath. Cold air made my lungs ache.

Her face crinkled around the eyes and forehead. "Can your father's approval make your life fulfilled forever? Is it enough?"

"That's the question I keep coming back to. Sometimes I see faces when I close my eyes—Ricky, whose father left before he was born; John, who lives in a ratty tenement with no running water; Tommy, who's lived on the street for as long as he can remember—dozens of them, Julie. I can't get them out of my mind."

"Do you really want to?" She turned toward me, her face inches from mine. "If you forget them, something inside you will be gone."

I squeezed her mitten. "How'd you get so smart in a backwater place like this?" I stood and brushed my pants. "We'd best get moving. A few more minutes and we'll freeze to that stone." I gave her a hand up, and we set off.

At the time I didn't stop to analyze the situation, but when we reached the others half an hour later, Honey's arched eyebrow and silent look brought me back to reality with a thud.

Chapter 6

Julie? Are you awake?" Honey asked from the other bed.

Under the quilt, I stretched and sighed, enjoying a strange, sleepy excitement. Was it because I'd faced the river and returned triumphant? Or was it something more?

"What time is it?" I asked.

"Seven. I'm thinking of knocking on Jim's door and asking him to go for a walk."

"Honey, you shouldn't knock on the fellows' door. Mother and Dad wouldn't like it."

She scuffed on her slippers and stood. "I'm not a child anymore, Julie. And besides that, Jim and I have an understanding." Her voice softened. "I wouldn't be surprised if he gave me a ring for Christmas."

"Do you really love him, Honey? You've had so many beaux. How do you know it's real this time?"

"Two good reasons, child. First, he's a sheik, and second, he's worth twenty-five thousand a year on his allowance. Just wait till he gets his inheritance."

"Honey! That's not love." I sat up. "How would you feel if he had an accident that disfigured him or paralyzed him?" I reached for her. "Don't do this, Honey. You'll regret it all your life."

She ignored my hand. "Save the sermon, sis. I know what I want. And what I want right now is Jim Clarke." She shuffled to the closet.

A moment later Millie burst in. "Oh, you're awake, Julie. I came to help you dress. Esther gave me a black dress to use for the play." She laughed. "I could put two of me in it and still have room left over. What a lark!" She headed toward the closet. "Say, I like that maroon sheath, Honey. It makes your hair glow."

Honey opened the adjoining door and called, "Lucy, Alice, get up! We have to work on our costumes today."

Alice mumbled, "Go away!"

"It's after seven," Honey said. "You've got two minutes to roll out, or I'm going for some cold water."

Lucy giggled. "This could be interesting, Alice. I wonder if the boys are up yet. We could get some glasses and. . ."

Millie said, "They went out for an early fling on the ice, all three of them."

Honey sat in the chair and ticked off the day's agenda. "Millie's dress is ready. Jim and Tubby can wear their usual clothes. Bob has a pair of knickers to play Peter Ruggles. Mother's white nightgown will do for Julie, but we ought to make a nightcap for her, too."

I pulled on a corduroy jumper, biting my cheek to keep from commenting on the nightcap idea. Arguing with Honey only made her more determined to have her way. I finished dressing, then hurried downstairs to help Esther knead bread dough. Better the kitchen than Honey's endless plans.

The men arrived at the breakfast table on time. Dad was already at the mill and Mother had walked to Shegog's for some thread, so the meal was livelier than usual.

"Throw them hotcakes on over, Bob," Tubby said. "On second thought, maybe I should just exchange plates—my empty one for the platter."

Lucy cut in. "Don't forget us girls, you hollow legs. We're hungry, too."

Esther trudged in, bringing the pungent smells of coffee and sausage with her. "Here, Millie, help Miss Julie." She set a platter beside me, poured my coffee, and hurried out, saying, "I've got more hotcakes on the griddle."

"What are we going to do while you ladies sew?" Bob asked between bites.

Honey said, "You can carry props from the attic. And we need a Christmas tree at the church. If we finish the dresses in time, Lucy, Alice, and I will go over and decorate it later today."

"I want to do my nails this afternoon," Lucy complained. "All this practicing is wearing me out."

Tubby sang, " 'O, Christmas tree. . .' Where do we find one?"

"Cut one down in the woods out back," Honey told him, as though it were a dumb question. "There are plenty of small spruces around."

Bob's voice dripped sarcasm, "This is getting better all the time. You think it's easy to chop down a tree?"

"You'll live, Bob dear," Honey told him. "After all, you and Tubby can take turns."

The big fellow sputtered. "What about Jim? What's he doing?"

A fork clinked on a plate. "Jim will be driving around Athens, collecting things." A paper rustled. "Here's the list."

Jim read, "A table and chairs from the parsonage, lamps and rugs from Mrs. Anders—"

"I found some darling old ornaments in an attic box," Honey interrupted, "and Grammy's old china set. We'll bring them down today."

"Hunky-dory!" Bob said. "Be careful today, Jim. You don't want to strain yourself with all that heavy work."

Honey answered before Jim could. "Cut it out, Bob! The pageant is tomorrow afternoon. Don't start griping now."

Bob and Tubby were unusually silent for the rest of the meal. At eight-thirty, we went our separate ways: the fellows outside and the ladies into the library.

Honey pushed a wad of flannel at me as soon as I stepped through the library door. "Put on this nightgown, Julie. I'll close the doors. You can change in here to save time."

"Why do I have to put it on now?"

"Just do it," she said sharply. "I want to see it for myself."

"Let me help you." Millie came behind me and pulled at the fastenings on my dress. Minutes later, I stood in the center of the room with soft flannel brushing my bare feet. After pulling two garments over my head, my hair felt like a tumbleweed.

A light knock sounded at the door.

Jim called, "Honey, I need directions to Mrs. Anders's house."

"Come in, Jim. Everyone's decent."

I whispered frantically, "Honey! I'm not decent."

The door slid back as she said, "Silly, tomorrow you'll be wearing that in front of a whole crowd."

"It's not the same." I wanted to die.

Too late. I could hear Jim's voice saying, "Just sketch a map on the back of your list, and I'll be on my way."

As soon as Jim strode out, Honey said, "I think we can make a nightcap from one of Dad's big handkerchiefs. I'll go up and fetch one."

I couldn't stand it any longer. "Why do I have to wear a nightcap, Honey? No one wears those anymore. I'll look ridiculous."

"The play was written in the 1800s, when girls wore nightcaps." She trotted away. The next moment I heard her shoes on the stair treads.

"Don't worry so much, Julie," Alice said around her wad of gum. "None of us are going to be fashion plates for this thing, you know."

I blinked back frustrated tears. "I just wish she'd listen to me sometimes. She acts like I don't have a brain."

Millie hugged me. I returned the hug, thankful for her concern but still uncomforted.

Honey came whizzing back and set a soft cloth on my hair. "Isn't Jim sweet? Whenever I ask him to do something, he does it right away. He's one in a million."

Alice giggled. "One with a million, you mean."

"Don't be crass." Honey laughed deeply.

"He's thoughtful and kind," I said softly.

"And he's mine." Honey snatched the cloth from my head. "Everyone had best remember that."

I reached for the buttons on my gown. "Are you through with me now?"

"Yes. You can run and play." Honey moved to the game table, where Alice and Lucy were working over their gowns.

"This is boring, you know that, Honey?" It was Alice and she wasn't kidding.

I groped to find the sleeves in my jumper as Millie said, "I'll go up and help your mother sew rings on the stage curtain. She must have a hundred left to do."

"I wonder how Tubby and Bob are doing." Alice cracked her gum and snickered. "I wish we could take a little hike and spy on them."

Lucy spoke up. "You'd be a dead duck. If you laugh at Bob while he's in a grump, he may break some ice and stick your head in the river."

"Now that would be a sight," Honey said as I reached the stairs. "I'll get my camera. Let's go."

Even Millie laughed that time.

Chapter 7

I couldn't believe how callous Honey was acting toward Julie. As I headed out to my car, I thought about the scene I'd just been through in the library. I'd been almost as embarrassed as Julie when I stepped inside the library and saw the poor girl standing there in a nightgown. Her face could have lit a town square.

As soon as Honey drew the map, I'd hurried away. What could explain Honey's behavior? Ever since we'd arrived, I'd been picking up little hints that things were strained between the two sisters, but I didn't think much of it. I'm not that close to my brothers. Those things happen in families.

The Oldsmobile purred like a warm cat as I headed down the gravel road. Shegog's Grocery loomed just ahead. On impulse, I parked in front.

The place smelled of freshly ground coffee and the coal smoke belching from the rusty potbelly stove in the back corner. It was a mom-and-pop affair with farm equipment on one side and dress goods on the other.

"He'p you, mister?" a grizzled old codger asked. His whiskers touched the top button on his faded flannel shirt.

"I'd like to make a phone call. I'll reverse the charges."

The shopkeeper nodded to the wooden box on the wall near the end of the counter. "There it is."

Our butler, James, had Dad on the phone in less than a minute. "I just wanted to check in," I told him. "We're having a swell time."

"Did you give that girl a ring yet?" The old man had a mind like a vise. Once it clamped on to something, it wouldn't let go.

I sighed. "No. I haven't found the right time." The diamond lay deep inside my inner coat pocket in a velvet pouch. I hadn't touched it since we arrived.

"Well, see that you do. With her pulling for you, you could be a senator some-day. She'll charm fat accounts out of the woodwork."

"Dad, I'm not sure I want to join the firm. I've been doing some serious thinking—"

"Well, think about this, then. I've spent a small fortune on your education, and I'm willing to spend more. But if you welsh on my investment, you're going to regret it. Do you understand me, son?"

"Yes, Dad. I understand." I held the silent receiver a moment, then said, "Have a merry Christmas."

He grunted. "Pete and his wife are in the country, and Ron is at a house party for the holidays. I'm alone with James and the cook. Call me before you leave Vermont."

"I will, Dad. Good-bye."

I left the store wishing I hadn't called. Dad had his ideas and I had mine. What was I going to do?

I aimed my roadster toward Stowe. Mrs. Anders lived near the north end of the narrow road in a square cottage with frost-killed marigolds lining the walk. My breath came out in white billows as I knocked on her door.

A rawboned woman opened it and looked me up and down. "Yes?"

"I'm here to collect the lamps and rugs for the Christmas pageant. Honey Simmons sent me over."

"They're right here." She pulled the door wider.

I had everything loaded and delivered in an hour. On the way back the roadster suddenly developed a cough. I reset the choke and listened closely. I'd have to check it out before Monday.

My thoughts drifted to Julie. Maybe I should talk to Honey about her sister. Maybe if I told her what she was doing to Julie, she'd ease up a bit.

I saw my chance when I reached the house and she said, "Let's go to the attic. I'll show you the boxes I need."

I dropped my leather cap on the newel post and followed her up two flights. The attic covered half the house. It was dusty, organized, and cold as the Arctic.

"That box," she said, pointing to a cardboard carton on the floor, "is the china."

"Honey." I ignored the props and turned her to face me. The look on her face said she expected me to kiss her. "It's about Julie," I said.

Her mouth tightened. "I've noticed you're spending a lot of time with her."

"Please try not to embarrass her." I wanted to smile, to ease the tension, but my lips felt stiff. It must have been the cold.

"I haven't embarrassed her." She sounded indignant.

"I can think of several times when you have."

"When?"

"Making her sit on the bed for practice when none of the rest of us had to get into our parts. Calling me into the library when she was wearing. . . Honey, you can't be so dumb that you don't understand what I'm trying to say."

"Jim darling, I haven't asked her to do anything that she's not going to do in front of a hundred people during the pageant."

"Just giving her the main part embarrasses her."

"I was trying to be nice to her."

"It's not working." I lifted the carton. "Let's go down. You're shivering."

"Wait a second. Why are you so interested in Julie?"

"She's vulnerable. I don't want to see her hurt."

"I wouldn't hurt Julie for anything. She gets stubborn sometimes, and I have to give her a little push." Her eyes narrowed. "You did the same thing when you took her to the river."

"That was different. She had a great time skating. She's miserable about the pageant. Can't you see that?"

"You like her, don't you." It was an accusation.

"Of course I like her. She's your little sister."

"She's two years older than me. And she's not the fragile flower you're making her out to be."

I bit back a sharp reply. "Forgive me for mentioning it." I turned away. "I'll take these to the car."

She followed me downstairs and disappeared into the library. I stopped to catch my cap from the post. Honey was usually so sympathetic. What had happened to her?

Two more lonely trips to the attic, then I drove to the church. With the pulpit to move and the props to arrange, I was busy until Bob and Tubby arrived—scratched and seething—dragging a four-foot spruce behind them.

Chapter 8

There you are, Julie!" Millie said. She pulled out my chair at the lunch table, and I sat. "Ham sandwiches and potato salad," she whispered, "at nine and three."

"I'm catchin' forty winks after this." Bob's lifeless voice was almost unrecognizable. "I'm beat. If I'd known we were going to be lumberjacks today, I wouldn't have gone skating before breakfast." Though I couldn't see anyone's face, when I'd come down for lunch I'd sensed that the party spirit had soured. The only one in a good mood was Millie, who seemed terribly amused.

"Don't fuss," Alice told him. "Exercise is good for you. Builds muscles."

"He's got plenty of muscles," Lucy said, "around his mouth."

"Can it, girls." For once, Tubby was serious.

"We'll all rest for an hour," Honey said. Her voice sounded dull. "Dress rehearsal's at two-thirty."

"I want to go shopping," Alice said. "I haven't bought a single Christmas present yet."

Even Jim sounded subdued. "After practice I'll take everyone on a drive to Stowe. I'd like to look around myself."

I leaned toward him. "Will you have room for me?"

"Certainly." His voice lost its apathy when he said, "Delighted to have you aboard."

We all filed upstairs when Millie started clearing the table. It was the first time my sister had been silent since she'd arrived.

"What's wrong, Honey?" I asked, lying back on the bed. "Did you quarrel with someone?"

She punched her pillow. "Tubby and Bob have turned into two spoiled cabbages, Alice is bored, and Lucy whines until I want to slap her. Even Jim's in a bad mood." The bed creaked as she moved. "The house party has gone wrong, and I'm not sure why."

"Maybe you're expecting too much of everyone," I said carefully, not wanting to rile her. "They came here for a good time, and you're putting them all to work."

"Well, that's just too bad, Julie. The pageant is tomorrow, and we have to see it through—no matter who likes it and who doesn't."

I turned away from her and closed my eyes. How could anyone get through to her? Sometimes her mind wore armor plating.

෨

Since we had to change into our costumes, we girls walked to the church half an hour earlier than the fellows. My tiny Sunday school class acted as a dressing room. We were constantly bumping elbows and losing things.

Honey flitted from Alice to Lucy, helping them with buttons, joining in their snickers, reassuring Lucy on the fit of her gown. Finally, Honey said, "I'm going out to see if the children playing the Ruggles family are here yet."

"Millie!" Alice yelped. "That dress makes you look like a pregnant elephant." She giggled. "Isn't this a panic?"

Millie laughed. "I put powder in my hair to make me look older. I'll be the first pink-haired cook in history." She pulled the nightcap over my curls and brushed stray strands away from my face. "You look like an angel," she whispered close to my ear.

I touched her hair. It was pulled back into a fat bun with wisps hanging down all around. Millie's springy mane was impossible to tame. How had she managed to fasten it up?

Honey opened the door and called inside, "Okay, gang. Let's go knock 'em dead."

"One look at us," Lucy said, "and they'll keel over for sure."

Dress rehearsal went surprisingly well. Only Bob had to be coached with his lines. Now that the props were in place and everyone in costume, I almost felt that I really was Carol Byrd. Despite the sad ending, it was a lovely story—one of my favorites.

At the end I sank into my pillow and closed my eyes.

From the audience Honey said, "Now the children sing, 'My Ain Countree,' and the curtain falls."

"What curtain?" Lucy asked. Her voice echoed in the empty auditorium.

"Mother will have it ready by tomorrow morning. We'll run a wire from there to there and slide the rings over it."

"Shouldn't we do it today?" Jim asked. "There may be a slipup if we wait too long."

"Mother's not finished with it yet," Honey said.

"Let's get the wire up anyway," Jim said, stepping down to the lower level. "Where is it?"

Honey's shoes made the floor vibrate. "In that box by the organ."

The cast began to chat. I threw back the quilt and eased out of bed.

The children gathered around me. "You look beautiful, Miss Julie," little Mary Parks said, swinging my hand.

Her sister Maud said, "Get that bug away from me, Billy! I'll tell your mama!"

"What bug?" I tried not to flinch. If only I could see that rascal, Billy.

"Don't worry, Miss Julie," Billy Gates said. "I've got it in my pocket."

"It's a spider," Maud said.

Billy got louder. "No it's not. It's just a beetle. They live in our basement when it's cold like this."

That was my cue to leave. "I want to change, Millie," I said reaching for her, "so I can drive to Stowe with the others."

"You want me to go along?"

"If you don't mind. I'd like to buy some Christmas presents. I haven't been Christmas shopping since. . .you know."

Millie gripped my hand, and we headed toward the classroom at the back of the church. Five minutes later, the other girls arrived, excited about our outing.

Jim's car had soft leather seats and a humming heater that reached to the backseat, where Millie and I stuffed in with Tubby and Bob.

"Meet back here at five-thirty," Jim said as he cut off the engine, "and I'll buy supper. There's a nice place just down the street, The Snow Goose."

"That's a lovely café," I told him when we reached the sidewalk. "I haven't been there in years."

Millie was buzzing inside. I could feel it.

Jim said, "Honey, I'm Christmas shopping this afternoon. Would you mind going along with the girls?"

"Of course not." The lilt was back. "See you in a while." She and her friends moved ahead. Her voice drifted back. "Where do you want to go first?"

"A dress shop," Alice said. "Do they sell glad rags in this hick town?"

Lucy added, "I want some chocolates. Big fat ones."

I turned toward Millie. "Let's go to Smithy's, Millie. I'd like to find a hand mirror for Mother."

An hour later, Millie and I were loaded down with packages.

"We'd best get back, Julie. It's five-twenty."

"Already? I've hardly gotten started."

"C'mon. I don't think I can carry any more."

I laughed, delighted. "I did get carried away, didn't I?"

"It sure is good to hear you laugh, girl. Here, hold my arm and let's go."

The wind had turned bitter. I tucked my chin deeper into my sheepskin collar.

Jim greeted us with, "Two down and three to go. Have you seen the other girls?"

I smiled. "Not me."

He took my bundle. "The trunk's open. I'll lay these inside for you."

"We haven't seen the girls all afternoon," Millie said. "I heard they were going to look at clothes."

Tubby groaned. "They could be hours. I'm starved."

Jim thumped the trunk lid down. His keys rattled. "The Snow Goose is less than a block away. Let's go ahead. I'll leave a note on the window."

I felt Jim's presence beside me as we entered the restaurant. He had a special smell, a mixture of wool and that heady cologne he always wore.

"I'll take your coat if you'd like," he said, while we waited to be seated. His hands felt whisper light on my shoulders. "Party of eight," he told the hostess, placing my hand on his arm.

The smell of seasoned steaks and coffee filled my senses. I sniffed hungrily. It felt so good to be out again. Jim read me the menu and placed the order moments before the tardy girls arrived.

"Sorry to be late," Honey gasped, sliding into a seat across from Jim. "We found a luscious place full of handmade, hand-painted carvings." She laughed. "The girls had to drag me out."

"We weren't trying too hard," Lucy said. "I spent two month's allowance. Give me a menu, Tubby. I'm famished."

The conversation turned toward Christmas plans. Tubby and Lucy had to leave right after the pageant so they could be home in northern Vermont for Christmas. Jim would drive them to the train in Waterbury. Bob and Alice would stay on. Alice's parents were in Italy, and Bob's single father was living it up in California—two poor little rich kids with no place to go for the holidays.

I listened to their insolent attitude toward their parents and thought of Mother and Dad. Maybe there were some things worse than a physical injury.

Christmas Eve was a miserable day. During the night the temperature rose to thirty-five degrees and rain came down in sheets. It beat against the windows and drove a chill into the house that the fireplaces couldn't chase away.

Lucy spent the morning packing her bags and worrying over a lost sash. Honey paced the floor with a case of nerves over the pageant that evening. I wasn't worried. Once she got to the church she'd be fine. As a matter of fact, I was feeling better about the pageant all the time. My part was easy, and the children had calmed my fears about how I looked to the audience.

While I was dressing, Mother came in. "Julie, I want you to put on this extra set of woolens. That flannel nightgown isn't nearly warm enough for the drafty church. And with this rain, it's worse. You'll catch your death up there in front. The heat never reaches up there. My feet turn to ice when I'm sitting in the choir."

"Mother, I hate those scratchy things. My long flannels will be enough."

"I'm afraid I'll have to insist, dear." She turned to Millie. "Help her with these, will you? I've got to put the finishing touches on more pies for tomorrow's dinner. Those boys have completely emptied the pie safe." She hurried away, ignoring my objections.

Millie didn't move.

"What is it? What's wrong?"

"I wonder where she found these." Pause. "I suppose they'll keep you warm enough. That's what counts."

"Millie, tell me!"

She stifled a snicker. "They're striped like peppermint candy, the leggings and all." Patting my arm, she said, "No one will see them, love. It won't matter in the least."

"Won't they show through the white gown?"

"Not with three petticoats over them. Don't worry, I'll check you over before anyone sees you."

We decided to leave the house at five to give plenty of time for our hair to dry. With rain still pouring down, there was no way to keep from getting soaked.

We stood in the hall, screwing up courage to make a dash for the car, when Lucy whooshed open her umbrella and grumped, "I don't know why I'm bothering. With that wind, this bit of silk is just a token of despair."

My shoes got soaked in a puddle on the run from Jim's car to the church.

"Just take them off," Millie said. "No one will know your feet are bare. Your legs stay under the quilt. I'll put the shoes on the radiator to dry."

"And get wet again on the way home." I touched my hair. "This feels like a frizzy mop. Oh, I wish it weren't raining tonight."

Lucy said, "Get a shingle bob like me and you won't have to worry about it." She stepped closer. "Hey, what are those?"

Alice nudged in. "Are you playing the part of a candy cane tonight, Julie?"

My face grew warm. "Mother insisted I wear these because of the dampness."

Lucy said, "They're pippin. Wish I had a pair." Then she laughed.

I bit my lip to hold back a sharp answer.

Soon, children swarmed over the church like bees over a clover field. Not only the ones in the play, but all their brothers and sisters with some cousins thrown in. I heard Honey calling to them, frantically trying to keep order.

Chapter 9

J im, please help me with the children," Honey said minutes after I stepped inside the church. Her face was flushed from chasing two speeders through the oaken pews. She pushed the delinquents toward me. "I've got to see to last-minute details, and they keep running around the church, yelling and knocking things over."

I took two grimy hands and said, "I'll put them all down front in the choir's chairs."

She smiled and touched my arm. "You're the greatest."

No stained glass or velvet in this church. The floor needed a coat of varnish, the wainscoting needed paint. It was a far cry from the cathedral my parents attended, but I felt a warm spirit here I'd never felt there.

I had the children sing carols for the next half hour. They were slightly off tune but made up for it with volume. By some miracle, everyone was ready at zero hour. I stayed with my choir, ready to slip behind the curtain at the proper moment.

Mary, Maude, Billy, and the other Ruggles children sat on the end chairs, so they could march on stage for Act Two: the Ruggles Family at Home. Cast members waited behind the curtain while Pastor Jenkins, a gaunt, white-haired gentleman, welcomed the folks and opened in prayer. Then Honey told about Carol Byrd's birth on Christmas morning and how her mother found a name by listening to the boys' choir singing at the church next door. On cue, my choir belted out "Carol, Brothers, Carol" and the curtain opened.

Act One passed without a hitch. Dressed all in white with a white quilt and lacy pillows propped behind her, Julie charmed the audience. When Millie's outlandish costume got a belly laugh, she blushed with pleasure. Tubby played jolly Uncle Jack to perfection.

Finally, the Ruggles children swarmed into Julie's bedchamber. Billy hung on the bedpost and swung on the backs of the chairs until Millie gave him a boot as she passed.

When they finished the meal and the children left the table, Julie said, "Oh, wasn't it a lovely. . ." Suddenly her face contorted—shock, realization, then stark fear.

She screamed and scrambled off the bed. Her foot caught in the quilt. She fell headlong into the back of a chair. The chair knocked Billy, and he landed against the Christmas tree, sending it and all the china ornaments crashing to the floor.

Julie's gown flew up to her knees, showing a wide patch of red-striped long johns and bare feet. The children pointed and laughed. Soon most everyone in the audience was laughing, pointing, and laughing again.

In the wings, Honey burst into tears and disappeared through a side door. Still squealing, Julie tried to kick her foot loose from the quilt. Millie ran to her rescue. Afraid she'd been hurt, I rushed to help. A second later, Tubby had the presence of mind to pull the curtain.

"A spider," Julie sobbed in Millie's arms. "It was on my hand." She sniffed, very unladylike. "Oh, I've ruined everything!"

Millie looked to me for help.

"You're not to blame, Julie," I said, touching her arm. "It could have happened to anyone."

"Let's get you home," Millie said. "I'll fetch your coat. You can put it over your gown and sneak out the side door, like Honey did."

"Honey ran away?" Julie pulled back from Millie. Her face full of dread. "She'll never forgive me. Never in a hundred years."

The children scampered down to their parents. Tubby and Bob and the girls slumped in chairs beside the overturned table.

I peeked around the curtain. The last of the folks were heading out the back doors. On a cold, wet night like this, the best place to be was home. I wanted to be there myself. Too bad I had to drive Tubby and Lucy to the train.

We found Honey already in the car when we loaded up a few minutes later. Since Mr. Simmons had his Model T at the church to take his household home, I headed right to Waterbury with Lucy and Tubby. We drove eight miles in silence. Lucy hunkered down into a corner of the backseat. Tubby slouched in front. They didn't offer any conversation during the hour-long wait either.

At eleven o'clock I hung my dripping coat on the Simmonses' banister and dropped my hat on top of it. They were too wet for the closet. I hesitated, too keyed up to go straight to bed. The library fire looked inviting.

Except for the glow of orange coals, the room was dark, the furniture black lumps in the shadows. My hands stretched toward the heat when I heard a sniffle. I peered through the gloom.

Huddled in a corner of her chair sat Julie. Her tear-smudged face wrenched my heart. She tilted her head. "Who's there?" she whispered. "Mother?"

"It's Jim." I knelt before her. "What's the trouble?"

Fresh tears flowed. "Honey won't speak to me. She's moved in with Alice. I've never known her to get so mad."

My lips tightened.

"If I weren't blind. . ."

"Now hold on." I pulled her chin up with my forefinger. "Being blind has nothing to do with it. Sighted people are afraid of bugs, too. Please don't torment yourself."

She touched my cheek. More than that, she touched my heart. The next moment, she was in my arms. I wanted to comfort her like I'd never wanted anything before. My lips found hers, tenderly, sweetly. I was in another world.

Chapter 10

Jim's kiss reached down to the deep recesses of my being. I lost myself in his arms, overwhelmed with his gentleness.

Honey's face slowly took shape and moved to the front of my mind. Trembling, I jerked away.

He immediately turned me loose. "Forgive me." His voice was haggard. "I had no right. I don't know what came over me."

I wanted to tell him it was okay, not to worry, but the words wouldn't come. I tucked my chin down.

He stood close to my knee. "I'd best go upstairs. Can I get you anything?"

An ember popped. The upholstery leather felt smooth beneath my burning cheek. I shook my head, unable to speak. I listened to his footsteps until they disappeared down the upstairs hall—savoring the bittersweet secret that no one in the world must ever know: I was desperately in love with the man my sister intended to marry.

⌒

"Wake up, Julie!" Millie said, shaking me. "It's Christmas morning. Everyone's waiting in the parlor. Go and splash your face while I get you something to wear."

I staggered next door to the bathroom. The icy water made my nerves tingle. Had I imagined last night? Dreamed it? No. Something in me had changed forever.

"Is Jim downstairs?" I asked Millie as she slid a scratchy wool dress over my head.

"Everyone's there. Honey's in a chair, tapping her toe. Alice and Bob are sitting next to each other on the hearth, looking like kids on after-school detention. Your parents are on the sofa, and Esther is making hot cider in the kitchen."

"What about Jim?" I said louder. Millie could be so infuriating.

"He's leaning on the mantel shelf, staring into the fire. I don't think he's said two words all morning."

With fumbling fingers, I pulled on a sweater and pushed cold feet into my shoes.

When I sat on the sofa next to Mother, she put her arm around me. "It's snowing, Julie dear. We've got a white Christmas."

Millie sat on the rug at my knee. Her hair brushed my arm whenever she moved.

Dad cleared his throat. "Let's have a word of prayer, thanking God for His special gift that first Christmas morning." His deep voice made the rafters ring. When he was through, he said, "Jim, since you're standing, would you do the honors?"

"With pleasure, Mr. Simmons."

Just hearing his voice made my heart skip. I pinched my lips together, afraid my face would betray the tempest brewing inside me. Would Jim kiss me, then give Honey an engagement ring a few hours later?

As Jim called name after name, Mother whispered what the gifts were. To Alice from Honey: a white feather boa. To Julie from Mother and Dad: a pair of skates.

To Honey from Jim: a painted wooden mouse on skis, three inches tall. "How lovely!" she exclaimed, but I sensed her disappointment. I drew in a slow breath that felt like the first one in days.

To Julie from Jim. . .

His fingers brushed mine as he placed the lumpy package in my hands. Mother untied the string that held the cloth around the gift. Alive with curiosity . . .seeing with my fingertips. . .I felt two tiny people on top of a flat box slightly larger than my hands. The top surface felt like glass, the sides like wood.

"Here, let me." Mother reached for something on the side.

Tinny, plinking music made the box vibrate. The people swirled around in time with "The Skater's Waltz." Enchanted, I ran my hand over the sides, found the stem, and wound it again.

"I found it in a tourist shop the day we went to Stowe," Jim said from somewhere far away.

I looked up. "I'll cherish it." The couple reminded me of my first time back on skates, a crisp breeze in my face and my hands clasped by a certain wonderful gentleman.

Esther's voice broke the spell. "Watch out, everyone! Hot cider coming through."

The rest of the day was a series of exhilarating sensations: a roll-and-coffee breakfast, a rousing round of carols at the piano, a turkey dinner with all the trimmings.

Suddenly time flew like a December wind. On Monday, only two days more, Honey and her friends would drive away. Would I ever see Jim again? Honey's ring hadn't appeared. Hope kindled a tiny fire beneath my left rib.

That night Honey snuffed out the flame.

It was past nine, and exhausted, I'd just climbed into bed, when Honey marched into my room. The music box stood on my bedside table where I could reach it.

"We have to talk," she said, standing over me. Usually when Honey started with those words she meant: I'm going to talk and you'd best listen if you know what's good for you.

I clamped my jaw and waited.

"Why are you chasing Jim? You know he's mine. I brought him here to meet the family because I intend to marry him. Then you get your head filled with juvenile. . ." She paused to take a breath, and I dove in.

"Honey, he's not a puppet. He's a man. All your life you've bossed everyone, including me. If you think you can do the same with Jim Clarke, you're in for a surprise."

"You know him better than I do?"

I tried to keep a lid on my temper. "You only see what you want to see. To you Jim is a rich fellow with a plush future. But that's not what he's really like. He's a sensitive guy who wants to work with poor city children. He may not be a lawyer at all."

She whispered her answer, but her words were intense. "He'll be a lawyer all right."

A moment later, her voice softened. "I feel sorry for you, Julie, shut up here with the social life of a caterpillar. It's no wonder you found one of the fellows attractive. I'm just sorry it had to be Jim."

This was really rich. "You'd rather I liked Tubby. . .or Bob?"

"Not seriously, silly. Just for fun."

My temper flared. "For your information, I didn't chase anyone."

"That's not the way it seemed to the rest of us. I'm sorry to tell you this, but it's embarrassing the way you've been mooning over him—leaning toward him at the dinner table, hanging on his arm. I'm not the only one who noticed. Lucy mentioned it to me before she left."

My face burned. Had I been forward with Jim? I tried to remember, to reexamine my actions. I rubbed my forehead. Everything was jumbled. I couldn't think straight.

Honey put her arms around me. "I feel bad for you. Truly I do." She sounded sorry. "We won't talk about it again, okay?"

I nodded and curled down under the quilt. I heard her turn out the light and close the adjoining door. With trembling fingers, I reached out to touch my music box. My shoulders heaved, and I hid my face in the pillow.

Despite my exhaustion, I hardly slept. Humiliation seared me like a hot poker. What must Jim think of me? Twenty years old and acting like a schoolgirl with her first crush. I'd made a royal fool of myself. How could I be so stupid?

"I'm not dressing," I told Millie the next morning.

Honey and Alice were downstairs getting into coats to go sledding on the hill behind our house. Runaway horses couldn't drag me outdoors with them today.

"Why are you still in bed?" Millie touched my forehead. "Are you sick?"

I pushed her away. "Stop treating me like an invalid. I'm not sick. I'm tired."

She perched on the side of my bed. "What's gotten into you, Julie? Yesterday, you floated on a cloud. This morning you look like you've been up all night eating stewed persimmons."

"I don't want any breakfast. You can bring me a tray for lunch."

She stood. "Suit yourself. I'm going sledding with the gang. If I stay to argue, I'll miss half the fun." She opened the door, said, "See you later," and scurried away.

I pulled the quilt over my ears.

I must have slept because when Honey and Alice burst into their room chattering like two jays and laughing between every sentence, they startled me. I traced the hands on my alarm clock. Eleven-thirty.

I might as well get dressed. No sense staying in bed all day. I felt in the closet for my flannel shirtwaist and corduroy jumper.

"I'm glad to see you're up," Millie said, startling me. "Time to come down for lunch."

"I told you. I'm not going down."

She flopped into the chair. "You really are in a pet, aren't you? Come on, tell Dr. Millie what the problem is."

Praying for courage to do what I must, I turned around for her to fasten my buttons.

"I've got a little job for you, Millie." I swallowed. "Don't try to talk me out of it. Just do as I ask this once. . .please."

"You're serious." She sounded worried.

I reached for the music box. This time I didn't wind it up. "Wait until you catch Jim alone, then give this to him. Tell him I can't accept it."

"Why not? It's a wonderful gift. You'll hurt him if you give it back."

I pushed it into her hands. "Please, Millie! Don't argue." Tears welled up behind my eyelids. "It's best this way."

She hesitated.

I waited for her to scold me. But all she said was, "I'll bring you a lunch tray," and then she went out.

I dug in my drawer for a handkerchief and sank into the chair. If I could hold on through today and tomorrow, Monday they'd all be gone and I could get back to normal.

Normal? Did that exist for me anymore?

Chapter 11

"Mr. Clarke." At Millie's words, I looked up. "Julie asked me to give you this," Millie continued, hurrying across the library rug. She thrust the music box at me like it was full of hot coals.

I stayed in my chair and stared at it. "Why?"

"She says she can't accept it." Millie set the wooden box on the hearth near my hand.

"Where is Julie? I want to talk to her."

"She won't come downstairs." The red-haired girl stepped closer and whispered, "I don't know what's happened, but she's in an awful pet. Looks to me like she cried all night. I can't imagine what's gotten into her."

My first impulse was to bound up the stairs and make Julie tell me what had happened. I let out a slow breath, trying to put the pieces together, and not liking the picture no matter how I turned it.

Millie darted from the room. I hardly noticed.

I picked up the music box and turned it over in my hands, remembering Julie's pleasure when she'd received it yesterday morning. What had changed her attitude?

I went up to my room to hide the music box before anyone asked questions I didn't want to answer. When I burst in, Bob stood before a mirror with a hairbrush in his hand.

"What's on for the afternoon, old man?" he asked without turning. "I've had all of the great outdoors I can stand for a while. Let's play parlor games after lunch."

I mumbled a noncommittal response and slid the box under the quilt near my pillow.

Bob picked up his sport coat and shrugged into it. "I wonder what's cooking for lunch. I could eat a moose."

I was hungry when I reached the dining room, but Julie's empty chair killed my appetite. I pushed away from the table before the others finished.

"What is it, darling?" Honey turned to me, mild concern in her eyes.

"I think I'll walk to Shegog's. It's nothing important." I forced a smile. "Be back in a while."

The moment I stepped through the door, the wind clawed at my face, pulled at my hat, and sucked away my breath. I pulled a wool muffler about my chin and leaned against a pillar on the porch. Going to the store was an excuse. I wanted to be alone, to sort things out.

Sunbeams glittered on the snow that covered every surface: the trees, my Oldsmobile and Mr. Simmons's Model T, the mill across the road.

Julie couldn't stand to be near me. Did it matter so much?

I tramped through the woods for more than an hour. Sorting through a fellow's priorities is never easy. For me it was sheer torture. All my life I'd craved my father's approval. I'd endured unspeakable agonies trying to please him. The trouble was, I never could. It came down to one question: What did I really want in life?

Two ways lay before me: a gorgeous wife, a topnotch job, fabulous wealth and social standing. Or a life of service, of living with the problems of others, of self-denial. The choice seemed ridiculously easy. So why was I so miserable?

I kept telling myself that Honey was perfect for me. I believed it, too.

Alice, Bob, Honey, and I played mah-jongg the rest of the afternoon. I laughed louder than anyone. Why not? I had everything going for me down to the last detail. . .special ordered by my father.

⌒

Sunday morning, Honey clung to my arm, smiling close to my face, tempting me. I didn't look at Julie when she came down with Millie and took her father's arm for the walk to church. I sat with Honey in the second pew—two rows ahead of the Simmons family—so I wouldn't have to make a choice about where to keep my eyes. Honey, warm and possessive, was enough for any man.

After the singing, Pastor Jenkins shambled to the pulpit. He looked almost too frail to get through the message. He stood quietly for a moment and took inventory of the congregation. His black eyes rested on me, and suddenly I felt like an eight-year-old on the first day at a new school.

"Open your Bibles to Matthew 6:28," he quavered. " 'Consider the lilies of the field, how they grow; they toil not, neither do they spin: And yet I say unto you, that even Solomon in all his glory was not arrayed like one of these.' " He cleared his throat. "Today we're going to have a little lesson on God's economics."

I looked at the shiny elbows on his black coat, at the worn edge on his collar, and I wondered what he could teach me, heir to a man who drove a Rolls and owned three massive homes. But during the next hour that old parson made more sense than anyone I'd heard since Dave Yancy left the university.

I also learned that keeping someone out of your line of sight won't stop you from seeing them. For a solid hour I had to keep pushing aside the image of liquid brown eyes and a sweet, natural smile.

After the service, we left the church. On the steps I paused to shake the old parson's hand and thank him for the message. As we walked away, I turned to Honey. "I have to make a phone call."

She latched onto my arm and smiled into my face. "Mind if I come along?"

Covering her glove with mine, I made myself grin. "Do you have to ask?"

"You've got something on your mind," she said, watching me.

"It's nothing. Honest."

We strolled across the road toward the store, and I glanced at the village people crossing the bridge, the same bridge Julie and I had skated under a few days ago.

"Is Julie ill?" I tried to sound casual. "She looks pale."

Honey tilted her head. "Why are you worried about Julie?"

"She's your sister. Why else?"

She laughed. "I suppose it's the Good Samaritan in you."

I stopped in midstride. "What's that supposed to mean?"

"I was referring to your charity work." She plucked at my sleeve. "It's terribly sweet of you, Jim, to want to help those poor urchins in New York. It shows your soft spot, I suppose."

"Honey, I'm not sure I'll enter law school next fall. I think God wants me to work with my boys full time."

She dismissed my statement with a toss of her head. "Your father would never allow it."

I swallowed hard, feeling as if I stood on the edge of a precipice. I knew what I should do, but did I have the courage to do it?

Shegog's lay just ahead, a thin gray spiral rising from its chimney.

She pressed her lips together as though deciding something. "Before you make your call, I want to tell you how sorry I am for the way Julie has been hounding you. You have to understand she's not used to social settings like—"

"Hounding me?"

"You know. Getting you to play checkers with her, keeping you at the piano."

"Honey, did you speak to Julie about me last night?"

"Darling, I couldn't let her go on like a giddy child. It's embarrassing to her and to the rest of us."

My blood pressure went up ten points. "How could you be so cruel? Julie would be devastated to think she's made a spectacle of herself."

"Exactly why she had to be told." She turned those wide, guileless eyes on me. "Don't you understand?"

Suddenly, I understood much more than Honey imagined. "My phone call can wait," I told her. "Let's walk by the river. We need to talk."

Chapter 12

Julie, what's the matter with you? You aren't ill, so why won't you come to dinner?" Mother asked, hovering over me. "Please come to the dining room with the rest of us."

"I can't, Mother. I just can't."

"Why not?"

I pressed my lips together. Finally, she got tired of asking and clumped down the stairs. I'd won, but I didn't feel like a winner. Roast beef and mashed potatoes are tasteless when eaten from a tray in a lonely room, even with French apple pie for dessert.

When Millie came for my empty dishes I told her, "My head feels like someone's pounding it with a hammer."

She touched my hair. "Poor dear. Let me get you an icepack. I'll be back in a jiff."

But Mother returned, not Millie. "Here's a spoonful of sleeping powder mixed with sugar," she said, "and a glass of water."

I swallowed, then shivered and gulped the cool liquid. Not that it took away the awful taste. I let my head fall to the pillow, more miserable than I'd been since the accident.

"Julie," Mother sat near me, "has Honey upset you? I want to know before she leaves in the morning."

"Don't blame Honey. She's only tried to help me." My eyelids felt heavy. "I'm the one. . ."

I didn't hear her leave.

~

"Julie? Can you wake up?" Honey spoke into my ear. "I've got something to tell you." She gently shook me. "Please wake up. We've got to leave soon."

The soft urgency in her voice brought me around. "What is it?" I rubbed my face, fighting off the drugged feeling that held me down. "I'm awake. What is it?"

She hesitated. "I want to apologize." She touched my arm. "Sometimes I get so caught up in things, I forget to think about how everyone else feels. We've been through this before, I know."

I waited for the rest of it. She meant it now, but there would almost certainly be another incident like the pageant. Honey couldn't seem to learn the lesson.

"I didn't mean any harm, Julie," she went on. "You really were a lovely Carol Byrd."

My anger softened. Honey had come home full of energy and expecting a great time. Everything had gone wrong. I felt bad for her.

"I forgive you," I whispered. I hugged her tight, wanting to say more but not knowing how.

She broke away, murmured "Bye," and hurried out.

Who told Honey she'd hurt me? Mother?

I threw back the covers and scooted to the window. Through the glass I could hear Alice's shrill giggle and Jim's voice calling good-bye. The car chugged to life. It sounded rough, more like Dad's Tin Lizzie than Jim's smooth Olds. I hoped they wouldn't have a breakdown.

Tires crunched over snow and gravel and faded away. Finally, sweet silence told me they had gone. I leaned my forehead against the cool pane. I'd expected to feel relieved. Instead I felt empty.

I turned toward the closet. I had to get to my piano and have a long session with Chopin. Only music could ease my emptiness.

Jim was gone.

I slipped into a housedress, any old one, and touched a brush to my hair.

The cool banister felt comfortingly ordinary under my hand. My slippers made a whisper on the stairs. I heard Millie laughing in the kitchen followed by Esther's booming scold. Mother would be tidying the parlor, taking down all the decorations. The household had returned to normal the moment the gang drove away.

Why couldn't I? I felt like a stranger to myself, half a person where a whole person used to be.

I turned toward the library door, my hand outstretched to find the knob. Inside my sanctuary, I closed the door behind me and leaned against it, smelling the fire in the grate, hearing it crackle, feeling its warmth.

Another smell—a man's cologne, achingly familiar. Did Jim stop by here this morning? His scent lingered behind to torment me.

I tilted my head, straining with everything inside me to "see" both past and present. Something was different, and it was more than just me.

A slow, melodious tinkle shocked me with the rush of a tidal wave. "The Skater's Waltz." My music box.

I gasped. "Who's there? Jim?" Tears welled over before I could stop them.

In an instant, Jim's fingers twined in mine. "It's me," he said.

"You didn't go." I was too astonished to be shy, too much in love to care.

"I couldn't leave you. I finally realized what a shortsighted fool I've been. If a man lives for money and prestige, he's nothing but a shell."

"But Honey—"

"Isn't right for me. I told her so yesterday." He lifted my fingers to his lips. "I won't be going to law school. When I phoned my father I expected him to disown me, but he didn't. For the first time in my life I heard respect in his voice when he said good-bye."

He pulled me closer. "I love you, Julie. You're sweet and sensible. . .and real. Will you marry me?"

"Oh yes." My hands reached for his face.

He pulled me into his arms and kissed me. My world exploded into a million dazzling lights that swirled and spun in a frenzy of colors. In the middle of it all I saw Jim, the part of him that no one else could see, the part of him that belonged only to me. Sometimes the heart has eyes of its own.

Christmas Flower

Colleen L. Reece

Chapter 1

T attered banners of crimson, green, and violet fluttered in the autumn sky over the tiny village of Tarnigan, like a shattered kaleidoscope spilling broken rainbows. Fantastic patterns painted the white hills and valleys in the shadow of the Endicott Range. The yellow glow from lighted windows paled by comparison, even those shining brightly in Nika Illahee, the Clifton-Anton home. The distant din of war had faded in the mid-1920s. Peace shrouded the top of the world.

High atop a snow-covered slope above the little village, a parka-clad girl with large dark eyes and wild roses in her cheeks caught her breath at the wondrous sight. She laid a mittened hand over her heart. Shoshana Noelle Clifton, "a rose, born on Christmas Day," pride of Tarnigan and all of north central Alaska, wound the fingers of her free hand in her malamute Kobuk's collar. He whined, then stilled beneath her touch.

Did the aurora borealis, she wondered, give her dog the same sense of tension it roused in her? She silently watched the display, held by its splendor, yet unable to shrug off a feeling of apprehension. For twenty years she had marveled at the northern lights. This night felt different, although she could not explain why. The beauty mocked her, bringing pain so exquisite she wondered if she could bear it. The northern lights seemed to whisper a single word to her: good-bye.

Shana flung her head back and cried, "God, what do You want of me?"

Kobuk stirred restlessly and whined again. The heavens glowed with the aurora's mad dance, and Shana stubbornly refused to give way to the growing coldness inside her well-wrapped body. Like snow figures created by laughing children and left to the mercy of the night, she and her now-silent dog remained still. The performance of lights reached its zenith and began to fade. Only then did Shana tear her gaze from the skies and command, "Home, Kobuk."

She turned and started for Tarnigan, spurred by nameless dread. Surely her fancy was running away with her, she told herself, but her momentum increased with every step, as though she could escape that single, whispered word. Soon she was running. With a joyous, "Woof!" Kobuk ran beside the fleet figure, as his father before him had run during Shana's younger years.

Halfway down the slope, a tall figure stepped from behind a cluster of giant spruce trees, halting girl and dog's impetuous rush. Strong, gloved hands grabbed Shana's shoulders and shook her. "You know better than to pelt down that slope," an angry young voice accused.

"Let me go!" Shana jerked free from the gripping fingers. Knowing she was in the wrong added fuel to the fire of her anger. "You aren't my keeper, Wyatt Baldwin. Just because Strongheart called you Little Warrior when you were born—"

"Don't forget Dad and Mom recognized even at that young age how appropriate it was and obligingly gave me my French name because Wyatt means the same," the young man taunted.

Shana knew without seeing that his ocean-blue eyes—so like Arthur and Inga Baldwin's—crinkled with mischief. "When are you going to grow up and treat me as I deserve?" she demanded. "The Bible says to respect your elders."

He shouted with laughter that brought an unwilling smile to her lips. "Never going to let me forget you arrived a few weeks before I blessed the world with my coming, are you?" His mirth died. "Right now you deserve to be tied to your bedpost, Shoshana Noelle. Running down the side of a mountain at night is just plain stupid."

Piqued because he was right and they both knew it, Shana brushed aside the comradely hand he held out to her. Not for the world would she tell Wyatt of the need she had felt to get away from the night. "Even if I fell down, which I didn't, it would be like landing on a feather bed," she muttered.

"Sometimes you're a featherhead, pal. Come on. Let's go home."

Shana sedately walked to the foot of the slope. Yet the moment her boots touched even ground, she gathered her muscles and sprang forward with the speed that made her one of the fleetest runners in Tarnigan. Even Wyatt was normally hard put to keep up with her and tonight she had a head start. Down the lane she sped, straight for Nika Illahee, her family's homestead, the name of which meant "my dear homeland" in Chinook. Wyatt's snow-muffled steps thudded close behind. A peal of laughter rang out when she reached the steps and burst onto the porch a single step ahead of him.

"You'll never catch me," she taunted between hard breaths.

The light from the windows showed his gleaming white smile. A burnished lock of hair had escaped his parka hood and dangled over his forehead. A curious biding-my-time glint in his blue eyes sent warning chills skittering through Shana's veins. So did his low, "I wouldn't bet on it" and the odd little laugh that followed.

The door swung open. "Are you two being chased by wolves?" Dr. Bern Clifton wanted to know. His dark eyes twinkled. "Daughter, you look more like your mother every day."

"Thanks, Dad." She slipped out of her parka, fashioned from a white wool Hudson's Bay blanket with scarlet trim and warmly lined with fur. Shana grinned at her mother, pretty Sasha Anton Clifton, whose coronet of gleaming dark braids interlaced with crimson ribbons made her look just a few years older than Shana. "That's quite a compliment."

"You're almost as good a nurse, too," Bern told her. He ran one hand through the soot-black hair that gleamed with silver threads. His black eyes twinkled. "Tarnigan's mighty lucky to have us, plus Wyatt's folks."

She fell silent, remembering. First, Dr. Bern Clifton, then his best friend, Dr. Arthur Baldwin, had come to Alaska by tangled trails. Both had found love and settled in Tarnigan. Shana privately considered her parents' and the Baldwins' love stories even more romantic than Sir Walter Scott's novels. She felt a quick flush rise to her face and ducked her head so it wouldn't show. Would she find love one day? The kind that shone in Inga's eyes for her husband, in Mother's eyes for Dad? If so, when? With whom?

Shana shot a sidewise glance at tall, handsome Wyatt, her best friend since cradle days. Why had he looked at her the way he did in the glow from lighted windows? Surely after all this time he wasn't getting notions about his playmate, was he? *I hope not.* Her mind quickly rejected the idea. *I wouldn't want him to consider marrying me just because I'm the only girl around. Or because he doesn't want me to be an old maid. I'll be twenty-one on Christmas Day, pretty old to be unmarried in the north.*

The sense of standing tiptoe on the very edge of something too fragile to put into words made Shana mentally back away. Wyatt glanced at her, as if the girl's close observance had caught his attention. His eyes widened, but he seemed no different than usual. Shana bit her lip and turned from him, relieved, vaguely disappointed, and disgusted with herself, all at the same time.

"You're different lately," Wyatt remarked to her a few days later. "Something's changed, hasn't it?" He gave her a long, thoughtful look, as though he were searching her thoughts.

Shana flushed and turned her face away. "Leave me alone, Wyatt. Sometimes people just need a little solitude for a change."

His eyes lingered on her face, but then he shrugged and walked away, leaving her alone as she'd requested. When he did not seek her out the next day or the one after that, she was irrationally peeved, and when she realized an entire week had gone by without Wyatt's presence, a wave of loneliness swept over her.

Still the time alone gave her a chance to finally pinpoint what troubled her. The compelling feeling God was calling her to use her nursing skills—skills the two doctors had taught her from as far back as she could remember—gnawed at her like a mouse nibbling rawhide thongs. With it came fear. What if He asked her to take those skills elsewhere? Away from Tarnigan?

"No!" she protested in a mighty surge of rebellion. "God, You won't make me leave everything I know and love, will You? I'm needed here." Yet was she, really? Both her mother and Inga Baldwin were excellent helpmeets for their doctor husbands. Shana could be spared, should it be God's will.

For days she denied the growing feeling in her heart, scoffing at the idea a person could actually be pulled toward a place she had never been except in stories. She shut her heart against the tales Arthur had told of the time he served in a place thousands of miles away, a place known only to Shana by fingering it on a map of the continental United States. A silly map, that had Alaska shoved off to one side as though it were of little importance.

Time after time, she stood beneath an iceberg-cold moon, the sky again alight with the aurora borealis. The low-hanging stars offered no answer. Neither did the flashing lights with which she had grown up. Yet amidst their magnificence, memories more vivid than the dancing heavens filled her mind. A small girl at her mother's knee, inviting Jesus to be Ruler of her life. A fourteen-year-old kneeling with her friend Wyatt, both promising to go wherever God might choose to lead them.

"Lord, when did my fascination with the valley tucked away in a fold of the Great Smoky Mountains in North Carolina begin to pull me toward 'the Hollow'? " she brokenly prayed. "When did the creeping suspicion I must one day go there take root in my mind? You know how I laughed at first. How ridiculous to believe You would expect such a thing of someone who loves Alaska as passionately as I do."

She shivered. Bern and Sasha had taught her since babyhood that God works in mysterious ways to accomplish His purposes. What if He asked her to leave all, including Wyatt? "Don't be foolish," she told her rapidly beating heart. "Never by word or deed has he spoken of anything except friendship."

Shana continued to struggle, saying nothing to family and friends, but pouring out heart and soul to her heavenly Father. Her mother's dark, troubled eyes, so like her daughter's, showed she realized all was not well. She said nothing and Shana appreciated it. For several years, Sasha Clifton had allowed her daughter to come to her, rather than attempting to discover what troubled her only child.

One night, Shana again climbed to her observation point. Helplessness swept over the girl, alone on a snowy hillside except for her faithful dog. Everything she held dear lay below her. She could not leave it. Yet how could she refuse, should going be God's will? A torrent of tears rushed to her eyes. Her cry echoed in the encroaching night, the cry of every follower who stands at life's crossroads, longing for guidance. "How can I know if it's really what You want?"

Kobuk laid one paw on Shana's sturdy boot. She dropped to the ground and hugged him fiercely. If she were called, he, too, would be left behind. Face buried in the dog's fur, she whispered her prayer of submission. "God, if it's truly Your will, I'll go. I know we're not supposed to ask for signs, but I feel so torn. Like a wishbone pulled two ways until it breaks, leaving jagged edges." Her voice trailed off. After a long time Shana slowly stood and started down the slope toward Nika Illahee, one hand resting on Kobuk's proudly lifted head. No running this time. No Wyatt, scolding and exasperating. Just the drained feeling she had done what she must. The outcome was hid in the mighty hand of God.

An uneasy, waiting week passed. Two. Shana regained some of her peace. Perhaps God didn't require such a sacrifice. Perhaps He was merely testing her to see if she were willing. Then, just a few days before Christmas, a letter arrived. It shattered Shana's new-found tranquillity like a thunderbolt from the blue. Dr.

Aldrich, the physician who had replaced Arthur at the Hollow wrote:

> *It breaks my heart to admit it, but soon I won't be able to carry on. I've tried in vain to find someone willing to at least assist. I know from the stories you share in your letters there's no chance you or your friend Dr. Clifton can come. Your people's need is too great. Do you know of anyone with even rudimentary skills who might help me? I have grown to love these people, as you predicted I would. I'll continue until I drop, but I shudder to think what will happen here when I do.*

Arthur read the letter to the Cliftons. His handsome face, so like his son's, looked troubled. Regret darkened his blue eyes. "He's right. Neither of us can be spared. We're the only doctors for hundreds of miles. When one of us is away on call, the other is needed here." He spread wide his sensitive surgeon's hands in a gesture of hopelessness. "There's nothing we can do."

Bern sighed. "If we only knew someone, anyone, who would leave all and go serve." His massive shoulders sagged. "Arthur, I am so sorry."

Shana felt her heart skip a beat. Then it began to pound the way it did when she ran long distances. Her mouth dried. Three times she started to speak. Three times words failed her. On the fourth try, her clear, steady voice rose above the hard beating of her wishbone heart. "Father, there is someone. I will go."

Chapter 2

If Shana lived to be older than the Endicott Range, she would never forget the pool of silence that descended following her announcement. She averted her gaze from the battalion of eyes staring at her and focused on the room she loved. Colored by the impending departure, the handcrafted furniture covered with buckskin, the wolfskin rug, even the oversize fireplace with its six-foot lengths of logs that warded off Tarnigan's far-below-freezing winter nights, all looked unfamiliar.

Would she ever see them again? Shana swallowed the obstruction that leaped to her throat at the thought. A minute or an eternity passed. She looked at Bern, jaw ajar in amazement. She had involuntarily called him Father instead of Dad. Had it sprung from the knowledge she must be considered an adult? Otherwise, his beloved daughter could never convince him she must carry out what she now knew beyond the shadow of a doubt was her calling.

Bern shook his head, as if disbelieving what he'd heart. "You?" His voice sounded hoarse, strained. "You want to go to North Carolina?"

"No, but I must!" Shana burst into passionate speech. "It's tearing me apart. I don't know how I can ever leave you and Kobuk and Tarnigan." She looked at her mother appealingly. "I've fought and fought. For a long time, I tried to convince myself it was just hearing Uncle Arthur's stories." Her lips quivered and she clenched her hands into fists. "Deep down, I knew better. Every time I thought of the Hollow, something deep inside me stirred." She paused and licked dry lips. "I can't fight any more. Wyatt and I told God years ago we'd go anywhere He sent us. I just didn't dream it would be so hard."

The dam behind Shana's eyes broke. She ran to her white-faced mother and buried her face in Sasha's lap. Drenching tears poured. The silence continued. At last Shana raised her head and looked around the circle of concerned faces. "I finally told God it—it was all right with me. I had to be sure, so I asked Him to send a sign."

Like puppets released from a spell, the others came to life. Sasha's lovely face twisted with pain. She stroked her daughter's tangled dark hair with the slim and shapely hand that had helped save more than one life. "Dr. Aldrich's letter."

"Yes." Shana glanced around the circle of friends.

A spark flamed in Arthur's eyes. Was he thinking of his own days in the Hollow, of the terrible need, of how he himself had worked with Bern to make Shana an accomplished nurse and helper?

Inga only smiled, but the look in her clear, fjord-blue eyes warmed Shana through and through. Inga understood. Had she not given up life aboard the *Flower of Alaska* with her ship-captain father to marry Arthur and live in Tarnigan, far inland from the ocean depths she loved?

Shana turned back to her father. Bern Clifton looked ten years older than he had short moments earlier. Yet even as she watched, he raised his head and squared his shoulders. Shana felt a rush of love. No wonder the Indians of Tarnigan called him Hoots-Noo, "heart of a grizzly."

"You are sure." Not a question, but a statement of confirmation.

"I am sure." The words fell from Shana's lips like a sacred vow.

Wyatt said nothing. He stood in a crouch, like a mountain lion waiting to spring. His eyes slitted until only a blue gleam showed between curly golden lashes. Only the whiteness of knuckles strained to the utmost hinted at his agitation. A wellspring of protest raged within, but he dared not utter it in the face of such perfect faith. He felt caught in a whirlpool, tossed to and fro. To deny the white flame of Shana's belief in her call would be an insult. To remain silent was to lose her. *God, how can You allow it?* he silently prayed. *Must I give her up, just when her eyes betray the dawning of a new kind of love?*

Never! He had loved Shoshana Noelle Clifton from the time her mother gently placed the little girl's hand in his and said, "Wyatt, even though you are a few weeks younger, you are larger, stronger. I cannot always be with Shana. When I am not, you must always care for her and keep her from harm."

Clear-eyed, knowing even at that young age his pledge must not be given lightly, the boy's clear blue eyes manfully gazed into Sasha's dark ones. He squeezed Shana's small fingers with his own slightly grubby ones and said, "I promise. For always."

"Thank you." Sasha's hand rested on the curly blond head like a benediction. It set responsibility burning in the boyish heart. Much later, Wyatt realized the poignant moment also marked the beginning of his journey toward manhood— and the day he would ask Shana to be his wife. No dark-eyed village maiden ever tempted. No laughing trapper's daughter or visiting cousin received more than a polite bow or smile.

With every year, Wyatt's love for Shana grew stronger. He scolded, teased, coerced, and praised. They took turns leading and following. The desire to outstrip Wyatt in canoeing and hiking and running made Shana fiercely competitive. His sunny smile and obvious pride in her accomplishments spurred her on to greater heights. He fought for her when necessary. A certain whey-faced shopkeeper who dared grab Shana with drunken hands when she was sixteen fell victim to Wyatt's clean-limbed rage and magnificent strength. Only the commandment "Thou shalt not kill" saved the man from death. Long before Bern Clifton learned of the insult to his daughter, the man fled in the dark of night again. The wounds inflicted on him by Wyatt's righteous indignation marked the transgressor for the coward and bully he was. He carried scars for months.

Never again did a man or boy lay hands on Shana. At the first sign of any unwelcome attentions by newcomers, someone in Tarnigan quietly took the strangers aside and related the shopkeeper's story. The usual response was a disbelieving, "That good-natured boy? Impossible." To which those who knew reminded through set lips, "Yeah. Cougars look like big pussycats, too, but they ain't!"

Cougars. Bears. Wolverines. Wicked men. Blizzards. Wind and rain and hail. Wyatt felt he could conquer them all. Now, faced with the greatest threat to happiness he had ever known, must he go down in ignominious defeat?

He straightened, a six-foot stripling whose slender build and buckskin suit covered solid muscle. He quickly marshaled the facts. One: He was Wyatt, a warrior. Two: He had promised to take care of Shana. He could not keep his pledge if thousands of weary miles stretched between them. Three: He had also promised to go where sent. He could still feel the solemnity of the moment when he and Shana knelt and dedicated themselves to following Christ wherever their heavenly Father might lead them.

A thrill shot through him. Like a heavy door thrown wide to welcome sunshine, a daring idea poured into him. Never one to waste time on regret, or to turn back once he had set his face forward, Wyatt took a single step toward Shana. Had a second or an hour passed since she had vowed in her solemn voice, "I am sure"? He neither knew nor cared.

Wyatt rose to his toes, then allowed his heels to hit the floor with a little bang of finality. Burning blue gaze fixed on Shana's tear-streaked face, he answered her vow with his own, in a voice that rang in the quiet room. "Mother. Dad. I am going with her."

This second bombshell brought a wave of protest. Wyatt ignored it, intent on watching Shana. Emotions chased over her expressive face like rainbows on a glacier, mingling, everchanging. Doubt. Delight. Disbelief. They warred for mastery even as she fell back a step and held out one hand, as if to keep Wyatt away. "You?" she said in a strangled voice. "You?"

"Yes."

"Are you going because you also feel a call or because of Shana?" Bern rasped. His eyes glowed like twin coals.

Wyatt met his gaze squarely. His muscles tensed but he didn't flinch. Too proud to deny, too honest to claim divine leading when he wasn't sure about it, he quietly replied, "I don't know. Maybe some of both." He drew in a ragged breath and expelled it. "Sir, it's only a few weeks until Shana and I are twenty-one. I am asking you to release me from my promise."

A curious smile tilted Bern's mouth. "I'm amazed you have kept it this long." Was it a hint of relief that brightened the dark eyes?

Wyatt felt bright flags of color wave in his face. "Have you ever known me to break a promise?"

"No." Mischief replaced Bern's grave expression. "Would you like to take Shana into the kitchen and speak to her there?"

Wyatt flung back his corn-colored hair. "No sir. Everyone here has the right to know. Do you want to tell them, or shall I?" He looked from puzzled face to puzzled face. A slight frown creased his mother's forehead. His father's eyes twinkled. Had Bern Clifton been unable to stay silent? No, for Sasha and Shana chorused, "What promise?"

At a nod from Wyatt, Dr. Clifton quietly said, "This young man came to me a good five years ago. He declared his love for Shana and asked permission to marry her when they were both old enough."

Wyatt's ears burned at the words and Shana's gasp, but he manfully took his medicine, never letting his gaze move from the girl's shocked face.

"Wasn't I to have anything to say in the matter?" Icicles tinkled in Shana's voice and a tidal wave of red swept into her tanned skin.

"Of course." Bern blandly went on, although his sparkling eyes showed how much he was enjoying himself. "Wyatt simply felt the right thing to do was to come to me, my dear. He gave his word he would not express his feelings until you were both twenty-one, unless you showed marked interest in another man. From the look on your face, I believe Wyatt has kept his promise. His honor is above reproach." Bern exchanged a meaningful glance with Sasha, who smiled tremulously in return. "Son." He extended a powerful hand. "If you can win my daughter, you have my blessing."

Wyatt tore his gaze free from Shana and knelt by her mother's chair. "Once you placed her in my care," he said huskily. "Should God grant me the gift of Shana's love, do I still have your blessing?"

Sasha looked deep into his eyes. Wyatt had the feeling she saw his very soul. Her lips curved upward. "With all my heart," she told him.

The revelation of Wyatt's love—or his audacity—proved too much for Shana. Hands over her scarlet face, she fled from his triumphant whoop to the safety of her room. She slammed the door, barely missing Kobuk's plumy tail, and threw herself on her bed. The malamute took his usual place on the bearskin rug next to it. "Go away," she ordered when Wyatt knocked.

"You have to come out sometime," he called. An exultant laugh followed. "When you do, I'll be here. I told you not to bet I couldn't catch you!" The sound of racing steps told Shana her scheming suitor had gone back to the main room. Was he even now gloating over the shock of his surprise?

The thought brought anger. How could he? How dared he complicate her life even more, when she already had more than she could handle?

Be fair, a little voice reminded. *He couldn't know you would be called to North Carolina. He did the honorable thing. Once he knew his boy's love for you had become a man's, he went to your father. He abided by your father's edict not to speak unless he saw you were beginning to care for someone else.*

Someone else? Preposterous! Shana's eyes widened. She pressed both hands to her chest, where her traitorous heart beat wildly. "God, am I in love with Wyatt?" she demanded in a whisper. Little things came back to her. His care through the years. His constant presence when she needed him. His comfort when her pet fawn died. His defense against the greedy, clutching hands of the drunken storekeeper. She shivered in revulsion at the memory.

Wait! Had that incident five years ago roused Wyatt to awareness of her as a woman? "God, I don't care for Him that way," she confessed. "At least not yet." A deep blush dyed her oval face. She stirred uneasily and allowed her hand to fall to Kobuk's ruff. She felt the dog's rough pink tongue against her skin. Loneliness filled her.

"Lord, if Wyatt goes, I could take at least that much of Tarnigan with me. Is it fair to him, when I'm not sure how I feel? Oh dear, just when I think I've made it over one obstacle, here's a new one, although Wyatt wouldn't appreciate being called an obstacle." Diamond drops sparkled in her long, dark lashes. Like the mountain ranges of Alaska, her life had become one peak after another, each higher and harder to climb than the one before!

Chapter 3

The next day brought a northern storm that rattled even closely shuttered windows. Winds straight from the peaks took the girl's breath when she stepped to the porch of Nika Illahee, and drove her back inside. Only fools or cheecha-kos, what white men would could tenderfeet or newcomers, exposed themselves to such fury unless they were far from home when the devil winds caught them by surprise.

Shana shivered. The previous winter she and Wyatt had been caught by the wind a few miles from Tarnigan. They had taken stock of the situation and decided their best refuge was to hastily construct a snow house. Kobuk snuggled down between them, adding his warmth to their shelter. When gray daylight came late the next morning, the three companions headed home. It took all their strength to reach the outskirts of the village before another arctic blast attacked.

Now Kobuk barked defiantly into the face of the storm and followed Shana inside. The Indians of Tarnigan had felt "the daughter of Clifton" would surely ruin the furry malamute by allowing him the run of her home. She had laughed, then proved how mistaken they were when twice Kobuk and his mistress bested the finest dog teams for miles around. Suspicion of the powerful dog's worth quickly died. Vindicated, Shana had the satisfaction of knowing all Tarnigan recognized Kobuk more than lived up to his ancestors' reputation.

In the living room, Shana slipped from her parka, knelt on the wolfskin rug in front of the blazing fireplace, and hugged Kobuk. "I'm going to miss you so much." She sighed. "I can't take you with me. You'd never be happy." A shadow crept into her heart. "I wonder if I will be. I know I must go, Lord, but why am I not happier about it? Shouldn't I be glad to serve You, no matter where?" She thought of missionary stories she had read. Of the hardships and struggle, the eventual realization it was all worthwhile. "Be patient with me, please, Lord," she prayed. "Surely once I get there. . ." Her voice trailed off. Long, snowy months stretched between December and a time safe to travel.

"Enough brooding," Shana scolded herself. She jumped up. "Remember, Shoshana Noelle Clifton, the Lord loves a cheerful giver. A cheerful goer, too, I'll bet!" She giggled and felt better.

Heavy thumps sounded at the heavy front door. It burst open, and a snowy figure flung himself inside, accompanied by a gust of frigid air. Wyatt Baldwin's strong shoulder pushed the door shut against the shrieking storm.

"Good grief, what are you doing out on a day like this?" the girl demanded.

"Just because it's stormy, does it mean a man can't call on his ladylove?" Mischief twinkled in Wyatt's blue eyes.

Shana's heart lurched, but she refused to dignify his jest with an answer. "Get yourself out of those wet boots and parka and to the fire before you catch pneumonia," she ordered. "Here. I'll put them to drip in the bathtub."

"I'll do it, but thanks, ma'am." Wyatt exaggerated his drawl. "Much obliged."

"I hope you don't think that's a southern accent," Shana said crushingly. "Even southern Alaska would scorn it."

"A humble thing, but my own." He fished a pair of worn moccasins from his parka pocket, slid them on, and disappeared in the direction of the bathroom. His curly golden hair shone in the firelight when he returned on silent feet, then hunkered down in front of the fire next to her chair and held his hands to its warmth. "Wonder if the Hollow gets blizzards."

"They get snow, but it probably doesn't last like ours." Shana stared into the leaping flames, wondering how to open a subject they must discuss—now, while Dad was in the kitchen watching Mother make dried-apple pies. "Wyatt?"

"Yes?" His sapphire gaze turned toward her.

She found herself strangely tongue-tied and mentally chastised herself. The young man before her was no stranger. She had shared her innermost thoughts with Wyatt Baldwin since they both learned to talk. Perhaps that was why she felt differently. All the long years she believed he was as open as she, Wyatt had carried the secret of his confession to her father. In some indescribable way, that secret, now that it had been revealed, had built a barrier.

Never one to back away from hard tasks, Shana crashed headlong into the invisible wall. "You mustn't go to North Carolina if it's only to follow me," she said in a low voice. Head bent, fingers laced together, she added, "I may not ever be able to care as—as you do."

Really, an unfamiliar little voice mocked inside. *Then why did your heartbeat quicken when Wyatt called you his ladylove? And why is your face redder than wild strawberries in summer?*

Wyatt's gaze was steady. "I'll take my chances."

Another wave of red shot up from the rolled-back, white collar of Shana's warm woolen gown. Wistfulness crept into her voice. "I wish you wanted to go for the reason I do," she faltered. "Don't you see? If it's just for me, you may find everything horrid and be sorry you ever left Tarnigan." She raised her head until her troubled dark gaze met his. "I will feel it's my fault."

For once, Wyatt's happy-go-lucky personality gave way. He reached up from his position on the rug and lightly touched her fingers before clasping both hands around his knees. He waited a long moment before he spoke. When he did, his face set in the lines of a man.

"Shana, I appreciate your honesty. We've never lied to each other and we won't start now. I wish I could tell you I feel as called to the Hollow as you.

I don't. I do have a tremendous curiosity about the place. I always have. God speaks to His children in different ways. Perhaps my belief that I have to go with you, coupled with the desire to see the place my father loved and served, is the Lord's way of nudging me in the right direction."

Again he fell silent. She considered what he had said. If only—

Wyatt broke into her musings. "I never want to make you feel uncomfortable. We're too good of friends for that. Now that you know my feelings, we don't need to discuss them further." His gravity slipped and he gave her the lopsided smile that changed him back to the boy she knew far better than the determined man she had just glimpsed. "One thing. If I forget and come out with endearments —such as ladylove, sweetheart, or darling—" He shrugged. "Well, just ignore them. I've been thinking those words for a long time—but that doesn't mean you've given me the right to use them." He broke into a hearty laugh, the last thing she expected.

Shana's hands flew to her flushed cheeks. She scrambled from her chair. "Wyatt Baldwin, you are outrageous!" she gasped.

He bounded to his feet. Strong arms inexorably drew her to him. Too surprised to struggle, Shana stood quietly. Wyatt's head bent. He whispered, "Then just this once, I may as well be totally outrageous." His lips touched hers, lightly, reverently. For the space of a heartbeat, Shana stood stock-still, filled with wonder at the kiss. She felt the hard beat of Wyatt's heart, felt his arms tighten as if he would hold her in a circle of protection forever.

A second, an hour, an eternity later, Bern Clifton's rumbling laugh in the kitchen separated the couple as effectively as a knife slicing bread. Wyatt's arms dropped to his sides. Shana stepped back. "How could you?" Her face burned with shame. After telling him she didn't care the way he wanted her to, how could she have submitted to his kiss? What must he think?

Tears of rage came. Without another word, she turned and ran—as much from her own traitorous self as from Wyatt.

He caught her at her bedroom door. "Don't run away from me," he said huskily. "I won't do it again. Not until you tell me it's all right."

She found her voice. "What kind of an apology is that?" she cried.

He proudly flung back his head. "I make no apologies, Shana. Saying I am sorry would deny my love. That I will never do." He wiped away a lone tear that escaped her tight control and left a silver streak on the girl's smooth cheek.

The gentle touch almost proved Shana's undoing. Feeling the need to sort out the new emotions rising within her, she opened her bedroom door and stepped inside. Wyatt backed away, but his gaze never left her face. Just before Shana closed the door, she saw a slow smile form on the lips that had kissed her so tenderly.

She flung herself to her bed. How could she face Wyatt again, she wondered in despair. His action had changed everything. No longer were they boy and girl, carelessly playing together in a land both harsh and wonderfully satisfying. Wyatt's inexperienced kiss had roused the sleeping womanhood in Shana as nothing else could have done. She tried to whip up resentment. "How could he, Lord?" Her attempt at fury failed miserably. There had been nothing rude in Wyatt's kiss, only the need to stake his claim, to let the woman he desired for his mate know the depth of his feelings.

What about her own feelings?

Unwilling to answer the pounding question, Shana hastily rose from the bed, rebraided her hair, tied it with the scarlet ribbons she loved so much, and smoothed her collar. If the dark eyes peering back from her mirror shone more brightly than usual, if color streaked her face, surely Dad and Mother would not notice. Wyatt must not. If he did, it would give far more significance to the little tableau in the living room a few minutes ago than Shana desired. With a quick prayer for strength, she swept out her door and into the living room.

The room stood empty and quiet, and both relief and disappointment swelled in her heart. She swallowed hard. Too bad if Wyatt had gone, just when she'd been prepared to pretend nothing out of the ordinary had happened. What was a kiss anyway? Her heart thumped against her ribs. She hated dishonesty, even when it was only herself she lied to. She could not write off as trivial an incident that had affected her so deeply.

She walked to the kitchen on hesitant steps. A cheerful room, it boasted windows on two sides, a colorful tablecloth and chair covers. "Where's Wyatt?"

Sasha looked up from her pie making. "He said he had to get home." She expertly pared extra dough from the plate she held aloft in one hand. "Did you get things settled between you?"

The innocent question set Shana afire. "I—I think so." They had, hadn't they? "He knows I'm making no promises. He also is intensely curious about the Hollow." She seated herself in a chair next to her father, who took his nose from a medical magazine long enough to raise a quizzical eyebrow. "Dad, is it really all right to let him go with me?" A dreadful thought occurred to her. "You don't think the people in the Hollow will feel we are doing something wrong by coming, do you? Together, I mean. After all, we aren't married or related."

"I've given it some thought," Bern admitted. "Your friendship has always been accepted here in Tarnigan. But the Hollow? Dr. Aldrich will know of course. Since the War and Armistice, conventions have been shaken. I don't know how much it's affected the Hollow. I do know they lost boys and men in the conflict."

"I wouldn't worry about it," Sasha put in, dark eyes confident. "If it's God's will for you and Wyatt to serve Him there, He will work things out." Her busy hands stilled. "I'd think anyone Dr. Aldrich sponsors would be given a fair trial. After that, your and Wyatt's own decorum will determine the way you are treated and whether you are accepted."

"Well spoken." Bern reached out a long arm and pulled his wife to his lap. "I do have a concern, Shana. You're a well-trained nurse and physician's assistant. What does Wyatt think he's going to be able to do in the Hollow?"

He posed the same question later that evening when the Baldwins braved the continuing storm and dropped by. "You can't just tag along after Shana," the doctor bluntly told Wyatt.

"I know. I wish I'd spent less time trapping and hunting and more time learning medicine from you and Dad, like Shana did," Wyatt mourned. "I can't change that, but I can follow you around and study. In short, take a crash course between now and spring. It will give me enough medical knowledge to intelligently follow orders. Right? Thanks to you all, especially Mother, I also have a good general education." He smiled at pretty Inga, who had carried out a regular program of schooling for him, Shana, and other Tarnigan children. "Maybe the Hollow can use a teacher. If not, I always have these." He flexed his muscular arms. "Shana might need a cabin of her own. So might I, and I'm just the person who can build them."

Wyatt restlessly shifted position and frowned until his silky, golden eyebrows came together. "There's just one thing. Would it be better if we arrived in the Hollow separately? Once we get to Vancouver or Seattle, I could hang around and take a later train." Hot color flooded his face. The apology he had withheld earlier flashed a wordless signal to Shana. "I don't want to do anything to dishonor you."

Shana shrugged the question away, not wanting to face the implication behind his words. But she did not want her witness to God's love to be marred by Wyatt's presence. Her mother gave her a small serene smile, and Shana sighed, remembering what her mother had said earlier. As usual her mother was right: If this was God's will, then He would take care of all the possible problems. There was no point worrying.

Chapter 4

Shana Clifton always remembered the months following her call to a distant place as a time of waiting, bittersweet, filled with both anticipation and regret. Once the fateful letter committing Wyatt and her to their mission sped on its way by *coureur de bois* (woods runner), Shana threw herself into holiday preparations with all her usual fervor. Every passing day brought a pang. She might never again spend Christmas in Tarnigan. Even if she someday completed the work God had for her to do in that faraway land and returned, things would never be the same. Time had a way of altering even the most beloved patterns.

With Wyatt's help, Shana smothered Nika Illahee in fragrant evergreen boughs, hauled in on a sled pulled by the prancing Kobuk. Satin ribbons as scarlet as the girl's cheeks formed bows and loops against the dark greenery. Candles stood waiting in every window, ready to be lighted on Christmas Eve in honor of the Christ Child.

Sasha busied herself with sewing simple gowns of sturdy material, their only beauty in the workmanship of nimble fingers. She whisked the dresses out of sight when Shana raced into the room, saving them for her daughter's Christmas birthday. Costly garments would set the girl apart from the women of the Hollow, so Sasha laid aside fine laces and contented herself with bits of bright trim on collars and pockets.

Only Shana's heavy silk traveling gown hinted at the riches she and her mother had inherited from Shana's grandfather, Nicolai Anton. Money from the sale of priceless furs Nicolai had taken in fair trade with Indians and trappers had helped provide much-needed medical equipment for Tarnigan. More than enough remained to carry Shana to her destination. She could live as comfortably as surroundings warranted, even supplement Dr. Aldrich's equipment, if necessary. Wyatt had saved most of what he earned by trapping, so he also had no pressing need.

If tears dampened the garments Sasha created with such loving care, only God knew. Along with wealth, the proud conqueror Nicolai had passed down a heritage of fortitude and endurance that silenced inner protest. Even an aching heart must respect the code of the north, the unwritten rule stating men and women must stand or fall according to their own choices.

Neither would Sasha allow Shana to carry away the memory of sighs and tears. She raised her chin and buried the loneliness creeping into her heart like permafrost under the tundra. She stored away each trilling laugh, every sight of girl and dog tussling on the wolfskin rug before the fire, each tender good-night kiss. In the months or years when obedience to God's calling separated mother and daughter by thousands of miles, Sasha would lift her memories from the treasure chest of her soul, and stroke them like nuggets in a chain of gold.

"Wyatt will care for her," Inga whispered to Sasha on Christmas Eve when the families joined others in the small church first pastored by Bern Clifton's father, who had been buried a few years before, not far from Nicolai Anton.

"I know." Sasha pressed her friend's fingers. Long years of friendship coursed between them—and the strength God gives those who love and trust Him.

Shana saw the look the two mothers exchanged, and her own heart was comforted. The two women would sustain one another in the loss of their children. Shana stared at the candlelit altar, wondering at herself. In the time since she accepted God's calling, a strange thing had begun in her life. Her body remained in the land she loved, acutely aware of all she was leaving. Her parents. Kobuk. The Baldwins. Her Indian friends, especially Strongheart and his lovely wife Naleenah. Yet at times she felt curiously detached, as if her spirit had already taken flight and gone.

Only Wyatt knew how Shana felt. She would never forget the poignant look in his eyes when she haltingly tried to explain. "I understand, Shoshana. I am the same." He raised his head and stared at the distant Endicotts, eternal watchmen over the valley in which Tarnigan lay. "I believe our hearts and minds are separating from what we hold dear to help make the actual parting less painful."

In a flash, Shana realized the truth of what he said. "Is this God's way of ensuring we will actually go?"

"Perhaps." He turned from the mountains, dropped gentle hands on her shoulders, and looked into her eyes. "Or His way of reminding that when His Spirit lives in us, we need not fear the future."

Shana said through trembling lips, "I am glad you are going with me, Wyatt."

"So am I." His blinding smile sank deep into her troubled heart. The next moment he changed from philosopher to facetious. "About time you admitted I'm a pretty handy guy to have around. Race you home. On your mark. Get set. Go!" This time she had no head start. Wyatt outdistanced her by a few steps.

Now the fragile moment shimmered in the candle-lit church. Shana bowed her head and silently prayed, *God, we can't know what's ahead. Help us take comfort from knowing You do. I still don't know why You're sending me so far away from all I know and love.*

A startling thought broke into her prayer. *Was this how Jesus felt when He left His Father to come to earth?* How could God stand it when He sent His Son, not to the warm welcome Shana and Wyatt would surely receive, but to a hostile world? What great love God had for His children to send Jesus to die for them! How could anyone refuse to believe in God, after He sacrificed His only Son?

How small her own sacrifice, when compared to the giving of Jesus' life!

> *Joy to the world! The Lord is come;*
> *Let earth receive its King;*
> *Let every heart prepare Him room,*
> *And heaven and nature sing,*
> *And heaven and nature sing,*
> *And heaven, and heaven and nature sing.*
> *Joy to the world; the Savior reigns.*

Shoshana Noelle, a rose born on Christmas Day, could sing no more. The peace and joy that first dawned in a rude Bethlehem stable flooded her soul. No matter what lay ahead, she could bear it—and bear it joyfully. She looked at Wyatt and thrilled to his deep voice singing the ageless carol. The same exaltation that had come to her shone in his uplifted face. His hair glinted in the candlelight, and his wide shoulders were set straight and strong. No wonder Mother had confidently placed her in his care!

A sense of awe stole through the girl. Tease he might, irritate her he surely would, yet the love of such a man was not to be taken lightly. On this Christmas Eve, more than ever before, Shana accepted the truth. Wyatt Baldwin, not quite twenty-one, was a man, full-grown and master of himself. The fact he had turned that mastery over to the Lord only increased his worth.

As though he sensed her intense regard, his gaze turned toward her. His blue eyes darkened. For a moment, Shana felt he was a stranger, an exciting man she scarcely knew. Her pulse sped, and she hastily looked away. When she glanced back, her childhood companion smiled down at her. Yet the disturbing glimpse of unknown, unexplored depths haunted Shana, and set her heart on tiptoe thinking of what lay ahead.

⁓

Christmas Day passed in a flurry of snow and laughter, with tears just below the surface. New Year's Eve came and went, ushering in sub-zero weather that froze the snow-covered valley to a rock-hard surface. One day as Shana ran beside a sled drawn by Kobuk and his mates, her face bright with the joy of exertion, the sharp premonition of homesickness to come struck her heart with such force that she stumbled and fell behind the dogs. Next winter she would be far away in another land. Why, she had only been in Fairbanks a few times, and never as far as Vancouver, British Columbia, but soon she would be thousands of miles from her home.

Jesus left His home, too, she reminded herself, recollecting her Christmas Eve experience. Again she felt herself withdrawing from the only life she had ever known, the sense of distance insulating her from pain.

Meanwhile, Wyatt had changed from outdoorsman to student overnight.

Most of the time he steadfastly resisted Shana's attempts to lure him for a run behind the dogs. The one time, he did go with her, he kept pace with her easily, shouting medical questions at her between strides.

"How do you splint a broken leg?" he bellowed. As soon as she answered, he fired another question at her. "What's the treatment for pneumonia? Why does moldy bread cure infection? What's the best relief for the pain of an abscessed tooth?"

She answered his questions automatically, while her fascinated eyes watched the way his muscles covered the snowy ground so easily, his mind absorbing the new information. It seemed to her that she was watching him stride forward into manhood. And yet when he suddenly gave her a sideways shove, sending her sprawling into a snowbank, she was perversely relieved to see him lapse back into boyishness. Giggling, she struggled to her feet, pelting him with snowballs all the while.

⌒

At last the long-awaited letter from Dr. Aldrich arrived. The Baldwins and Cliftons gathered before the fire in the living room at Nika Illahee. Arthur read:

Dear Arthur,

God is so good! I cannot stop thanking Him for the strange paths by which He accomplishes his purposes. Long ago when I first heard your stories of the need in the Hollow, I felt as called as Peter, Andrew, James, and John must have felt when Jesus quietly said, "Come. Follow Me."

My work here has not been easy. Fighting poverty, poor diet, and mountain superstitions means giving everything I have, knowing many times it will not be enough. Each time I lose a patient, a small part of me is buried along with the child, the mother, the bearded mountaineer who has "fotched" my mail. Or whose callused grip of my hand makes me fear for my bones. Or who has bestowed on me a rare smile of unconscious charm.

I often think of the English preacher and poet John Donne's immortal lines from his 1624 Devotions for Emergent Occasions:

"No man is an island, entire of itself; every man is a piece of the continent, a part of the main; any man's death diminishes me, because I am involved in mankind; and therefore never send to know for whom the bell tolls; it tolls for thee."

Think of it, Arthur! Three centuries have come and gone, yet Donne's words are as relevant to life in this secluded Hollow as if the poet had been born and raised here. I know you in Tarnigan must share my feelings, the necessary interdependence of those who live far from so-called civilization.

Forgive an old man's ramblings. They come from an overflowing heart. I also felt the need to let Wyatt and Shoshana know that no matter how hard the tasks here in the Hollow, it is all worth it. My people join me in rejoicing at the coming of your son and your friend's daughter. Don't be concerned about Mrs. Grundy and her raised eyebrows. We're too far back in the hills to slavishly follow her manners and morals. Besides, I have explained to those here the impossibility of Dr. Clifton leaving his work long enough to bring his daughter to the Hollow. These people accept the practicality of his appointing your son to act as her brother and protector. It is as natural as breathing for the older children in families here to look after the "least-'uns." As a sop to conventions, Nurse Shana, as she will be called, will live with a young widow and her small child. Emmeline is a little older than Shoshana and highly respected. I once had hopes of training her as an assistant, but young love, early motherhood, and the loss of her husband interfered.

Is Shoshana knowledgeable enough to pass state nursing exams? What about Wyatt? My people have great respect for my certificate. Mounting others on the wall of the whitewashed cabin I use for a clinic would raise esteem.

My lamp is sputtering a warning the oil is nearly gone, and daylight nears. I look forward to spring and the coming of the two courageous young people. Their youth, strength, and dedication may be the salvation of the Hollow.

Below the signature were a few scrawled words, punctuated with a heavy black exclamation mark:

Wyatt and Shoshana won't have to ride muleback into the Hollow, as you and I did, Arthur. A road of sorts now permits automobile travel. Advise day of arrival. I will make sure they are met!

"What a grand person!" Shana exclaimed. A thrill of pure excitement flowed through her. "Dad, do I know enough to get my certificate?"

Bern Clifton considered. "I don't know why not. What do you think, Arthur?"

The mischief in the blond doctor's eyes made him look only a few years older than his son. "She might squeak by."

"Well, I like that!" The corners of Wyatt's mouth turned down and he leaped to Shana's defense. "Hasn't she helped with every malady known to mankind? Didn't she stitch up the trapper she found mangled by a wolverine when we were miles away from Tarnigan? Wouldn't he have died if she'd run all ladylike and shrieking to get one of you?"

Arthur's eyes almost disappeared in laugh wrinkles. "Seems to me she did." His merriment subsided. He turned to Shana, whose face shone with pleasure at Wyatt's spirited support. "I'm only teasing. You will pass. Easily."

"Thanks to you and Dad, Mother, and Inga," Shana murmured gratefully. She smiled at Wyatt. "If you study as hard between now and when we leave Alaska as you have been since Christmas, I won't be the only highly trained assistant."

He flushed beneath her warm approval. "Thanks for the lollipop, pal. What I don't learn here, you can pound into my head on the way to North Carolina."

Chapter 5

Winter reluctantly loosened its grip. Streams and rivers freed from their icy prisons babbled with the ecstasy of being alive and free-flowing once more. At daybreak on a late spring morning, the two missionaries and an Indian guide set out on their long journey. Heads high and unafraid, eyes damp but shining, they faced whatever perils might arise between their points of departure and destination.

"I won't look back," Shana promised herself. "Jesus said in the ninth chapter of Luke that he who puts his hand to the plow and looks back is not fit for the kingdom of God." She bid farewell to family and friends as composed as though she would return by nightfall, then followed Wyatt and Mukee up from the valley floor.

Alas for Shana's good intentions. Kobuk broke free from Bern Clifton's firm hold and caught up with the travelers atop the rise from which Shana had so often observed Tarnigan. She felt herself tremble when the dog flung himself on her with a joyous bark. She fought the urge to bury her face in his fur and never let him go. "Home," she sharply ordered. "Home, sir!"

The malamute trotted a few steps down the slope. He halted, looked back, and whined. His pricked ears and rigid stance showed puzzlement that his mistress did not follow.

"Home," Shana called again. Her voice sounded thin. "Kobuk, go home."

The dog threw back his magnificent head and howled. His desire to stay warred with years of training. Body drooping, he backed away a few steps and dropped to his haunches. His excited barks shattered the stillness.

"Ko–buk." Faint but clear, Dr. Bern Clifton's voice rang in the morning air. Ko–buk echoed from the hills.

With a look of reproach Shana knew she would never forget, her canine friend headed back to Tarnigan. Through blurred vision Shana saw Kobuk reach the group of miniature figures in front of Nika Illahee. A final mournful howl floated up to the three on the hill. Shana turned away. Mukee's impassive face softened into kindliness. "Kobuk, he be all right."

Shana said nothing. Could a dog raised and loved as the malamute had been, adjust to the absence of the person he loved most on earth? She had heard of animals that sickened and died when separated from their masters. "Please, God, don't let that happen to Kobuk," she whispered. Child of the wild, she saw no incongruity in asking God's protection for her dog. The One who knew when a sparrow fell would surely show compassion on a lonely, abandoned malamute.

Wyatt's face wrinkled in sympathy and he wordlessly held out his hand. Shana laid hers in it and felt strength flow into her. Without another backward glance, they left the crest of the hill and began their arduous journey.

To Shana's relief, the trip itself brought a measure of healing. The wilderness grapevine had long since broadcast the news that son and daughter of the Tarnigan doctors would soon tread the Alaskan mountains and valleys. The trio found welcome in remote and unexpected places. Vaguely familiar French and Indian faces appeared, their owners grinning and chattering with delight when the nomads of the north arrived at cabin or village. Shana recognized former patients. Wyatt discovered trappers he had met while running his lines. All shared what they had, and the visitors gladly accepted the rude shelter and coarse but strengthening food offered.

Other provision for their care had been made. In spite of knowing the uncanny way those who dwell far from civilization communicate, Shana and Wyatt found it hard to believe just how quickly word could travel. "How could they know?" they marveled when Mukee calmly pulled an overturned canoe from its shelter of bushes by the side of a rushing river.

A rare smile blossomed on Mukee's lined face. He grunted and his obsidian-like eyes shone. "Perhaps the birds of the air tell them daughter of Clifton and son of Baldwin come." He motioned them into the canoe, picked up a paddle, and sent the craft flying over the water. When the stream changed course from the direction they needed to go, Mukee waited until his charges clambered out, then beached the canoe far back from the water's edge.

"There will be other streams and rivers," Shana said. "Shouldn't we carry it?"

The corners of Mukee's mouth twitched. "Other rivers, other canoes," he said. "We use. We leave. Mukee bring back when he come again."

The guide's prophecy proved accurate. Only once did they fail to find a canoe when needed, placed there by unseen hands. That time, two bronzed Indians awaited their coming and safely transported them on their way.

"We be here when you come," they told Mukee.

"How will you know?" Wyatt demanded, fun dancing in his blue eyes. "It will be many days."

Shana covered her mouth to keep from giggling at the Indians' scornful dismissal of Wyatt's ignorance. "We know."

"Will they wait here?" Wyatt asked after the others left.

Mukee shook his head, a mute reminder that people who dwelt in the wilderness had better things to do than stand by the side of a river or stream until he arrived. Time enough to go there when needed.

At last the travelers, whose trek together had firmly cemented their friendship, reached Fairbanks. Mukee immediately replenished his supplies and turned back. Shana silently watched him go. She mentally reviewed the paths his moccasin-clad feet would retrace, each stretch of white water, every lonely mile. Only the excitement of purchasing tickets to Anchorage and boarding the Alaska Railroad could overcome the sadness of parting from their faithful guide.

A new world opened to Shana and Wyatt. Eyes used to far distances and few people widened at the crowds in Fairbanks, and then at Anchorage, where they took passage on a steamer bound for Vancouver and Seattle. At dinner time, Shana slipped into the dark silk traveling dress her mother had made, the dress that had ridden from Tarnigan in pack and canoe. When she shook out the wrinkles, the exquisitely stitched garment had no need to hide in comparison with more glamorous gowns. Shana's lovely face, velvety dark eyes and hair, and strong white throat rose above the dark silk like an exotic white flower growing in rich black earth. More than one man cast wistful glances at the girl. A few attempted to scrape an acquaintance but fell back from Wyatt's black scowl, assuming he must be a relative.

Unconscious of the power of her charm, Shana was more concerned with the unaccustomed sight of glaciers and heaving seas than with her clothing. She and Wyatt spent every daylight moment at the rail of the ship. The Inside Passage especially appealed to them, with its forested islands, fjordlike coast, tumbling waterfalls, and glimpses of wild animals.

Seattle left them both confused and eager to leave. "Like squirrels in a cage," Wyatt disgustedly labeled the inhabitants who hurried to and fro. Neither he nor Shana rested during their one-night stopover. They agreed the scream of fire engines, the rattle and rush of a city that seemed never to sleep, outweighed the beauty surrounding Seattle. Even distant Mount Rainier on one side and the snowcapped Olympic Mountains on the peninsula across blue Puget Sound couldn't make up for "too many people in too small a place," as Shana called it.

The cross-country railroad trip brought more wonders. "Who'd have dreamed it would be like this?" Wyatt murmured, nose pressed to the window glass with the curiosity of an unselfconscious child. Shana, who rode facing him, did the same, much to the amusement of fellow passengers. "Alaska has a lot of different kinds of land but precious few cities and fewer villages. Here you can't go more than a few miles without coming to a little town."

"Wait till you get to the desert and the plains," the kindly man across the aisle advised. "You'll travel many a mile 'tween towns and more 'tween mountains."

Shana turned brilliant eyes toward the weather-beaten speaker who said he'd be getting off in Denver. "If I had to live where I couldn't see mountains, I think I'd die," she told him.

The man's keen gaze bored into her. "Just how I feel, ma'am," he said heartily. "That's why I picked Colorado when I went to ranchin'. You say you're from Alaska? Well I reckon Colorado comes 'bout as close to matchin' your home for mountains as anyplace I know."

Shana and Wyatt fervently agreed when they saw the mighty Rockies.

They told their new friend good-bye in Denver. Before he left them, the rancher said, "The Great Smokies ain't like our Alaska 'n' Colorado mountains, but accordin' to pictures, they're mighty purty. Good luck with your doctorin' and nursin', young'uns. If you ever come back this way, look me up." He smiled until his eyes almost disappeared in crow's-feet, then ambled up the aisle and down the steps. The whistle shrieked a warning. The engine rumbled to life. The train chugged forward, gathering momentum with every turn of the wheels that carried Wyatt and Shana toward their new home.

"I hope the people in the Hollow are as friendly as this man," Shana soberly told Wyatt.

"If they aren't, we can always come back and look him up," Wyatt drawled. "He'd probably give us a job punchin' cows."

"Why would anyone want to punch a cow?" Shana demanded.

Wyatt exploded into mirth, but lowered his voice. "Haven't you ever read western novels? Men who work with cowherds are called cowboys, cowpokes, and cowpunchers."

"Who cares what a cow heard?" Shana grinned at him, but relented when he rolled his eyes. "Of course I've read western novels." A little trill of laughter escaped her. "When I was fourteen I was madly in love with Gene Stewart in Zane Grey's book *The Light of Western Stars*."

"You were!" Wyatt sat up as though she'd dumped an icicle down his back. "How come I didn't know anything about it?"

"My goodness, Wyatt. Don't tell me you'd pry into the secrets of a fair young maiden's heart."

"You bet I would!" His blue gaze brought an unwilling smile to her face. He grinned, gave a mock sigh, and placed one hand over his own heart in an exaggerated gesture. "Aw shucks, Shoshana Noelle. If I'd known years ago you had a yen for cowboys, I could have been one. Can't you just hear me yelling yippy-ki-yi and herding caribou your way?" Awe crept into his laughing eyes. "All this time and I never knew how to make an impression."

He paused and added irrelevantly, "I never heard of North Carolina having an overabundance of cowboys, did you? Especially in the Hollow."

Shana felt warmth steal up from the collar of her dress. "Don't be silly. I'm not going to the Hollow to catch a cowboy or any other man."

"Indeed, you shouldn't be," he pompously approved. "Not when you already have an outstanding specimen of Alaskan manhood biding his time until you decide to say yes to his offer of hand and heart."

"I certainly am glad for your lack of conceit," she mumbled.

"Faint heart never won fair lady," Wyatt reminded. He closed one eye in a wink. "I just want you to keep in mind that if a pore, lonely cowpoke wanders into the Hollow, I saw you first!" He yawned, stretched, and added, "We can't get to North Carolina any too soon for me. These train seats weren't meant for my legs." He shifted them restlessly, trying to find a place to stretch out their length. Shana giggled at his frustration.

Many a quiet laugh brightened the lengthy miles for Shana and Wyatt. Time after time those around them said things that tickled their funny bones. Such as calling trickles of water that wouldn't make a respectable creek in Alaska "rivers." Or pointing out "mountains" in the distance that rose no higher than the smallest Tarnigan foothills. Only their laughter kept their long journey from deflating their spirits.

$\sim$

At last, after days of travel, they reached Asheville, jumping-off place for the Hollow. Shana's heart pounded. Tarnigan, Kobuk, even her parents seemed part of a different lifetime.

A stocky, silver-haired man with dark eyes stepped forward. He held out a gnarled hand. "Miss Clifton? Mr. Baldwin? I am Dr. Aldrich. Welcome."

Shana's spirit soared. Time, hard work, and worry had bowed the doctor's shoulders. The three robbers had been unable, however, to dim his unquenchable spirit. More important, Dr. Aldrich's look of gratitude and compassion made the travel-stained, weary girl feel that somehow she had come home.

Chapter 6

T he scenery is like a series of masterpieces painted by the matchless hand of God," Shana breathed to Wyatt. Fascinated by her introduction to her new home, she forgot the jouncing of Dr. Aldrich's old car over what he called "a road of sorts." Loveliness surrounded them, the Great Smokies at their best. Mountain laurel crowded close to the trails, great treelike shrubs wearing glossy dark green leaves and pink or white flowers. Some wore purple markings.

"What are those?" Shana pointed out the uncurtained car window toward clumps of trees, some thirty feet high and more. Waxy white clusters shone brilliant against the gray branches. Her eyes felt enormous from trying to take in everything at once. Her ears rang with the songs of countless unidentified birds.

"Those?" Dr. Aldrich glanced in the direction she pointed. "Dogwood." He tightened his hold on the wheel of the bucking vehicle. "According to legend, Jesus was crucified on a dogwood tree. The tree supposedly felt such terrible pain and shame, Jesus had compassion on it. Until then it had been a mighty tree. Jesus said never again would it grow to such large proportions that it could be put to such a use. It's also said Jesus caused the four bracts—the modified leaves—beneath the small, greenish-white flowers to form in the shape of a cross. Then He put a spot of scarlet in the center to remind the world of His shed blood." The doctor smiled sheepishly. "It's just a legend, but I have to admit, I never see a dogwood without thinking about it."

"That's great. Are there other legends?" Wyatt wanted to know. Sun shone on his hair and turned it to molten gold.

Shana saw warm approval in Dr. Aldrich's face before he replied, "Oh yes. See those redbuds? The ones with reddish-brown bark and heart-shaped leaves? They're called Judas trees. Legends say after Judas betrayed Christ, he hanged himself on a redbud tree."

Shana looked at the tall trees with the black-veined design on their trunks and shivered. "Don't they bloom?"

"Earlier in the spring, before the leaves appear. They're a sight to behold." He smiled at his enthralled passengers. "Of course, before then you'll see an autumn to remember. It's one of my favorite times of year." The winding, upward road grew steeper. Dr. Aldrich shifted to a lower gear. "We're almost to the top of the hogback. Close your eyes and don't open them until I tell you."

Wyatt winked mischievously before obeying, then shut both eyes. Shana did the same. "You don't need to tell us what we're going to see," Wyatt boasted. "Dad said the valley lies tucked in the folds of the hills like a cornhusk doll folded into a bit of leftover calico."

Dr. Aldrich chuckled. "He did, did he? Sounds just like him." The car slowed, chugged, and came to a stop where the road flattened. "I'm going to open the door and help you out. Keep your eyes closed," he warned. The doctor suited action to his words and cleared his throat. "All right. Take a gander for yourselves."

Shana opened her eyes. Blue haze that gave the Great Smokies their name shimmered in the distance. Thick forests composed of more than two hundred species of trees spread over the highest and most rugged portion of the Appalachian mountain chain. They stretched from where the watchers stood to farther than the keenest eye could see.

Long moments passed before she tore her gaze free from the horizon and reluctantly let it drift downward. A small feeling of dismay unnerved her for a moment. In spite of Arthur's warning, she simply hadn't been prepared. She and Wyatt had secretly decided passing years would surely have brought change, improvement. They had not. The westering sun, eager to retire for the night, ruthlessly exposed both the picturesqueness and shortcomings of the Alaskans' new home. So had it done more than two decades ago when Wyatt's father first stood on the hogback and looked into the Hollow.

Patches of corn and other vegetables snuggled up to log cabins in small cleared areas that feebly held back the looming, encroaching forests. Hounds bayed, their deep-throated cries clear in the still air. The laughter of children mingled high and sweet with the ring of pick and shovel on rock where men wrestled out stumps and cleared more land.

Shana involuntarily reached for Wyatt's hand. Thank God he had come with her, no matter what his motives! His fingers tightened on hers and swept away some of the forlorn feeling in her heart. She firmed her lips and lifted her head to stare again at the mountains. Why mourn that the valley itself held poverty, hard work, apathy, when she had those glorious, ever-present ridges above her?

" 'I will lift up mine eyes unto the hills, from whence cometh my help,'" she softly said.

Wyatt continued the quotation from Psalm 121. " 'My help cometh from the Lord, which made heaven and earth.' "

"My motto as well," Dr. Aldrich told them. "Are you ready to go on? Go down, I should say." He chuckled again.

Shana and Wyatt silently climbed into the car. Waves of weariness dulled the new nurse's senses. They jumbled her impressions until only Wyatt and that mountaintop moment remained clearly in her mind. Down, down, down, the old car crawled. Here and there, figures in denim and calico raised curious faces. Men raised their hats. Women bobbed their heads. Children stared.

Dr. Aldrich waved to all. So did his passengers, but their host and sponsor didn't stop the car. "Time enough later for you to meet the folk," he told them.

"Right now, you two look pretty done in."

Wyatt yawned mightily. He grinned at Shana when she couldn't help following suit with a yawn of her own. "Lead me to a bed. Any bed. Or a hunk of ground under a tree. It really doesn't matter."

"We can do a bit better than that," Dr. Aldrich said dryly. "You'll stay with me, at least for the present." He motioned to a small whitewashed cabin at the near end of a large, cleared area. A short dogtrot, or covered passage, connected it to a similar, but larger cabin. "Our clinic," he explained proudly.

Our clinic. Two small words that unequivocally welcomed and accepted Wyatt and Shana as partners against sickness. Wyatt straightened. A spark kindled in his blue eyes. Shana felt some of the fatigue drain from her body.

Dr. Aldrich didn't stop but drove slowly over the dusty road that led past a few discouraged-looking buildings. Shana felt her lips twitch when she noticed a freshly painted sign over the door of the largest. "Mercantile" rather than "General Store" seemed a bit pretentious for such an aged building. On closer examination, she revised her first impression. Old and sleepy-looking it might be, but a neatly mended screen door kept out flies, and the windows on either side of the door shone brighter than sun after a lazy glacier.

"Is the store always this way—or is the shininess in our honor?" Wyatt mischievously asked. His eyes sparkled and Shana's lips twitched in sympathy with his rising spirits.

"A little of both. The windows are always clean, in spite of the dusty road," Dr. Aldrich told them. "The newly painted sign is definitely in your honor." He grinned. "Actually, so is the sign itself. There's never been one before. When the storekeeper put it up, it sure made a stir." He laughed reminiscently. "Some folks 'lowed it was purely pretty. Others said 'twas all foolishness; there weren't nary a body for miles around but who knew where the store was!" The doctor's reproduction of his beloved mountaineers' speech held no malice and his passengers laughed along with him.

They reached the far end of the clearing. Dr. Aldrich halted the car before a double cabin attached by the same covered dogtrot as his own cabin and the Hollow Clinic. Rough and unpainted, time had laid a kindly hand and mellowed the boards to weathered gray. Wild roses clambered up the supports of the communal porch, whose worn floor boards showed evidence of a recent scrubbing. Starched white curtains fluttered at the window of the cabins. Their coarse material fit their humble surroundings, yet bore mute witness to someone's loving care. Twin water buckets rested on each end of the porch railings.

"Your new home, Nurse Shana," Dr. Aldrich quietly told her. "The left-hand cabin. Emmeline Clark and her son Gideon share the one on the right. Good. She's coming out now."

Wyatt's low, "What a beauty!" turned Shana's fascinated gaze from the unexplored mysteries of her new dwelling place to the young woman slowly coming down the steps. She mentally echoed Wyatt's admiring appraisal. Emmeline's coronet of pale-gold hair framed a pure oval face, shy blue eyes, and a hesitant smile that silently pleaded *please like me.* Her full-skirted, blue-sprigged calico dress failed to hide high-arched, shapely bare feet but stole not one whit from her natural dignity, as she gracefully walked toward Dr. Aldrich and the newcomers.

A small, male replica peered from the shelter of his mother's arms. Shana judged him to be about two. She glanced at Wyatt, who hadn't taken his gaze from Emmeline since she first appeared. Something sharp and hurtful thrust into Shana's heart. Never had she seen Wyatt show interest in any girl except herself. Now he looked thunderstruck. *As well he might,* jealousy taunted. *This mountain girl is as lovely as the wild rose blooming over the doorway.*

Dr. Aldrich beamed and said, "Emmeline, this is Nurse Shana. I know you'll be friends."

"I'd admire to," Emmeline replied in a low, musical voice. "Folks are all so glad you came. Gideon hardly ever cries. With the dogtrot between, we won't be a bother to you." She held out a slim, workworn hand.

Shana marveled. No wonder the doctor had coveted this girl's services. Her smile alone could bring as much healing as all the medicine in his black bag! She pressed Emmeline's hand and spoke more to the wistfulness in the other girl's eyes than to what she had said. "I am so glad we'll be living together." She glanced at the dogtrot and laughed. "I mean, be neighbors. Did you make the curtains and plant the rose?"

Emmeline's face lighted up as if a hundred candles flamed behind her eyes. Her laugh reminded Shana of a waterfall in spring. "The rose has been there as long as the cabins. I fixed up inside for you. Folks gave what they could. Would you like to see?"

Shana respected her the more for making no apologies. "Very much."

Wyatt found his tongue. "Not before I meet this young lady," he objected. "I'm Wyatt Baldwin. I'm not a doctor or a nurse, but I'm learning."

Emmeline turned her smile on him. The sword in Shana's heart thrust deeper at the delight in Wyatt's face when the girl said, "Many a man and woman here remember your doctor pappy and what he did for their kinfolk. I welcome you." She curtseyed quaintly, then turned back to the other girl, eyes eager. "Come and see, Nurse." Still holding Gideon, she mounted the steps, her slender back straight as a soldier at attention.

Shana crooned with pleasure when she stepped inside the cabin. Plain, white-washed walls gave a feeling of restfulness. The wood stove had been polished to within an inch of its life. A rag rug covered most of the scrubbed floorboards. Packing boxes nailed to the wall served as cupboards and hid behind plain white curtains that matched those at the window. An unmatched collection of freshly washed dishes sparkled on the shelves. A bright afghan mercifully hid the sagging sofa's defects.

Shana peeked into a small, curtained alcove and exclaimed in delight. It contained a narrow bed covered with the most beautiful red-and-white patchwork quilt Shana had ever seen. Another braided rug lay beside the cot. A small table held a shiny kerosene lamp, well-filled and artistically shaded by a rose-red paper shade. A coarse linen runner covered the top of an old chest of drawers on which stood a plain white pitcher and bowl.

Shana thought how little those in the Hollow had, how they could ill afford to give. She blinked to keep back a rush of emotion. She turned to Emmeline. "It's beautiful. I can never thank you enough."

The mountain girl's eyes widened. One hand absently patted her son's shining blond hair. After a moment she softly said, "There's no need to be thankin' us. It's we who are beholden."

Shana valiantly blinked back tears at the response. Barefoot and simple, Emmeline Clark, child of the woods, might be, yet Shana realized the girl's heart was as pure as mountain snow.

Chapter 7

Strange as it might seem, growing up in Tarnigan gave Shana Clifton and Wyatt Baldwin a boost in adjusting to life in the Hollow. Thousands of miles and customs separated the two places, yet they shared a common need: Residents had to be both self-reliant and dependent on neighbors in order to survive. Any doubt or suspicion on the part of those who lived in and around "the Holler" soon vanished like fog on a brilliant day.

Shana's first day in the Hollow began with a rooster blasting the morning air with his cock-a-doodle-doo. His arrogant stance and loud crowing clearly implied the bird's belief that the sun got up every morning just to hear him.

Shana stirred, pulled her covers higher against the cool air coming in the wide-open, screened window. Dr. Aldrich had told her folks in the Hollow never locked doors or windows. His eyes twinkled when he said, "It's considered downright unneighborly, insulting, even."

"You don't have crime?"

"A few moonshiners in the hills. A mild feud or two that breaks out mostly in shouting matches or rivalry at rifle contests. Nothing that will touch you. Just stay on the main trails if you have to visit patients without me. Folks can be a mite touchy about strangers wandering around where there might be a still."

The rooster crowed again, louder and more insistent this time.

"All right. I'm getting up." Shana threw a warm flannel robe over her night-gown, thrust her feet into deerskin moccasins that brought back memories of home, and pattered from alcove to sitting room. She touched a match to the already-laid fire and watched the sweet-smelling wood shavings burst into flames, then hopped back in bed until the cabin warmed.

A smile of pleasure curled her lips, remembering how Emmeline suggested Shana lay her morning fire the night before. "That way it won't take near as long to warm up your cabin," she explained. " 'Course in winter, you'll put in a backlog and keep a fire all night. It gets cold here."

Shana laughed outright. "Not as cold as in Tarnigan. I've run with my sled dog Kobuk in weather that's far below zero."

Emmeline's blue eyes opened wide. They reminded Shana of the deep blue shadows found in the massive Alaskan glaciers. Or cloudless summer skies. "How excitin' that must be! I've never been anywhere much except the Hollow and to Asheville a few times." Her face shadowed. She started to speak, then broke off.

Shana saw hunger in the other girl's face. "What is it, Emmeline?"

"I want to be somebody, somethin' more than what I am."

The eternal cry. The germ of an idea popped into Shana's mind. "If given a choice, what would you like to do?"

Emmeline didn't hesitate. "Be a nurse. Like you. If I hadn't married so young, I'd have learned what I needed to know from Doc Aldrich. I still want to, but how can I?" She hugged Gideon so fiercely he looked up at her in surprise and wiggled to get free. "It takes all my strength just to raise enough crops to keep body and soul together and care for my boy."

"Do you regret marrying young?"

A poignant light came to Emmeline's sensitive face. "No. I loved Gideon's pa always. 'Twas natural for us to marry soon as we got old enough. We were happy. When my man died, I had our son." She stroked Gideon's pale gold curls. "Nurse Shana, I want better for him. I want him to have more than a mule and a patch of worn-out land. I'd do anythin' to get it for him."

For the first time, Shana felt the power having more than enough can bring. "Is there a woman here who would look after Gideon so you could work with Dr. Aldrich and Wyatt and me?"

Clear red stained Emmeline's cheeks. "I reckon, but I'd be too proud to ask unless I could offer them a sum. Doc Aldrich don't know that though."

Shana touched the other girl's hand. "I inherited money. More than I need. I've already spoken to Dr. Aldrich about sending for medical equipment the clinic doesn't have. Emmeline, will you let me pay for Gideon's care while you learn nursing?" She held her breath. In the time she had been in the Hollow, Shana had learned the mountain people found it far easier to give than to take, or be "beholden" to others.

Before Emmeline could answer, Shana quickly added, "You know God called me to North Carolina. It may be for the rest of my life." Her lips quivered at the thought of permanent separation from Tarnigan. "On the other hand, it may be only for a time. Don't you see? Dr. Aldrich can't live forever. Should God call me away, the people here will have no medical help, unless someone is trained. You could also earn money to help with your dreams for Gideon."

Generations of ancestors who possessed little more than pride warred with the truth of what Shana had said. The struggle showed in Emmeline's face. At last she let her son slide to the floor, and rose in quiet dignity. "There's a granny-woman among my kinfolk who'll be glad to keep my boy. She said so long ago, but I couldn't bring myself to let her unless I could pay his way." The flush receded from her face. Her eyes shone with anticipation. "If you're sure you want to do this, I'm beholden."

"I do, with all my heart."

Emmeline gave a little cry and pressed Shana's hand to her cheek. "You won't be sorry. I'll make you proud." She caught Gideon up and ran out, happy tears streaming from her glittering eyes.

News that the Widow Clark was aimin' to study medicine with Doc Aldrich and his fotched-on helpers hit the Hollow like a bomb. As usual, the inhabitants reacted in different ways. Some thought it a good idea. Others, notably the unmarried men, found it a pure shame. Such a pretty widow could get any man she wanted with the snap of her fingers. Hadn't some of them already said so to her face and offered to be pa to her boy?

At Shana's insistence, Granny King kept mum about the fact she would receive a small sum for keeping Gideon. "I don't mind buttonin' my lip," she told the new nurse. "Some folks might think it was right down onneighborly to take money for watchin' a young'un." She sighed. "Truth is, hit's an answer to prayer. Gettin' old in the Hollow ain't easy and I never been one to take charity."

"This certainly isn't charity," Shana reassured. She'd fallen in love with the little old lady the first time she met her. "You're allowing Emmeline to gain knowledge that can help the whole Hollow, maybe even save lives."

Black eyes twinkled in the walnut-shell face. "Nurse, you kin talk the birds outta the trees." She cocked her head to one side and grinned. "No wonder that feller of yours wouldn't let you outta his sight. I'll dance at your weddin', if you don't wait too long to get hitched."

Shana laughed and felt color rise from the neck of her cotton gown. She patted the wrinkled hand, promised to drop by again when she could, and escaped.

Now a familiar ache replaced Shana's smile. Every day she saw less of Wyatt. He had taken to his lessons like an otter takes to the sea. He whooped with delight when he learned Emmeline would be studying along with him. After the first week he confessed, "I never saw the like of our new student nurse. She gobbles up Dr. Aldrich's medical books so fast it's all I can do to keep ahead of her, in spite of studying last winter and this spring."

His frank approval sent Shana's heart to her toes, but she had to be fair. "When Emmeline works with me, I seldom have to show her anything twice."

"I'd like to see her spend some time in a training hospital after you and Dr. Aldrich teach her what you can here," Wyatt commented. "The Hollow offers almost everything she will need to know, but not all. We haven't faced them all yet, but according to Dr. Aldrich, the Hollow never lacks for variety when it comes to ailments." He ticked off on his fingers. "Influenza. Broken bones. Measles, mumps, chickenpox, consumption, rheumatism, croup, scarlet fever. Gunshot wounds, some accidental, some questionable—" He sighed. "It's really not that much different from Alaska. I remember a few wounded trappers and Indians being packed into Tarnigan under mysterious circumstances."

Shana nodded, then watched Wyatt's blue eyes darken as he changed the subject. "About Emmeline. Think she'd go?"

"I don't know. Why don't we wait and see?" Shana's treacherous heart beat fast with hope. In the short time since she reached the Hollow, she had learned to love Emmeline as the sister she never had. Yet sharing Wyatt's time and attention with the other girl made the prospect of Emmeline's absence loom promising and attractive.

Dog in the manger, she scolded herself. *You turned Wyatt down. You told him to count on nothing. Now when he shows interest in Emmeline, you want to snatch him back. You're jealous of one of the sweetest, most Christlike girls you've ever known.*

"I am not!" she protested aloud. Wyatt raised his brows at her in surprise, and Shana flushed and turned away. *It's just that I never thought Wyatt would turn out to be so fickle,* she told herself. *A few weeks ago he was swearing undying love for me. Now. . .* She couldn't finish the thought. What if Wyatt gave up on a girl who had taken his friendship, even his love, for granted? What if the protective nature she knew so well reached out to the mountain girl who fiercely longed to be someone and was willing to do whatever necessary to make it happen?

"I don't think I could stand it," she whispered to herself later that night when she was alone in her room. With a lightning flash of illumination she realized the truth. She loved Wyatt. Not with the childish adoration carried through the years into girlhood. She loved him with every beat of her heart, with the love she had so often seen in her mother's and Inga's eyes when they looked at their husbands.

The realization kept her tossing and turning all night long. At last, as morning's light brightened the windows, she sat up in bed and put her hands to her aching head. "God, why did it take me so long to know?" she cried into the stillness of her cabin. "Why did I have to come half a world away from Tarnigan to realize I can never marry anyone but Wyatt? I want to be his wife, to bear his children. Have I put him off too many times? Is it too late?"

Self-loathing brought Shana out of bed. In all the novels she had read, she had despised heroines who awakened to the preciousness of a fine man's love only when another woman came onto the scene. Shallow, she had called them. Now she understood. Her blind eyes had remained closed until a catastrophic shock shook her very foundations. She quickly dressed, scorned breakfast, and braided her hair into two fat braids. Honest to the core, she knew she must tell Wyatt of her stupendous discovery.

A merry laugh outside her cabin sent her to the door. She flung it wide and stepped outside. At the other end of the dogtrot, Wyatt stood smiling down at Emmeline. Gideon leaned against Wyatt's leg, arms wrapped around it. Shana bit her lip, undecided whether to call a greeting or go back inside.

Shana shifted her weight. A board creaked under her foot. Wyatt looked up. "Morning. Ready to go to the clinic? We'll drop this young man off on the way." He picked up Gideon, set the child on his sturdy shoulder, and said, "Ow! Stop that, you rascal," when Gideon buried his chubby hands in Wyatt's golden curls and hung on for dear life.

The completeness of man, woman, and child shut Shana out and drove a splinter of pain into her heart. She mustered her poise and smiled at Emmeline, dewy fresh in her simple cotton dress with its white collar and cuffs. "I'll be along in a little while. I haven't had breakfast."

"All right. Coming, Emmeline?" They went off together like three children happy just to be together.

The day's beauty turned clouded and gray. Shana waited the length of time it would normally take to eat breakfast, then slowly walked the dusty road leading to the clinic at the other end of the clearing. She passed the mercantile, too dispirited to smile at its incongruous sign. Now that her childhood playmate obviously admired Emmeline so much, how could Shana tell him her feelings had changed? It wouldn't be fair to hold him to a promise that his heart could no longer keep.

Pounding footsteps raced toward her and broke into her misery. Her heart lurched. In all their years of acquaintance, she had never seen Wyatt so distraught. The gray-faced man reached her, grabbed her arm, and gasped, "Hurry. It's Emmeline." He dragged Shana toward the clinic at full run.

Shana couldn't speak, only feel. What had happened to bring agony to Wyatt's eyes, agony that sounded a death knell to the love Shana had not recognized until it was too late?

Chapter 8

Shana and Wyatt burst into the Hollow Clinic. Emmeline lay on the examining table, white-faced and silent. Blood stained her left hand and the white forearm where Dr. Aldrich pressed a heavy pad, obviously torn from a petticoat. He ignored his nurse's frantic, "What happened?" and barked, "Get the suture tray. She may need stitching."

His tone of command freed Shana from her daze. She ran for the tray of sterilized instruments and supplies always kept ready for emergencies. Sewing up gashes in patients was a common need in a community that worked with ax and saw, plow and hoe, guns and knives.

Wyatt stood to one side. Shana wondered why he looked so ill. His short term of study with the Tarnigan doctors had exposed him to far worse sights than a wounded arm. A moment later, Dr. Aldrich uncovered the wound and Shana understood Wyatt's concern. No jagged gash marred the rounded arm, but deep punctures. Tooth marks. Shocked, Shana asked again, "What happened?"

Wyatt passed an unsteady hand over his face. "We left Gideon at Granny King's. I suggested taking a shortcut through the woods to the clinic. Halfway here, the bushes rustled. A wild dog sprang toward me from the side of the trail." He swallowed and huskily added, "Emmeline leaped in front of me. When she lifted her arm to ward off the attack, the dog sank his teeth into her."

Emmeline's eyes looked enormous, but she whispered, "Wyatt grabbed a downed tree branch and killed the dog. If he hadn't been there. . ." Her whole body shook as with a chill.

"If I hadn't been there, you would never have taken the shortcut," Wyatt fiercely flailed himself.

"No use crying over spilt milk," Dr. Aldrich told them. His heavy eyebrows knit into a shaggy line across his furrowed forehead and he warned Emmeline, "This is going to hurt." He drowned the wounds with antiseptic, let them bleed freely, and poured more antiseptic over them. He finished off with a generous dose of evil-smelling carbolic acid and a mixture of herbs Shana didn't recognize. "Local medicine." He grunted. "Draws the poison out."

Shana barely heard him. Fear brushed its wings against her, then clutched with both claws. What if the wild dog were rabid? If not, why would he attack? Her fear increased. She thought of the Indian who had staggered into Tarnigan after being bitten by a rabid wolf, and the horrible death that followed. *Dear God, please don't let that happen to Emmeline*, she silently screamed. *Save her. She loves You and longs to serve. Please, God.*

Shana looked at Wyatt's bowed head and knew he was praying for the girl who had risked her life to save his. She felt comforted. Had not Jesus promised in Matthew 18:20 that where two or three gathered in His name, He would be in the midst of them? Surely God would spare one so pure and willing to serve as Emmeline! *Thank You for hearing and answering our prayers*, Shana's heart cried.

⌒

God did hear and answer their prayers.

"The dog wasn't rabid," Dr. Aldrich told Shana and Wyatt the next day. "I examined him, and I couldn't see any signs of sickness. One of the men recognized the animal. Says the dog was a mean stray that had been beaten until he hated every human he encountered."

Shana breathed a sigh of relief and tried not to notice the look of joy on Wyatt's face. When Emmeline had faced death for Wyatt, how could Shana begrudge her his love? She blinked away tears of gratitude and pain.

Emmeline's wound didn't even infect, thanks to the quick medical attention. As the torn flesh healed, Shana tried to open her wounded heart to God's healing grace. Eventually only small scars remained on Emmeline's arm, and she was able to resume her studies and training. But Shana's heart still felt as torn as ever.

⌒

One sunny afternoon when business was mercifully slow, Dr. Aldrich called a meeting of his "staff," as he designated his nurse and two helpers. His thick white hair waved wildly above his keen black eyes. He didn't shilly-shally but went straight to the point. "Wyatt, Emmeline, how would you like to spend the next six months in Charlotte, working harder than you ever have or ever will?"

Shana felt her heart leap to her throat. Wyatt cocked his head to one side. An eyebrow lifted and a wary look came to his face.

Emmeline finally said, "Charlotte?" The mountain girl's eyes turned round as the silver moon that sailed above the Hollow. "That's better than a hundred miles from here, and it's got more folks than grass blades in a meadow!"

"I know. It also has a topnotch hospital run by one of the finest surgeons I know." Dr. Aldrich fitted the tips of his fingers together. "I'd like to put you two under his tutelage until Christmas."

Emmeline twisted her fingers until they shone white. "I—I thought you'd be teachin' us everythin' we needed in order to help folks."

"You'll learn a heap more during your six months in Charlotte than I can show you here in years," Dr. Aldrich told her. "When you come back, you'll be far more valuable to me and to our people."

Shana felt the blood drain from her face. A lifetime ago, she had wanted Emmeline to get training away from the Hollow. After the other girl's courageous act, Shana bitterly regretted her selfishness. Now with a quirk of fate, not only Emmeline but Wyatt would be gone for six endless months.

"What about Shana?" the young man demanded.

Surprise filled Dr. Aldrich's face. "She will stay here and help me of course. I've already arranged for her to take exams in Asheville and get her nursing certificate." He considered for a moment. "Emmeline, do you think Granny King would mind moving into your cabin while you're gone? Gideon's used to it."

"I'm to leave my baby?" Emmeline paled and put her hands in front of her.

"Only for six months. Child, you once told me you would do anything in the world to get a better life for him than what most of our mountain folk have." The doctor's face wrinkled in sympathy. "Perhaps it's too much to ask, but if you will go, stick it out, and learn, it will be the finest sacrifice you ever make."

Shana thought Emmeline aged ten years in the next ten seconds. She bowed her head. When she raised it again, she quietly said, "I'll go. For him." Without another word, she rose and started for the door. Dr. Aldrich's voice stopped her with one hand raised to open the screen.

"Wyatt? How about you?"

He stared at the doctor. He looked at Emmeline. Last of all, he turned to Shana in wordless appeal. An eternity later, he asked, "Well?"

Could a heart ache this much and not shatter into tiny pieces? Shana wondered. Desolation rose within her. Long, lonely months stretched ahead should he choose Charlotte. Yet how could she protest? Ever since the accident, Wyatt had treated Emmeline more tenderly than ever, as if she were a delicate piece of porcelain that suddenly showed previously unsuspected depths of strength. Longing to beg him to stay, Shana said in a colorless voice, "You have to do what you feel is right."

He stared at her for a long moment, and the eyes she knew so well were unreadable. "If Dr. Aldrich believes we can learn faster, I have no choice." Now that the die had been cast, Wyatt reverted to his usual, laughing self. "Emmeline, we can keep each other company in our banishment to Charlotte. Right?" He grinned.

Shana barely heard the murmured reply. Pride inherited from both her father and mother sustained her. If Emmeline could forsake her child for six long months in order to ensure a better future for him, then Shana Clifton must ignore her aching heart and give her best to those in the Hollow.

෴

That pride carried her through the parting with Emmeline and Wyatt. She took care not to be alone with him and tossed her head when he looked deep into her eyes. Yet his questioning gaze remained in her mind long after the *chug-chug* of

Dr. Aldrich's old car faded on the other side of the hogback.

The same pride also sharpened Shana's mind when she took the tests for her certificate. She did well on both written and oral exams and thrilled when she received a letter of commendation from the board of examiners.

Summer passed, the hard work broken only by brief letters from Charlotte and longer ones from Tarnigan. Sickness ravaged the community until Shana had little time to think beyond its forested borders. She traveled into the mountains on foot and on muleback, tending the sick, fighting the belief fever patients should be bundled and made to sweat in a room devoid of the slightest bit of fresh air. Nights found her too tired to do more than tumble into bed until roused to a new day, new worries over the people she had come to love.

Autumn lived up to Dr. Aldrich's predictions. Shana reveled in the gold and red, the orange and russet tones of leaves that drifted onto forest trails and paths. The mornings grew colder. Frost sparkled on twig and branch. Granny King said her "rheumatiz" told her they'd have a hard winter. "Bet you can't wait for Em'line and your feller to come back," she teased.

Shana didn't reply. Time enough at their return for folks in the Hollow to learn Wyatt no longer cared. Emmeline's last letter had been straight from the heart.

_____

Did Wyatt tell you what's happened? she wrote. I never thought I'd love another man, and I'll be beholden to God for the rest of my life. It's so wonderful. He wants to be a good pa to Gideon, too. Don't tell Dr. Aldrich (we want to surprise him) but we plan to spend the rest of our lives in the Hollow. Nurse Shana, none of this would have happened if God hadn't led you to North Carolina. We aim to wait and get married in the Hollow. Will you stand up with us?

_____

Even though Shana had feared such a thing, the reality rocked her senses. Her first thought was to flee, to return to Tarnigan and forget North Carolina, the Hollow, and the false-hearted Wyatt Baldwin. She shook her head. No. God had called her here. Until He directed otherwise, here she must stay—even though it meant watching Wyatt and Emmeline's happiness at the expense of her own. Would they live in the cabin at the other end of the dogtrot? The thought was unbearable.

Chastened by prayer and the determination never to let anyone but God know the extent of her wounds, Shana relied more heavily on her heavenly Father than ever before. The last leaves of autumn lay buried under winter's first snow. A skiff of ice in her water bucket reminded her that Christmas and the return of the happy couple lurked just ahead. Shana threw herself into caring for the sick, studying her Bible, and making certain passages her own. The Psalms came alive to her as never before. She relied heavily on those that promised a shield, protection, strength, memorizing them and repeating them whenever she thought of the future. From disbelief and anger, through acceptance, Shana worked her way to a fragile peace.

Now the days raced along. A week before Christmas. Six days. Five. Four. Three. Wyatt and Emmeline were due on the twenty-third. Fortunately, nothing beyond the usual drip of colds and hack of sore throats plagued the community. Dr. Aldrich went to Asheville, leaving Shana in charge of the clinic. A few hours later, snow began to fall. When darkness came, Shana wearily trudged home. Snow crunched beneath her feet. Never had she felt so defeated. Even telling herself Christmas was for celebrating Christ's birth, not wondering how she could live through the holidays without betraying her feelings, didn't help.

Dr. Aldrich, Emmeline, and Wyatt didn't come that night. Granny King looked wise. "Don't fret yourself, child. They'll be here for Christmas, no matter what. What Doc says, Doc does."

Christmas Eve dawned clear and bright. Inches of white laid their gentle hand over the Hollow, softening its rough edges, beautifying the unlovely buildings. Wreaths made of wire covered with cedar boughs and red calico bows hung on her door and Shana's. A large package from Alaska rested beneath a tiny tree the girl had forced herself to decorate with carefully strung popcorn and cranberries.

Gideon raced down the dogtrot on chubby legs. "Momma come today?"

"I hope so." The sooner she faced meeting Wyatt and Emmeline, the sooner she could begin to fade into the background. She hugged the child, sent him back to Granny, and nerved herself for the ordeal.

They came just before dusk, honking the horn and hollering like banshees. Shana peered from her window when the car came to a halt in front of the double cabin. The last rays of daylight shone on Emmeline's laughing face, on bulky Dr. Aldrich, on a tall stranger. Shana's fingers curled into tight buds. Emmeline and Wyatt must have brought a minister. She turned from his pleasant countenance and gazed at the man she loved. Why must he look so handsome, so happy, so unattainable? Hot tears she had dammed threatened to spill. She turned from the window and whispered, "God, I can't do this alone."

The door burst open. Wyatt bounded inside and across the small space between them. "Shana?" His strong arms circled her. "I know I promised to wait until you said I might, but hang it all, it's Christmas!" His lips, cold from the clean outdoors, found hers.

For the space of a heartbeat, she returned his kiss, forgetting everything except her love for the man who held her. Then she tore free, eyes blazing. "How dare you?" A sob of pure fury escaped her.

"Sorry." He didn't look at all repentant. "As I said, it's Christmas."

"What would Emmeline think if she knew you were in here making love to another woman?" Shana raged.

A twinkle appeared in his eyes. "She'd tell me faint heart never won fair lady. That's what she's been telling me ever since we went to Charlotte. So has John."

Shana's head reeled. "John? What on earth are you talking about, Wyatt Baldwin?"

"Dr. John Wilson. He fell in love with Emmeline the first time he saw her. It didn't take her much longer, a day or two, perhaps." Wyatt's teasing gave way to startled recognition. "Shoshana Noelle, you didn't think—you couldn't have thought—" He caught her by the shoulders and his mouth set in a grim line. "Thanks for trusting me," he said sarcastically.

The dam broke. "How could I know? Emmeline's letter never mentioned John's name, just yours."

"And you cared this much?" Wyatt put a finger beneath her chin and tilted it up. "Why, Shana!" Wonder and gladness rang in his voice.

The final barrier between them crashed. "Ever since we came here. I was going to tell you, but you were always with Emmeline, and she's a wonderful person, and—"

Wyatt stopped her pitiful explanation the only way he knew how. With a kiss. This time Shana responded with all the love she had secretly hoarded, the way mountain squirrels stored up nuts for winter. At last she broke free, flushed and happier than she had been since leaving Tarnigan. "Wyatt, please don't ever frighten me so again."

"Only if you promise not to get foolish notions. Haven't I proved you're the only girl in the world for me?"

Made daring by her newly declared love, Shana couldn't help saying, "You have to admit. Emmeline is lovely."

"Of course. So is a columbine, or a wildflower. I just happen to like black-haired, black-eyed girls with lots of sass." Wyatt cocked an eyebrow in the endearing mannerism she had missed so much. "Going to be a good girl and marry me tomorrow? A preacher's coming, and I can't wait any longer for you to be my wife." He looked at her with eyes she felt examined her very soul. "People in the Hollow will have to be our family, Shana. It's too far for our folks to come, even if it weren't the dead of winter."

Shana thought of Nika Illahee, her dear homeland. Those she loved more than life itself would be getting ready to celebrate Christmas. Dad, Mother, Arthur, Inga. Strongheart and his Naleenah. A pang of homesickness went through her. If only she could be married in Tarnigan, in the church where Benjamin Clifton had proclaimed the Word of God until his death. Yet as Wyatt said, it was just too far.

But wait! Didn't the best of Tarnigan stand before her, strong and tall? The same dear boy, now a man, who had stood beside her all the years of her life? The love in Wyatt's eyes came from a heart that beat true and always would. It shone brighter than the aurora borealis in all its splendor. She nodded, and rested in the circle of his arms. As long as Wyatt Baldwin loved her, she was home.

The next morning, Shoshana Noelle Clifton donned the simple white gown and veil she had found in her Christmas package from Tarnigan. Emmeline's delight over a matching gown and veil completed Shana's happiness. Through a sheen of tears, she wondered, *How did Mother know?*

"I've been keeping the mail service between North Carolina and Alaska busy." Wyatt grinned. "We decided your twenty-second birthday would be about right for a wedding. After all, Shoshana Noelle, when else could a Christmas rose be wed?"

Epilogue

Tattered banners of crimson, green, and violet fluttered in the sky over the tiny village of Tarnigan. Fantastic patterns painted the white hills and valleys in the shadows of the Endicott Range. The yellow glow from Nika Illahee's lighted windows paled by comparison.

High atop a snow-covered slope, a parka-clad girl and man stood gazing at the beauty. Months and years had fled since Wyatt Baldwin and Shana Clifton left Alaska to answer the call of God. After Dr. John Wilson had arrived to help Dr. Aldrich and Emmeline in the Hollow, Wyatt had been accepted in medical school. Shana continued nursing. The same day Wyatt received his license to practice, he and Shana left for home. Alaska was growing. She needed her sons and daughters.

The Baldwins raced to Tarnigan a few steps ahead of a winter storm. How good it felt to be clad in the clothing they wore when they left so long ago! To paddle a canoe, tramp for miles without seeing anyone, then be welcomed in isolated places as though they had left only days before. Although they knew they should have waited until spring, their goal was to reach Tarnigan by Christmas. Tonight, Christmas Eve, they had at last reached their goal.

"Look, Wyatt," she said. "Someone opened the front door of Nika Illahee." She laughed. "The wilderness grapevine must still be working." Her grip tightened. "Someone's coming out."

He laughed, the same joyous laugh she'd loved since childhood. "Not someone, darling. Something." Wyatt cupped gloved hands around his mouth and called, "Hallooo." "Hallooo" came back from the hills.

A frenzy of barking echoed and reechoed. Shana felt her heart leap. "Is it. . . do you think he—?" Heedless of the steep slope, she began to run. Down, down, down. Halfway there, a furry avalanche hit her head-on. Girl and dog fell together and rolled in the snow. "Kobuk. Oh Kobuk, you remembered!" Shana buried her face in his fur and wept.

The malamute gave a single howl, then quieted beneath her touch. Wise in the ways of the north, Shana heard in his cry the story of waiting, watching, hoping: the eternal hope that never dies in the hearts of those who love deeply. It rang in her heart like a paean of praise. God willing, she and Wyatt would never leave Alaska again. From now on their Christmases would bloom here, in their one true home.

Bittersweet

Rebecca Germany

Dedication

To my mother, Wanda Royer, for sharing ideas and memories;
also to the community of Tappan for historical inspiration.

Prologue

September 23, 1936
Cleveland, Ohio

Gracie, I'm so glad I caught you in."

The phone against her ear, Grace Rudman relaxed against the entryway wall of the boardinghouse and set her handbag down in the telephone nook. Her brother's voice was a soothing balm as she prepared to start another stressful day of job hunting. If anyone could sympathize with her situation, it would be Guy. No matter what, she could always count on her older brother to understand.

Six months ago, when Grace had left Tappan, she had been desperate to escape the small hometown and get to the busy city. After graduation, she had worked hard in the little store on Tappan's sleepy Main Street, saving all her money, until at last she had enough to leave. She'd needed to get away from the people who loved her, especially her father, who couldn't understand that she was no longer a little girl. Everyone had seemed to think that she would simply settle down and be a farmer's wife, something safe and boring.

After her high school graduation, David Matthews, Guy's best friend, had acted so surprised when she'd said she wouldn't marry him, as though she could have lived the rest of her life on a farm outside Tappan with someone who had always been like another older brother to her. Marrying David would have been like never leaving home at all. She had desperately needed to get away and find a life of her own, something new and exciting and independent.

Finding that life, though, was proving to be harder than she had anticipated, and she was tired today, tired and a little scared. Hearing Guy's voice made her realize how much she missed him. She loved her brother John, too, of course, but Guy was the one she had always been the closest to in the family, and until these last few months he had been the one in whom she had always confided. Tears sprang to her eyes, and she wished he were standing beside her so she could lean her head against his shoulder.

"I know you city gals can be very busy with work and high society," he was saying, "but you haven't called home lately. When will you get home for a visit? We haven't seen you since you left in March." His voice was soft and playfully pleading, one of his endearing qualities.

Grace blinked away her tears and resisted the appeal in her brother's voice. *Long-distance calls and train trips are out of the question when you're down to your last dime,* she justified. Instead, she said into the heavy black receiver, "I may plan a trip home soon. I miss you, big brother."

"The job keeping you busy…?"

What job? The last three were only temporary positions. She had relied on her substantial savings to get her by until…

"…or maybe some sweet talker has stolen my little sister's heart?"

Oh, if you only knew the half of it. I'm such a fool. Grace couldn't bring herself to tell Guy about Gerald. She glanced around the narrow hallway and frowned. Two boarders entered the ornate front door and were greeted by Mrs. Schumacher. Speaking with the other boarders didn't stop the landlady from continuing to time Grace's phone call. A limit of ten minutes was strictly enforced. Grace sighed. This was not the place or time to go into her troubles.

She spoke in a quiet tone, holding the receiver close to her mouth. "To say the least, I do find myself very busy, but the men of this city have lost their appeal." She sighed again, wishing she could go into more detail. The face of Gerald Renner floated through her mind.

"Well, what I really called to say was that Dad wanted me to let you know—" Guy's voice crackled through the phone wires.

"Wait! I know what he wants to ask me," Grace stubbornly interrupted. Her father was strong and loving, but his overprotective nature balked at giving his daughter the freedom she craved. Grace had fought to prove her independence, yet with every fiber of her being, she longed to go home. But to admit defeat when she had had such large dreams…

Grace continued, "I'm sure he wants to know if I have had enough of city life, if I've blown my savings, if I still go to church, if I'm in any trouble, if I…" She ran out of breath.

"Sure he's concerned for you. We all are!" Guy assured her. "He didn't ask anything, but he just wanted me to tell you that Mrs. Miller's dress shop in Dennison is expanding and she is hiring new help with room and board included. I guess he's thinking that you could live closer to home and still have your independence."

Grace hesitated. The job sounded very tempting, but she wanted to make her own choices. Still, the thought of home brought a lump to her throat, especially when she realized that her familiar home and the entire town of Tappan would soon be underwater.

As though he'd read her thoughts, Guy said, "With the water conservancy damming up the valley, things are pretty interesting around here." Guy had his usual positive outlook, but Grace was sure her parents were distraught over the threatened loss of their home. "It would be nice to have you close so you could come home on weekends," Guy added. "Mom and Dad still won't sign the papers that will deed their land to the water conservancy, but more and more of our neighbors have given in. Whatever happens in the end, things here are going to be. . .well, challenging. It might be easier if the family could face it all together."

"Uh. . ." Grace saw Mrs. Schumacher tap the little watch pinned to her lapel. "I'll think about it. Things are busy around here right now. I'll. . .I'll try to call home soon."

Grace hurried her good-byes. She hadn't had a chance to share her own worries with Guy, but she promised herself she would splurge and call him again soon, in another week or two. The next time she and her brother talked, Grace told herself, she would confide in him. She knew Guy would understand. Guy would never say "I told you so."

She smiled to herself, cheered by the thought that her big brother would always be there for her, and then she collected her handbag and marched determinedly for the front door. She still had one hope left if she wanted to be a success in this city—find Gerald Renner and make him give her back her hard-earned money.

Two hours later, she found him in a crowded diner, sitting at the counter in a stylish pin-striped suit and polished leather shoes. She took a deep breath and came up behind him. "I need my money back, Gerald," she ground out, trying to keep her voice low in the crowded diner.

Gerald spun around on his stool. His initial surprise was replaced by a cocky grin on his dazzling handsome face. He stood, towering over her petite frame, and removed his bowler from the next stool.

"Please sit, doll," he droned. "May I order you a coffee or soda?"

Grace stood rigid, holding tight to her resolve. "I have been trying to reach you for over a week. The job at the courthouse turned out to be only a temporary typing position, and I need my savings to pay my rent at the boardinghouse."

"I told you I would get you a car with the money." He sighed. "Please, take a seat, dear. You're drawing attention."

She ignored him. "I don't know how I let you talk me into an automobile. I can't even drive," she spat out and crossed her arms tightly in front of her. Of course, she had driven the horse-drawn carts across her father's fields, but that hardly counted.

The bell on the door jangled as people streamed in and out on this first day of fall. The waitress jarred Grace on her way past, but Grace remained rooted to her spot by the pie case.

"Even if I owned a car, I would have to sell it." Her voice started to rise. "I couldn't afford the gasoline."

Gerald gave a pacifying chuckle and took her elbow in an attempt to draw her back to the stool. She resisted.

"Grace, you want to make it in this town, don't you?" He turned his piercing gaze on her, and her strength began to waver. He had hit her weakest point. "A young woman like you needs a car and a stylish wardrobe to move up in this town. You'll see. Once you have your own automobile, things will turn around for you."

Grace sighed as she finally slumped to the stool. "Then where's my auto? I know I had more than enough money to get at least a used one."

"Well. . ." Gerald's laugh shook. "It will be another week or so before I can get things worked out. . . . Business has ben keeping me running. . . ."

Grace's anger returned. "Where's my money, Gerald?"

"What do you say we go out and paint the town red tomorrow night?" he suggested, ignoring her outburst.

"My money?"

"Sure—I'll bring it along. If you're really certain you don't want that car." Gerald ducked his head over his cooling pie of meat loaf.

❧

Two weeks later, Grace tossed her hat into the corner of her room and lowered herself to the lumpy armchair. She released her thick brown hair from the clasp at the back of her neck. The room was stuffy with the heat of Indian summer. Her feet ached from a long day of job searching, and she longed for a leisurely soak in a tub. If only the one boardinghouse bathroom didn't have a time limit.

After Gerald had stood her up for their date and couldn't be found, she had given up her private room and moved in with another girl, who, like Grace, was only a little over a year out of high school. The arrangement was helping Grace afford to stay in the city, but she was desperate for more than temporary work. Her goal to rise to the top of society was going nowhere but downhill—fast.

She felt herself drifting toward sleep when a knock sounded on the thin door.

"I have a wire for you," Mrs. Schumacher started in her thick clip before Grace had the door opened.

"Thank you."

Mrs. Schumacher held the door open and continued briskly, "Have you seen today's paper? That man you have been seeing since you got here last spring is a wanted criminal."

"Gerald Renner?" A lump formed in her throat.

"Jah, that's the one. He's been robbing good people blind and is now on the run from the law. I could tell he was no saint. I even—"The robust woman broke off her report. "Why, are you ill, child? You look positively sick."

Grace's loose hair curtained her ashen face as her head hung forward.

Mrs. Schumacher grasped the young woman's shoulders. "Do you need to sit?" she asked before a new thought overtook her. "Did that scoundrel take advantage of you? Did he leave you. . .in a compromising state?"

Grace shook her head and murmured, "Only. . .my money." She forced herself to face the realization that she would probably never see her hard-earned money again. It wasn't fair. Even though she hadn't seen Gerald for two weeks, she had held on to the hope that he would eventually bring her the money or a car. She couldn't keep the tears from streaming down her face.

"Oh. . .I should have paid more attention to your money troubles," the large woman moaned as she hugged Grace's slender, petite frame to her ample bosom. "You poor girl.

"Call me if you need someone to talk to. I'll even go with you to make a report to the police." The woman's eyes were unusually moist.

"Thank you, Mrs. Schumacher," Grace finally said as she swiped tears from her streaked cheeks and recollected her rigid composure. She remembered the wire. . .and though her common sense told her otherwise, she couldn't help but hope that it was from Gerald, explaining what he had done. Mrs. Schumacher handed her the message.

Grace tried to smile politely as she closed the door softly behind her landlady.

She retreated to her chair. *I had a feeling that something like this was coming,* she thought. *How could I be so stupid? I even thought he cared for me! How will I ever get back those months of wages? All that time I stayed home and worked in the Tappan store was wasted.* Her blank stare looked past the tiny third-floor window, beyond the four close walls.

I should have married and settled down like any normal young woman. David made a perfectly good offer, but I had to see the world. . .though this is far from what I had in mind.

For some reason the thought of David Matthews sent more tears streaming down her face. She remembered the way he had looked at her the last time she'd seen him, and she saw again the love and hurt in his eyes. A strange yearning filled her.

She gulped back her tears and slowly unfolded her telegram. And then she simply sat frozen, staring at the words in front of her, unable to make sense out of them.

GUY IN BAD ACCIDENT. *Stop.* FATHER IS SICK. *Stop.* TAKE TRAIN HOME SOON. *Stop.* JOHN

Grace choked and read her brother's words again. They couldn't be true. Not Guy, who was so dear to her, to her entire family, and to his best friend, David— to the whole community, in fact. Nothing could happen to Guy. He was like the ground she walked on, always there, always dependable. Surely God would not let this accident have hurt him too badly, surely he would be fine soon. And Father never got sick. He was so strong; he'd always been strong her whole life. *They'll both be fine,* she tried to tell herself.

But a cold chill settled over her, telling her otherwise. *How can all this be happening at once? Oh God, what are You doing? Please. . .heal my brother and my father.*

Her prayer brought her no comfort. Dread filled her heart, a terrible sense of foreboding. She jumped up and began to pack. As she stuffed her clothing into a trunk, a new thought occurred to her: she would have to admit to her family that she couldn't even afford to buy her own train ticket home.

Grace moved to the bed to weep in despair. *Lord, where are You in times like these?*

Chapter 1

December 18, 1936
Dennison, Ohio

Three months later, Grace walked to the depot to catch a ride home from Dennison to Tappan for the Christmas holidays. After Guy's death and her father's declining heath, she had known she could not return to Cleveland; her family needed her to be closer to home. She had taken the job at Mrs. Miller's dress shop, the one Guy had told her about the last time she'd talked to him. The job was not a bad one, but it was boring, and the last months had been a dreary blur of sorrow and discouragement. After her experience with Gerald, she had no desire to return to Cleveland—but she felt no excitement about living the rest of her life in Dennison either.

Going home today brought her no excitement either. Her parents' house was not the same since her father's illness and Guy's death, and she almost dreaded her visits there. Things were too different; Guy's absence was too painful; and soon the entire town would be gone, flooded by the new dam.

Reaching the depot, she stood rigid by the window, too tense to sit on one of the long benches. She was here to meet Mr. Matthews, her family's neighbor and her only way home today from town. She could see that he had already gone out to the platform to await the train, even though a stiff, cold wind was blowing. The chill had hit with force this past week and Little Stillwater Creek was almost frozen over.

Grace looked now toward the creek, trying to think of something besides the man who would soon be arriving on the train. A train's whistle could be heard as it neared the station from the direction of the neighboring town, and her stomach clenched with nervousness.

This would be the first time in eighteen months that she had seen David Matthews, Mr. Matthews' son, Guy's best friend—and the man who had once asked her to marry him. David could not come home for Guy's funeral, and Grace could only imagine the grief he suffered alone. Her own sorrow had been unbearable and she could barely remember details of the day.

She turned now and looked over the waiting room, thinking perhaps it would be better to sit than be found waiting by the window. But most of the seats had been taken. Being the holiday season, the depot was extremely busy on this Saturday afternoon with shoppers traveling to and from the bigger cities and other people who were already making the journey home for Christmas. Grace could see no comfortable seat available in the small waiting room, so she turned back to the window, pulling her black woolen coat closer as the door opened to receive a new flow of travelers.

The brick-lined platform was full of people, large carts of luggage, and boxes. Grace had to crane her neck to find Mr. Matthews where he waited eagerly for his son to alight the train that could now be seen chugging into the station. Grace imagined David sitting awkwardly on the train, out of place among all the finely dressed people. Of course he wouldn't be wearing the farmer's overalls that he always used to wear, but she could picture him in an ill-fitting suit, his old misshapen hat jammed on his head. She wondered how a farm boy like David had managed all these months in the city. She had been surprised when David had found employment in Detroit.

The last time she and David had spoken, she had been filled with ambition and plans. The memory of her rejection of his marriage proposal was between them now, but she would have been embarrassed to face him even without that, now that all her fine plans had come to nothing.

Working every day along with her four roommates in Mrs. Miller's dress shop was getting old for Grace. She was growing to hate the tedium of the stuffy upstairs workroom with its treadle sewing machine that pumped all day long. The widowed Mrs. Miller had been unusually kind though at the time of Guy's funeral, advancing Grace the money to move closer to home. Grace owed her much and she felt obligated to stay with the position and do a good job.

But it had been a long, busy week at the dress shop, and even if she dreaded facing again the changes in her home, she was glad for the extended holiday. She could have been home by now if only her brother John had picked her up at the dress shop like he usually did for her weekend visit. Then she could have avoided this embarrassing meeting with David, at least for a little longer. But John had said he was occupied today with his own business, and he had made the arrangement for Mr. Matthews to pick her up instead.

Grace frowned as she thought of her brother John. Since Guy's death, he seemed to have distanced himself from the family, spending more and more time with his new girlfriend. His changed attitude toward his family was one of the many disturbing changes that Grace faced each time she went home—but where Guy's death and her father's illness filled her with sorrow, the change in John made her feel frustrated and angry. *How can John be so selfish? Doesn't he understand that we need him now more than before?*

Grace pushed away her anger with John and scanned the passengers descending from the train. Her eyes were drawn to a handsome young man in a well-tailored navy suit. The brim of his stylish hat had slid to one side and hid his face from her view. He held his head high as he scanned the area, and she wondered if he were in town on business.

She continued to watch as he neared the building, but quickly the young man's hat was sent off with the wind by Mr. Matthews's jovial greeting. Red hair glistened in the winter sunlight. She felt her mouth drop open as she recognized David as the stylish gentleman.

She recalled the last time she had spoken with him. David had been wearing his old overalls, his dull red hair allowed to curl over his ears. He had been well-toned from the years of farmwork, but the same hard work had always seemed to give him a tired look. This new David was nothing like she had expected.

David retrieved his hat and followed his father to the door. Grace found herself lifting a hand to check her long hair clasped at the back of her neck, a luxury she afforded herself and chose not to cut to fit new fashion fads. David spotted her even before he stepped up over the threshold and gave her a warm, broad smile.

"Gracie, how are you?"

Grace was surprised by his use of her childhood name. Only Guy had used it in recent years, and the name made her eyes sting.

David's voice was soft and kind. He took his hat in his left hand and gently squeezed her shoulder with his right. "I'm so sorry I couldn't make it home for Guy's funeral." Grace detected moisture in his eyes. "You know he was like a brother to me, too, but praise God, he's with Christ."

Grace couldn't find her voice. This attractive, confident gentleman barely resembled the friend of her childhood. Neither did he appear to have even a flickering memory of their last conversation, when she had flatly rejected his offer of marriage. He seemed to have captured everything she had once sought after—worldly charm and sophistication. His change lacked the pride and haughtiness that many of her friends had displayed however. But were his show of faith and sympathy honest? Honesty and faith had become very important to Grace.

❧

Grace sat in the rear seat of Mr. Matthews's Ford Phaeton on the ten-mile trip to her home near the village of Tappan. She still had barely said more than hello to David, and now he and his father were enjoying their first reunion in nearly a year.

"That's a nice suit you have there, son. That Detroit car factory must be treating you pretty good," Mr. Matthews noted.

"It was past time for me to buy a new suit and I could only afford one, so I decided it should be a dandy."

Father and son chuckled over this wisdom.

But strangely, it bothered Grace that David might care so much about appearances. She ran her hand across the lap of her sturdy navy work dress and sighed inaudibly. Was she jealous of David or simply disappointed? After all, hadn't she always secretly scorned his ordinary, worn, farming clothes?

"Have you bought one of those new cars yet?" Mr. Matthews asked his son.

"I don't need a car. The city offers great transportation, and I ride a train to work every day," David stated. "I could get a good deal from the company, though, and may take advantage of it someday."

Grace smothered a cough, thinking of her failed attempt to buy a car.

"I'm up for a promotion," David told his father. "Supervisor. They could let me know by New Year's."

David's father was thrilled, but Gracie wrestled with strangely troubled emotions as the car traveled through the frozen farmland. They crossed the railroad tracks at Station 15, and Grace recalled the awful day when she first learned that her brother Guy had been killed at that crossing. There had been little left of his barely used Chrysler.

"Yes, that's the place," Grace heard Mr. Matthews's soft reply to a question David must have asked. "Such a tragedy."

David turned and looked over the high seat back. "Gracie, I don't know what to say."

"Don't. . .I'm fine. He was your friend, too," Grace said softly and quickly turned to avoid his eyes as she swallowed against the nauseating emptiness in her chest. She kept her defenses firmly in place. The less she talked about such things, the better she could cope.

Within a couple of miles they would be passing through Main Street in Tappan. The town had become a refuge to Grace after her big-city experience last summer. She hated to think that it would all be underwater someday, and she wondered how David would view the village in comparison to Detroit. Would he think that the small town was so little that it would be of little loss to the new lake?

"Look, there it is," David called out, pointing to the new dam. "It's huge. I can't believe it's done." His voice reflected awe. Did she also detect regret, or was it just her wishful thinking? *Misery enjoys company*, Gracie realized.

She followed his pointing finger to the massive dirt and cement structure. The dam had been completed in October and was already collecting water that would eventually cover their beautiful valley.

"Has anyone moved yet?" David asked.

Mr. Matthews answered, "Just the Cloughs and the Masons since the dam went right through their properties. Most of the rest will go in the spring, while some will stay till the water pushes 'em out."

Grace squirmed on the cold leather seat. Would it take a flood to move her family out?

⌒

It would have been hard for David not to notice the decline of the Rudmans' once prosperous farm. Tall weeds lined the drive, still harboring traces of the last snow. Tractor and bulldozer tracks from the dam construction made muddy ruts across the western fields and through broken fence lines. The Rudmans' remaining livestock were crowded into a barnyard pen.

Mr. Matthews pulled the car up along the side of the peeling farmhouse as Grace's older brother John rushed out to meet them. "I'm sure glad you're home, Grace," he almost shouted. "Hey David, welcome back."

David offered Grace a hand out of the backseat, but she seemed to shrink from his slightest touch.

John filled the sudden silence with annoying chatter. "Mother's been like a ruffled hen all day long. She gets so anxious, and none of the church ladies were able to stop in and lend a hand today."

Grace straightened her shoulders and marched through the kitchen door. David grabbed her small suitcase and started to follow her, but John stopped him. "Let me take that. You'll be wanting to get home."

David stared at John, not understanding his cool welcome, and John ducked his head as if in shame.

David felt his father approach. "Son, I told you Mr. Rudman was sick, but. . . I failed to tell you that he isn't getting better."

"If that's all, then I'll see him now and not wait," David said and sidestepped John to the door.

The kitchen was a jumble of half-finished projects. Biscuit dough was rolled out but not cut. Unwashed dishes were stacked in a sink full of soapy water, and the teakettle whistled on the old coal-fueled water heater. Grace stood in the middle of the room with her coat over her arm and her shoulders sagging.

"Grace," Mrs. Rudman's high-pitched voice preceded her pencil-thin body around the doorway, "your father will be so excited to see his little girl."

She seemed like the same energetic woman David remembered as she fussed over her grown daughter, yet a veil of false gaiety shrouded any feelings of joy.

"Oh David!" Mrs. Rudman's eyes teared immediately as she reached for the boy she had known in the man before her. "How I have longed to see you again. Guy will. . .well, we all want you to stay to supper."

David ignored her slip. "I would love to, but I must go home to see my mother first."

"Of course, I'm sure she has a whole spread laid out for your return," Mrs. Rudman said.

"Is Mr. Rudman awake?" David asked. "I would like to say hello."

"Well. . .he doesn't take many visitors. He—" Mrs. Rudman stammered.

"I'll just take a minute."

"I wish you would wait until he is better," Mrs. Rudman said sadly.

"Oh Mother," Grace moaned with impatience, "I'll take him in. You can't keep all of Father's friends away. You just don't know if Father will—" Grace stopped as her mother's face clouded.

Grace motioned for David to follow her and they entered the front parlor. A rocking chair was placed between the fireplace and the piano with a good view out the window toward the town in the east. But Grace's father was leaning dangerously forward in the chair with his head rested against the windowpane so he could look to the west where the new dam hid the setting sun.

David quickly took hold of Mr. Rudman's shoulders and eased him back into the chair. It was obvious that this man was not the robust farmer that David had once known. Grace straightened the quilt on her father's lap as David surveyed the vacant look in the man's eyes and the droop to the left side of his face.

"Hello, Father," Grace soothed. "I brought an old friend."

"Good to see you, Mr. Rudman," David forced around the lump in his throat.

"David will be here for Christmas and will come to visit again." Grace spoke clearly and precisely to her father, then led David back to the kitchen.

She stopped in the hall. "I'm sorry you weren't told," she managed to say without looking at him.

"When did the stroke occur?"

"The day of Guy's death. That was the hardest blow, but he hadn't really been the same since the conservancy first came to take the farm." Her eyes shone, betraying the moisture that had gathered.

David longed to ease her stiff shoulders and comfort her, but it seemed as if she had placed a prickly wall between them. His hand reached for her.

She stepped back. "You'll want to be getting home," she offered and excused herself up the back stairs.

David promised Mrs. Rudman that he would return for a piece of her custard pie the next afternoon, then walked slowly to the car where his own father waited patiently. John's car was gone; he had already taken off to follow his own whims. David wondered why John would leave so soon after his sister's return home.

Oh Lord, how the Rudmans need Your comforting assurance, he prayed as he settled into the car.

Chapter 2

The waves were deep and numerous. Beams of winter sunlight highlighted their crests, while their troughs were rich in dark color. There would be no containing the waves, and they splashed out in every direction. Though wild, they invited the curious spectator to take a closer look.

David could hear the preacher's voice in the background as he delivered Sunday's message and his Bible lay open on his lap to the book of Luke, but David's gaze was glued to a head of gorgeous mahogany hair two pews in front of him. He had never given Grace's hair much notice before; he remembered her best in braids. Now she styled her hair in becoming waves that reflected the sunlight to its greatest advantage.

When he had left the valley about eighteen months ago, everything about Grace had consumed his thoughts. While living in Detroit, though, he thought he had come to the point that Grace, and marriage in general, were not as important to him. He had found that he had much to offer his job and community, and he still had much to learn about love.

Then why did the slightest tilt of her head catch his attention and the changes of light on her hair fascinate his imagination? Why did he long to understand all that she and her family had been through since their last parting?

David joined the congregation in the closing hymn and prayer and he moved with his parents toward the center aisle. Many people wished to greet him, and they clogged the center aisle as they offered handshakes and kind words.

From David's side he could see Grace trying to squeeze through the press of bodies. He turned to meet her squarely. "How are you this morning, Gracie?"

"Fine, thanks." She smiled, but continued to inch down the aisle.

"And where is your mother today? I missed her fine piano playing."

"She couldn't leave Father alone and insisted that I come in her place." Grace sounded tired. "I need to get home right away to help her," she sighed, unable to move farther down the aisle.

"Come." David took hold of her elbow and pulled her back toward the front of the church. He was almost surprised that she didn't resist him.

They slipped through a small door at the right and through the pastor's study. Few of the parishioners would think of disturbing this private chamber, but David felt like he was on a mission of mercy to see Grace home with speed.

Another small door led to the rear of the church where dead briars clawed at the siding in the biting wind.

"Now," David said, "where did you leave your car?"

"John dropped me off on his way to meet Melissa, his fiancée, for church up the valley."

"You weren't planning to walk home in this wind, were you?"

"It really won't take long. I walked it almost every day when I worked at the store," Grace flatly stated and started at a fast pace down the alley.

David fell in step beside her, skirting nearly frozen mud puddles. They walked in silence, turning onto Rose Street and leaving the village's limits. Two carloads of people from church passed by, waving cheerfully.

Then Grace broke the silence between them. "Your parents will wonder where you went," she stated simply.

"Yes," he acknowledged. "You should have let us drive you home."

She didn't respond, but bowed her head to the force of the wind.

"Gracie…" He had many things he would like to ask her, but he didn't know if she would answer. Instead, he found himself saying, "Do you remember how when we were all kids, you, Guy, John, and I would explore the woods on that hill over there?" He pointed to the right and Grace turned to look.

"Sure, but the 'castle' rock with the interesting hiding places is gone—" Her steady voice broke. "They blasted out the side of the hill to get rocks for that dam."

"So many changes we can't control."

"Be glad you haven't been around to witness the worst of it."

David could hear her bitterness and chose not to speak for several paces. His parents drove slowly up beside them, but he waved them on even as the wind whipped around them. Liberated strands of Grace's hair danced around her sad, little face.

David chose a new topic. "How has John been? Where is he working?"

She took a deep breath. "I don't see a whole lot of John. He works for Melissa's father at a county office in Cadiz and spends most of his time with her family. He has very little time for the farm…or helping Mother. He can be so juvenile that you would think he was the youngest."

David hid the smile generated by her sibling frustrations. He had never had brothers or sisters to relate to. The Rudman children had been his extended family.

"One could say," David reasoned, "that John has a lot on his mind and is trying to avoid anything stressful or—"

"Then he needs to grow up!" Grace was adamant. "We'll get through this, but…"

"Yes, you will make it, and I agree that everyone should do his share. Would you like me to talk to John?"

"Sure, if he'll listen…" She slowly changed her mind. "No, it really doesn't have anything to do with you."

"Call me anytime you need a big brother," David offered.

Grace didn't reply and her pace quickened as her driveway neared. She hurried along the rutted lane without looking back.

David stopped, but called, "I promised to stop in later for some of your mother's pie."

"Fine" was the only answer the wind carried to him, and he turned to the east to follow the road on across the creek to his home.

⌒

"Can you imagine a place that will seat 36,000 people?" Grace overheard David asking Mr. Rudman. There was no response and David continued with enthusiasm, "I went to a Tigers' baseball game after the additions to the stadium were made and it was fantastic!"

Grace leaned against the wall in the hallway thinking it was nice of David to offer to sit with Mr. Rudman and carry on a one-sided conversation without knowing if anything he said was heard or understood.

David had arrived in time to share a piece of pie with Mrs. Rudman before evening church service. Then he volunteered to sit with Mr. Rudman while Grace and her mother attended church, but Grace felt it was her duty to stay with her father. She straightened the kitchen and found other odd jobs to avoid sitting with the men in the parlor. But when nothing more needed her immediate attention, she found herself drawn to the parlor door by David's rich voice.

Now David had moved on to Detroit car manufacturing and was explaining the attributes of the V-8 engine to Mr. Rudman. Then he extolled the virtues of the brand-new Zephyr that Lincoln had introduced. David worked at Mr. Ford's factory where the Zephyr was made. Grace understood very little of the jargon—she was still waiting to learn how to drive an automobile—but she enjoyed David's enthusiasm and felt herself relaxing.

"The Lord knew what He was doing when He sent me to Michigan. I wouldn't have believed I could be happy outside the farm. But now my work in Detroit will make it easer to see the farm go," David quietly said.

Grace came to attention and stood stiff. *Lucky you. If I had married you, farming would still be the only thing you knew and you would be faced with losing your livelihood. I did you a favor.*

Grace turned to the back stairs and climbed slowly. *Why does it seem that God clearly directed you, David—and not me? If marriage wasn't the right choice for me, neither was going to the big city.*

She entered her bedroom and looked around at this haven that would be gone much sooner than she would like to think about. Her window faced up the valley and she could see David's family farm. Mr. Matthews had already torn down the large barn for lumber, and the house would be moved as soon as possible to a new location on the ridge.

Friends and neighbors were moving on, finding new direction for their lives and starting over. But Grace felt that her life was at a standstill. Her mother refused to make any decision about their farm without Father's direction. John had dealt with it by mentally removing himself from his family and the farming duties. Grace knew her dressmaking job was her future no matter what happened to the farm, though she didn't like it.

"Grace!" her mother shrieked.

Grace jumped up from the edge of the bed where she had been resting and raced down the stairs. Her mother met her in the hall, still wearing her coat. Grace could hear her father coughing intensely.

"Help me get your father in bed, now! So much company has given him a setback," Mrs. Rudman spoke sharply.

David stood over Mr. Rudman rubbing his shoulders and offering soothing words. He met Grace with an apologetic look. Mrs. Rudman refused David's assistance, and she and Grace shouldered the limp man's weight between them.

When Grace returned from settling her father in the downstairs bedroom, David hadn't moved from the parlor. "I'm sorry about that; I didn't mean to excite him," David said.

"It's not your fault," Grace assured him.

"But Gracie. . ." David tentatively started, "I think your father was trying to say something before the coughing started. Does he ever speak?"

Grace was surprised. "He usually never makes a sound."

"He has this cane." David pointed near the rocking chair. "Does he ever use it?"

"No. . .but. . .I think he could. Though he doesn't seem to have it in him to try."

"Can I come again tomorrow? I would like to try talking to him again."

"I don't think Mother will allow him to be disturbed for a few days. You better not come."

David moved to the back door. "Gracie, I. . ."

"Thank you for coming," she quickly said, not wanting to hear any more apologies—or anything. "We. . .I mean, I think Father enjoyed your company."

A pained expression crossed David's face, but he left without further words.

Chapter 3

David stayed away the next day. Grace's father spent most of his hours in his bedroom, and Grace's mother kept her busy creating a magnitude of Christmas delights which included sugar cookies, cherry turnovers, mincemeat pies, braided date bread, and much more

Tuesday morning, Mrs. Rudman put coal in the little stove that heated the hot water pipes and started the fire going. Grace watched as she moved on to lay wood in the old cookstove. Grace's father had offered to buy a new electric range not long after electricity reached their corner of the world, but Mrs. Rudman remained faithful to her stove even while her kitchen had the conveniences of an electric refrigerator and some small appliances. Today the heat from the stove would feel good as a chill seeped in around the window frames.

Grace got the recipe box from a window shelf and laid out her grandmother's recipe for Ozark Pudding. She read through the instructions.

2 eggs
1 teaspoon vanilla
1 teaspoon baking powder
1½ cup sugar
½ cup flour
1 teaspoon salt
2 cups apples, diced
1 cup nuts, chopped

Beat eggs and vanilla, add dry ingredients. Fold in apples and nuts. Spread in greased 8-inch square pan. Bake in a hot oven (375 degrees) for 50 to 60 minutes.

Then she laid out her ingredients. She could mix up the pudding quickly and it could bake while she took a tin of cookies into town for the widowed Mrs. Douglas. Normally Mrs. Rudman would invite older folks like Mrs. Douglas who had no family to join the Rudmans for Christmas dinner, but she had declared there would be no company this year.

Grace was peeling apples when a crash came from the bedroom. She and her mother raced to the room and found Father sitting on the floor with the bedside table upset beside him.

He looked up at them as they entered the room, and Grace saw something in his eyes, an expression that reminded her of the father who had been gone for a long time. But then he lowered his eyes and moaned, long and loud.

Grace noticed that his cane was clutched in his right hand. She said nothing but pointed her mother's attention to it.

Mrs. Rudman frowned.

They worked together under the strain of lifting Mr. Rudman to the edge of the bed and set to the task of changing him from pajamas to day clothes with little comment about the incident.

Grace was sponging his face clean when a loud popping noise came from the kitchen. She sighed, laid aside her washcloth, and prepared to investigate the noise. Suddenly an explosion rocked the house and filled the bedroom with a gray, acrid smoke.

Mrs. Rudman screamed. Mr. Rudman began making muttering noises. Grace was frozen to her place near the door. She was unsure what could have created the explosion and what she would find outside the room.

There was loud banging on the front door of the house, and finally Grace was able to propel herself into the front parlor. She felt like her body moved in slow motion. The smoke was still thick from the direction of the kitchen and she opened the door.

"Thank God, you are all right! How about your parents?" David rushed past her and toward the smoky kitchen.

Grace was still rooted to the spot.

"The water heater exploded. There's no fire, but a lot of mess." David pulled her outside to the porch. He took her shoulders and drew her to him. Grace took a deep breath of the fresh air mixed with his freshly washed hair and allowed David to hold her. "I was just coming up the drive when the kitchen windows blew out and I saw smoke. Where are your parents?"

Grace came alert and pushed away from David's warm embrace. "They're in the bedroom," she said, shaking her head and losing hairpins.

David helped Grace move Mr. Rudman to a chair on the front porch. It was a very cold morning and they wrapped him tightly in several blankets and quilts. Mrs. Rudman, who still seemed to be in shock, sat on the top porch step mopping a continuous flow of tears.

"I'll inspect the damage," David announced and headed through the front of the house to the kitchen. This time Grace stayed right on his heels.

The room was swiftly clearing of smoke but everything was black with soot, ashes, and hot coals. Two of the three windows were blown out as well as the glass in the china hutch. The coal water heater lay in a crumbled mass of iron with hot coals spilled around it and steam from broken water pipes clouding it.

"Frozen pipes," was David's only comment.

Grace picked her way over the dirt and coals to where she had been preparing her pudding recipe. Her apples were black with soot and a hot coal sat in the middle of her recipe card, charring her grandmother's script. Red coals were everywhere, smoldering on the floor, table, counter, and almost every other surface.

"We need to pick these up," Grace said and reached for a spoon and large crock.

David opened the remaining window and the door, then took a snow shovel from the back step and started scooping up coals from the floor.

"Look there, Gracie!" David pointed to the ceiling.

In the ceiling, embedded at least two inches deep, was the door from the water heater's fuel bin. Grace thought about how her mother and she had been working near the water heater just minutes before it burst.

"Praise God you weren't in here at the time," David said.

"Father fell out of bed, and mother and I were dressing him when it exploded," Grace said with wonder. If only her father could understand what he saved them from.

"It is good that you happened to be coming this way," Grace commented as she watched David work. She brushed coals from the counter into her crock. "What brought you by?" she casually asked.

David smiled. "I couldn't stay away."

Surely not from me!

"I wanted to try talking to your father again. Maybe his mind is not as paralyzed as it has seemed. Certainly he has every right to be depressed and withdrawn. . ."

Of course, that's all it is, a good deed toward my father. . .but if he thinks he can make a difference. . .

"The water heater," Mrs. Rudman said from the doorway. "Father always thought to check those kinds of things," she continued without emotion. "Can we move him into the parlor now?"

"Certainly." David hurried to the task.

"I think I'll lie down," Mrs. Rudman told Grace as she trudged up the stairs. "Oh, and the man from the conservancy is headed up the drive. Would you send him away?"

"Uh. . .yes, Mother."

Gracie laid her cleaning supplies on the table and looked around at this latest disaster. So much had happened to her family in the last few months, more than any normal family should have to endure. They were all running out of the strength to deal with new crises. When would this testing end?

She met Mr. Richards at the front door and explained the morning's events, apologizing that neither her father nor mother was available to talk with him.

The man was kind, but he explained, "Miss Rudman, surely your family realizes that the conservancy has made its best offer. We have obtained rights to all the property surrounding this farm—over 2,000 acres total—and the valley will begin to flood as soon as the spring rains come. You can hold out as long as you wish, but it doesn't change the fact that a large lake will begin to form here in less than a year." Mr. Richards stepped off the porch and prepared to leave. "Please have a representative from your family come and see me at my office in town at your earliest convenience. We want to make this change as smooth as possible. Good day. . .and merry Christmas."

He tipped his black hat to Grace as he got into his car. She watched him leave their property and looked to the west. The dam was a large, ugly mound of dirt. Its very presence was choking the life from her family's farm. It had already completely concealed any evidence of two other farms.

Then she looked toward the creek. It still looked innocent enough, though its waters had been allowed to pool downstream at the new gatehouse. She remembered many summer days of wading in the cool stream—and many springs when it spilled over is banks. Grace realized that someday people would boat over this land and pull fish from its waters. Would she even recognize where their farm had been?

A tear slipped down her cold cheek, and she turned to go back inside. David met Grace inside the front door.

"He's right, Gracie. None of us can stop this lake now." He was leaning against the wall, charming in his soot-covered clothes.

Grace was frustrated that his simple words and good looks would stir her emotions. "I know, and I'm sure Mother knows, but I can't make the decision for her."

"I'll continue to pray," he said while his gaze roved her face.

"Perhaps you should pray that God doesn't send us another disaster." Her temper flared.

A frown creased his gentle brow. "Please, don't blame Him. Your family is still together. You just need to trust Him for your future."

"Don't preach at me, David. My family is a shadow of what it used to be," Grace blurted out before she slowly began to calm down. "I know the Lord can turn out all things for the best—" she took a deep breath "—but I just don't think I can take another ordeal."

David's hand reached for her, but she plodded toward the kitchen, pulling on her last reserve of energy.

⌒

Grace and David worked together all afternoon on repairs to the kitchen. David's father came with two men from town to help board up the broken windows and remove the trash. Grace's mother had stayed in her upstairs bedroom all day, and Grace checked her often to see that all was right.

It was past the supper hour before they had a chance to sit down. Mrs. Matthews had sent a warm casserole over in the late afternoon, and Grace was relieved of cooking in the disarrayed kitchen.

David sat with Grace in the parlor while she spooned the noodle casserole into her father's mouth. She had found a tin of undamaged cookies, and

David munched them contentedly.

"Thanks for all your help today," she offered without looking at him.

"You're welcome. I'm just glad I was here."

"I'm sure this isn't the restful visit home you had planned."

He chuckled. "At least I have been here among family and friends who are most dear to me." He meant what he said, and if he had known the extent of the Rudmans' troubles, he would have found a way to come home sooner.

He watched Gracie wipe her father's face and tuck his quilt around his lap. David marveled at the strength she had shown, not just today but ever since he had returned home. He had always admired her energy, but before it had been demonstrated in her zest for her own life, creativity, and dreams.

Some of her spark might be gone, or buried, but her determination was still strong. *She would have been a good wife for me. . .and she still would be a good wife. But I'm past that point in my life. I don't have to marry right away. I can take my time and save money for a home.*

He watched the loose curls of her hair bounce with each move and admired the tilt of her pert nose. Would she wait? He shook his head, and his cheeks flamed from the ridiculous thoughts he'd been having. *She still sees me as a brother, and that isn't likely to change.*

Chapter 4

Christmas Eve came to the valley on Thursday under the grip of an extended cold spell. A light snow dusted the ground, masking some of the scars from the dam construction. The creek appeared to have frozen solid and some of the youth were excited about a hastily planned skating party for that afternoon.

The morning was very still throughout the house. Grace's mother had not stirred, and like the last two days, Grace didn't expect to see much of her. She had been staying close to her upstairs bedroom.

Grace prepared her father for the day and settled him into his chair near the parlor window. On impulse, she turned the radio on for him, and livestock prices were the topic of the moment.

She anticipated spending her morning in the kitchen working on a new batch of bread. She missed the sunlight the two boarded-up windows had given the room. The dirt from the explosion had been cleared away, but the damage was still very obvious.

She was startled when someone came clattering down the staircase.

"John! I didn't even know you were home!"

"I slipped in late last night. I needed to come by for a few things and I figured I'd spend the night."

"Well. . .we've missed seeing you. Where have you been staying?"

"I have a friend or two down in Cadiz way. I see you've kept pretty busy though," he remarked as he circled the room. "If this house keeps falling apart, we won't have to worry about moving it." He laughed at his joke.

Grace didn't enjoy his humor and her anger rose. His careless attitude sickened her. "Mother and I could have used your help. Luckily David was here and he rounded up some men to haul trash and board up the windows."

"Ah, David, the lost son returned. I'm sure Mother certainly enjoys having him around." John's eyes narrowed with the thought. "Though lacking in Guy's flair for pomp and circumstance, he still could do no wrong. I, on the other hand, worry my parents sick about everything—my education, my job, my choice of a wife. . ."

"Nonsense. Why are you so bitter?" Grace couldn't understand his attitude. "We miss you and want to get to know Melissa. Can you bring her over tomorrow?"

"I doubt it." He gathered his coat and a small bag from a corner chair. "Gotta go. See ya later, sis." He was out the door before Grace got in another word.

Midway through the morning as Grace was placing her raised dough in the oven, Mrs. Rudman entered the kitchen for the first time after almost two days of solitude. She wandered around the room, running her hand along the marred countertop and surveying the other changes to her large kitchen.

Grace watched her slow, deliberate movements. Though her hair was sprinkled with silver, she still had a look of youth and refinement about her. Grace had always admired her mother and hated the lines that worry and grief had etched into her face.

"Well, Grace dear." Her mother finally turned to her with a sweet smile. "I have lived in this same house since the day of my marriage to your father. I shared it with his parents for nearly ten years, and I raised my children here. The property around here has sold and our farm will flood whether or not we sign it over to the conservancy. It will be sad to see the place go, but the conservancy has made a very fair offer." She sat down in a wooden chair that had lost an arm in the blast.

Grace continued to watch her mother in silence, but she noticed a definite peace about her that had not been present for many months.

"The Lord and I have had a long talk. He has made me see that I can't go back to the past, the present is constantly changing, and the future is His alone to determine. Nothing I can do can change these facts." She held out her hands to Grace. "My sweet daughter, I think so often of your brother Guy, and finally, I can be happy for him. He is with his Savior." She drew a work-roughened hand along Grace's cheek. "I highly recommend the comfort it brings when you place your trust in the Lord."

Grace hugged her mother and felt she understood the transformation of her attitude. Her mother had grasped onto the faith that Grace had acknowledged but not yet placed her whole trust in.

" 'Lay up for yourselves treasures in heaven, where neither moth nor rust doth corrupt, and where thieves do not break through nor steal.'" Mrs. Rudman quoted. "We will take what we can with us to remember this old place by, but it will forever remain in our hearts."

She patted Grace's cheek as unbidden tears came to the young woman's eyes.

"Your father and I will move in with Aunt Maggie in Bowerston. She is no young thing and could use the company," Mrs. Rudman continued with a voice full of new purpose. "In fact, she offered the idea to your father back in the summer."

"John and Melissa will marry by March and live in Cadiz." She rose from her chair and hooked her arm around her daughter's waist. "As for you, my dear, dressmaking is a fine vocation, but I do wish you would marry, too."

Grace swallowed hard. *You sound as if I can just snap my fingers and make it happen.*

"It's sad that things didn't work out with you and David last year, but with him home. . ."

"Mother!" Grace choked. "I hardly think that's an issue anymore. With Guy gone, David is even more like a brother to me."

"Exactly!" Mrs. Rudman smiled and dismissed the topic with a flick of her wrist. "That bread is already starting to smell wonderful. You are a good cook, dear, but why don't you take the afternoon and enjoy yourself with the kids at the skating party? You haven't had any time for socializing since you've been home."

"I. . .I don't need to play when there is so much to get ready for Christmas."

"Your skates are in the attic," Mrs. Rudman stated and gave Grace a playful shove toward the stairs.

᠎᠎᠎

The ground was cold beneath Grace as she sat on the bank of the stream to lace her skates. She pulled the laces tight and the one in her right hand snapped. It was old and frayed.

"Having trouble?" David's voice boomed from over her head.

A chill tickled her spine, and she hoped it was due to the slight breeze blowing across the frozen landscape.

"I've got it. Thanks," Grace smiled up at him. David looked tall and strong from her vantage point. Even under a blue stocking cap, his face was handsome and friendly. She quickly lowered her gaze and knotted her broken lace.

"Can I give you a hand up?"

"It's not necessary—thanks," she blurted, uncomfortable with the emotions churning inside her. She felt like a schoolgirl with a crush, a woman starving for affection, and a stranger come home, all in one. She couldn't comprehend the power he had over her, and it had been like this ever since the day he stepped down from the train.

When Guy was alive she had thought of David as merely Guy's shadow. She had always been fond of David, of course, but she had thought of him almost as an extension of her beloved brother, not really important in himself. Suddenly, he had emerged from Guy's shadow, taking her by surprise. She wondered now if all along he hadn't been more important to her than she had ever realized.

"Well. . .okay." His shoulders dropped as Grace watched him move onto the ice-covered creek and into a group of young townsfolk.

She eased to her feet and struggled for a footing on the bank. She wobbled, nearly fell, then balanced herself against a sapling.

She brushed dirt, snow, and dry grass from her pleated plaid skirt and navy stockings and straightened her coat that sported large, hand-carved buttons. The buttons were a luxury that Grace's mother had griped about, but Grace enjoyed the way they made a sensible, sturdy coat feel special.

Finally, she took a tentative step onto the ice and waited for her ankles to adjust to the skates. Her body teetered like an intoxicated idiot before she got the hang of it.

A shoulder bumped into her, upsetting her precarious balance and seating her hard on the ice.

"Oops," Thomas Cord chuckled. "Reality hurts," he sneered. "You Rudmans think you can hold out and make the conservancy pay you a bundle for an ugly strip of used-up farmland? My dad got top dollar for the best farmland in this valley." He towered over her with his gangly teenage frame. "The conservancy doesn't care if your place floods—now that they own everything around it." He glided away, obviously pleased with his performance.

Grace saw David making strides toward her, and she shot him a warning glare. She gingerly got to her feet and worked at establishing her balance once again.

David hung at a short distance from her with a young girl at each elbow trying to gain his attention.

Grace slowly glided upstream away from the majority of skaters. She knew that some people in the valley looked down on her family for holding out on the conservancy. Many thought that the Rudmans were greedy for money, but there were still those who cared enough to understand the family's plight and sympathize.

Soon Grace was joined by the pastor's daughter, Lydia, and her friends. The lighthearted chatter of the girls made a nice diversion for Grace's train of thought.

Often, though, her attention was pulled to David. She found interest in his skating partners. No doubt, David was used to having several young women on his arm in the city. A handsome young man with a good job was quite an attraction, and it didn't hurt that he had a friendly, clean-cut personality to go with it.

Grace shook her head free from the web of thoughts. *The gal who reels him in will sure be lucky. That is. . .if she's smart enough to say "yes."*

❧

David longed to go to Grace, to defend her and ease her discomfort. Her stubborn show of independence frustrated him. Pain pierced his heart when she made it clear that she didn't need his assistance.

He watched her now as a group formed around her. She smiled easily at the youths and talked freely with them. She tried to figure eight with Lydia and laughed about their crooked lines. Then she clapped and cheered for a child who demonstrated a simple spin. When she glanced at him, though, her face lost its animation, as though she had immediately erected a wall around her emotions. He longed to break through her guarded borders and see her at ease like that with him.

In the past he had seen her as a carefree tomboy, following her brothers and him into the woods on childhood adventures. He had been present as she had talked freely of her dreams and desires with her brother Guy, but always it had been Guy's attention she craved and David was ignored.

David turned his attention to one of the young women at his side. She had an annoying giggle that hurt his ears while the other exaggerated her wobbly footing on the narrow blades and blotched his arm with long, sharp fingernails.

He quickly tired of their prattle and found himself watching Grace more as as she skated with the pastor's daughter, warmed her hands by the bonfire on the bank, and wandered upstream alone.

David grew edgy when Grace went beyond a low hanging tree and followed the curve of the stream out of his view. He could no longer manage polite conversation with his companions and soon broke away from the group.

He skirted the clusters of skaters and kept close to the shore as he wound his way upstream. He was putting a good distance between himself and the other skaters when he heard a splash ahead of him. David sped along the frozen creek, sending snow flying out behind him.

Chapter 5

Grace enjoyed the solitude of the upper stream. The arching trees provided a canopied effect with their snow-frosted branches. She could hear the song of an unseen cardinal while the voices of the skaters grew dimmer. She knew some were headed downstream toward the new pond at the gatehouse, while she entertained the thought of continuing her course all the way home.

Here the stream had widened and she moved toward the shore, unsure that the ice in the middle would be solid. The cardinal seemed to be following her as its song came to her loud and clear. She looked up to spot him on an overhanging branch.

The ice cracked beneath her blades and Grace tilted. Snow covered the ice and she couldn't determine the direction of the crack. She inched forward and closer to the shore.

The ice gave way underneath her. She gasped and dropped over two feet to the rocky creek bed. Her left ankle buckled and the frigid water instantly soaked her nearly to her waist.

She wanted to cry, to scream, but she felt stiff as if frozen in place. The water flowed freely under the icy crust.

She heard a strange scraping noise behind her, then David yelled, "Gracie, are you all right?"

She turned to him with relief. "David! Thank the Lord you've come."

David approached her from the shore side and inched toward the break in the ice. He reached out to grasp her under the arms and pull her up. Her feet came out of the water flailing for a solid footing. Her wet skates slipped on the ice, and David gripped her tighter, popping a loose button on her coat.

"My button!" Grace wailed.

"Sorry," David said as he set her on her feet. Then he quickly swept her up into his arms and tight against his chest, nearly knocking the air from her lungs. Grace desperately searched for a place to rest her arms and finally settled them on his rock-hard shoulders. She was strangely thrilled by the strength evoked from his sheltering arms.

He started a swift pace downstream, and suddenly Grace started kicking and wiggling.

"Stop! My button," she cried. "Go back, David. We have to get my button."

"You're about to freeze! What do you want with a button?"

"But I don't have an extra, and they're very unique. . .and expensive. Go back, please," she begged.

David stopped and stared down into her eyes. "Gracie—" His breath caught suddenly as their gazes locked.

She looked away and thrashed her feet again. "Put me down, David. This isn't proper."

"Why ever not?" his voice rose abruptly. "I'm just a *brother* helping his kid *sister* who happens to be nuts about a stupid button and on the verge of becoming an icicle." He punched his words at her, echoing those she had spoken to him when she had rejected his proposal.

"Now why are you mad at me?" Grace nearly shouted with indignation. "I'm not the one who lost the button." She found that anger clouded the troubling emotions that his embrace and gaze had stirred in her and put distance between them.

All of a sudden he dropped her to her feet and pushed away from her. He shook his head without another word and backtracked toward the break in the ice.

Grace shivered as his warmth left her. Her skirt still dripped and her legs felt numb. Anger had gotten her nowhere and she felt more confused than ever. Those many months ago, she had said she did not want him, but now she desperately wanted to be back in his arms and know he cared.

She brushed clumps of damp snow from her crocheted mittens. The blood in her left ankle began to pound and her legs started to shake with cold. Grace no longer had the will to stand. She sank to the ice with her legs folded beneath her.

It had started to snow. Big, fluffy flakes floated down from the sky, instantly changing the scene. They covered everything they touched with a veil of white.

"Here's the button. Can we go. . .oh Gracie, you're going to be sick with cold." David knelt before her and held the button out in his palm. "Truce?"

The button was already a forgotten issue for Grace. "Why did you come after me?"

"I. . .well. . ." David's brow furrowed. "Let's get you home."

He gently scooped her into his arms, and she curled herself against his warmth, locking her arms around his neck. He carried her as if without effort and soon the voices of the other skaters grew closer. Someone shouted as they came into view, but Grace was shivering with cold and she no longer had a clear picture of her surroundings. She leaned into David's warmth and surrendered her plight to his will.

⌒

"What happened?" Lydia squeaked as David neared the group at the fire.

David stumbled up the bank and was instantly surrounded by curious young people. "She broke through the ice and is soaked." David pointed out the obvious.

"Lydia, would you get my shoes from over by that oak?"

Lydia hurried to the tree while David lowered himself to a log.

"Let me drive her home," a young man from town offered.

"Thanks, but I'll see her home." David finally had Grace willingly in his arms. He wasn't in any hurry to give her up.

"Where's your car, man?"

"I—" David forgot that, like Grace, he had walked to the creek.

"Borrow my car—or better yet, I'll drive you both."

"Thanks," David sighed. He would have willingly carried her home if he had to.

Quickly, he traded his skates for shoes, enjoying the solid base on which to plant his feet. Then he gathered Grace close to his heart again and carried her to the young man's car. He held her in his lap and loosened her skates as the car bumped along a pasture road and up Grace's drive.

❧

Grace opened her eyes as the warmth from the kitchen touched her face. She could feel David's chest rumble as he spoke with her mother, but the words were fuzzy. The muscles in David's arms strained as he carried Grace up the stairs to her bedroom and laid her on her bed. She felt his breath tenderly brush her cheek. Then he spoke quietly with Mrs. Rudman at the door and left.

A flood of emotions too jumbled to describe overtook Grace and tears started to flow freely. She wanted David's arms around her once again. She needed his warmth and tender touch. She longed to feel loved and cared for. She yearned for her father to be the pillar of strength he had always been for her. He would tell her how to cope with the present and plan for the future.

Grace longed for John to be part of the family again, to share their joys and sorrows together. She wanted to have the opportunity to know his fiancée and welcome her into their midst.

She cried for Guy and wished her brother back among the living. He would have had cheerful encouragement for her. Perhaps he could have spoken to David and made him see that she had changed, that she desired to know him as more than a brotherly friend. She needed a second chance for love to grow.

Grace felt her mother's arms fold around her and rock her gently as the tears continued to flow.

Lord, thank You for restoring peace to Mother. I do want to trust You for everything. Please grant me the peace and patience I need so much. If You will guide me, I know I can endure these times of trial.

Grace eased away from her mother's embrace and sniffed, "Thanks."

"Let's get you warmed up."

Mrs. Rudman helped Grace undress and lower herself into a hot tub of water. The water instantly revived her senses.

Before long her mother had her gowned in thick flannel and tucked into bed with a hot water bottle to warm her feet. Grace still didn't feel warm, but sleep came quickly.

When she woke an hour later, she saw her mother in a bedside chair, dozing over a Bible that was opened in her lap. Her attention was abruptly moved, though, to a pounding downstairs. She swung her legs out of bed, but when her feet hit the rag rug, she gasped. Pain throbbed through her left ankle and Grace gripped the footboard. As she adjusted her weight to her right foot, her mother woke.

"Why are you out of bed?"

"Someone's downstairs."

"I'll go. It's most likely David. He promised to return." Mrs. Rudman set aside her Bible and left the room, but she soon returned. "If you feel up to it, you should come down to visit with David. You—we all—should enjoy every chance to visit with him before he leaves again for Michigan, and he was so worried about your getting sick."

Grace raised her eyebrows at her mother's retreating form. Leave it to her to play matchmaker. Certainly, Grace liked the idea of being matched with David, but she didn't want a romance with him to be because of the efforts of someone else. She wanted to know that David wanted it, too.

Oh. . .Lord, why can't I leave this in the past? She started to change into a clean dress. *Because David Matthews is the best guy who ever showed he cared for me, and I turned him away.* She yanked her dress over her head. *But I was immature and foolish back then.* Slowly she buttoned the closure. *Have I really changed that much? I still can't deal with my emotions. I melt at the slightest look or touch from him. He would laugh if he only knew.*

"Grace." Mrs. Rudman opened the door with a worried frown. "Has your father come up here?"

"Why, surely not."

"I know. I usually help him walk anywhere he goes, but now I can't seem to find him anywhere." Mrs. Rudman seemed close to tears. "This is so strange."

"He has to be here somewhere. Did you look on the porch?"

"David is looking outside right now. I'll go and see if he found him."

Mrs. Rudman hurried down the stairs. Grace moved to follow, but her ankle didn't appreciate the weight applied to it, and she had to hobble slowly down the stairs.

"I didn't see any sign of him around the house or the barn," David was telling Mrs. Rudman in the kitchen. "I didn't even see any footprints to follow."

"He has to be in the house somewhere," Grace declared.

"Then I'll check upstairs again," Mrs. Rudman sighed.

"I'll make another circle around the house," David said.

Grace limped into her father's bedroom, looking in every space and even opening the closet. She shuffled on to the parlor and found her father's rocking chair empty. The quilt that usually rested across his lap was folded haphazardly on the floor nearby.

Grace was looking out the window when David came back in with snow capping his head in white.

"I went ahead and checked the root cellar and springhouse, but found nothing," he reported.

"I don't understand where he could have disappeared to. He can't walk far alone."

"Gracie. . .where is your father's cane?"

"Here—well, usually it rests right here against the wall." Grace met David's wide gaze. "But he never uses it. . ."

"I think I had better extend my search outside."

Grace followed David through the house. Her limp wasn't nearly as pronounced as it had been. They met Mrs. Rudman in the kitchen.

"Nothing upstairs, not even a clue," she moaned.

"I think I'll do more looking outside, maybe talk to some neighbors," David said.

"His cane is gone, Mother," Grace interjected.

Mrs. Rudman shook her head in despair. "Should I ring on the telephone for help?"

"But. . ." Grace couldn't believe it had gone this far.

"Yes," David said, "It may be time to bring in extra people. Tell anyone who answers the ring to start their search here and fan out. But some should also look in town. Someone could have picked him up at the road and given him a ride in."

Grace sank to a kitchen chair, weakened by worry.

David continued to organize details of the search. "Then I suggest you call John and demand that he get here to help. And don't take any excuses."

Mrs. Rudman's face reddened with the shame of already letting her son put so much distance between himself and the family.

"I'll take the car and start looking between here and my home," David said as he buttoned his coat.

"I'm going with you," Grace suddenly announced.

"No," David said firmly. "You've already had a full day, and you don't need to get cold again."

Grace stood and braced herself for a fight. "I'm either going with you, or I'll start my own search."

Chapter 6

David stared at Grace. He couldn't believe how vulnerable she could look one minute and how very stubborn the next.

Mrs. Rudman cleared her throat and went to the phone to give the ringer several quick cranks. She was soon announcing the disappearance of Mr. Rudman across the party wires.

David stood rigid, meeting the challenge in Grace's eyes. He would never forgive himself if she went off on her own and caught her death of cold or found another patch of ice to fall through, but this was a fight he hated to back down from. He wrestled with himself, then ordered, "Dress in your warmest clothes and layer up. You'll ride in the car, but if you dare get out and start prancing through the snow, I'll bring you right back here. Do you understand?"

Grace's eyes narrowed at the ultimatum, but the corners of her lips twitched with the joy of even a small victory.

David shook his head at her as she collected her coat, a sweater, and a blanket. He would always thank God that if nothing more, he had been like a brother to this wonderful young woman. They might never have more between them, but as long as he could hold on to her friendship, he would feel blessed.

"At least five families responded to my call." Mrs. Rudman broke through his reveries. "Plus the reverend will start the search in town."

"Good." David led a bundled-up Grace to the back door. "We'll let you know as soon as we find him. Don't forget to call John."

Snow swirled in when they opened the door. They plowed through a good two inches of the white stuff and climbed in the car. The snow was getting heavier and sunset was swiftly approaching. Time was of the essence.

David drove to his home to inform his parents of the situation. His father was on an errand to town, but his mother promised to go to Mrs. Rudman and wait with her for word.

Grace waited patiently while David made a sweep around his farm for any signs. When he returned to the car empty-handed, she met him with a new idea. "I feel like we should check down by the gatehouse."

"Why? There's nothing down there. I think he would have headed to a neighbor's house or to town."

"I know it doesn't make a lot of sense, but I have a gut feeling about it." She shrugged.

"Okay, it can't hurt to look around." He told his mother the direction they were headed and quickly returned to the car.

They followed a good road for only a short distance. The road to the new gatehouse was a rough track through old pastureland. The car jolted in and out of ruts. Grace struggled to stay in her place on the leather bench seat.

David turned on the headlights as the shadow cast by the dam deepened, and their beams shone out over the bulldozed land to where it rose sharply at the dam's base. He stopped the car at the foot of the dam and turned to Grace.

She leaped from the car and started a brisk inspection of the snow up to the water's edge. David scrabbled from the car after her.

"I told you to stay in the car or I'd take you straight home," he yelled over the car's engine.

"And I told you I had a feeling we'd find something here." She stooped, picked something up, and held it toward the car lights.

David moved closer. It was a mitten. "It's small. Do you think it is his?"

"I don't recognize it." Her face crumbled in defeat.

"It was likely left by a skater." David surveyed the area and found nothing more.

Grace sat on the stump of a once great tree that had been sawed and hauled away for lumber. Soon silent sobs rocked her frame.

David approached her slowly, wanting to give comfort but afraid of being rejected. He bent his knees and brought his face level with her. Cautiously, he placed his hands on the stump on either side of her. "Gracie, I—"

"You know," she interrupted with a whimper, "this very afternoon, I asked the Lord to grant me peace and patience to weather the storms in my life. I didn't ask Him for a new trial." She slammed both fists into David's shoulders then left them there as she gripped his coat collar. "I can't lose my father like this." She was adamant as she stared into his face.

"It'll be all right, Gracie."

"But you don't understand what I've been through," she cried. "No one really understands."

"I understand." David tried to hug her to him, but she kept her arms stiff between them and rubbed her fingers along the wool of his coat.

She gave a brittle laugh. "Do you remember the last day I saw you before you left for Detroit?"

"Don't..." David didn't want to rehash the past or hear any hollow apologies.

But she continued, "I told you of my inflated dreams to leave this valley and see the world. Do you know how many months it took me to save enough money before I left for Cleveland? And do you know that within five months I was flat broke, living in a run-down boardinghouse?"

"Gracie, you don't have to..."

"I fell for a guy with all the right stuff..."

David hung his head. He didn't want to hear that she was in love with someone else.

"...or so I thought," Grace continued. "He promised to introduce me to fashionable people and teach me how to fit in." She swung her arms out to her sides. "He lavished gifts on me and made me feel like a queen. Then he took my money with a crazy promise to buy me an automobile. According to him, the right kind of car would give me a foot up in the world."

She brought her arms in with a shiver. "I was so foolish—naive—that I handed my whole savings over to a handsome cad and never saw it again. I couldn't even pay my own way home for Guy's funeral. I took a loan. . .now I'm stuck in this job. . .no reason to dream—" Her voice broke.

"Oh honey, I'm sorry."

"See, you were better off without me," she continued. "Failure follows me on every side."

"What?" David cupped her face in his hands. "Everyone learns by mistakes. Mistakes don't make failures." His thumbs massaged along her jawline. He had never desired to kiss Grace Rudman more than this moment.

She still glowed with the sweet blush of innocence, but now a maturity and a touch of wisdom also adorned her. She radiated with winter's touch on her cheeks, and her eyes, staring back at him, glistened with. . . Could he dare to call it hope? A hope for them? Hadn't they put that in the past and settled for friendship?

He felt himself drawn to her. Her lips shined like a fresh ripened apple. Their breaths mingled in a frosty cloud.

Unexpectedly, a shot rang out and echoed through the valley. They jumped to their feet as one, craning to determine the direction of the shot. Could it be one of the searchers?

Soon another shot followed.

"It sounds almost like it came from the top of the dam," David said. "I'll go check it out while you get back in the car."

Immediately, David started the steep ascent up the embankment. He slipped several times as he attacked the dam wall from an angle.

"Umph!" came from behind him. He turned to see Grace sliding down to the foot of the dam, her arms flailing out to steady her descent.

"Gracie, please, go back to the car." He tried to keep his voice gentle but strong.

She picked herself up and started the climb again. Her face was set with determination as she strained with each new step. He watched as she neared him, puffing for each breath. She flung her hand out to grasp his arm. David reached for her and drew her up to meet him.

"Do you know that you can be very stubborn?" David asked, stifling a chuckle.

"I get it from my father. . .and if he had the will to walk all the way out here . . .I can get myself to the top."

She pulled away from him and dug her toes into the dirt. Her left foot slipped and she cried out. David steadied her.

"My ankle," she gasped. "I twisted it in the creek."

"Oh Gracie, why didn't you say so?" David sighed.

They were more than halfway up the eastern side of the dam now. David put his arm around her waist to steady her as they looked across the ridge. It was much lighter here and the sinking sun was still visible in the cradle of nearby hills.

A short distance along the leveled top of the dam was a group of five people. Sitting on the ground, looking out over the valley and town of Tappan, were two older men. Standing around them were three teenage boys, one carrying a hunting rifle. David and Grace hurried to them as fast as Grace could manage on her weak ankle.

"Father," Grace called out as they neared the group.

Mr. Rudman turned to his daughter with a very lopsided grin and grunted what could have been her name.

She dropped to her knees and wrapped her arms around his thin shoulders. "Oh Daddy. . ." Grace whimpered as tears started.

David approached his own father who was seated next to Mr. Rudman. "How did you come to be here, Dad?"

"Well," Mr. Matthews began slowly, "I was headed to town when I met up with an old friend. We hadn't seen each other in a very long time and decided to take a drive. I parked my car along the road at the other end of this giant dam while we took a little stroll."

David frowned at his father's casual description. He looked to Mr. Rudman and saw a mischievous glint in his tired eyes. "I should paddle you both," David muttered under his breath, but he was overjoyed to see a visible change in Mr. Rudman's spirit.

One of the boys spoke up. "You're right, Mr. Rudman, the shadow of the dam is spreading across the whole valley." It was Thomas Cord. He eyed Grace with an apologetic tip of his head.

Mr. Rudman bobbed his head in agreement.

"One day everything under that shadow will be a great lake," Mr. Matthews stated. "It will draw hundreds of people for fishing and boating vacations, but better yet, this here dam will save many homes in the outlying areas from being threatened by yearly floods."

"So, it's a case of our sacrifice for the good of the majority?" Thomas asked.

"That's. . .right," Mr. Rudman sputtered. "Be. . .proud."

Grace hugged her father tighter.

Three carloads of people had arrived and were making their way along the ridge to the little group. David recognized his mother and Mrs. Rudman with several folks from the community. Mrs. Rudman ran to her husband and clasped him in a tear-filled reunion.

"Here we have a beautiful view of our valley," Mr. Matthews declared with a sweep of his arm.

The group came to a muted halt as each individual stared across the farms and town that made up the community of Tappan. The shadow of the dam was slowly ending the day for the close-knit community.

Someone started to hum "Silent Night," and soon the voices of friends and neighbors joined in song. Slowly descending snowflakes sparkled in the last rays of the sun.

David touched Grace's shoulder, and she gave him a smile that warmed him clear through.

Chapter 7

Despite their plans to have a quiet Christmas, the Rudmans' house was full of visitors on Christmas Eve. The gathering of friends at the dam had followed the Rudmans home, and Grace served them hot chocolate, cookies, and fresh-baked bread with preserves.

More visitors arrived later to hear the events surrounding Mr. Rudman's disappearance, and soon the house was overflowing with holiday cheer.

It was still unclear what motivated Mr. Rudman to go on his excursion and why he was suddenly able to say some words after months of virtual silence. It was a moment to celebrate, nonetheless, and Grace welcomed the festive atmosphere in the house.

"It's an answer to our prayers," Mr. Matthews told Grace. "God's still doing miracles."

Mrs. Rudman sat down to the piano and started playing carols. Some joined in merry singing, while others continued to visit freely. There seemed to be people everywhere. Grace waded through the masses in the parlor with a tray of sugar cookies, smiling and chatting with old friends.

Someone grabbed her arm and pulled her into the empty front stairwell.

"David!" She caught her tray as it tilted. "What are you up to?"

"I. . ." He opened his mouth, then grinned like a mischievous child and shrugged. "I guess I wanted to wish you a merry Christmas before I go." In a lightning flash, he bent down and brushed her cheek with a feathery kiss and was gone.

Grace stood transfixed at the bottom of the stairs, her breath caught in her throat. Dreamily, she dropped to one of the wooden steps, balancing her tray on one hand and her rosy cheek in the other. When had a kiss ever been as sweet? What bitter irony that David Matthews now only treated her like a sister.

⌒

Christmas morning, Grace trudged down the stairs after stealing almost an hour of extra sleep. The day before had been such a draining day, and they were up late visiting with their unexpected company.

She entered the kitchen to the smell of oven-fresh cinnamon rolls, her favorite.

"Merry Christmas, my sweet," her mother sang, her face wreathed in smiles. "Go get your gifts. We will do an exchange before the 10 a.m. church service."

Grace skipped back upstairs and soon returned with three gaily wrapped packages. In the parlor, her father was sitting straight in his chair and decked in his best Sunday suit.

She kissed his weathered cheek. "Merry Christmas, Daddy!"

A movement in the corner caught her eye, and there stood a small, fresh pine tree.

"Oh!" she gasped.

"Merry Christmas, little sister," John said, popping his head around the little tree.

Grace squealed and captured her brother in a tight hug. John hugged her back and whispered in her ear, "I'm really sorry for being selfish and leaving you here to shoulder all the problems. I came as soon as I got word about Dad, though I missed all the excitement."

"It's forgiven," she smiled up at him.

The family had much to celebrate as they draped the little evergreen in ribbons, glass bulbs, and glittery tinsel. Then they exchanged gifts with each other in expression of their love and thanksgiving. The fact that this would be their last Christmas in the sturdy old farmhouse was far from their minds. Being together was the answer to every wish and prayer. They even openly shared memories of Guy and could laugh together about the past.

The Lord had brought them much healing. The sun reflecting through the window off the fresh-fallen snow couldn't have shone any brighter this morning than the smiles on the faces of the Rudman family.

～

Grace sat beside her father at the little church on Tappan's main street, ready for Christmas worship. John and his fiancée, Melissa, sat directly behind them. The sanctuary was filled with the low buzz of joyous worshippers as they waited for the special service to start. Mrs. Rudman had taken her traditional place at the piano and was playing a Christmas hymn.

The Matthews arrived and took seats in the pew across the aisle from Grace and her father. David smiled their way and Grace's heart started to thump in response. He was wearing the new suit he had worn home on the train. Its classic style fit him well.

Grace thought of all the things that had happened in the week since their reunion. David had been near her or her family almost every day—often sacrificing precious time with his own family. He was sweet and considerate, a gentleman, and just like a member of her family.

She knew that when he left for Detroit on Monday that parting would pain her greatly. There would be no guarantee when he would return, and with the community's scattering in wake of the dam, it would be less likely that they would visit regularly again.

Lord, she almost chuckled out loud, *if David Matthews is not the man You have designed for me, then You must have someone pretty spectacular in my future. . . because at this point I can't think of anyone better than David.*

Grace had to pull her gaze away from David's brownish-red locks, his chiseled features, and his perfectly shaped, strong hand that rested on the back of the pew as he tilted forward to speak with someone. She took a deep, cleansing breath as her father leaned closer, touching her shoulder.

"The best. . .dream. . ." he whispered in a raspy and halting voice, "is usually . . .what God. . .places. . .within reach."

Grace quickly looked at her father. He was settling back against the pew with a satisfied smile. She glanced around to try and gather what he had been referring to. Across the aisle, David sent her another smile, and instantly her cheeks flushed a rosy Christmas red that matched the new dress she wore. Her father couldn't have guessed what she had been thinking.

The pastor's entrance to the platform saved her from her tortured thoughts. He introduced a group of schoolchildren who reenacted the Christmas story. Then a choral group led the packed congregation in Christmas songs. Grace sang with her whole soul, enjoying the blend of voices.

The second half of the service turned to a time of reflection on the church body and surrounding community. The pastor had a special announcement.

"By Easter Sunday, if all goes according to plan, our church building will have been relocated to a hill six miles east of here. The elders have settled on a fine spot that was donated by a faithful church member."

There was clapping and whoops of joy. No longer did the church people have to worry about tearing down the beloved building.

But when her parents moved to Bowerston, her family would be worshipping at a different church among new friends. Grace would miss the fellowship with these dear people.

She turned her head and found David watching her. His gaze was deep and serious. Were his thoughts similar to hers?

It was slow getting through the lingering churchgoers at the end of the service. No one seemed in a hurry to get home to their individual holiday celebrations, but preferred to talk about where neighbors were moving to and how many would still be around for Easter.

At home, Mrs. Rudman had a feast prepared. John and Melissa joined the family for the meal along with an older couple from town and the widowed Mrs. Douglas who had been invited at the last minute. Mr. Rudman was also present at the table for the first time in many long weeks. He still needed help managing his food, but it was good to have the family together again.

Grace relished the occasion, eating until she was almost miserably full. Her mother's cooking was always wonderful, and she had made all of the family favorites for the holiday celebration.

Grace also feasted her eyes upon those around the table. She was so pleased that John had decided to join them and bring Melissa. Melissa had a subtle beauty and quiet nature. Her straight blond locks contrasted with John's deep brown ringlets. They made quite a handsome couple, and it was obvious that they were deeply in love.

Before they were through with dessert, there was a knock at the door. John answered it and ushered David into the dining room. Grace's cheeks warmed at the sight of the young man. She chided herself and tried to continue with her dessert, but all appetite for food had left her.

Mrs. Rudman pulled a chair up to the table for David and placed him between Grace and herself. David casually brushed Grace's shoulder as he sat down to a large bowl of cream-covered date pudding. Lightning struck through Grace and zipped out her toes. Each new encounter with David seemed to awaken startling new awareness within her. At least separation from David should keep her from going on these bumpy emotional rides.

Grace sat back in her chair and sipped from her water goblet. She listened as David conversed with the others around the table. He fit in naturally. He and John teased each other, and Melissa blushed at his charming compliments. Even Mrs. Douglas was not immune to his charms.

"Now, David dear, I hear you are headed back north to Detroit and you still don't have a wife," Mrs. Douglas stated frankly.

Grace fidgeted in her chair, brushing a hand through the ends of her loose curls.

"Yes, you heard right," David smoothly replied, "but I would gladly take you with me to fill the position."

Everyone around the table burst into laughter. Mrs. Douglas reached across the table and playfully swatted at David's arm.

"I'd go in a second, my dear boy, but the move would be too much on this old one. In fact, I'm staying put until the lake is at my back door. But you young ones have to make a life for yourselves beyond the ghost streets of an old town. Just take an old woman's advice. Remember where you came from and take it with you wherever you go. This town will always, then, be remembered by the wonderful children it produced." Merry chatter continued around the table, and Grace observed with little to contribute. Her mind tumbled as she mulled over Mrs. Douglas's words. *I can always be proud of who I am because of where I came from.*

David leaned toward her, touching his shoulder to hers. "You don't have the Christmas blues, now do you?" he quietly asked Grace.

"No, certainly not. I got everything I wished for."

"Everything?"

"Yes, my father is better, John is home, and Mother has come to a peaceful plan for the future of the farm and their home."

"What about you?" he pried.

"I. . .well. . .uh. . ." She looked at him with a frown. His eyes showed an honest concern. "What do you want to know?" she almost whispered.

His eyes crinkled with a slow smile. "Will you take a ride with me later?

Dad still has the old sleigh in the barn, we've got a horse that should pull it, and there's a good coating of snow for the runners. Should I bring it over later?"

Grace swallowed hard, a nervous flutter tickling her stomach. "Um...should we invite John and Melissa?"

"I came to see just you today," was his low, rumbling answer that thrilled and scared her at the same time. It was the same thing he had said the day after her high school graduation when he came to propose. That day ended with her flat rejection. How would today end?

Chapter 8

The chill air nipped at their cheeks as the sleigh cut through the snow. Grace burrowed farther under the quilt while David encouraged the horse to a faster trot. Grace's sudden giggle delighted his ears and he spurred the horse even faster.

It was a picture-perfect Christmas day. Sunlight glistened on the snow and their breath hung suspended in the still air. Smoke from the occasional chimney drifted straight up to meet the clear blue sky.

David guided the sleigh around the perimeter of the valley's bottom then through the main part of town. They waved to a family that was hurrying in out of the cold. Then David slowed the horse as they started the incline up Mill Hill Road. He halted the horse at the bottom of the path to a hillside cemetery and stepped out of the sleigh.

"Would you like to visit your brother with me?" He lightly suggested as he offered her a hand out of the sleigh.

She gave her hand without a word, and he kept it as they climbed the steep, snow-covered path. Small granite headstones covered the slope before them. They located Guy's plot with little trouble.

"Guy would have loved this day," Grace said into the stillness. "Winter was always his favorite time of the year."

"He loved building snow caves," David said.

"And snow forts," Grace added, "with snowballs."

"And eating snow ice cream," they laughed together.

"A kid couldn't have had a better brother," David reflected more pensively.

Grace slowly brushed snow from the carved stone. David watched her tender ministrations. She pocketed her spare hand for warmth and seemed to search for something within the depths of the deep coat pockets.

"I'm missing a mitten. I had it on when we left the house," Grace said.

"Then it's probably in the sleigh. Here, wear one of mine." David probed his own pocket, and as his hand reached the glove, something hard touched it. He pulled the hard, circular object out and held it toward Grace in the palm of his hand.

"It seems I still have your most precious of buttons, my lady," he said with a bow.

"Wonderful!" she cried. "I have truly missed it. You were so good to rescue it for me."

Her eyes were alight with joy as she turned her face to him and closed her hand over the trinket. David's insides knotted. How he longed to gather her close to him and call Grace his own. He had never been in a better position to make plans for a future—a family of his own. But to be twice rejected could spoil a beautiful friendship. He would have to continue to pray for God's divine guidance.

David turned from Grace and the moment was broken. Grace shivered. She had felt so sure that David was close to saying something. Perhaps something very important. She reached out to steady herself against the stone. It was like ice under her hand.

David abruptly handed her his glove. She slipped her right hand into his large glove, enjoying the soft leather. He continued to scan the view below, and Grace moved to stand beside him.

The town sat directly below them. Bathed in a blanket of white, it was beautiful. To their right rose the wall of the dam, standing sentinel across the mouth of the valley. And to their left the valley stretched long and wide.

David reached down for a broken branch and sent it sailing into the brush. There was a long silence between them, and Grace used it to reflect about life in the valley below. She leaned against a large monument and pulled her coat tight against her slight frame.

All of a sudden, David surprised her by saying, "I may leave for Detroit tomorrow. It shouldn't be hard to change my train ticket. . ."

"What?" Grace came to attention.

"I had a wire from one of my bosses on Wednesday. I meant to tell you about it yesterday. . .but then there was your accident and your father's disappearance. . ."

"Well, what was the telegram about?" she probed, while she tried to look him in the face.

He turned away from her, staring out across the valley below. "I have been offered the supervisor's position that I had wanted."

"That's great!"

He was strangely silent.

"It is great, isn't it?" she asked, suddenly concerned.

"Sure. . .sure. It is a secure position with good pay. I guess I wasn't prepared for the possibilities it opens. The new opportunities." He turned his face heavenward.

Grace sighed, not understanding his hesitancy. "Then you are leaving Saturday so you can accept the position?"

"Yes, they want me to return as soon as possible." He shuffled his feet in the snow, sending tiny snowballs rolling down the slope.

She reached for his arm, touching his sleeve at the elbow. "David, I'm really happy for you. Things seem to be working out for you in Detroit." She paused to focus her thoughts. "You deserve the best."

He spun to face her and clasped her hand. "Gracie, you. . ." He stopped and closed his eyes. After a moment of quiet he shook his head. "I hear a car coming down the hill. I better tend to the horse. Stay longer if you wish." He turned quickly and bolted down the path to where the horse was tethered.

Grace was shocked by his brisk manner. It was almost like he was fighting some unseen fear. If only he could understand that she was happy for him. He really did deserve the best of everything, even if that meant that his future wouldn't include her.

She walked back to the marker on Guy's grave. *I sure could use some brotherly advice.* But it was the words of her father that came to mind. *"The best dream is usually what God places within reach."*

She was already well aware that David Matthews was the best guy she had ever been acquainted with. Her problem was that she had rejected a perfectly good man. *I just wasn't ready then. I had to do some growing up.* She stared at the motionless gravestone. *I think I'm ready now, Lord. But what kind of man would want to go through the humiliation of asking a second time?*

Lord, he leaves tomorrow. I'd ask him if I could. It's just too late for us.

A thought struck her with force. How badly did she want David in her life? What was she willing to risk if she really loved him?

She looked down the hill to where David petted the nose of the bay. The car had already passed by and was entering town.

"The best dream is usually what God places within reach," vibrated through her mind.

Her feet suddenly took flight. She slipped and skidded down the steep slope and passed David before she was able to stop her forward motion. She limped on her left ankle and stepped back in front of him.

"You can't leave tomorrow," she panted.

"I don't understand."

"Not before we settle something."

He stared at her, undoubtedly thinking she was acting strangely.

"When you asked me to marry you, I had to refuse."

He grimaced and grasped the horse's bridle.

"Wait," she cried and hurried to continue, "I had to see the world to know what I was missing. I needed to do some. . .growing up."

"And. . ." He looked impatient with her speech, and she almost faltered in her plan.

"I needed time before I could see that," she searched for the right words, "sometimes the best things God has intended for us are right within our reach." She longed for him to understand. "David, what I'm trying to say is, if you would ever ask me again, I would now be more inclined to say 'yes' to your proposal."

He dropped his hold on the horse and took a step toward her. She placed her hands out in front of her in a defensive stance.

"But I will understand if you say you have moved on to new avenues of your life—"

Her words were stalled as David drew her flush against him, and with deliberate slowness, he lowered his mouth to hover above hers. Her breathing caught as she lifted her gaze to meet his dark eyes. What she saw in their depths caused her to relax against him.

Then his lips touched her, the heat searing her wind-chapped skin. She responded to his deepening kiss with all the pent-up longings she had been trying to suppress. It was better than a homecoming; it was as natural as a sunrise.

"Gracie my love," he moaned as he pulled away, "I have wanted to ask you that particular question since I saw you at the train station, but. . ."

"Who wants to ask the same question twice?" She supplied.

"Yes, I guess that's how it was." He smiled and lightly pressed his lips to hers again.

He turned to hand her into the sleigh.

"But. . .where are we going?" She was confused. He hadn't asked her "that" question yet.

"Home."

"Home?" Her voice came out flat. Her foot felt weighted as she lifted it into the sleigh.

"I need to talk to your father." He climbed in beside her and smiled at her confused expression. "Yes, even before I ask 'that' question."

With one hand holding the reins and the other holding tight to Gracie's hand, David steered the horse and sleigh through the sleepy town of Tappan, along the still pastures of the valley, and to the weathered and worn farmhouse where they would plan their future together. A future made bright by a rich heritage and the goodness of God.

Epilogue

Grace pushed open the sliding glass door and stepped out onto the shaded deck. A cool summer breeze blew across the lake and played with her silver-edged hair. The fresh air felt good to her tired body. She had lugged boxes and scoured cupboards all day long.

Suddenly, David was there, wrapping his arms around her from behind. "The boys and I have all the living room furniture in, but I'm sure you will want to do some rearranging."

"You know me too well," she chuckled.

David hugged her tight.

"Who would have guessed that we would ever buy a retirement home on Tappan Lake?" she mused. "What do you think Mother and Daddy would have to say about it?" She stared across the bay to another area of waterfront homes. "We knew the family that once owned the property under this section of water, and the town is only marked by a much-visited boat launch." She felt close to tears.

David gently encouraged her. "They would say you have a lovely home on a beautiful lake. It's a far cry from the old farmhouse where you grew up, my love."

"Yes, but does it have the charm of a house that has seen a lot of living?" Grace wanted to know.

"It's home, and we will make many memories with our children and grandchildren," David insisted. "We will tell them of what used to be and teach them how to make the memories live in their own lives."

They watched as their two grown daughters walked out onto the dock, their auburn hair highlighted by the afternoon sun. Julie was just out of graduate school while Karen was a wife and new mother. David and Grace were proud of their beautiful daughters, just as they were of their three older sons, all husbands and fathers.

"God blessed our life in Michigan and now He has brought us full circle," David told Grace as he planted a sweet kiss on her earlobe.

About the Authors

Award-winning author **DiAnn Mills** is a fiction writer who combines an adventuresome spirit with unforgettable characters to create action-packed, suspense-filled novels. DiAnn's first book was published in 1998. She currently has more than fifty books published. She speaks to various groups and teaches writing workshops around the country. She and her husband live in sunny Houston, Texas.

Multi-published author of numerous award-winning books, **Loree Lough** is also a frequent guest speaker who encourages other writers. She lives in Maryland with her husband of (mumble-mumble) years, where she's determined to stay until she succeeds in prying the secret Old Bay Seasoning recipe from McCormick employees.

Gail Gaymer Martin, multi-award–winning author, has been blessed with 52 published novels and nearly 4 million books in print. CBS local news listed Gail as one of the four best writers in the Detroit area. She is the author of Writing the Christian Romance from Writers Digest. Gail is a cofounder of American Christian Fiction Writers and a member of numerous other professional writing and speaking organizations. In her earlier professional career, Gail was a teacher of English, literature, and public speaking at the high school and university levels and still enjoys teaching workshops at conferences across the US. She lives in Detroit, Michigan, with her husband and is active in her church, especially in the music program. Visit her website at www.gailgaymermartin.com.

Sally Laity has written both historical and contemporary novels, including a coauthored series for Tyndale House, nine Heartsong romances, and twelve Barbour novellas. She considers it a joy to know that the Lord can touch other hearts through her stories. Her favorite pastimes include quilting for her church's Prayer Quilt Ministry and scrapbooking. She makes her home in the beautiful Tehachapi Mountains of Southern California with her husband of over fifty years and enjoys being a grandma and a great-grandma.

JoAnn A. Grote lives on the Minnesota prairie, which is a setting for many of her stories. Once a full-time CPA, JoAnn now spends most of her time researching and writing. JoAnn has published historical nonfiction books for children and several novels with Barbour Publishing in the Heartsong Presents line as well as the American Adventure and Sisters in Time series for children. She enjoys researching and weaving her fictional characters' lives into historical backgrounds and events. JoAnn believes that readers can receive a message of salvation and encouragement from well-crafted fiction.

Peggy Darty is the author of 31 novels, ranging from inspirational romance to romantic suspense to mysteries. Recently widowed, she is the mother of three children and the grandmother of three little boys. Writing is her passion and she hopes to inspire readers with themes of hope, forgiveness and trust.

Rosey Dow is a bestselling and award-winning author. Her novel, *Reaping the Whirlwind*, won a 2001 Christy Award for excellence in fiction. A former missionary and lifelong mystery buff, Rosey now makes her home in Delaware where she writes and speaks full-time.

Colleen L. Reece was born and raised in a small western Washington logging town. She learned to read by kerosene lamplight and dreamed of someday writing a book. God has multiplied Colleen's "someday" book into more than 140 titles that have sold six million copies. Colleen was twice voted Heartsong Presents' Favorite Author and later inducted into Heartsong's Hall of Fame. Several of her books have appeared on the CBA Bestseller list.

Rebecca Germany works full-time as a fiction editor and has written and compiled several novellas and gift books. She lives in Ohio, where she enjoys country life.